DESERT
VARNISH

KAREN COCHLOVIUS

KWELA BOOKS

This is a work of fiction. While some of the events, institutions and characters in *Desert Varnish* may bear a superficial resemblance to actual incidents, companies and people, they have been fictionalised for the purposes of this novel and are not meant to portray reality.

The quotes on pp. 55, 98 and 106 are from the Bible. The book, *Sophie's Choice,* referred to on pg. 98 is by William Styron.

The quoted song lyrics are from: pg. 87, 'Blowin' in the Wind' by Bob Dylan; pg. 89, 'Child in Time' by Deep Purple; pg. 91, 'When the Levee Breaks' by Led Zeppelin and 'Bold as Love' by Jimi Hendrix; pg. 106, 'Diamonds on the Soles of Her Shoes' by Paul Simon; pg. 121, 'Alabama Song (Whiskey Bar)' by The Doors; pg. 133, 'Yellow Roses' by K.Devine/S. Nichols; pg. 170, 'Big Time' by Peter Gabriel; pg. 216, 'Dangerbird' by Neil Young.

Other pieces of music referred to are: pg. 241, 'Tatazela' by Juluka; pg. 256, 'A Whiter Shade of Pale' by Procol Harum; pg. 258, 'Una Furtiva Lagrima' by Gaetano Donizetti.

Kwela Books
40 Heerengracht, Cape Town 8001; P.O. Box 6525, Roggebaai 8012
kwela@kwela.com

Cover design and typography by Nazli Jacobs
Set in Berkeley
Printed and bound by Paarl Print, Oosterland Street, Paarl, South Africa

First edition, first printing 2003

ISBN 0-7957-0169-1

My thanks to:

Anne Schuster who encouraged this book
from start to finish,
and to Jon who has supported me
along this journey.

PROLOGUE

As I climb, my thighs ache. My day pack bites into my shoulders and my boots chafe my ankles. I pant. I stop, struggling for breath. I look up. Above me, the basalt cliffs loom: black, vertical, forbidding. Their deep resonating voice rolls down the green slopes towards me. Calling me. Their clean fragile lines sing, high and sweet, willing me closer. I start to climb again. I follow the call, as I have always done . . .

Into the ground, through that black tunnel; finally emerging into the light of the open veld and the desert. Lured at last into the swarm of corporate takeover and bloody acquisition: elevated copper results, assets, TurnStone. TurnStone, leaving no stone unturned.

I left behind my past, my luggage. Only the small notebooks tucked into the waistband of my shorts were a reminder of my time spent in northern Namibia. I was angry, yes. But the anger had subsided, had been left behind to settle. That was not the voice I answered to. My voice lay deep within stone, deep within the earth. And I was accountable to it.

I added those notebooks to the others. There were sixteen in all: black, hardcover, each the size of a hand. I spread them out in a circle around me. I pried the covers open. The pages were warped from water and sweat, soil and sun; some of the entries were difficult to read. Sketches, maps, sample positions – words trailed across them. They made no sense to anyone but me.

I began to tear. I tore out the entries and pasted them on blank sheets. Pasting the memories together. Then . . . I started to write. I wrote with my head bent and my arm twisting across the page. Words flooded memory. I wrote as if words were water and pages dry dune sand. Memories, places and faces; the past eclipsed the present. I wrote. Words linked arms across the pages and formed sentences, sentences marched towards chapters and the chapters marched towards this book. This book you now hold in your hands. Its pages lie open, pale subscriptions to my soul.

My chest heaves, my eyes water. High above me the cliffs rumble, they roll, they churn. Those basalt cliffs call and I must answer. I climb, higher and higher. Back to those cliffs that whisper my name, back into those gullies that hold my peace.

PART ONE

CHAPTER ONE

Don't Let It Rattle Your Cage, Man

The thing about working in the tunnel was that it did not get better; it only got worse. Even after two months, the fear devoured me. Daily, the men rode into the tunnel with me, rocked by the rhythm of the train. Daily, the three shifts each worked eight hours. Hard, heavy, physical work. Men's hands occasionally slipped, faces grew tired, attention wandered and legs ached. The Tunnel Boring Machine was only as good as these men, and I was afraid.

I arrived on a warm Thursday morning. The Ash Tunnel construction offices were set in a dip between rolling hills of yellow grass, just outside the small town of Clarens. A stranger's arm pointed out Carter's office to me. Carter: my new supervisor, my new boss. He worked in the brick building furthest from site, two doors from the entrance. I knocked on the open door and waited.

A large, middle-aged man, with the first touches of grey in his dark hair, stood behind his desk, which was stacked with paper and reports. Behind him were rows of office partitions, but Carter's desk stood apart, in a corner, away from the hustle and bustle of dusty paper activity. He flicked through a report, wearing the flat, amicable smile of someone who had other things on his mind.

I knocked again. 'I'm Robyn Hartley, the new geologist.'

Carter still did not look up. He scratched a thoughtful finger against his cheek and glanced towards the door. His mouth opened slightly.

'God dammit,' he said, 'they sent me a bloody woman.'

Silence. My heart sank. So this is what it would be like.

I hovered in the doorway. Carter lowered his navy-blue eyes to his desk for a full three seconds, chewing his lower lip. Finally he took a deep breath and gave a concerned smile – concern for himself, I thought.

'Well come in, come in. Don't just stand there. It's just the last time they sent me a bloody woman, I ended up doing all her shifts,' he sighed. 'Robyn – of course. Female.'

He motioned me into the seat in front of his desk and I sat down. I had no response to give. I studied my fingernails; they were dirty like his.

'You find the place all right?'

I nodded. Carter tried smiling, but the frown that hung over his eyebrows somehow ruined it.

I tried to fill the silence. 'Where will my office be?'

Carter did not reply. I studied his desk. There was a fork-shaped stick lying amongst the paper. The wood was freshly cut – not all the green shoots had been trimmed away.

'Right,' he said suddenly, 'we should show you the tunnel then. No time like the present.'

'Now? In these?' I looked down at my jeans.

Carter's eyes shifted around the office, distracted, and then lit up. 'We should get you some overalls then, shouldn't we?' He loped out of his office, was gone for two seconds, and then stuck his head back through the door. 'What size are those great clodhoppers of yours?'

I followed his look, with surprise, to my feet. 'Er, six woman's or five man's.'

'Right.' Carter patted the doorframe, smiled at me and, unable to hold it back any longer, gave a long, slow, sad sigh.

He reappeared with a neat, folded pile of grey overalls. 'Try these on. Smallest they have. Should fit, you're not too fat.' He attempted a teasing wink and held up a large pair of white gumboots. 'Only male size seven, I'm afraid. We don't have too many dainty feet around here. They'll have to do for today. I've ordered some your size. There's a toilet for women around the corner, you can change there.'

I pulled on the overalls. They fitted well enough, but a man's fit, so they were loose around my waist and tight around my hips and thighs. The top was too large, so I rolled up the sleeves to expose my hands. The gumboots looked ridiculously big on me. I clumped back to Carter's office and knocked tentatively on the door. Carter had already changed into his grey overalls. In contrast to the stiff fold-creases in mine, his looked worn and used. He looked up, as if with surprise, to see me standing at the door.

'You know I'm deaf, don't you?'

I shook my head.

'Yup, most people don't. I lip-read mostly, only have ten percent hearing in my left ear. I am not ignoring you, which is what most people think I do.'

He eyed the overalls. The frown in his forehead evaporated for a second and the corners of his mouth lifted. 'Well, old chap, we'll make a tunnel geologist out of you yet.' He handed me a clean, white hard hat. 'Adjust that to fit you.' He picked up another, dirty, with *CARTER* and *GEOLOGIST* marked in black ink on its sides.

I followed Carter out of the office building, past the parking lot to the tunnel construction site. The site was all activity, humming with various tones of grinding. Vehicles, earth-moving equipment, dust and people.

Carter lifted his hand to the passing figures: 'Afternoon, afternoon.' He pointed up to a huge corrugated-iron construction on our right. 'That's the segment factory. That's where they make the segments to line the tunnel.' Outside the factory, pale grey, arc-shaped concrete segments, each the size of a small boat, lay piled in each other's concave curves. 'Those will be taken in with the next train. Each segment weighs a ton and a half, so don't get caught between one of them and gravity. How it works,' continued Carter, 'is that once the TBM has drilled through a section of tunnel, a mechanical arm lifts each concrete segment and places it against the tunnel wall. The segments fit into each other and form a perfect ring. So as the TBM eats its way through the mountain, the walls are lined and prevented from caving in.' Carter looked at me suspiciously and gave an involuntary wink. 'You *do* know what a TBM is, don't you?'

I nodded quickly. 'Tunnel Boring Machine,' I said, hoping it sounded like I knew something at least.

Carter looked at his watch impatiently, 'Worst thing you'll find about this job is the waiting for the trains. It's the only way to bum a ride in and out of the tunnel.'

He clicked his tongue, sighed and loped off to the closest pile of segments and sat down heavily in its inner curve. I noticed he dragged his right leg slightly; the knee seemed stiff. Following him, I sat down in the adjacent pile of segments. He placed his stiff leg over the other and crossed his arms over a slightly bulging stomach.

'You hurt your leg in there?' I pointed to the gaping, black hole leading into the tunnel. I turned my head to face him as I spoke, pronouncing the words clearly, so he could lip-read.

Carter shook his head. 'Not in there.' He glanced at his watch. 'Another fifteen minutes wait, at least,' he sighed. 'My leg. Let's see. When was it? Ten years ago. Now: I always work alone. I don't like assistants, never have. Not like Dicky. You haven't met Dicky, but never mind, you will. He needs some lackey to follow two paces behind him when he maps. Anyway . . . I like to work alone. One day I was in the field mapping for a road construction project. I slipped and fell into a deep trench and broke my leg.' Carter's hand involuntarily slipped to his thigh. 'There was no one around. I shouted until I was blue in the face. Then I realised that if I didn't get myself out of there, no one would. I dragged myself out of that trench with my arms and my good leg. Did some extra damage there.' Carter was rubbing his leg now, as if to soothe the memory.

'I got out, eventually, but then what? I had to get into my bakkie and drive myself to the closest doctor. Now, that small-town doctor was a tough one,' he chuckled. 'He patched me up, put my leg in plaster and looked at me over his spectacles and said, Carter, you said you drove here? That's right, I told him, sweat running down my face. Well Carter, he said, if you drove here, there is no reason you can't drive yourself back.' His whole body shook with laughter, as if the joke had been on him.

Glancing up, and sensing from my smile that his story had fallen on fertile ground, Carter scratched the corner of his mouth and continued. 'Born deaf you know, only because of my mother that I speak so well. She would not let me slur my words. I had to speak clearly or she would refuse to understand me. Yup, thanks to her, most people don't even know I'm deaf.' He looked at his watch once again. A muffled horn blasted from the interior of the mountain and a *chug chug* sound grew louder. A train, carrying skips loaded with rock, burst out into the sunlight and with a metallic screech came to an abrupt halt.

The train tugged the skips to a ledge, where they were tilted one by one onto waiting trucks below. When all the skips were finally emptied, Carter hurried forward and spoke a few words in Sesotho to the driver. He turned and motioned me to follow him as he squeezed in behind the driver's seat. There was just enough room left for me to wedge myself in next to Carter.

'God,' he said, patting his stomach, '. . . getting too fat for this. They don't use the passenger carriage between shift changes, so at times like this you'll have to bum a ride with the train driver while he's taking the loaded skips of rock out or carrying the empty ones in. But then you have to squeeze in behind him. Here we go.'

The train pulled forward. *Chug chug*, it began its journey back into the mountain: my first time into the tunnel. I wrapped my fingers tightly round the back of the seat. The train picked up speed and began to rock. Small yellow lights flashed above us, reflecting off the steel tracks, as we disappeared into the black hole. In the dark I could feel the driver's back leaning against my fingers and Carter's stomach against my arm.

Fifteen minutes later, about five kilometres down the tunnel, the brakes screeched the train to a standstill. Carter gave me a gentle push and I stepped out into another world: bright lights, dust, noise and action. I stared at the commotion in wonder, and then looked up at Carter.

He bent down to my ear and shouted, 'Follow me, step where I step, nowhere else. Okay?'

I nodded my head anxiously. He tapped a knuckle against the hard hat I was holding and pointed to the top of my head. I put the hard hat on. It was not yet adjusted to my size, and slipped over my eyebrows. I pushed it back.

Carter leant towards my ear again. 'Should have got you ear protection, dammit, I forgot. Mind you, the crews don't wear the earplugs anyway.' He gave me a wan smile. 'I, of course, can't hear all the noise. You ready? Follow me.'

Without waiting for a reply, Carter marched ahead, into the blinding yellow light. I followed him, step for step. My gumboots flopped uncomfortably and my overall top hung to mid-thigh. The white hard hat tilted over my forehead, my blonde-brown hair tucked inside it. A newly born, ugly grey chick with feet too large and half an eggshell perched on her head.

As we walked past, men dressed in grey and blue overalls stopped working. A large man with a muscular frame and a black moustache folded his arms as he watched our progress, and frowned. Carter lifted a hand to greet him. Our observer did not reply, just took off his hard hat and wiped the thick black hair, wet with sweat, back from his face.

'That's Mallet,' Carter informed me. 'He's in charge of this crew. Stay on the right side of him.'

'Carter,' Mallet caught his sleeve. 'Your geologist, Dicky. He held up the TBM for *forty-five minutes* yesterday.' Mallet's voice was harsh, even above the deafening grind of machinery.

Carter's smile flattened, and he shook his head heavily, almost sympathetically. 'I'll speak to him.' He tugged at my sleeve.

I followed Carter along the metal walkway, and collided with his bulk as he stopped abruptly. 'Stay here,' he shouted at me above the roar. 'Don't move.'

I nodded obediently. Beneath a cloud of red dust, a conveyer belt churned fragments of rock past us. My throat felt agitated. I coughed and reached out to touch a rock that had fallen off the conveyor belt and into the gutter beside it. I wrapped my fingers around the angular surfaces: sleek natural fracture plains of mudstone. My fingers involuntarily slid back and forth, soothing the rock, soothing myself. Carter caught my hand.

'Don't *ever* put your hands anywhere near the conveyor belt while it's moving. *Ever*. You'll lose all your bloody fingers!'

I felt my eyes grow wider.

Carter attempted a smile: '. . . and you'll have nothing to pick your nose with.'

The deafening rattle of engine died down suddenly. Silence hung in the air like the suspended dust.

Mallet ducked under the conveyor belt and inched over to us. He tapped his wristwatch, 'Five more minutes and you can go in. They're just pulling the conveyor belt out of the cutter head. You have *fifteen minutes* in there, Carter.'

Carter nodded.

Mallet looked at me. His complexion was ruddy, his jaw tense and beneath his moustache, his lips very red. 'Fucking crazy to go into the cutter head. It's safe on *this* side of the TBM, where the walls are protected by the lining. There's nothing to protect you from the falling rock on the other side. I had to drag a man out of there once. Unconscious. A rock fell on his head. Good thing he was wearing his hard hat.'

Still staring at him, I stumbled after Carter. Only when Carter pulled me under the conveyor belt did I rip my eyes off Mallet.

Carter turned on his haunches to face me. 'Look, Robyn, touch what I touch. Step where I step. Okay?'

'Okay,' my voice sounded dry.

'Right, let's go.'

I followed Carter's big boots, climbing under and over dusty steel beams, keeping my hands close to my body, my fingers tucked into my fists. I walked into Carter's stationary backside. He pulled me closer and pointed to a large mechanical arm above us. I looked up. *Dong*, my hollow hard hat hit a metal beam. I straightened it, suddenly relieved I was wearing it.

'That's the arm, it picks up the concrete segments and places them against the tunnel wall. As I explained, the segments make up a full ring, which supports the rock once the TBM has cut though it. Anyone caught between one of those concrete babies and the tunnel wall will be squashed like a bug.' Carter's thumb left an imprint on the toe of his black gumboot, and his eyes rested in mine for a few seconds.

He ducked under a couple more beams and then eased his tall body up. He patted the floor of a narrow metal chamber that lead into the dark at the height of his shoulder. 'Okay, Robyn. We've crawled under the conveyor belt and past the arm. Now we're about to climb into the cutter head. It's much more confined in there. That's where you'll do your mapping from.'

Carter heaved up his weight and disappeared into the dark chamber. I hoisted myself up after him, my forearms straining under my body weight. I landed in a soft bed of dust. I could not breathe. I coughed and gagged, wiping the muddy spit across my face. Carter stirred up more dust as he crawled on all fours in front of me. A light emerged ahead of him. *Dong*, I hit my hard hat on a metal beam again. I adjusted it, spitting out a mouthful of mud. As the space opened up, I crawled beside Carter. A soft, hazy glow of yellow light hung silently around us. A metal face loomed in front of us. It echoed our voices.

Carter panted, 'This is it, Robyn. This is as far as we can go through the TBM. On the other side of this metal wall is the mountain. That's the rock face you will map every day. Just make sure you complete it in fifteen minutes.'

The air was stale. Our world was isolated by thick metal, and I could hear nothing but Carter's echoing voice. I did not like small spaces. I did not like being confined. I could not breathe. I began to panic. I closed my eyes tightly. What would I do? Slow, even breaths.

'You can stand again here,' Carter pulled me up by my sleeve.

I rose slowly, holding my hard hat.

'Right, old chap . . . you okay?' he frowned.

I nodded bleakly.

'These – ' Carter pointed to a large, open gash in the metal wall beside him and then to another three, one beside me and two above us, 'are the portholes. You have to climb into these to see the rock face.'

The portholes radiated out from the centre of the cutter head like open mouths in silent, obscene laughter. When I crouched down, I could see the dusty rock through the ports. That was the mountain. I stretched my arm out and touched the broken face of rock. It felt warm. Peering through the port, I could see the entire rock face. It was larger than the confined cutter head: just over five metres in diameter, the same as the tunnel.

Carter pulled out a hanky from his pocket and dabbed his forehead. The sweat ran down his face in fine streaks through the red dust. Rivulets of blood.

'Just map in the sedimentary beds, and what they are, sandstone or mudstone, that sort of thing, oh, and the thickness and dips of the beds.' Carter wiped his mouth on his sleeve. 'Always record the overbreak, that's the amount of rock that has collapsed from the ceiling. This slick mudstone always caves in. Dicky will show you how he maps.'

I reached out and touched one of the numerous metal discs suspended like UFOs in the cutter head in front of us.

'Those are the actual cutters, the blades, they spin and break the rock as the TBM moves forward, eating its way through the mountain. The broken rock lands on the conveyor belt, which usually lies where we are standing, and the rock is fed from here onto a series of conveyor belts towards the back of the TBM, where it's loaded into the skips and carried out by train and dumped. Right old chap, you got it?'

I stared at Carter.

'Easy as pie,' he added, as if to convince himself. 'Just go in with Dicky a few times, you'll soon get the hang of it. But remember, time is money and money is time. You can only stop the machine for fifteen minutes to map, and it must be between shift changes.'

Step for step, I followed Carter back through the malicious cross-cutting beams of the TBM to the waiting train. Mallet watched us leave, then unfolded his arms to look at his watch. He nodded at a man next to him. Less than fifteen minutes.

The train seemed to have shrunk in size – for looming beside it, with his back to us, was a huge man. Arms like dark mountain ranges emerged from the torn sleeves of his overalls. Carter, who stood over six feet, lifted an arm to pat the man's shoulder. He turned to face us. His face was lined, lived-in. Tight grey curls like burnt ashes emerged from under his hard hat. His eyelids were heavy, giving him a sleepy, watchful look. He flicked his hard hat with a fingernail – a type of personalised salute.

'This is Robyn, new geologist. Robyn, Sipho.'

Sipho glanced down at me, then back at Carter. 'She take as long as Dicky?'

Carter gave a humourless smile. 'We hope not, Sipho, we hope not. Well . . .' He made a gesture to leave.

'Be safe. I wish that you are safe here.' Sipho's heavy eyelids dropped onto me. He had a hard mouth, wide. It smiled briefly.

'Thank you,' I mumbled.

I watched him lift a barrel and carry it off, a weight two men would have struggled with.

Carter was urging me into the train. I climbed in beside him, behind the driver. The train rocked us out. Fifteen minutes later a small circle of light appeared in the distance. It grew larger and larger and then exploded around us as we burst out of the tunnel. Carter and I squeezed out of the driver's compartment and clumped back to the offices.

As we reached the entrance of the building, he turned to me. 'Why don't you clean some of that muck off? You can use the showers here. Usually you'll be able to go back to your room to clean off. Once you're done, I'll introduce you to Dicky.'

In the ladies' shower I watched the water stream a muddy brown off my body. I spat the grit from my mouth, blew it out of my nose, washed it from my eyes. Finally, I dried myself off and pulled my shirt and jeans back on. I rolled up the filthy overalls and walked back to Carter's office.

'Right, old chap . . . let's find Dicky.' Carter loped off between a row of office partitions. Strange faces looked up from worn desks, weighed down with paper and grubby hard hats.

Carter thumped a fragile office partition. 'Dicks dearie.'

A small man with a neatly clipped grey beard and large, silver-framed glasses looked up. His hair was thick, grey and coarse, and he had a large red birthmark on his right cheek.

'This is Robyn Hartley, she'll be helping us out in the tunnel. And sharing your office,' said Carter.

Dicky stood up and extended his hand. His touch was cool and limp.

'Well,' Carter punctuated the silence between us, 'I'll leave you two to get to know each other. Take Robyn into the tunnel a few times, Dicks, show her the ropes. Let her see how one of the older buggers does it.' Carter nodded to himself, as if in agreement, and left.

Dicky and I studied each other, the smiles on our faces uncertain. Through his spectacles, his eyes shifted through a variety of greys. Behind him, his desk was cluttered with maps and pencil crayons. At his feet, below his desk, a row of rock samples peered out. Additional samples wallowed in a large orange tub of water. The rest of his collection stood above his bookshelf, basking in the frail winter sunlight. All the rock samples were yellow or red-brown. Sandstone or mudstone – I recognised them from the tunnel.

'So . . .' Dicky tapped his thumbs together and eased his small backside onto his desk. 'Is this your first job?'

'Second, I worked for the government in Pretoria before this.'

Dicky gave a tight, satisfied smile. 'So this is your first real job then.'

'Second,' I corrected, placing my overalls on the empty desk, which faced a blank office partition. Unlike Dicky's, which faced an open window looking onto a hill of yellow grasses.

My first job . . . where time had blurred in the filling-out of white forms. As flavourless as the tea twice a day; as starched and empty as the maze of corridors you had to negotiate to get to me on the tenth floor. My first job, where the corridors smelt of Dettol and nothing. Mostly nothing – or if you sniffed closely, near the air vents and drains, the smell of wasting life. If you followed the row of flickering neon lights, you'd have found me sitting behind my heavy wooden desk in the corner office. The desk was empty apart from two shifting blocks of paper and a yellowing telephone. Six months and three thousand forms later, I left. I wiped away the taste of Dettol from my mouth. I wiped away the mind-blowing routine and suffocated lives. *Clump clump*, my footsteps echoed down the corridor. *Ping*, the doors of the lift opened and closed behind me . . . *three, two, one, ground*. Grounded, I returned to the world of the living.

Dicky bent down and selected a rock from the basin. He wiped it on a grubby towel and delicately bit the corner of the rock. He chewed thoughtfully. 'Mmm . . . a silty mudstone, not a muddy siltstone, as I had originally thought. It's the only way you can tell the rock types apart, tasting them. Want a bite?' He held the damp specimen out toward me.

'No, no thanks. I had quite enough in the tunnel this afternoon.' I patted my stomach.

Dicky laughed but his eyes did not soften.

'Well,' Dicky licked his lips as he returned the rock to its rightful habitat, 'time for me to go. I feel quite weak. I don't think I've had enough protein for the day – can make you quite dizzy. I need a ham sandwich. Or perhaps I'm coming down with something.' He touched his forehead with the back of his hand. 'I'll meet you at the tunnel tomorrow morning. The train leaves at six. At six, mind you. They won't wait. I must say . . . an unpleasant lot. But you'll find that out soon enough. That's why I take Orbit in with me. My assistant. Don't trust one of *them* going into the cutter head with me.'

Dicky packed a clipboard, compass and geological hammer into a muddy backpack, stroked his beard and suddenly turned back to me. 'Orbit's been my assistant for almost two years now. When I first got him, he wanted to learn to map. I considered it at first, but I re- alised it takes the experience of a qualified geologist. One with an eye for detail, if I may say so myself. Orbit bothered me for a while about it, but now he's happy to just carry my pack. I need him to pass equipment to me in the cutter head. That's all. And for safety. It's safer with two. Well,' he smiled briefly, 'see you on site tomor- row.'

I trailed after the other strangers out of the site offices, climbed into my VW Beetle and drove around the hill back into town to the single quarters. I had been allocated room number nineteen. It was pleasant: two single beds with pale blue bedcovers (which I pushed together to make a double), a table and a chair, a TV and private bath- room. A sliding door led on to a tiny veranda and garden enclosed by a high wall. I sat on one of the beds and unpacked my two boxes of possessions. I arranged my small collection of books onto a shelf: a couple of Kunderas amongst the Steinbecks; Cormac McCarthy, Pat Barker and J.D. Salinger. I rearranged them in alphabetical order and felt marginally better. I sighed. Glancing at my watch, I saw it was almost dinner time. I went to find the single-quarters restaurant.

The restaurant was mostly empty, except for a couple of tables crowded with men, some of them still in their overalls. They looked up to watch the stranger enter and then resumed eating. I sat self-consciously alone. Staring at my plate, I half-heartedly ate the brown outer rim of my steak. I did not want to send it back for more cooking, lest I should draw the attention of the busy tables.

A thick, stocky figure slid onto the chair next to mine.

'Roth,' he said, grinning and holding out a hand. I shook it. Sky-blue eyes crinkled in a broad tanned face. A head as round and bald as a bowling ball. He looked about fifty, and spoke with a pronounced accent, not one I could place. Starting from the back of his neck, he rubbed an awkward hand over his large head. 'That's right, I said to myself, that's the new geo. That's the one Carter told me about. Well, anyone raining on your parade? No, not yet. Fresh as a newly hatched chick here, aren't you? Going to work in the tunnel with us? I don't work with the underground crews myself, as such. Mechanical engineer, I am. Go in now and again, just to check the TBM.' Roth gave me a toothy grin. 'Say, Robyn. Say we go and wet the tonsils? Get a beer.'

I nodded. 'Where?'

'The Lodge up the road. Outskirts of town. It's where we all go. Every night.'

I slid out of my chair to follow Roth. I didn't want to be left alone to think about my current situation just yet. Not yet. And I only wanted to speak to Terence about it once I had given it some thought. Terence would be arriving the following night, Friday, for the weekend, anyway.

I drove behind Roth's bakkie (tunnel issue) and parked beside him at the Lodge. Following him, I pushed my way through a throng of men, some of whom I recognised from the tunnel that morning, and into the bar. Roth sat down at the bar counter and sunk a powerful hand onto my shoulder, pushing me down onto the bar stool beside him. He shook my shoulder.

'What can I get you?'

'Beer. Black Label, thanks,' I replied, wrestling off my thick jacket, sleeve by sleeve.

Roth ordered the drink from the young, vacant-looking man with a goatee beard behind the bar. He repeated the order good-naturedly while rubbing his bald head. He turned to me, still smiling, and gently took my hand.

'Man, it's a heavy load. Keeps me away from the family. It's an anvil, it is. It's our anvil, working in the tunnel.'

I considered removing my hand. I did not particularly like being touched, and he was almost a stranger. But something in his eyes made me leave my hand extended between us. They were as gentle as a cloudless summer sky, and they caught alight when he smiled. I liked his smile: it was filled with affection and warmth. And mischief.

Roth patted my hand. 'You can hear I'm from Liverpool. Well, originally, been in South Africa for many years now. Not lost the accent though.'

I gently retracted my hand. Roth twisted around in his bar stool. Pulled out his stiff leg and stretched it out more comfortably in front of him.

'What happened to your leg?'

'This splint? Rains on my parade, it does. I've always worked in construction, used to work high up, man. High up in them scaffolding. And then one day I fell. Maybe three stories. The scaffolding collapsed right under me – right under me, man. I fell and this leg,' his thick forearms wrapped around his thigh, 'this old leg of mine was crushed beneath me and I was unconscious. This old Roth sitting in front of you was almost a goner, man.' Roth took my hand once again and pulled me closer. His blue eyes grew wide. 'I woke up in a hospital. In them crisp, white sheets with nurses and doctors running around me.'

His voice dropped to a whisper. I strained to hear him over the drone of voices in the pub.

'I had the biggest experience of my life. Thought them angels had come. Thought the heavens had opened and them angels were sounding them trumpets.'

He looked at me.

'What?' I asked. 'What happened?'

'Whoooie!' Roth exclaimed loudly, pulled back his hand and threw back his head, 'Those drugs they gave me, man. Whoooie!' Scuse me while I kiss the sky . . . Purple haze, man, I was floating. Wonderful drugs they gave me. Never had a feeling like that again in me life. Scuse me while I kiss the sky!'

His eyes crinkled amongst the laughter lines, searching mine for a reaction; he seemed pleased when I laughed with him.

'Your first day in the deep dark hole. With them trolls. What do you think of our tunnel?'

I felt my chest constrict; it was difficult to reply. I shrugged my shoulders instead and gave a sick smile. Roth stood up and sunk his tough hands in my shoulders, sinking his fingers expertly into all the tense muscles. Against my will, I felt my back ease, grateful for his touch.

'Don't let it rattle your cage, man.'

A young man sitting on my left, short with a dark crew-cut, turned to watch. He chuckled softly into his beer, 'Roth gives a good massage. A throw-back to the old days – he was a boxer, then a trainer. Knows how to prepare his fighters to get back in the ring. He gives us all massages.'

'That's right, man,' Roth continued to work my neck and back, 'I was a fighter, had the body for it, just not the soul. I'm a lover, man, not a fighter.'

He patted me on the shoulders. I wriggled them and drained the last of my beer.

'I must be off. I have an early start in the tunnel tomorrow.' I stood up to leave.

Roth nodded his large pinball head at me. 'That won't be worrying you for long. You'll be in here with the rest of us. We leave the tunnel for the day. Come here at night. No man, can't let it get to you.'

I drove back to the single quarters, climbed under the pale blue covers and set my alarm. I drifted into a shallow sleep, waiting for the alarm to yell.

Which it did, reliably, as the hand struck five-thirty the next morning. I pulled on my overalls and then my all-weather padded trousers and jacket over them. Bleary, half asleep, only ready to wake with the sun a full hour later. It was freezing. I swore silently. It was only May: real winter was still on the way.

Only a few minutes later, I drove through the security gates and into the noise and bustle of the construction site. I parked beside a row of concrete segments and went to stand beside the passenger carriage with a crowd of unfamiliar faces. There was no sign of Dicky. I stamped my feet to keep warm and breathed into my scarf. Five to six. The large padded figures beside me, carrying hard hats and headlamps attached to heavy, square batteries, bent over and climbed into the carriage. I followed them.

Inside the carriage, an invisible line appeared to divide the crew – blacks on one side facing whites on the other. I sat in the first empty space, facing the white tunnel workers, beside the man I recognised as Sipho. He cast his serious eyes onto me and gave me a single nod. There was still no sign of Dicky. I looked at the row of men opposite me and into the eyes of Mallet. He was rhythmically grinding his jaw. He looked at his watch. He and Sipho looked at each other. Sipho gave another nod.

'Go,' Mallet thumped the carriage wall behind him, commanding the driver.

'Wait. Wait!' Dicky, dressed in the same padded clothing as the rest of us, was climbing on board.

A thin man with a vacant grin followed, carrying a pack and an enormous pump-action water bottle. I wiggled aside to make room for them.

Dicky sat down beside me, gasping cheerfully for breath. 'Morning, gentlemen.'

There was no reply.

'This is Orbit,' he told me.

I greeted his assistant, who nodded his frozen smile and shoved the bottle and pack protectively between his knees.

Mallet leant forward to Dicky. 'Next time . . . Next time you're late, we are leaving without you.' His head jolted as the train released its brakes and we started to rock into the mountain. The lights of the carriage flickered on.

Dicky gave a hollow laugh, ignoring Mallet and turned to me, 'I always bring a water bottle, to wash the dust off the rock face. Can't map without it. Actually I quite enjoy mapping . . .' Dicky's voice was lost as the train and tracks clacked into an even rhythm.

Above us in the tunnel, yellow lights flashed at constant intervals. Heads rocked silently. Large worn hands held lamp batteries on stained overall laps. It grew steadily warmer, increasing to a comfortable temperature and then getting steadily hotter. And hotter. My all-weather clothing grew suffocating. Jammed between Dicky and Sipho, there was no room for me to pull it off.

Fifteen minutes later the train shrieked to a halt, metal on metal. We had arrived at the TBM. I followed the hunched figures out of the door and, imitating them, pulled my padded outer clothing off. I followed Dicky and Orbit along the same route of metal walkways I had walked the day before with Carter. Dicky cut a small, neat figure in his overalls, rather like an action toy – The Miner. His gumboots, much like his hands, were large in proportion to the size of his body.

Figures moved aside to let Dicky walk. One voice mumbled, 'Don't take too bloody long in there today, Dicky.'

Orbit's dark face looked feverish. I caught his eye, his grin broadened.

Through the metal beams, below the conveyor belt. I clambered up into the cutter head, landing in the now anticipated carpet of red dust. On all fours I crawled after Dicky and Orbit until we reached the cutting edge of the TBM. We stopped outside the portholes leading to the rock face. I watched Dicky climb into the lowest porthole. His small figure was a convenient size: only a woman or a small man would fit into those ports. Never Carter.

Boop-boop, Orbit pumped the water bottle. The sound hung in the thick dust and confined silence. Dicky wiggled himself into a comfortable position, waiting for Orbit. After five minutes, Orbit handed Dicky the water bottle.

With the attached hose and nozzle Dicky squirted the rock face, pondered it until the rock had dried, and then squirted some more.

The pressure in the bottle ran low. Dicky handed the water bottle back to Orbit. Orbit pumped for another five minutes. Dicky took the bottle. He squirted, he pondered. Back and forth this continued for twenty-five minutes. I glanced anxiously at my watch.

Finally satisfied, Dicky called, 'Compass, Orbit.'

There was no response.

Orbit had closed his eyes. I tapped his shoulder, and he looked up at Dicky with surprise.

'Compass, Orbit,' repeated Dicky.

Orbit fumbled in the bag, found the compass and gave it to Dicky with a glazed expression. Dicky leant through the port towards the rock face and took a reading. And another.

From deep within in the TBM, a voice rumbled menacingly: "Thirty-five minutes, Dicky."

Dicky looked at me and smiled; a small, satisfied smile.

'My pencil and clipboard, Orbit.'

Orbit searched for the requested tools and handed them to Dicky. Dicky began to draw the map.

"Forty minutes, Dicky. If you don't get out of there now, I'm coming to fetch you!" The voice was closer, louder, angrier.

Licking the tip of his pencil, stroking his thick moustache, Dicky continued to work.

"*Dicky!*" a voice ripped from behind me, its edges torn loose with furious hostility.

I jumped, we all did. *Dong*, I hit my hard hat on the metal beam above me. Figures loomed in the murky light behind us.

"Get the fuck out of there. Now!"

Dicky jumped out of the port and was on all fours, scurrying through the dust out of the cutter head, Orbit behind him. I was close on Orbit's heels.

Out of the cutter head, past rows of furious eyes and heads turned away, I walked behind Dicky.

He stopped to talk to me. 'They're always like that. Try to bully you into taking less time. It's impossible. I keep telling them that. And Carter. You need at least forty-five minutes to understand the rock.'

Mallet stormed past us to the train. On the way he passed Sipho and pointed two fingers into his eyes and chucked his fingers back to the TBM. *Keep an eye on things.* Sipho nodded and strode into the light and dust, wiping the oil from his hands. His figure was so large, he temporarily blocked out the glare.

'Make them wait until you're taking a load of skips out,' Mallet instructed the driver. 'Don't take them out now. He – ' he turned and pointed a thick finger at Dicky, 'can wait.'

Dicky swallowed his smirk as Mallet stormed off. Orbit's face turned grey, his smile as bright as ever.

Dicky patted his forehead and neck. 'Think I'm getting a touch of fever. Probably glandular. Yes, I think I can feel my glands are swollen.'

Friday afternoon. Two days in the tunnel. It felt longer, much longer. I returned to my room to wash the fine dust off my body, floss it out of my teeth, scrub it from my neck and ears. As I dried off and pulled on my clothes, I heard a diesel engine and the familiar rumble of a rattletrap parking outside my room. Terence.

I opened the door to see the large, battered Isuzu bakkie, still splattered in Swaziland mud. The driver's door, with the circular badge of Red Earth Exploration, was bent inwards, allowing access in and out of the vehicle only through the passenger door. A few months ago, one of Terence's field staff had stolen the vehicle to visit a nearby shebeen. Not really knowing how to drive, he had jammed his foot on the accelerator instead of the brake, spinning the vehicle off the muddy track and into a fence pole. Terence had let him off with a warning, but in the meantime, as the geologist in charge, he was stuck with the faulty vehicle. He edged across the seat, moved something out of the way and climbed out the passenger door. He smiled and waved.

Terence's hair, as pale blond as the Clarens grasses, had grown long and straggly. As usual he had rough, dark-blond growth on his chin. He seldom shaved, allowing his beard to grow until it bothered him and then shaving it off on impulse. Terence's jaw, when tense, could seem hard and unyielding; but his eyes were always gentle, carrying an almost wounded look. They were eyes that insisted on seeing the truth in all situations. Yet devoid of any sentimentality. They shifted colour according to what surrounded him, from blue through grey to green. With the darkening sky behind him, they were the colour of choppy grey seas. Crow's feet formed around those eyes and I buried myself in his arms. That familiar smell of Terence: pine forests and cinnamon.

'I've got something for you,' he told me and strolled back to the vehicle. He had an easy way of walking. Slim and athletic, he handled the long walking distances required of his work on the Swaziland border with ease.

I followed him and peered into the bakkie. Between the numerous Led Zeppelin and Tom Waits tapes was a bundle wrapped in a dirty blue blanket. He lifted it out and delivered it into my arms. From the centre of the folds, wild hazel eyes glinted up at me. It was a small golden spaniel puppy. A long pink tongue unrolled from his mouth.

'He stinks,' I said.

'He probably rolled in something on the farm. My crew gave him to me. They found him abandoned along the road. They already gave him a name, a Zulu name: Bonginkosi. Bongi for short.'

'Bongi,' I repeated, lowering the blanket to the ground. The puppy tore out and snorted through the grass, propelled by a spinning tail. As he ran into my room I jogged after him, just in time to see him run out the sliding door and with one bound, clear the garden wall. I looked at Terence helplessly.

'He'll settle in.' He threw down his bag and put an arm around me.

Sure enough, Bongi reappeared at the front door and charged back into the room. Room number nineteen, now home to Bongi and me. Shut in the room, Bongi collided with the glass door a few times and then slunk between the furniture. Terence lay back on the bed and I lay against his chest.

'Tell me about your new job.'

I sighed, 'I don't know what to say. Hopefully I'll get used to it.'

'Underground is no place for anyone,' Terence ran a hand through my shoulder-length hair.

'The walls are lined. They won't cave in. Not like a mine.'

'Still, angel, be careful. It's underground.'

I scrambled off the bed and looked under the table for Bongi. I found him under a chair, gently chewing the lamp cord. He had already chewed though the plastic coating and was gnawing on the wires.

I unplugged the cord and smacked him on the nose. 'No, Bongi, no.'

He sat up. For the first time I noticed how bow-legged he was. White-blond hair stood out from the top of his head in an oddly human way. I tried to cup his silky little head, to comfort him. He jolted around and sunk his sharp teeth into my hand.

'Oow! You little bastard.'

Bongi jumped up onto the bed behind Terence. *Thump thump*, his tail knocked the bedspread, while he eyed me with suspicion. Terence stroked his long ears, laughing.

My fear in the tunnel did not diminish, even after two months. It only got worse. Was I waiting for something to save me? Reason perhaps. Reason would dissolve my terror. But reason stood back – or perhaps the fear was reason at work. The tired men, the lethal machinery . . . When was I safe, when not? I had to trust these men; trust them with my life.

The tunnel worked on three shifts a day and so did I. From early morning I was underground, in the late afternoon I wandered the surrounding sandstone hills with Bongi, and in the evenings I sat in the pub with new-found friends and colleagues. Gradually I began to feel like one of the crew.

In the tunnel, after I had finished mapping and stood waiting for the train, I would be invited for coffee. The coffee room was a three-by-one-metre cubicle at the back of the TBM, insulated from some of the noise. The coffee was weak and served in grubby styrofoam cups. Magazines about guns or girls were strewn over the bench. The breasts on the naked girls were enormous; the covers on the gun magazines all looked the same. I sat with the crew in my filthy overalls, my boots caked with mud. The heavy battery for my headlamp lay beside me. I got to know something about the men. Small details about their lives: son's new bicycle, a remedy for their sick dog, a farm left behind.

Even Mallet once sat down beside me. I moved my legs in surprise.

'Just be grateful this isn't a gold mine. I worked two kilometres under before this. I worked with Sipho, he was on my shift. We worked at the face where we had little space to move. Long hours in fucking lousy conditions. One night the stopes gave in, we all got out in time, except one. A metal rod cut his legs clean off. Sipho and I carried him out. Let me tell you one thing,' Mallet looked at me, 'he didn't make one sound as we carried him out. Not one sound.'

He stood up. 'Just appreciate that these tunnel walls are lined. It's safe. The rock can only cave in on the other side of the cutter head. And you have got to be fucking crazy to go there.' He pushed past my muddy boots and back into the bright lights and grinding noise of the TBM.

Carter had increased my shifts. When I arrived, I mapped three times a week, as did Dicky, while Carter took the remaining shift. Now Carter's plans had changed. He was not permitted to work underground, as he was too senior. I was to map four times a week, and already, Carter was speaking of increasing my shifts again. The arguments between Dicky and the crews were ongoing, and Carter wanted to decrease the amount of time Dicky spent in the tunnel. Dicky resented this, naturally. He insisted he needed more time to map the rock face.

I kept my part of the deal with the crew. I completed a map in fifteen minutes, recording only the bare detail of the rock. The shift inspector, always an older man than the rest of the crew, recorded the time I spent in the cutter head. He would nod if I came out within fifteen minutes. That nod kept me going. That nod kept me mapping. That part of the job I liked: being part of the crew, being useful.

Only in the late afternoons, as I walked through the hills, was my underground fear permitted to surface and dissipate. Walking in those hills, I even forgot about missing Terence. I stopped counting the days to his next visit, stopped wondering if he would be able to visit this weekend, or would it be the next? Walking, I forgot everything but the hills and grasses, the mountains and sky. I was high, high above the tunnel, high above my fear.

Late one afternoon, I stood in the hills above the town, the cold light of day fading and the first town lights beginning to blink. A dog barked – even its bark sounded cold. I wrapped my scarf more tightly around my head, my eardrums vibrating. I had not known I could get this cold.

Beside Clarens lay the township of Kgubetswana. It had grown dramatically since the start of the tunnel. There was work, for some. Those that were employed supported the many others that were not. Crowded and poor, Kgubetswana was a township of small plots and big dreams. Smoke rose from fires already lit; fires to ward off the deathly cold which rattled and shook the insubstantial corrugated-iron walls.

Further in the distance I could see the grey clouds gathering over the Lesotho mountains, and between the mountains and the town I could see the construction site. The distant sound of the site, busy twenty-four hours a day, floated up to me. Bongi sat watching the view beside me, his head cocked thoughtfully to one side. In two months, he had grown from a gangling pup into rather a handsome spaniel. His front legs were no longer bow-legged. His coat was a shiny caramel, his long ears wavy silk. He still had the odd tuft of blond hair on his head. He tore past me as I continued to walk, almost tripping me in the process, and sped down the path.

A siren bleated. I stopped walking. *Beebaa beebaa.* Yes, it was a siren. My eyes slid across Clarens and Kgubetswana to the construction site, straining through the last light of the day. The machinery on the site had died down. Silence. And then suddenly an ambulance, its lights flashing and its siren now loud and clear, burst onto the road. *Beebaa beebaa . . .* it sped from the tunnel site past Clarens.

I pulled up my jacket collar, tucked my nose into my scarf and followed Bongi. He was already waiting for me at the VW Beetle. I drove us to the Lodge, where I slipped a leash onto Bongi's straining collar and walked through the throng of bodies to the bar.

The bar was, as usual, busy. But there was a greyness to the tone, a severity to the noise. Mallet stood at the bar. I'd never seen him at the bar. In the tunnel, he'd told me he preferred to drink at home. He was still wearing his filthy overalls and gumboots. He drained a glass of gold liquid – brandy, I guessed – and slammed it on the bar. Beside him sat Roth and on his other side was a young technician I recognised from underground, Cas. Cas had cruel, brittle-blue eyes and a slightly deranged smile, and moved with the contained energy of an elastic band. He spun around to watch me sit next to Roth and wiped a hand through his spiky blond hair.

Roth took my hand as I sat down. Bongi climbed under my bar-stool.

'What happened?'

'An anvil man, it's a goddamn anvil.'

'What happened, Roth?'

Mallet turned to me. 'They almost killed him.'

'Killed who?'

'That surveyor, that Brit,' said Mallet.

I nodded. Weekly, a surveyor came into the tunnel to check the alignment of the TBM with laser precision.

'He was working under the mechanical arm that lifts the segments,' Mallet continued. 'The TBM was down, and the foreman had a couple of the guys carry the control box with them.'

I nodded again. Once all the controls in the driving room of the TBM were shut down, they could be overridden by a hand-held control box – an extra safety feature.

'Some fucking idiot placed the control box on a ledge above them and then knocked it off. He caught it and activated the starter button. He activated the mechanical arm. The surveyor was lying between the tunnel wall and the segment. Those segments weigh one and a half fucking tons and the arm started to place it against the tunnel wall, trapping him in between.'

Roth sunk his big head into his hands and rocked it. 'No, man.'

Mallet turned to go. 'They stopped the arm just in time. Just before it fucking killed him. But it crushed his spine and he's going to be in hospital for some time.'

'It . . . wasn't your shift?' I asked.

'No, not mine. I was in the tunnel to check an air vent.' Mallet shook his head, 'He was our side of the cutter head. He should've been safe.'

Roth and I watched him leave.

'Fat lot of good his fancy education did that surveyor, his *degree*. You need savvy to be in there, you need to know the way machinery works. Thought his degree would save him,' Cas snorted, and turned his back to us.

'The sky fell on that surveyor, man. Just like Chicken Licken.' Roth squeezed my hand, which lay limply on the counter. 'You and me, we're still here. Can't let these things rattle your cage, man.'

That night I drank too much. Many small glasses of clear liquid. It wasn't too unusual – I had begun to drink more heavily. We all drank like that. We drank in the face of fear, we toasted its bruised existence. Besides, I didn't want to go back to my room, I didn't want sleep to find me. Bongi sat beneath my barstool with a hangdog expression. He was as morose and irritable in bars as he was exuberant in the hills. But I wanted him close that night, I wanted to sink my hand onto his soft head and stroke his long ears.

I drifted into a vodka-drenched sleep – I think it was vodka. Grinding blades tore me open, dust suffocated me. I awoke tearing blankets from my body. Winter froze me within seconds, and I pulled back the covers. Then I slept with tiredness in every muscle and every bone. But as I slept, the rotting breath of fear drew closer. Blades, blood, blackness, bewilderment. My nights were always more fearful than my cold, dark mornings.

The next morning I rose groggy, my throat sore and irritated from the constant tunnel dust. I rinsed my mouth out with salt water and took an aspirin. I bundled on my all-weather clothing and drove past Kgubetswana to pick up Orbit, who was now my assistant too. Mechanically I drove to site, parked and climbed aboard the passenger carriage.

I sat in the carriage between Sipho and Orbit. I leant my dizzy head back against the metal wall. I would do the work, I would map the rock face. I always did. In fifteen minutes. Brakes screamed their release. The train chugged, first slowly and then breaking into a rhythm. Into the mountain. The lights in the carriage flickered and then went out – the bulb was gone. We rocked in the darkness. Someone turned their headlamp on and off. As we rode into the stomach of the mountain, it grew warmer.

And in the blackness, a voice rose. Sipho. A lion's rumble. A deep resonating voice. A harmony so powerful and sad, it melted the frost on my fingers and nose. Rocking with the train, the rest of us were quiet.

Then another voice rose to accompany his, and another. Until all the Sesotho voices had risen in harmony with Sipho. Flowing into him – tributary streams flowing into the main valley. Washing through me, washing like the water would wash from Lesotho through this tunnel. Their water. Our privilege. The harmony of the Lesotho hills and lives linked to nature, to the soil, to the cattle and the heavy grey clouds that gathered above the mountains. I felt the words, although I could not understand them. All the time I prayed the journey and this heavenly sound, like drops of water in my dry painful throat, would never end.

But the train did slow down, screech to its predictable halt in the light of the TBM. We sat there in silence, the light having extinguished the sound. We each waited for another to be the first to stand, unlock the bolts and slide open the carriage door. No one moved.

Cas started to laugh, silently, exposing his crooked front teeth. Then called out in a flat accent, 'Their singing is just like their brains. They sing the same things over and over.'

Sipho's dark handsome face was once again silent and closed. He was the first to rise, unbolt the carriage door and slide it open. I felt too heavy to move.

CHAPTER TWO

Patron Saint of Tunnels

I had worked in the tunnel for six months. For six months I had climbed through the machinery, mapped the rock face. The weight of the lamp battery, the anticipation, the dust, rocking against the men's padded shoulders – all this was by now familiar. I worked on automatic. I mapped in fifteen minutes.

That morning, the brakes scraped metal on metal and the train slowed down. Figures rose, hunched. The door of the carriage rolled open on its coasters. Even before my gumboot hit the walkway, I knew something was wrong.

Silence. There were no footsteps milling around, no grinding of machinery. No clanging, no banging, just . . . silence. It drifted around us. Brushed up my spine and crept around my neck. Blood pounded in my ears: *what-is-wrong, what-is-wrong* . . . I stood motionless. The morning shift emptied out of the carriage and congealed around me.

Mallet's shift was currently working nights. Usually the night shift stood waiting for the train. That morning, however, they drifted around us, seemingly oblivious of our arrival. I placed my pack carefully on the metal walkway so my hammer would not ring out. I waited. In the distance I saw Sipho wipe his hands on a rag; he was watching Mallet. Mallet stood stationery, his hands on his hips, staring at his boots.

Sam pushed past me. As the inspector, he was responsible for recording events on the shifts. All events. His senior years and brusque manner assured him a certain authority with the crews. His grey eyes, which peered out from beneath a bushy overhang of eyebrows, often made me uncomfortable – as if they had seen too much in a lifetime spent working down mines and in tunnels. Sam walked over to Mallet. Mallet said something and Sam nodded. He walked back to me. What?

Later, Sam told me, *let them leave, get them all out of here.*

My eyes began to smart and my breathing became rapid and shallow.

I stood waiting in the doorway of the coffee cubicle. Beside me on the bench was a magazine cover of a girl thrusting out her tanned breasts and licking her top lip. Around me in the TBM the conveyor belts were clean and empty, and the walkways shone. The entire TBM sparkled. I had never seen it this clean before. The night shift lifted their batteries and removed their hard hats to wipe their brows. They milled about, but no one moved towards the waiting train. Mallet remained motionless. His mouth open, he took big, slow breaths that made his chest rise and fall. Sam pushed past me into the coffee room. He sat down on the girlie magazine and pulled off his hardhat as if it contained some unbearable weight

'A man lost, lass, a life lost.'

'Who?'

'A man from Lesotho. One of the night shift. He was cleaning under the conveyor belt while it was moving. He stood up and was decapitated.' Sam released a staggered breath. 'Who's to blame, I don't know. He shouldn't have been working there. Whose fault it was, doesn't matter. A life has been lost, one of the crew.'

I pinched my nose, which had begun to run.

'They wrapped up the body and then the head and took him out of the tunnel. They laid him outside and some of the men cleaned the TBM. Washed away the blood, cleared away the rock. They removed all traces of the accident.'

Sipho walked past us towards Mallet. He stopped beside the cubicle and looked at Sam and myself. 'It could've been anyone of us. Any one of us. You or me.'

We watched Sipho gather Mallet's square battery and lamp and wrap them in his thick blue jacket. A few of the night shift glanced at

Sipho and, taking his lead, started moving towards the train. Mallet continued to stare at the walkway, his hands on his hips, his chest rising and falling with slow deep breaths. Sipho climbed into the train and without looking up Mallet followed, as if pulled by a magnetic force. Mallet pulled off his hard hat and climbed into the carriage. The last of the shift came after him. The metal door clanged. *Chug boom, chug boom,* the train took its precious cargo out into the safety of the sunlight.

The death echoed in the tunnel. We trod carefully, we were quiet. The men took their positions. The machine was ready. The TBM would start again and the tunnel would continue: Mallet's shift had ensured that. I worked quickly, completed the map and left, and a train took me out immediately.

I closed my eyes to the rocking motion. Daily, the shifts boarded the train. Each eight hours heavy with work; the yelling, the friction, the production. The loyalty. No one had noticed the bonds forming. One life, one of the crew.

Back in the site office Carter took the map. For once he showed little interest in it.

'How was it in there?' he asked

'Quiet,' I swallowed, 'really quiet.'

Carter shook his head, sighed and walked over to his window. He stared outside at the green summer grasses. 'You've seen the statue hanging above the tunnel entrance?'

I nodded bleakly. I had seen her. She was just a colourful patch in the corner of my eye as I rode daily into the tunnel.

'That's the Patron Saint of Tunnels. She's meant to keep all the men in the tunnel safe. Someone brought her from South America. Now the shifts will not go into the tunnel unless her lamp is burning. Last night,' he rubbed a coarse hand over his face, 'last night her lamp went out.'

I was quiet. From now on, I too would not enter the tunnel if the Patron Saint's light was not burning.

Chansa waved at me from across the conveyor belt of the TBM. He was the new engineer from Kenya, who had moved into the single quarters next to me, room number twenty. Chansa had arrived shortly after the death in the tunnel, as if the Patron Saint had taken one life and sent another. He was as quiet, level and calm as the Serengeti Plains he came from. He looked foreign. He was too tall, too dark, his cheeks bones too defined and his eyes too almond-shaped to have come from Southern Africa. Engineers had come from all over the world to work on this project, but Chansa was the first one from East Africa.

Bongi had immediately become good friends with Chansa, spending long periods of time in his room. The first time it happened I went over to retrieve him, and found the two of them in Chansa's garden. Chansa sat smoking, one leg crossed over the other and his gaze fixed on the sandstone hills in the distance. Bongi lay at his feet, asleep, his ears as fluid as honey. I left Bongi. And immediately liked Chansa.

Chansa continued to check the conveyor belt fittings. I placed my pack on the walkway and sat on it, waiting for a train to take me out. I had been working in the tunnel for eight months, and Carter had increased my shifts again: I was doing five, sometimes six tunnel shifts a week. My nightmares had got worse. I drank more. My throat infections were more frequent. But I continued to work.

I pulled out my black notebook from the inner, most protected pocket of my jacket. I removed my ink pen, black with a gold nib. Terence had given me the pen as a gift, one he could ill afford.

Three days until your next visit, I wrote to Terence. The pen influenced my handwriting: it trailed over the sweat-crinkled pages with an artistic flourish I found difficult to recognise as my own. Terence visited whenever he could – every second weekend, sometimes every weekend; whenever his project did not need him. Letters dropped off and picked up at post boxes bridged the time between.

It's been over eight months that I've worked in this tunnel. Eight long months. Why don't I just get out? Perhaps like the TBM, I can only move forward and eat my way out of this black hole . . .

I wrote over the sketch of the daily rock face. It didn't matter, I redrew the maps for Carter anyway; and Terence, despite his wariness of the TBM and underground life, enjoyed getting letters stained with red tunnel dust, covered with scribbles of the daily rock face. He said it gave him more of an idea of what it was like to work in the tunnel and, as a geologist, he could make sense of the sketches of rock beds, their dips and thicknesses. The dust and circular maps so different from his mapping in the Swaziland hills, where he strode the muddy tracks amongst the forests and rocky waterfalls.

'Robyn.'

I looked up. Chansa's slender arms made the rolling motion of a train and pointed in front of him. I gave him a thumbs-up and stuffed my notebook and overall top into my bag. I now just wore an old T-shirt or vest with my overall pants, it was much cooler and easier to climb up into the ports without my arms being restrained by coarse canvas. All my overall pants were by now stained with oil and eaten in patches by battery acid. I had replaced the tunnel-issue gumboots with my leather hiking boots. They felt more comfortable and had more of a grip for climbing in and out of the cutter head. The distinctive chug of the train grew louder.

'Orbit, train,' I called.

He sat talking to a couple of men in a dark corner. He looked up and smiled – a smile I still did not know how to interpret. Nervous or vacant? I had tried to rekindle Orbit's interest in learning to map, in learning a little about geology, at least enough to assist me in taking samples. But Orbit had become too comfortable. For two years he had worked for Dicky, doing nothing but follow him around the tunnel. Now he followed me. In the afternoons he sat behind the office kitchen door hoping no one would see him. There was no reason to change; Orbit was quite happy with the way things were. He rose slowly and followed me into the train. Orbit was of no help to me. The shifts were beginning to check the cutters while I mapped in the cutter head. There were now other hands to help if I needed my equipment passed to me. But with Orbit, I suppose there were always two of us: he looked out for me as I looked out for him. Perhaps that was the most important reason of all to keep him.

Chansa boarded the train with Orbit and me. As the departure horn blasted, another a long, lean figure sprung aboard. Cas. He slid the door of the carriage closed, slunk to the back of the carriage and collapsed in the corner, removed from the grasp of the overhead light. The train broke into a rhythm. The yellow lights in the tunnel flashed past, the window bars printing a cross-hatch of shadow onto Cas's face.

'How are you today Robyn?'

'Fine, Chansa, fine.'

Chansa shook his head and laughed softly, 'Just dirty I see. It's not a good job, the one you have. Better to work on the other side of the cutter head. Much safer.'

'I know.'

I glanced at Cas. He was watching me.

'When are you going back home again, Chansa?'

Chansa's smile was slow, the humour in his eyes a little sad. 'A long time from now, Robyn, months from now.'

'A long way from home,' sung Cas softly, 'such a long way from home.'

Chansa held his easy-going smile; he had a natural confidence.

'With a degree you can travel far, far from home. Get work any-where,' Cas continued in a soft sing-song voice.

Chansa gave a brief nod of acknowledgement, but he did not look at Cas. He leant back and closed his eyes, dozing with the rock of the train.

'Yes sir,' Cas spoke to himself, 'get work anywhere. Take work from others.' He leant forward in his seat, watching Chansa. Chansa's eyes remained closed.

Orbit glanced at me and his smile broadened.

The train burst into the sunlight and came to a stop. Cas rose and opened the door, and then suddenly stepped back to let us pass. I stepped out, followed by Orbit and then Chansa. Cas gave Chansa an elaborate bow. We walked across the yard to our respective vehi-cles. Cas's lanky legs jogged past us. He suddenly spun around and danced a small jig, ending it with a flourish and a show-time smile. We continued to walk. I kept my expression studied and pleasant, my eyes on the concrete floor ahead of me. I did not want trouble with Cas. Orbit took the path back to the offices. I climbed into my Beetle. I heard Chansa's car door close and his vehicle drive off.

Back at my room, I bathed. Washing the grime from my body was as much a routine as any of the tunnel work. I had recently cut my hair into a short bob, which was easier to wash every day.

Finally clean, I returned to the site office. Dicky was working in our office, facing the window, his back to me. With each decrease in his underground shifts and increase in mine, Dicky stewed with more resentment: Carter did not appreciate his eye for fine detail, Carter did not realise the time it took to deliver work of his standard.

'Morning,' he greeted me with a bright smile, sliding the top drawer of his desk open.

I sighed inwardly. Only two things lay in Dicky's top drawer: his Bible and his Medical Encyclopaedia. Both books were regularly consulted, the pages marked, the paragraphs underlined.

'Yes. Yes, it must be. I have all the symptoms.'

The Medical Encyclopaedia.

'I have a fever, my complexion is blotchy. Possible chickenpox.'

'Haven't you already had that this year?'

Dicky shot me a glance. I smiled.

Appeased, Dicky trailed his finger down the page, 'I think I should visit my doctor. I just feel better having being poked and prodded. Although she always tells me the same thing –' Dicky spoke in a high voice: 'Dicky, you've got Irritable Bowel Syndrome.'

Dicky looked pleased; he appreciated being awarded the medical title. He folded the pages back to B – Bowel. The book fell open to the well-used page.

'Irritable Bowel Syndrome,' he repeated with satisfaction.

I rubbed my ears and swallowed. Dicky's voice bothered my ears. Another throat infection was starting. Every time my throat was about to recover completely, the work in the tunnel reagitated the infection. I could not call in sick every time. Besides, arranging a substitute to map in the tunnel at the last minute was difficult. I had to reach Dicky or Carter before six in the morning, make sure they caught the train in time. It was easier just to map the rock face myself. Get it over with.

I regretted it on the days my throat was bad, though. What was just a mild infection out in the fresh air became a throbbing pain in the hot interior of the mountain. My limbs slowed down, I felt as if I was wading through tar. Then I mapped with merely a slow-witted recollection of the routine, carefully moving from one port to another. Chipping samples off the rock face to carry out into the daylight, in order to verify my hazy underground observations.

Dicky was quiet. My ears relaxed in the silence: they could heal.

I heard Dicky pick up the telephone and dial. 'Yes, the Senior Partner please. Thank you.' His tone was bright. 'Yes, Dicky here . . . Well actually I was calling about Carter, he doesn't seem to understand what mapping underground entails . . . He expects a geologist to complete an underground map in fifteen minutes, *fifteen* minutes . . . well, it's just impossible . . . Oh, you must? . . . Oh, goodbye.'

Silence. I continued to work. Out of the corner of my eye, I could see Dicky look at me. What did he think? That I couldn't hear him? I leant over my work, shuffling through my record of maps, busy. Dicky was dialling again. He was put through to a manager on the tunnel site.

'Yes, Dicky here. Fine, thank you. Well, I was calling about Carter . . . about the mapping underground. Carter doesn't understand what mapping in the tunnel requires . . . that's just not enough time . . . other geologists can? Well, only if they're cowboys like Carter (I saw Dicky shoot me a glance) . . . the underground crews are an unpleasant lot, they'll get away with what they can . . . speak to Carter? Well, I have . . . Oh, goodbye.'

This time I turned to look at Dicky. He was staring down the empty phone with surprise. Did he not know that Carter had no enemies? I didn't know a person on site who would take sides against Carter, including myself. He worked hard; he did a good job. Everyone liked him, and if there were those that didn't, they kept it to themselves.

I awoke coughing. My throat felt like sandpaper. My ears throbbed. I looked at my watch – twenty to six. I would never be able to get Carter or Dicky to the tunnel in time. I changed into my overalls, pulled on my boots and stared glumly at the holes running down the right leg. Battery acid. I loaded my pack into my car, drove past Kgube-tswana to pick up Orbit and drove on to the tunnel site.

Almost nine months after my arrival, summer lay gently on the hills surrounding the site. The morning air was pleasant and the grasses were green from summer rains. I stood waiting for the train in just a T-shirt, overall pants and my hiking boots, with my lamp, battery and hard hat under my arm. My throat felt as though I'd swallowed a handful of razor blades. I climbed on board with the rest of the morning shift.

As the train rocked into the mountain, it became warmer. And warmer. The pressure in my ears increased. It felt as if someone was steadily pumping air into my skull and it would soon burst. I climbed out with the shift and checked the equipment in my rucksack: hammer, clipboard, pencil, compass. I did not need much else.

As we reached the TBM, Orbit took my pack. He insisted on carrying it in the tunnel. I preferred to carry my own equipment, but Orbit somehow thought carrying my equipment justified his presence in the tunnel.

'They've pulled the conveyor belt out and the cutter head's ready for you, lass,' Sam lifted a bushy eyebrow. The shifts' cooperation with me still surprised him. The night shift now pulled the conveyor belt out of the cutter head, and I no longer had to wait for the morning shift to do it. My work now slipped easily between the night and morning shifts, interrupting both of them less.

'Go in with Sipho while he's checking the cutter blades. There's safety in numbers,' Sam pressed his lips firmly together and ticked off a column on his clipboard. Counting down my minutes.

Mallet stood beside Sam. He nodded at Sipho and glowered at me. Since the death on his shift he no longer took the time to speak to me unless it was strictly necessary. I was an outsider to his shift, to his men; an accessory, paid for by another contractor. These days, Mallet was preoccupied with being in all places to watch his crew. He prowled around the TBM, watching, shouting, calling. Or he stood next to Sam, the inspector's position being the most favourable for seeing the TBM operations.

Sam and Mallet watched Sipho, Orbit and I duck under the conveyor belt. I felt dizzy, top-heavy, my head an overblown balloon. I followed the two men through the metal beams. Sipho reached the cutter head and heaved up his mountainous form. Orbit's small figure followed. I braced my arms and pulled. My elbows almost buckled but I fell onto the level of the cutter head. Waves of fine dust churned around me. I coughed, light blurred and sparkled in the distance. My arms felt so weak. How would I climb from port to port? The dust was suffocating me; I could not breathe. I stopped crawling to pull a rag from my pocket and tied it around my mouth. I thought of Dicky's comment about cowboy geologists as I crawled on all fours through the dust.

I pulled myself under a metal overhang while Sipho attached the light enabling us to work. He had begun to coordinate the checking of the cutter blades with my mapping. It killed two birds with one stone, Sam told me; saved on the down-time of the TBM. I liked having Sipho with us. It was an additional person in the head and the extra light he provided was always welcome. I just felt safer having him around. Orbit was crouched under another overhang. I reached over and took the bag from him, and wiped the mud off the buckles to open them. It was so warm, so dusty . . . the dust shone like flakes of gold. Sipho's figure blended in with the light.

'Robyn.'

A deep voice.

'Robyn.' Hands shook my shoulders. I was in a warm, soft bed. Why did these hands not leave me? I wanted to sleep. A deep, dark sleep. Strong, rough hands lifted my head and jammed it between my knees. I looked up. Sipho's sweating jawline, his dark eyes.

'You blacked out.'

Black, black was nothing. I closed my eyes. Sipho shook me. I looked from him to Orbit. Orbit was still smiling. I lifted a hand to Sipho – stop. I looked again at Orbit. He had not even realised I had passed out. Orbit was the one man that I relied on to stay alive. I had thought we looked out for each other.

'Leave the map today, Orbit,' I pushed the pack towards him and turned and slid through the corridor of dust out of the cutter head.

I climbed down, my knees buckled and my weight fell. Sipho was right behind me; he caught my elbow, and followed me out, step for step. Orbit trailed behind us, smiling. What if Sipho had not been there? What if I had been in one of the upper ports when I passed out? The fall could have been lethal.

Sam and Mallet watched our progress. Sam's bushy eyebrows sunk as he looked at his watch. I had been less than three minutes; I could not have mapped. I took my elbow back from Sipho's hand.

'What happened?' I heard Mallet ask Sipho.

'She blacked out.'

I felt Mallet watch me as I walked down to the train. It was not only his eyes I could feel on me, but the entire shift's. I could feel their words once I was gone. Their words would burn.

The only woman working underground and she just is not tough enough. I could have told you that.

There would be laughter.

I could have told her that the tunnel is no place for a woman. Fainting!

When I was gone, they would laugh.

I climbed into the passenger carriage, which was fortunately waiting. I closed my eyes, ignoring Orbit who sat down next to me. I just wanted to get out. Every day I did this crazy work, but today everyone had seen how weak I really was. The train swung into motion. It took me out, out of the tunnel.

On site I climbed out of the train, pulling my pack out of Orbit's arms. He released his grip, smiling. Standing on the concrete floor of the construction site I looked up at the offices, the machinery and activity around me. I looked up at the tunnel entrance and the small statue with the blue halo above it. The Patron Saint of Tunnels. Her light was burning. I slung my pack over my shoulder and walked back to my car.

Above ground, the pressure in my ears immediately decreased, the pain in my throat subsided. My limbs could move with ease. I drove back to my single-quarters room. I just wanted to wash the mud and grime from my body. I wanted to remove all trace of the tunnel, and douse my throat with whatever medication I could find. I drove feeling broken and defeated.

I drove around the corner to the single quarters. Bongi was sitting outside my door. He should've been with Chansa. Chansa was working night shifts, and Bongi was spending the days with him. He cocked his head at the sound of my car. When he saw me he jolted across the road to greet me. Tyres skidded, a blue car swerved past me. Brakes.

'Bongi!' I screamed.

His little body lay in the road. The driver of the blue sedan came running and stood by helplessly as I picked up Bongi's soft body. His head rolled over my arm. I was running. Back to my car. And driving to the vet. Forty kilometres away in Bethlehem. I drove as fast as I could. Bongi did not move. Just as I reached the outskirts of town I saw him shift a soft paw. His eyes opened and dimmed with pain.

'It's okay, Bongi. It's going to be okay,' I touched his ear.

The vet, an indifferent man in a white coat, agreed to see him immediately. He laid him on a steel table and kneaded the unconscious dog. He looked at me over his spectacles. Walked to the basin and washed his hands. Dried them on a towel, one by one.

He turned to me and cleared his throat. 'No internal injuries. Nothing too serious. He'll make it, it's just a broken leg.'

I nodded, shuffled my feet. Speechless. The vet frowned, looking at my filthy overalls, my muddy gumboots. I could feel the tears roll down my cheeks.

After the vet plastered the small leg, he handed me the floppy dog with the comical stiff appendage and watched me carry him back to the car. I laid Bongi on the back seat, climbed into the car and held on to the steering wheel. But the tears would not stop. I just felt so tired.

Back in Clarens, in room nineteen, I laid Bongi on my bed with a bowl of water beside him should he come to. I bathed, changed into clean clothes and drove to the town's resident doctor. He was a young man with a friendly manner and grubby coat. He peered down my throat and then in both my ears.

'Mmmm,' he noted with medical satisfaction, 'badly, badly infected. Your inner ears are actually bleeding. I will have to book you off work for at least a week.'

For the first time that day, something like hope lit up inside me. A week out of the tunnel. I could relax, I could recover. I stared at the doctor's stethoscope as he spoke, keeping my emotions in check – if I breached that dam wall, I might drown.

The doctor dug in his drawer and handed me a bottle. 'Take three a day, until finished. Stay out of that tunnel.'

In my room I swallowed the first of the antibiotics and dialled Carter.

'What's that? Robyn? Hell, hang on, let me turn up the volume on this thing.'

He listened quietly while I explained my predicament.

'Take your time this week. Sort out those ears. Dicky and I will take on your shifts. Or I will, if the crews won't allow Dicky in.'

I was surprised – Carter was taking it very well. He did not substitute my shifts lightly.

'Robyn,' Carter said, just as I was about to put down the phone, 'there was an incident in the single-quarters bar last night.'

I waited. I never went to the bar in the single-quarters, only the Lodge up the road. All the men I was friendly with went to the Lodge. A rougher crowd hung out in the single-quarters bar, and nights there often ended in trouble.

'It was about Chansa.'

'Chansa doesn't drink,' I put Carter straight.

'He was buying cigarettes, apparently. That fitter and turner, Cas, attacked him. It was racial. He did a pretty good job on Chansa before the others managed to pull him off. Broke his jaw and three ribs.'

'No,' I sank my head into my hands, 'not Chansa.'

'But Chansa is fine now, Robyn, don't worry about him. He's in hospital. He'll be flying back home to Kenya in the next couple of days. He won't be coming back.'

'And that bastard?'

'Cas's gone,' Carter said, 'lost his job before daybreak. Had to get out of town before daybreak too. Left everything here, including a girlfriend.'

I rubbed my brow, remembering the pale girl who always wore long sleeves and heavy eye make-up to cover her bruises.

Carter sighed, 'It's terrible. But Cas has gone and Chansa's on his way back home. There is nothing more to do. Just concentrate on those ears, Robyn, and we'll see you in a week's time.'

I packed a tog bag full of clothes and threw it into my car. I carried Bongi and gently laid him on the back seat. I drove to the one place I wanted to be to recover, to the one person I wanted to be with. To the Swaziland border, to Terence.

After four hours of driving north-east, green forests began to crowd the roads and puddles erupted around the tyres. The car jolted off the road and onto an unmarked track. A twist and a turn and Terence's caravan appeared in a deep green field. It was a small lop-sided caravan with torn shade-netting and a rusted look. Terence was content living alone there, while the rest of his field crew lived in their own private camp over the hill. Mottled black and white cattle in the field looked up at the sound of our engine, and Terence looked out of his caravan door.

He stepped out wearing thick, heavy field boots, khaki shorts and a colourfully printed T-shirt he had bought at a local market. He had at least a week's growth on his chin. He strode over to the vehicle and opened the door, and looked from me to the backseat. Bongi attempted a weak thump of his tail. Without a word Terence lifted him up, his plastered leg standing out at an odd angle.

'Leave your stuff, I'll come back for it now.'

I climbed the three steps up into the caravan after him and watched him lay the dog at the bottom of the bed. I lay down with my head on the pillow. Terence lay down behind me, our bodies fitting easily into a spoon position. His bristly chin pricked my arm. Only then did he ask, 'What's happened?'

'Bongi was hit by a car. His leg is broken but other than that, he's fine. I've got a bad ear infection, I've been booked out of the tunnel for a week.'

I felt his fingers stroke my arm, 'It's good you came here. It's good you came here to recover, both you and Bongi.'

I closed my eyes. Suddenly relaxed, almost happy.

'Robyn.'

'Mmm?'

'You don't have to work in that tunnel, you don't have to work underground. You could stay here.'

I wrapped my hand over his, 'I must go back.'

'Terence, *Sawubona*,' a deep voice called from outside.

Terence sat up quickly. 'I must go. It's my crew, the drill company must've arrived and I need to show them where to set up the drill. They'll need food supplies for their camp, permission to stay on the farm.' He placed a hand on my leg. 'I'll be back later.'

With a bound he was off, the caravan door swinging behind him. I heard voices mumble outside and his old diesel rattletrap start up and leave. I drifted into a calm sleep.

Over the next few days I slept, waking only when Terence came into the caravan. Even then, I drifted off while I heard him clatter around the tiny kitchen and gas stove. I ate in bed: pastas, stews or his favourite recipe, roast chicken. The oven was only just large enough to fit the bird. On the fourth day I slept more lightly. I had completed the antibiotics and my ears had improved. The blood, however, had dried in my ears, leaving me temporarily deaf. Terence's voice that morning had sounded soft and muffled. I could only hear the cattle ripping the grass when they stood right beside the caravan. Bongi had recovered enough to sit outside in the long grass and watch them. I watched the shadows of gently swaying branches brush across the bed. And I fell asleep again.

I dreamt I was in a corridor.

A woman wearing a white laboratory coat rushes up to me. She is carrying an oil candle and is wearing a colourful blue halo. Her feet are bare and I can see her red robes under her coat. Her brightly made-up face has an expressionless, waxy sheen. She motions me towards an open door.

'It's all waiting for you. You must do it, we have all had to do it.' Her voice has an assumed authority, a business-like superiority.

I step inside the door. Inside the room it is dark and frightening. I want to leave.

'You must do it. We have all done it,' she repeats.

As my eyes adjust to the dark. I can make out a dimly lit table. Microscopes and scientific equipment lie waiting for me. I step closer and then recoil. Inside two round containers, floating in a clear fluid, are my two dismembered hands.

'I have begun the procedure, now you must finish,' she tells me from the door. 'The rest of your body is hanging behind the door.'

I turn around to look at her in horror. But she is gone. From behind the door I see a dark shape hanging on a hook. My body. I step back from the table. Revolted, terrified. I cannot. I cannot harm myself. I cannot do this to my own body.

I will not.

I back out of the room into the brightly lit corridor. I will never harm my body, I will never harm those square functional hands of mine. At the edge of the corridor I catch a glimpse of the red tails of the Patron Saint of Tunnels' coat as she disappears.

I awoke suddenly, with a resolution I had not felt before.

CHAPTER THREE

Derailed

A year after I arrived to work in the tunnel, the TBM crews broke the world record. Three weeks later, with three shifts, each working eight hours a day, they broke their own world record: twenty-four rings of concrete segments built within twenty-four hours, each ring a metre and a half in width. A Swedish manager, a fat man with a red face and a jovial smile, threw another celebration party at the single-quarters bar. The sponsored alcohol flowed, faces lit up, drunk and laughing.

'We are the best,' he roared above the noise, standing on the bar counter, 'we are the world's best tunnellers!'

Glasses and cans lifted. Beer flowed like mountain water.

'We must fight to stay ahead. Other tunnels are being built in Europe. They will take the world record from us. We must go *faster*.' The manager lifted his glass, 'To the three underground crews. To their foremen . . . and mostly to the foreman making the best time – Mallet!'

The men roared. Mallet was caught in a swaying tide of beer and men. He lifted his glass and one side of his thick moustache rose in acknowledgement to the toast. He drained his glass with the Swedish manager, whose beer ran over his pink chin and drained over his straining shirt.

Bongi sat beneath my bar stool, watching the raucous crowd sullenly. Carter, Roth and I sat back from the crowd, around a small table. Dicky had not arrived for the celebration, perhaps because he now seldom worked underground. The ground crews no longer tolerated any more hold-ups; fifteen minutes was all the geologist would be given to map. Carter had given me Dicky's remaining underground shifts.

Roth hunched his boxer shoulders over his beer and rubbed a hand over his eyes.

Carter's smile looked strained. 'If only they'd work a steady pace, they would make better progress overall and without all the trouble. All the derailing.'

'No man, they're acting like a hell-hound is on their trail,' said Roth.

'Well, I've shown my face,' said Carter, 'now it's time for me to leave.'

Roth and I watched him push through the jostling throng of men just as the bar broke into another cheer.

'Don't like this place. No man, it's got a strange vibe, like that fellow that beat up that Chansa engineer,' Roth shook his bowling ball head, 'No, I prefer the Lodge up the road. We can have a beer, play some darts without being worried about trouble, know what I mean?' He gave me one of his summer day smiles and took my hand.

'Sure, Roth,' I took my hand back and patted Bongi. He gave a low rumble until he sniffed my fingers.

'The crews are acting like they're on LSD or something, man. Going like a bat outa hell. Hooie, going to bust through that mountain.'

Bongi and I followed Roth out of the bar, Roth's limp so much more pronounced than Carter's. There was another toast, another cheer. The race was on.

The tunnel production was being constrained by one thing: the time taken for the train to tow the full skips, laden with rock, out of the tunnel and bring the empty skips back in. The train towed as many as six laden skips out now, each skip weighing over twenty tons. A second train engine was attached to the back of the skips, allowing the trains to shunt in and out of the tunnel with minimum disruption. Yet the rate at which the tunnel rings were laid did not increase. The train *must* move faster, the managers urged the tunnel foremen. Do what you have to keep the world record. The foremen told their drivers: faster, faster, break the fifteen-kilometre-an-hour speed restriction. And the managers turned a blind eye.

The drivers pushed the train's powerful engine to its maximum speed. The engine strained, the train rocked from side to side. Faster, faster, the loaded skips hurled after the speeding train. Until one of the skips would fly loose from the railway line, screeching the train to a halt and toppling twenty tons of rock over the tracks. Derail. The rock had to be moved by hand and shovel, causing the TBM to shut down for hours at a time. Yet the managers continued to urge the foremen and the foremen urged their drivers, *faster, faster*. The world record was what mattered.

With each derail, there was a combined sigh of relief that the driver had not been hurt and that the passenger carriage was not being towed. The drivers, however, were more cautious towing the crews in and out of the tunnel. They were wary of the inspectors on board, who did not answer to the foremen. It was only when the drivers travelled alone, with only the dark as their witness, that they pushed the engines to their full capacity. Toppled skips, broken rock, bent tracks. Derail after derail.

I walked into the office cubicle and put my muddy pack on my desk.

'*So be earnest and repent . . .*' Dicky read aloud, without looking up. He trailed his finger over the fine print on the yellow tissue paper. I sat down and began to work. After sharing an office with Dicky for over a year, I was accustomed to his readings, either from the Medical Encyclopaedia or the Bible. I flattened the pages of my notebook, the only outward sign of my irritation. I focused on redrawing the beds of yellow sandstone, recording the grain size, the colour and the strength of the stone.

'*Here I am! I stand at the door and knock. If anyone hears my voice and opens the door . . .* You would think people would listen to the truth. Like the partners of Carter's company. I told them no one could map in fifteen minutes.' Dicky paused to stare out of his window at the sandstone hills, sighed and continued to read: '*If anyone hears my voice and opens the door . . .*'

There was a loud thump on the partition wall. I jumped. Lena, the tea lady, peered into our cubicle carrying a tea tray.

'Too much of that will make your eyes go sticky,' she barked at Dicky.

Lena was a stout woman with a huge, motherly bosom. She was wearing a grey overall top over a floral skirt and takkies. She had a tendency to use English, her second language after Sesotho, in an expressive way.

'You are meant to feel that here,' Lena thumped her chest, and then pointed at her head, 'and not here.'

Dicky's smile was small and strained. He stroked his neat beard. 'Lena. I see you've brought me some tea.'

'Tea is at three, it is only half past two now. This tea is only for Mr Carter.'

'Ah, Carter,' Dicky lifted his eyebrows.

Lena sucked in a deep breath and pursed her lips, 'Yes, Mr Carter, not you. Why you always on the phone whisper-whisper about Mr Carter. I hear you speak to those men that come to visit us in suits and ties. Whisper-whisper.'

'I think *Mr* Carter is waiting for his tea,' Dicky told Lena, keeping his finger on the biblical passage.

Seizing the opportunity to escape Dicky's recital, I followed Lena out into the corridor to Carter's office. I carried my daily tunnel map with me. Dicky watched me leave, disappointed. He closed his Bible.

'That Dicky,' Lena complained, 'he is always reading that Bible. That Bible should be home, next to your bed. Not in dirty offices like this.' She snorted. 'What's he think? He a preacher? I don't think so. His eyes, they're too mean, look like two grey coals that won't burn in a fire.'

Lena tapped on Carter's door and walked in. 'Tea.'

Carter looked up, 'Tea! Thank you Lena, you're a star, old chap.'

'I thought I was your "old chap",' I said, placing my map on his desk.

Carter laughed. 'Lena's taken your place.'

'Dicky still "dearie" to you?' I asked.

Lena pulled a face. 'Dicky, the preacher.'

'Dicky dearie, the thorn in my side,' Carter replied.

'He's the whole thorn tree.' Lena left.

A forked stick, neatly trimmed and freshly cut, lay on Carter's desk. Sap oozed from its fresh wound.

'What's that?'

'Oh . . . um,' Carter glanced at his empty doorway, ' well . . .'

I picked it up. It was flexible.

'It's uh . . . for water divining.'

'You? Water divine?' I asked, excited.

'Well, it's not *exactly* an accepted science. Most people don't believe it. Mock it, in fact. But I find it pretty useful. As you know, the dolerite dykes contain most of the groundwater in these parts. Hold it in the rock fractures. Now, many of the dykes have a surface expression and can be mapped on the ground, thereby allowing us to predict where exactly the tunnel will intersect them. But some don't. So I like to walk the path of the tunnel on the surface with a divining rod. Try and predict any trouble before we hit it. Prepare the shifts so they can have the grout team ready and waiting. Grout it up before too much water washes into the tunnel. Besides,' he smiled, 'it makes us geos look good to predict things so accurately. The engineers can't believe it.'

'Would you show me? Could I walk with you?'

'Well, old chap, as I said, it's not exactly an accepted science. I wouldn't really want to . . . ' Carter rubbed his chin, uncomfortable. He seemed relieved when he was interrupted by a bang on his door.

The Swedish manager.

'Carter. Production's going well. We completed twenty-two rings yesterday. Not the world record, but close.' He dabbed the sweat on his forehead and leant back in order to shove his hanky back into his pants. 'Your guys are doing okay, Carter. Finish mapping in fifteen minutes. It's the trains that are the problem, they take too damn long hauling the skips in and out of the tunnel. They must move faster.'

Carter gave his flat smile, 'But uh . . . travelling at speed, they keep derailing. And with the time taken to clear the tunnel, we average less rings a week than if we were working at a steady pace.'

The manager shook his round face, 'No no, it's the world record.

We must fight to keep it. The tunnellers in Europe are catching up. They will beat us soon. It's all about our reputation.'

The following day, the underground shifts broke their world record once again. Twenty-five rings built in twenty-four hours. The third world record. The Swedish manager threw another party, free drinks for everyone. This time I did not go. I had taken to spending more time in my room anyway, and was only going to the Lodge every other night. This gave me a chance to catch up on my sleep and clear the alcohol from my head.

From my room I could hear the brawling shouts from the single-quarters bar. I lay on my bed reading a letter from Terence while Bongi cleaned the burrs from his paws. At each raised cry from the bar, he stood up and trod circles on the bed.

'It's okay Bongi, relax.'

There is talk of closing the project if we don't find something soon, wrote Terence. *I'll miss this place: the forests, the waterfalls and the rivers. I don't think I'll be lucky enough to be placed in an area as beautiful as this again. I may even be moved to a mine; I've told IOE that I want to stay in exploration.*

He described two white owls he had seen in a gully and a small buck he'd startled in the woods.

Be careful underground. Things are more likely to go wrong if the crews are all fired up. Try to make sure you get the passenger carriage to take you in and out. Are you sure you want to stay?

Before I completed Terence's letter, I had already begun my reply.

Terence, I cannot leave now, the tunnel is over two-thirds complete. The end is in sight. I can't walk away. Yes, the crews are crazy. And I am still frightened to work in the cutter head. But I need to stay. There is only one way out for me and that's to break out the other side of the mountain with the TBM.

Worried I'd got a little carried away, I stopped writing. But that was the way I felt. I had to finish this tunnel. I had come too far to turn back.

I miss you . . . I trailed my ink pen across the page. *Weekends are not enough.*

A roar broke out in the distance from the single-quarters bar. I left the pen and page on my bedside table, turned off my light and fell asleep with a pillow jammed over my head.

Automatically, I woke up at half past five. I no longer needed an alarm clock. I changed into my overalls and my all-weather clothing, wrapped a scarf around my head and pulled on gloves and a woolly hat. Winter had almost arrived. It was cold, but for some reason, winter did not eat into my bones as it had done the previous year. Perhaps I had grown used to it.

I drove to the site alone. I no longer used Orbit as an assistant; Carter had agreed there was little need for him to accompany me into the tunnel. He would try and find something more useful for Orbit to do. For the first weeks out of the tunnel, Orbit was difficult to find. He hid behind the kitchen door drinking cups of tea and bothering Lena, or skulked out back amongst the old geological samples. When found, he would lift a random sample and shift it, as if working. Meanwhile, inside the office, a collection of maps needing colouring grew beside Dicky. With a flash of inspiration, Carter put him to work beside an indignant Dicky (this sort of work needed a trained eye, an eye for detail).

The first afternoon I returned to find the two of them working together, Dicky fussing about Orbit using the wrong pencil crayons, not sharpening them frequently enough or not sharpening them at all. The fuss slowly subsided after the first week and by the end of the second week they were working contentedly side by side. They had divided the pencil crayons equally between them. Orbit had taken over my chair, which he grudgingly gave back to me when I returned from the tunnel.

A month out of the tunnel there was a definite change in Orbit. He began to dress more formally, no longer wearing his blue tunnel overalls. Now he wore pants with deep presses and shiny black shoes. Lately he had even started to wear his old maroon school tie. He smiled less often and less sheepishly and had begun to speak more. He greeted me in the late afternoon, and once even scolded me for bringing my dirty tunnel pack into the clean office. Carter, standing at the office entrance, closed his eyes and silently shook with laughter at my indignant look. Until eventually I too had to laugh and, mimicking Roth, complained, 'An anvil it is, that tunnel!'

'I'm never going back in there,' Orbit told me, sharpening his pencil and placing it beside his Bible – he now went to Bible study with Dicky. That suited me; I preferred to work alone.

The train hooted and I climbed aboard, and while the Patron Saint of Tunnels held her lamp aloft, we rocked into the mountain. I leant back against the carriage, between the large bodies of Sam and Sipho. My throat had cleared over the last couple of months. An infection still flared up now and again from the tunnel dust, but the extra sleep I was getting prevented the infections ever getting too serious.

Inside the tunnel I worked quickly, pulling off my all-weather clothing and hurrying after Sipho into the cutter head. I avoided Mallet's volatile gaze. Mallet was driving his crew hard, in pursuit of world records. But at the same time, his moods were getting blacker and he was more irritable. He continued to prowl around his crew while they worked on the TBM, torn between urging them on and keeping them safe.

I heaved myself up into the cutter head after Sipho, crawled through the dust after him and sat wedged under an overhang while he set up the light.

'I'm an old man,' he suddenly announced.

'Nowhere near,' I laughed.

'Too old for this, it's time to go back.'

'Home? Lesotho?' I asked, stepping on the cutter blades to haul myself up into the upper port.

'Home, Lesotho.' He took off his hard hat and wiped his brow. From above I could see how grey his hair was.

'All this time, I have worked in the gold mines up north. All these years I have worked with Mallet. When he got this job I came with him. A tunnel, not a mine. Closer to home but not home,' he sighed. 'My wife, my children, my farm and my cattle. It's time to go home.'

'Will you go now?'

'At the end of this tunnel. When this tunnel is finished. After that, Mallet will work without me.'

I briefly stuck my head out of the port to look at Sipho. He was bending down in the hazy light, his body too large and powerful for the confined space.

The rock face was slick and fractured, and the overbreak (the unprotected half-a-metre of roof above the face) was severe. Over forty-five centimetres of ceiling had collapsed. I crawled out of the cutter head. It was too dangerous to map; more of the ceiling would soon collapse. I moved out of the way, waiting for Sipho to finish checking the cutter blades before I followed him out.

Sam, the inspector, tapped his pencil while I walked up to him. 'Lass?'

'There'll be no map today, Sam. It's too dangerous to work in there, the overbreak is too bad. The roof will just collapse.'

'Rather you than me telling that to Carter, lass.'

I held Sam's gaze. I was not mapping that rock face.

I knew Carter would not be pleased. He thought the ports provided enough protection to the geologist. The previous time I had come out of the tunnel without a map, Carter had lowered his gaze, rubbed his bristly chin and given me a look that translated into *don't pull this one too often*. He'd never seen the tunnel face when the rock was bad, though.

'There's a train waiting to take the next load of skips out now. Mallet's at the back there, you'd better hurry,' Sam chucked his head to the back of the TBM.

The conveyor belt was still emptying rock into the last skip. Mallet was watching it when he saw me.

'Get in the back,' he shouted at me, 'We're not wasting time sending out another train just for you. You'll have to get this one.'

'Back?' I shouted, alarmed.

'Back. The second train towed at the back.'

The rumble of rock died down, and Mallet dropped his voice to a normal level. 'We're attaching the second train to the skips so we can shunt them back in without delay. Saves time.'

We watched two men link the train, back to front, on to the line of six skips, each skip laden high with rock.

'Get in,' commanded Mallet, irritated. I climbed in and sat on the empty driver's seat. Mallet whistled at the driver in the leading train, the horn blew and I was off.

Sitting in the towed train was certainly more comfortable than wedging myself behind the driver. I watched the lights of the TBM grow smaller and smaller, the rhythmic clang the only sound in the tunnel. Although the engine of the second train was disconnected, the speedometer was still working. The needle flickered. Rocking smoothly, the train quickly rose to its optimum speed.

Fifteen kilometres an hour.

The needle continued to swing.

Seventeen, eighteen, nineteen kilometres an hour.

The train started to lurch. I dug my fingers under my seat, suddenly aware of a rising and unexpected terror. My shoulder slammed against the metal wall of the train.

Twenty, twenty-two, twenty-four kilometres an hour.

The train swung wildly, side to side, side to side. I eyed the open door with horror; I would be flung wide. Yellow lights flashed past. I lurched forward. A skip had bounced off the rails – I could feel the weight swinging loose. Twenty tons of flying rock and metal. *Bang*, the skip landed back on the rails. The train rocked discordantly along the track.

Twenty-six, twenty-seven, thirty kilometres an hour.

The towed train, carrying me, flew clean off the rails. Swinging, airborne, interrupted by screeching metal as it hit the tracks. I hung on to the seat, bracing against every unpredictable wrench and hurl, blind with fear, wretched with terror. I wanted to scream at the driver, *stop, stop the train*. But he was one hundred and twenty tons of flailing rock and metal away from me. I would be crushed. I would die. A small heap of blood and bones beneath tons of metal and rock.

The ride out of the tunnel was a ride into the gaping jaw of hell. I could not weep; real terror does not allow that. Each lurch flung me to my death, only to yank me back into the horror of being alive.

The train shot into the sunshine. I was out of the tunnel. I was out, I had made it. I was alive. I pried my hands from the seat and stumbled onto the bright, sturdy concrete. Blue sky on an indifferent Tuesday morning.

I tossed my pack from my body. It landed on the concrete in a crumpled brown heap – a wounded animal. I walked past the loaded skips and past the driver and stood on the tracks in front of him, a boot on each rail. I lifted my hands to my hips. A scream rose. Words tore from me, every second word a *fuck*.

The driver's face closed. A stupid face, one that would never know reason or fear.

'You could have *killed* me, you could have killed *yourself*!'

The driver's face set like tunnel grout.

'*Fuck* you,' I told him.

My panting slowed down. I felt somewhat better. I looked up to see the Patron Saint of Tunnels. That witch. Her light was burning. I picked up my pack and threw it over my shoulder. Around me, all the site office doors were open. Staff stood silently watching me, jokers emerging from a pack of cards. I walked back to my car.

Heavy footsteps caught up with me. 'Robyn.'

I climbed into my car, but a hand caught the door before I could close it. It was the Swedish manager, his face red. He was panting.

'Robyn, we will dock the driver's monthly bonus. You know, teach him a lesson.'

Dock the driver's pay? What about the foreman pushing the driver, and the managers pushing the foremen? What about the world record?

'Don't do that.' My loyalty quickly shifted back to the men in the tunnel; I was uneasy standing alongside management. But I could have been killed.

'No, we must dock his pay. He must learn,' the manager turned abruptly and marched back to the offices. I watched him throwing his arms in the air, chasing the onlookers back indoors.

Having cleaned and changed in my room, I returned to the office. Orbit and Dicky sat working side by side. Dicky flashed me a smile. Orbit looked at my face and scrambled off my chair. He sat on his own.

'You see here,' Dicky pulled Orbit's attention back to the book they were reading, 'Elevated temperature, occasional nausea . . . bacterial. We probably both have it. It was probably the tea Lena gave us. The milk must've been off.'

Lena stormed into our office. 'What's that? I heard my name. What's that you said, Dicky?'

Orbit gave Lena a worried smile.

'Oh, nothing,' Dicky said lightly, 'we just thought the milk in the tea you served us could've been off.'

'Off?' Lena's voice rose an octave, '*Off*? You saying that Lena's tea is poisoning you?'

'What's going on here?' Carter arrived at the door.

Lena flew at him, breast first. 'You watch out for him, Mr Carter. He says my tea makes him sick. From now he can make his own tea.'

Dicky's smile dimmed. He did not like that idea so much. 'It may have been my sandwiches,' he began.

But Lena had already left.

I handed Carter a map. Using the previous week's mapping, I had made a rough prediction of the day's map. It was the best I could do.

He took the page from me, studied it for a second. 'Sam called me about the rock face. Actually, old chap, we all *heard* you this morning.'

Behind me Dicky sniffed a laugh.

Carter ignored him, 'Listen, old chap, why don't you come with me into the field. I have something to show you.'

I nodded. I wanted to get away from the tunnel, from the offices, from the staff.

'Dicky, would you chaps like to come along?' Carter asked.

Dicky shook his head with a bright smile. 'Too much work. Calls to make.' His hand slipped to the phone.

Carter nodded, not disappointed.

I followed Carter out into the parking lot and climbed into the passenger seat of his twincab Toyota, carrying my pack with me. I didn't know what work Carter wanted to do. Not that it mattered – I just wanted to get out into the sunshine.

'Do you mind if we fetch Bongi?'

I felt like his company, the closest I could get to Terence at this minute. Carter hesitated and then swung the vehicle in the direction of the single quarters.

Bongi sat waiting outside door number nineteen watching the

activities of the street and houses below. Out of plaster for over two months, his leg had healed easily. He bolted for the bakkie as I called him, clambered over my lap and took his rightful place as navigator between Carter and me. He leant heavily against Carter for more room. One look from Carter, and he shifted back to my side.

Carter drove out of the small town and along the open road towards Bethlehem. He turned off onto a dirt road and came to a stop. Fields of yellow wheat surrounded us. A wall of sandstone, the colour of sunsets, lay behind us.

'You can leave that here,' Carter pointed at my pack, 'just follow me.'

Carter walked along the gully towards a willow tree. Bongi tore through the yellow wheat into the distance.

'Heading in a straight line towards that sandstone hill, is the direction the tunnel will be taking. You'll see the red-and-white survey pegs if you look carefully. The TBM is currently somewhere under where we are standing.'

I thought of the dark, the noise and activity beneath us. On a quiet afternoon, sunshine and yellow wheat. It seemed hard to believe.

'Now, rule number one, always carry a penknife.' Carter pulled out a knife. He walked to the willow and cut off a small branch, trimmed away the leaves and tested the forked stick for flexibility.

'That'll do,' he announced. His eye caught my smile. 'Well, old chap, let's see what the tunnel's future holds.'

I followed his long strides into the wheat. He stopped abruptly and held out the forked twig. He pulled it taut between his fingers. Then he took long careful steps. After about ten minutes I saw him slow his pace, his forearms strained. The stick bent earthwards, seemingly beyond breaking point. Then after a few minutes it began to level to its original position. He rubbed his chin thoughtfully and walked back to me.

'Seems there's something big there, old chap. Your turn.'

I took the divining rod and held it the same way.

'No, keep it taut, Robyn. Flex that V between your thumbs. Keep the stick level to the ground, pointing away from you. Taut, okay? Right, now walk.'

I took slow steps, one after the other, along the same path Carter had walked. My thumbs strained, pulling the fork apart. Nothing, I felt nothing.

Carter saw the distressed look on my face.

'Come back here. Try again. You using those hands? Pulling tight? Try again. Walk at a steady pace.'

I walked the same path. Bongi came bounding through the long wheat, only his long tail visible, to see what I was doing. He trotted alongside me. I finished walking the line. Still, nothing.

Carter strode up to me. Bongi's eyes brightened at the approaching prey. He sunk onto his stomach, convinced he was hidden by a few blades of grass. As Carter approached Bongi pounced, sinking his sharp teeth into his shoe.

'Damn dog,' Carter shook him off, 'no discipline.'

Bongi jumped back playfully, wagging his tail.

'Here, fetch that.'

Bongi gave chase to the invisible ball.

'All dogs should know some basic commands,' Carter began.

I pointed at the stick, worried he was about to start lecturing me on his favourite topic around Bongi. Disciplining a dog.

'Ah, right,' Carter looked at the divining rod. 'Look, Robyn. We can try something, I've heard it works. Don't know why. Perhaps it's about connecting a current, or one person passing it on to another. We can give it a try. Take one side of the fork.'

I did as I was told. Carter held the other side.

'Now with your other hand, hold mine,' Carter held out his hand with some embarrassment.

I took it; it was large and dry.

'Now walk with me. Keep the stick taut.'

I felt it, gradually at first and then with the force of the earth behind it. My arm shook with the strain; it took all my strength to prevent the stick being torn from my hand. Gradually the divining rod eased up to its original position.

'There is something big as hell down there, Robyn. You felt it? Right. Do it alone.'

I positioned the stick between my thumbs. Held it level to the ground and walked. A gentle tug. I continued to walk. The divining rod tugged and then twisted to the earth. I kept walking, the muscles in my arms straining to keep it level. The force eased and then dissipated.

I turned to Carter. A smile split across my face.

'You felt it. It's a big dyke all right. Let me just take some measurements and I'll plot it up on a map when we get back to the office. Then I can warn the shift to have the grout team ready and waiting.'

I walked back to the spot. Pulled the divining rod taut. It bent earthwards with a power my arms could barely contain. I could feel it. The force of nature. From cloud to tree, root to soil. Above that hollow tunnel that would soon be filled with the Lesotho waters, with the sandstone wall to my back, knee-deep in yellow wheat, the force of water made my arms ache and my slow footsteps listen.

CHAPTER FOUR

Hole Through

I had been sitting waiting on the metal walkway inside the tunnel for almost four hours. I no longer waited in the coffee room. I sat on my pack, leaning back on a drum, and thought of Terence.

We had walked the hills and slopes overlooking the Lesotho mountains over the weekend. It was a bright sunny day and the grasses had already turned to winter gold. Terence appeared preoccupied: he walked with his hands thrust deep into his pockets, his forehead wrinkled in concentration. He had recently had his hair trimmed to collar length, and for once he had shaved. He stopped to study the distant mountains.

I walked up to him. 'What will you do?'

Terence shrugged. 'Go. I have little choice. I'm still under financial obligation to the Red Earth Company for the next year.'

Bongi came bounding through the long grass and Terence bent down to pat him. He wiggled in delight, propelling himself in circles.

Terence sighed as he straightened. 'Never wanted to work on a mine; I wanted to stay in exploration. At least it's open-pit. I'll be living in Thabazimbi, fifteen kilometres away from the mine. It's not exactly the same as living in a caravan with an entire farm to yourself.'

'It's so far from here.'

'About six hours drive north, I would imagine.'

'Too far to visit on weekends.'

Terence nodded and pulled me close. His eyes looked almost green against the winter grasses. 'You could come with me. I'd be given a house. Otherwise . . . we'll make a plan to see each other, you'll see.'

I looked at the grassy hills, the cliffs of sandstone and the mountains in the distance. I thought of the TBM churning beneath our feet. I thought of the crews and their recent hostility. I said nothing.

Inside the tunnel, I took out my black notebook and pen and began to sketch the skips being filled with rock. The earplugs I wore filtered most of the TBM's deafening grind. I felt a large, familiar hand on my shoulder and looked up to see Roth. I pulled my earplugs out.

He bent down beside me and looked at his watch. 'Don't let them rattle your cage, man.' He put his arm around me and squeezed.

I extricated myself from his grip. His kindness made me feel weaker, and I needed to be strong.

Roth grinned at me and pulled my hard hat over my eyes, 'I'll see you at the Lodge later tonight. Don't let them rattle your cage. No man, always look up at the sky. That's right, man. I can see what a heavy load it is, an anvil. I can see that. But you can't leave because of something like this. I won't let you.'

He closed one eye and walked back into the bright lights of the TBM.

I was not planning to leave. As wretched as I felt, I had not come this far to be pushed out now. I had worked in the tunnel for over a year. Thirteen months. It was a month since the driver had almost derailed me, but still the crews would not take me out of the tunnel.

The day after I shouted at the driver, I boarded the passenger carriage as usual. As I sat down heads turned away, and no one returned my greeting. Mallet climbed into the carriage last and sat opposite me.

He stared at me. 'Do you know what you've done?'

I felt my stomach sink.

'Three hundred rand was docked from the driver's pay.' Mallet leant towards me. His lips looked red and moist beneath his moustache.

'He almost killed me, he almost killed himself.'

'Three hundred rand, that's a lot for a driver.'

'I didn't ask them to dock it.'

'It was docked *because* of you.'

I leant back, folded my arms. 'He almost killed me.'

'Down here we stick together. Don't expect my crew to take you in and out of the tunnel. You can wait until the skips are full. Don't expect anything from us anymore.' Mallet leant back, focusing on the space behind me. I was no longer visible to him.

Since that day, a month ago, I sat waiting for the trains. Word spread quickly from Mallet's shift to the other two. Eyes were averted, heads turned away. The crews' trust in me, the trust that had taken a year to develop, just slipped away as if it had never existed. Overnight I had become their enemy, overnight I was a traitor underground. That geologist bitch.

Working as part of the crew had kept me going. The crew had watched my back. But for these men now, I was no longer present. My safety lay squarely on my own shoulders. It was a heavy, empty feeling.

Inside the tunnel, I never waited less than three hours for a train to take me out. Occasionally I waited five. I returned to the site office late in the afternoon. Carter would glance at his watch and visibly bite his lip. He knew something was going on. He kept quiet though, hoping I would ride it out. He could not afford to have his second geologist out of favour with the crews. There was little point in complaining to him – we both knew it was my battle. What could he do? And I knew he counted on me to get those daily maps.

As abruptly as I was discarded from the underground crews, the crews stopped aiming for the world record. There was no more pushing for speed, for production. The drivers travelled at their previous fifteen-kilometres-an-hour speed limit. Perhaps the crews were satisfied: they had scored a hat trick, three world records. Or perhaps the Swede with his pink cheeks and sweating face had instructed them to stop. Whatever the reason, the pressure was gone. Nineteen rings of segments a day, three shifts a day. No more.

The skips finally full, the train engine started up. I looked at my watch. I had waited just over four hours. I rode out standing behind the driver, travelling at a steady fifteen kilometres an hour. Out of the tunnel, I drove back to my room to wash and returned to the office. It was late afternoon.

Dicky wiped away his suppressed smile with satisfaction. 'I told you they were an unpleasant lot.' His eyes shone.

'Who?' I sat down heavily, tired.

'The shifts, the men working underground.'

I shrugged. 'Well, hopefully it won't last.'

Dicky sniffed a laugh. 'It's been over a month now.'

'Where's Orbit?' I changed the subject.

Dicky was fishing rock specimens out of a basin, drying them and placing them on his desk. 'Don't know. The map work finished, and then I realised there was a lot of work to do sorting all my samples. I have hundreds, as you can see. But Orbit appears to have disappeared.'

I eyed Dicky's rock collection sceptically. Even though Dicky was not mapping in the tunnel, he collected samples from the skip dumps almost every day. He lovingly washed them and added them to his office collection. They all looked the same. They had been breeding at a remarkable rate and were now encroaching onto my side of the office. His bookshelf was lined with samples, as was the floor beneath his desk. Sharp brown noses peered out into the sunlight. More bowls of water had been added to our office, habitat for his freshwater specimens.

Dicky tenderly picked one up and bit its nose. He chewed thoughtfully, 'Orbit doesn't seem to like working with rocks. He obviously doesn't have the stomach for it.'

I glanced at Dicky to see if he intended the pun. Obviously not. He spat the mud into a cloth. 'There is a lot of detail to record with these rocks. Although Carter wouldn't believe it. But then that's the thing with Carter, he does not have the ability to record detail.'

I sighed inwardly.

'I have been calling a few people. Speaking to them about Carter. I think they are finally beginning to see my point. He's just not . . . cut out for this. You know,' Dicky swivelled in his chair to face me, 'I've always known that I would be a geologist. Lecturers said I wouldn't make the course. It took longer than it should have. But I did it,' Dicky smiled. 'I did it.' There was mud on his teeth.

'Whisper-whisper.' Lena stood at our office entrance.

'Ah, Lena, have you made me tea?' Dicky winked at me as if this was a shared joke.

Lena sniffed, 'You make your own tea. I've come to speak to Robyn.'

I looked up at Lena.

'Not here, in the kitchen.'

I followed Lena into the kitchen.

Orbit sat behind the kitchen door wearing his neatly pressed pants and shirt. He smiled apprehensively at me.

'Hi, Orbit. Not working with Dicky?'

He shook his head.

'This one, he's too shy for work. Hides like a rabbit in the long grass,' said Lena.

'Ah well, I think your next job should be in an office. Nothing to do with rocks.'

'Robyn,' Lena commanded my attention back, not wanting to waste too much time on Orbit, 'I want to ask you something. I have seen you in the hills taking pictures.'

I leant back against the sink, tired after the long day in the tunnel. 'I take photographs of birds, mountains, that sort of thing.'

'I want you to come to my house and take pictures of my boy. My baby boy, Jabu. Now, after work. In ten minutes,' Lena pointed at her watch. It was almost five.

At five, Lena and Orbit stood beside my old Beetle, waiting for me.

'You coming along?' I asked Orbit with surprise.

'Orbit is coming along for the free ride, Robyn,' Lena replied for him.

Orbit climbed into the back seat, Lena took the passenger seat beside the driver's. We drove past my room to fetch my manual Pentax. Before I could stop him, Bongi jumped into the back seat beside Orbit. The four of us drove up the hill to Kgubetswana. Bongi stood up on his hind legs, sticking his nose over Lena's shoulder and out of her window.

'Shoo,' she smacked him on the nose.

Slighted, Bongi sat back on his haunches and stared, unblinkingly, at Orbit. Orbit clutching nervously onto the back of my seat.

Lena pumped her arms over her generous bosom, directing me between the dirt roads. 'Turn left. Right. Past the post office.' She waved at a group of women, and shouted at a chicken sprinting across the road. 'Shoo, shoo! No, through here. Stop, stop here.'

I parked beside a small brick house. It was surrounded by shacks. Slinging my camera bag over my shoulder, I followed Lena. Orbit stumbled out of the car, in hurry to get away from Bongi. I shut the indignant spaniel in the car.

'No, Robyn,' Lena directed me away from the brick house, '*This* is my house.' She pointed to the shack beside it.

I stared at the red shack. That was Lena's home? I thought about the ruthless winters, the frost, even snow.

Lena opened the door, which sunk on its hinges, and showed me inside. The shack was only large enough to enclose a double bed and a dressing table. A Bible and a hairbrush lay on the table. Fine needles of light pierced the tin roof and speckled the blue bedspread. There were no windows in the room.

Lena straightened the bed cover. 'Sit here.'

I sat down. The bed was soft and comfortable. Lena left, and I waited with my camera bag on my lap.

'Robyn, you can come out now,' she called.

I stepped back into the courtyard. Lena was holding a large, chubby baby on one hip and a chair in the other. The chair she placed against the brick wall, the baby she handed to me. He sat nonplussed in my arms, smelling of a cooked lunch. He had pumpkin on the side of his mouth, and I wiped it off with a finger. Lena disappeared into the brick house and returned with an armful of clothes. She dropped them in the dust and sorted through them. She tied a leather thong around Jabu's neck and another around his waist, and propped him up on the chair, splaying out his fat legs to balance him.

'First take Jabu like this, Robyn.'

Jabu stared back at me. His dark curls shone in the late afternoon sun. I bent down on one knee and focused the camera. *Click.*

Lena picked him up and lay him in the dust. She pulled on a tiny pair of white trousers and a top with a red sailor's bow. Jabu the sailor.

'Now like this,' Lena propped him back in the chair. *Click*. Jabu began to slowly slide down the chair.

'Robyn.'

I looked up from my camera, 'Yes, Lena?'

'I know men that work in the tunnel. Many of them live in Kgubetswana. I know the trouble you are having, they are boycotting you.'

'They are what?'

'Boycotting. Refusing to take you out of the tunnel. They don't want you to work there. Just like I won't make Dicky tea; I'm boycotting Dicky's tea.'

'It's fair enough that you won't make Dicky tea, he can make it himself. But in the tunnel, that driver was going too fast. He almost killed me and he almost killed himself.'

Lena hoisted Jabu up and lay him back in the dust. She changed him into another outfit. Tiny trousers and leather lace-up shoes. Lena's little man.

'I'm telling you only what I hear, Robyn. The man, he was driving too fast. You are right. But they can do what they want. You are only one woman and they are many men.'

'They must forget, Lena.'

Lena shook her head and balanced Jabu back onto the chair. Orbit had found his old school tie in his pocket and put it on. Smiling, he edged closer and closer to Jabu's chair. He stood up straight for the camera.

'Orbit move, move,' Lena pulled him away.

'What about a photo with you and Jabu together?' I asked Lena.

Lena laughed, embarrassed. She walked over to Jabu and picked him up. She held him up in front of her like a cabbage, waiting for their picture to be taken. I sat with my camera to my eye, ready. Orbit's smiling face inched closer into my camera view. Lena's arms suddenly grew tired, she hoisted Jabu onto her hip and nuzzled his cheek. Jabu laughed. *Click click*. I zoomed closer. Her love and pride. *Click click*. I zoomed out. Orbit stood beside them. *Click*.

Lena sat down on the chair with Jabu on her lap while I changed the reel of film.

'Robyn. You must go to work every day. You are wrong if you think they will forget. They will not forget. But if you go into the tunnel every day then the men boycotting you will see that they cannot scare you.'

I caught Lena's eye and nodded. Jabu looked up at his mother and lifted a hand to her mouth. She kissed his tiny palm and rubbed her nose against his. Lena, in her grey tea jacket, with her son, Jabu the prince. *Click click.*

Carter sat next to me in the passenger carriage, squeezed between me and Sipho. This was the first time he had been into the tunnel with me since my day of arrival. There had been a mumbled *Carter, Carter* as he boarded. No one greeted me. Six weeks after the speeding train incident, the men were only just starting to thaw: a nod here, a favour there. No one took me out on the trains though. The boycott still stood.

'Almost at the end of this tunnel, Robyn. Another kilometre to drill, another month of work. How long you been with us now?' Carter asked me, above the chug of the train.

'A year and a bit. About fourteen months.'

'Seems longer.'

'It seems forever.'

'Another month's work and then the Hole Through. Ever seen one of those?' Carter asked me unnecessarily.

I shook my head.

'When the TBM drills out the other side of the mountain into fresh air. They usually make quite an occasion of it.'

'What will happen to the crews after that? All the tunnel staff?'

'The men work on the site. They disassemble the TBM, shine it up. Put it together like new for the other sections of tunnel to be drilled.'

'Not much for geologists to do then.'

'Ah, we can keep you busy for a couple of months. And then we'll be starting the next one.'

It was easy to forget that this was just one section of the conduit. Another tunnel? I could not even imagine it.

'Thought I'd better come in with you today, Robyn. According to my measurements they should be very close to that dyke. Of course I can't tell them we detected it by water-divining. I just call it mapping. I've alerted the grout team – one call, they'll be in the tunnel. We need everything to run smoothly now that this tunnel is reaching its end. Touch wood.' Carter tapped his knuckles against his hard hat.

Twenty-five minutes later, the train stopped. Carter and I followed the others out of the carriage onto the walkways.

Sam lifted his bushy eyebrows at us. 'The cutter head's ready for you Carter, lass.'

Sam was one of those who had kept their neutrality with me. He still greeted me in the tunnel, spoke to me on the train. He waved us through, making a note on his clipboard.

I followed Carter through the TBM, slipping over and under the metal beams with ease. I made it to the cutter head before him and heaved myself up into the dark corridor, onto the thick carpet of dust. I spat it out as I landed, wiping my mouth on my sleeve. I crawled towards the light. The dust turned to mud before I reached the cutter head.

Carter groaned behind me, 'God, I'm too fat for this. What's this? It looks wet.'

I pulled myself up into the topmost port. My arms were accustomed to lifting my weight now, and my legs kicked free as I scrambled into the port. Time was still money; I would need to map. Carter squeezed his upper body through the lower port, grunting loudly.

'It is wet, Carter!' I shouted. I could see his yellow spot of light on the rock face below me.

'It's the dolerite dyke all right. Pretty fractured, should be holding a lot of water. And from our water-divining traverse it must be over twenty metres thick. Bugger.'

As if encouraged by our presence, the water started the gush from the rock face. An underground waterfall. My upper body was drenched.

I heard Carter spit out a mouthful of water. 'See the contact with the sandstone?'

'I'm looking.' I took the headlamp off my hard hat and scanned the rock face. 'Can't see a thing. There's water everywhere.'

'Not much we can do here, Robyn. Grab a sample for the record.

The tunnel contractors get paid more for drilling through hard dolerite like this. It wears the cutters out.'

Carter and I leopard-crawled out of the cutter head. Water flowed around us like a river. I wiped the mud from my eyes. Finally we dropped out of the cutter head with the stream of water and wiggled through the metal beams. I waited for Carter to catch up. *Dong*, his hard hat hit a beam, and he grumbled.

Mallet stood waiting for us out in the open.

'At the moment you're drilling through a dolerite dyke. There's a strong flow of water from the fractures,' I told him.

'Hard to estimate, but the flow is getting stronger by the minute,' said Carter, clumping up behind me. 'I've got a team waiting outside the tunnel. They can begin to grout up the fractures immediately. Stop the flow of water into the tunnel before it gets too serious.'

Sam was already putting down the phone. 'They're on their way. Looks like your prediction was spot-on, Carter.'

Carter wiped the mud from his eyes and grinned, 'What can I say? Us geologists have magical powers.'

'Don't know about that. But you've probably saved a day's production here.' Sam looked at Mallet for confirmation.

Mallet stood with his feet apart and his arms crossed. His head started to rock. Then his face split and he began to laugh. A deep, theatrical *ha-ha-ha*. Except it was real. I looked at him in surprise, and then at Carter and myself. We were covered in mud, our faces brown, our hair and overalls drenched. Smiling sheepishly, I wrung out the tails of my top and emptied the water from my gumboots, one by one.

Mallet shook his head, still laughing. 'Get the driver to take them out.' He looked at me. 'Take Robyn out, take her out in the passenger carriage.'

The boycott was over.

Carter nodded his flat smile; I could see he was pleased.

I trundled after Carter, my wet overalls clinging uncomfortably. So it was as easy as that – a laugh. If you didn't count the six weeks of waiting it out and growing a hide as thick as a rhinoceros, I thought wryly.

'Robyn,' Mallet stopped me, 'this is my daughter. She's finishing school this year.'

A young girl stepped out from behind the conveyor belt wearing a hard hat and overalls too large for her. She had her father's dark eyebrows and spark of temper behind her eyes. I smiled at her. She stared back, her eyes dropping down my muddy frame.

'She is getting straight As at school. She wants to study engineering.' Mallet could not disguise his pride. 'She'll be the first in our family to go to university. I just thought I'd bring her down here, to make sure she never wants to work underground.' He gave me a conspiratorial nod, turned briskly and walked off. His daughter followed, her large boots clumping uncomfortably.

I took my hard hat off as I followed Carter into the carriage. The engine started and the train took us out, chugging at a smooth, even speed.

Well, while we were all getting things out in the open . . . 'Carter.'

'Yes.'

'I thought I should tell you something. It's about Dicky. He, er, has been making some calls about you from the office.'

Carter studied me as yellow lights flashed above us, lip-reading. 'What kind of calls?'

'That you're not doing your job properly. You don't know what mapping needs. That sort of thing. But he's phoning all the managers of the associated companies, it could hurt you. I thought you should know.'

Carter sat motionless, gently rocking with the train. The flashing yellow lights caught his heavy frown. 'The little *cunt*,' he said eventually.

I looked at Carter with surprise. I had never heard him swear before.

The Ash Tunnel, which would guide the Lesotho water on its final stretch before it emptied into South African rivers, was almost completed. For over fourteen months I had been held underground by an invisible force, a gravitational pull. But that force was growing weaker by the day. I could feel it – just like the water diviner rising back to its original level. Carter expected me to stay on for the next tunnel. Another tunnel . . . the thought sunk to my gut. But where did my foundations rest, if not on the sandstone of Clarens?

Terence had already closed his project on the border of Swaziland and moved to Thabazimbi. The mine pit, he complained, was as hot as hell. Hotter, and more humid. It was like working in a red oven. The work was tedious and uncomfortable, but this didn't irk Terence as much as the fact that the mine did not really need him – they already had too many geologists. Red Earth Company had allocated him a house in Strelitzia Street, like the others of his grading. He said it was painted a strange colour to disguise the pink dust from the mine. Should I want it, there was room for me and Bongi there.

Terence had promised to make the effort to be in Clarens for the Hole Through. It wasn't far off: every day the train ride into the tunnel got longer, and it now took twenty-five minutes to get to the TBM. The factory had stopped producing concrete segments; less than a thousand would be needed to complete the tunnel. There was a tangible excitement on site. The underground crew began counting down the days.

Twenty-nine, twenty-eight . . . nineteen . . . sixteen days. The crews spoke of nothing else. In the offices, the staff behaved like proud parents, as if they had coaxed the crews and TBM through the mountain.

'I can feel it, Robyn,' Roth stuck his head into my office, 'I can feel it. The anvil's getting lighter.' He pretended to shift a weight off his powerful shoulders, the shoulders of a boxer. But a lover not a fighter. He winked and loped off.

Smiling, Dicky watched Roth leave. He began to hum. 'Carter says sixteen days before the Hole Through.'

'Sounds about right, there's less than three hundred rings left to place.'

I glanced back to Dicky and Orbit. Orbit had been coaxed back out of the kitchen and was once again colouring in maps. He sat a good distance from Dicky and his collection of rock specimens, as if nervous they might scuttle out from under the desk and attack him. Dicky bit into a rock.

'They called me in,' he told me with his mouth full.

'Who?'

'Carter and all the managers.'

'Why?' I asked slowly.

'Because . . .' Dicky lowered his voice to a hoarse, comical whisper, 'they accused me of *insubordination*.'

I carefully unpacked my notepad and clipboard.

'Yes, insubordination. They found out I was making those calls about Carter.'

I waited for Dicky to point the finger of blame in my direction.

Dicky hummed a tune as he spat out the mud and wiped his mouth. 'I was *reprimanded*. Carter said this was my Final Warning. I'm not allowed to fight with the underground shifts when they start the next tunnel either.'

Clearly Dicky was satisfied. He had now been awarded two technical disorders: Irritable Bowel Syndrome *and* Insubordination.

'What you eating the rocks for? Your wife not feed you?' Lena deposited the tea tray with a crash on my desk. There were three cups on it.

'Well, I can't believe it, Lena. You've brought *me* tea. It must be Christmas,' said Dicky.

'Hmm,' Lena looked away. 'For you, Orbit and Robyn. Nobody can stay mad forever.'

'Tunnel is coming to an end,' I told her. 'Only about sixteen days left.'

'Another tunnel drilled with that machine. The machine replaced people. Why don't they let the people of Lesotho build the tunnel?'

'I don't know. I suppose it would take too long to build it by hand.'

'It would mean more work for more people, longer.'

'I suppose it would,' I sighed, feeling at a loss. My view of this great water project was limited to the daily rock face, watching the rise and fall of sedimentary beds.

Lena's stern face lit up as I handed her a photo album. There had been a choice of only three albums in the photography shop in Bethlehem. I had chosen a large one decorated with silver snowflakes, which I thought Lena might like. She opened the book and laughed.

'Me with Jabu. And Orbit! How did he get in there?'

Orbit patted his pocket, his copies of the photos safely in place.

'Jabu,' she turned a stiff page, 'and Jabu. Jabu's first picture book. Robyn, Jabu will finish school. He will get good work, not work in a tunnel or on a farm. Not serving tea.'

I peered over her shoulder at the photos again. Jabu in his different outfits, the same expression. His back to the borrowed brick wall. Jabu the sailor, Jabu the warrior.

'I know, Lena, he's a prince. And you're his mother.'

As the last days of the Ash Tunnel unfolded, the excitement of the underground crews rose. Suddenly there were less than a hundred rings of segments left to line the tunnel. That was five or six days' work. Which of the three shifts would be the one to drill the Hole Through? After all these months, the TBM was ready to surface. So were we. Exhausted and stale, we wanted it to end. Forty-two rings, then ten, and then . . . one. The TBM was stopped. They would save the last ring for the Hole Through the next day, to be drilled in the presence of the invited guests. Fifteen months after I had arrived, the tunnel would be completed.

The next day, the day of the Hole Through, I sat between Terence and Carter on a grandstand made of rough pine.

Terence leant back, his arm resting behind me. 'It's over,' he said, glancing at me. He looked pleased.

I knew he was happy to be away from Thabazimbi for a couple of days. Although he had been living there for almost two months, he had not yet adjusted to working on a mine, living in a mine house. It would be better when I lived there, he told me. We'd have each other. I handed him one of the free caps they were distributing. He put it on, casting a shadow over his eyes.

Roth leant forward. 'You're right it's over, Terence,' he said. 'Time for the monster to take a breath of air. Time for the TBM to kiss the sky. Time for me to go back to my family and my little grandson. Been here too long, know what I mean.' Roth pushed his cap from hand to hand; his bald, brown head was accustomed to the sun.

Few of the underground crew had been invited to the Hole Through – only the foremen, the inspectors and some of the site engineers. The geologists were permitted to attend. Most of the people on the stand were strangers, guests invited from the cities. Sitting on the stand, we all stared ahead at the great bullseye painted onto the rock face. The paint had run in red streaks down the rock. Flags, those of South Africa and Lesotho, lined the pit walls around the bullseye.

Mallet and his family sat in front of us. I recognised his daughter. Mallet stared at the cap he was holding, looking unhappy. I knew he had wanted his crew to drill the Hole Through. Instead, he sat watching like a tourist.

'Who are all these people, man?' mumbled Roth. 'Never seen them before in my life. What have they got to do with the tunnel?'

I nodded in agreement as I loaded film into my camera, feeling at odds with my emotions. Like Mallet and Roth, I felt territorial. It was *our* tunnel, we had built it. Although we had counted down to this day, wanted the end to come, we suddenly felt cheated. The tunnel was being taken from us, claimed by strangers sitting among us with their removed, amicable expressions. Our work, our sweat was suddenly reduced to a collection of tourist flags and a bullseye.

Carter sighed heavily beside me. 'Your first Hole Through. The end of one tunnel, and then we begin again.'

'Carter, I don't think I'm going to be here when you start the next section of tunnel,' I said slowly. 'I'm going to Thabazimbi with Terence.'

Carter nodded slowly, sighed. 'Remember I told you that this was no job for a woman?'

'Yes,' I replied warily

'Well, I was right.'

'Oh? How's that?' I lifted my chin, expecting an argument.

'I was right. I still say it's no job for a girl. But with you, well, it somehow worked.'

I frowned at Carter. Was that meant to be a compliment?

'Listen old chap,' he continued before I could interrupt, 'I've never told you, but some years ago I got pretty sick. My whole body seized up with rheumatism. I was as rigid as a pole. Could not move – when

I tried, it was absolute agony. I took everything the doctors gave me, nothing worked. It only seemed to get worse. But they needed the pits to be mapped and I was the only geologist. I said I would do it. Two men drove out to fetch me, they had to carry me out of bed and put me in the bakkie. Drive me to the pit where they placed me in a man-size bucket and lowered me down the hole. My knuckles were too swollen to move, so they jammed a recorder between my neck and shoulder and as they lowered me, I called out the depths and the geology. Then they pulled me up and carried me back to bed. I can't tell you what it was like. Having strangers carry you, having your wife feed you. My boys were too young to understand. I was helpless.'

'What did you do?'

Carter did not hear me.

'What happened?' I touched his arm

'Oh, what happened. I had tried everything. Then we heard about these tablets with gold in them. They were absorbed into my body, they immediately eased my joints, lubricated them. After being practically paralysed, I was cured within weeks.'

'Well, they should cremate you when you die, you could be worth something,' I smiled, although I could feel my eyes betray my sympathy for Carter. 'I'm pleased they found a cure.'

'So am I, believe me, so am I. What I'm trying to say, Robyn, is that it taught me to never give up. I was told I would never walk again and look at me now. I learnt never to take *no* for an answer. To never give up. So if you're leaving, just remember that. Take that with you. Also, remember that it's the everyday things that are precious; that's the gold that eases the joints. Savour them and don't lose them. Don't take them for granted. Before my illness I forgot to take time to appreciate life, to find the humour in a situation, to laugh. Not any more.'

On the Carter Scale this was unusually personal.

'Like Dicky, I want him to learn to persevere in the right direction. Dicky swims against the current just for the sake of it. He loses strength that way.'

At the sound of his name, Dicky, seated a row away, turned and waved. He was sitting next to Orbit, both wearing their tunnel caps. I waved back. A sound like distant thunder made us all look up.

'What's that?' Someone whispered.

Terence took my hand. He studied my face and knitted his fingers into mine.

There it was. An unmistakable growl inside the stomach of the mountain, a giant bellyache. The distinctive grinding of the TBM. We strained our ears; the rumble grew louder. Cameras were ready, focused.

The bullseye shook. A slab of rock fell from the rock face. A slab that size would have killed me in the tunnel. More slabs fell, and then the bullseye began to crumble. A glimmer of whizzing metal could be seen in the top left-hand corner; the sound was deafening. And then the entire rock face collapsed.

The roar died down. The flat steel face of the TBM looked at us. Four ports lay open, gaping mouths – ports I had hunched in daily to protect myself from falling rock. Sixteen cutter blades stopped spinning and stared back at us in glazed insolence. Blades I had balanced on to climb up into the ports.

A hand holding a South African flag appeared from a top port. In the lower port, a boot and the Lesotho flag emerged. The men squeezed through the ports with difficulty, where I had slipped through with ease. The crew spilled out, forming an odd, filthy line in front of us. They shuffled their gumboots and blinked in the bright light, as if they'd drilled through to a foreign land.

Terence put his arm around me, reading my strained face. 'Well done, angel.'

The bench creaked and Mallet rose. He pushed past the polite legs and tourist flags and walked down the stand. He shook the first man's hand. And the next, and the next; welcoming them through. They had made it. We had made it.

An embarrassed cough, and a suit rose. Figures followed in Mallet's steps, congratulating the men. I sat with my hand in Terence's and my heart in my throat. Fifteen months, three shifts a day, twenty-four hours a day, the TBM had drilled. Our section of the tunnel was completed; it would be joined to the larger chain of tunnels. But for our time, we had been the link between Lesotho's thunderclouds and South Africa's expectant rivers.

PART TWO

CHAPTER FIVE

Sing Ta Na Na

I pried the mussel loose from the rock with my penknife and dropped it into my bag. Its beard was slimy, and I stood up wiping my hands on my jeans. Water lapped over the rocks and onto my feet. Down the coast, the low tide had exposed a landscape of mussels. Terence worked a few hundred metres away, and Bongi sat behind me, on an elevated sand dune, keeping an eye on us both.

The sea was still and flat, the sun weighed heavily on the horizon and in the distance, small boats lay motionless. On this desolate west coast, they were probably not fishing boats but diamond trawlers. The conditions were perfect for diving.

His bag full, Terence made his way back to the sand dunes. Over the quiet rustle of waves I could hear him sing: '. . . *how many roads must a man walk down before you call him a man?*'

His voice was even, a little rough at the edges. He buzzed the sound of Bob Dylan's harmonica into an empty beer can and dropped his packet of mussels onto the sand.

By the time I had filled my packet and strolled up the dune, a driftwood fire was crackling. I emptied my mussels into the bucket, sat down and unrolled my jeans to dry in front of the fire.

Terence handed me a cold beer. 'Cheers. To us.' He knocked his can against mine. His eyes, blue as the ocean, crinkled.

'To us.'

A crow squawked above us. Bongi stopped licking his paws and sat up.

'We'll call this Crow Bay. To us,' I toasted the sun.

The harsh coastline caught alight. The orange sun flattened and fractured as it sank, strip by strip, out of sight, bleeding into the sea. I dropped the mussels into a pot of boiling water as Terence stirred the butter, white wine and garlic over the flames.

To us. Only a month ago, Terence, Bongi and I had left Thabazimbi in the far north, to head south to the remote west coast near Lutzville. We had left without looking back. Behind us we left oppressive heat and a scarred skyline, scarred as the result of collapsed mine workings. Behind us we left 10 Strelitzia Street.

Actually, the street name had been spelt incorrectly, so we left behind *Sterlitzia* Street instead. How I had hated that bland, empty mine house, oyster-coloured, like all the other houses. Oyster-coloured to disguise the dust from the mine. The grass in our yard had remained brittle and yellow, indifferent to how many times it was watered. An enormous camel-thorn tree had cast a tangled shadow over the dying lawn, the branches twisting into a deformed dance as if pleading with the merciless blue sky. The heat was unforgiving: hot, oppressive, humid. In the six months we stayed there not one cloud drifted over us. From early morning, the inhabitants scuttled behind shady trees and thatched lapas. Air conditioners hummed behind drawn curtains.

In the north, dense bushveld enclosed Thabazimbi, hiding a world of birds, lizards, buck and snakes. But this thorny paradise was off-limits. Six-foot fences enclosed private game reserves. I could no longer do what I loved most: walk in the hills with Bongi. We walked the suburban streets instead, Bongi straining at his collar as we circled the blocks back home. He was as frustrated on his leash as I was on mine. What to do with the rest of the day? What to do with the rest of my life? Time weighed heavily on my shoulders. An anvil. I felt disorientated. For too long I had been mapping the serious side of life, for too long I had been underground. Now I had surfaced – to become the live-in girlfriend of the *Engelsman* geologist, Red Earth Company, grading C3.

Bongi handled his free time more constructively. He learnt to climb the camel-thorn tree by chasing blue-headed lizards up its trunk. He spent the late afternoons lazing in its shady branches, his limbs dangling, watching the world below with the bored intensity of a wild cat. As if, now that he could no longer survey the world from his sandstone hills, he could at least keep an eye on the neighbourhood.

One afternoon he watched two cops walk across our lawn.

The older one pointed up the tree, 'Is that a cat or a dog?'

'A dog,' I told him.

The younger cop's jaw slackened as he looked up. The older cop scribbled in his booklet, tore out the page and handed it to me.

'What's this?

'A fine.'

'For my dog climbing a tree?'

'No lady, for your dog not having a license. Does he have a license?'

'You want my dog to have a license to climb the tree?'

'No lady, all dogs must have a dog license. Or a cat license will do.'

The cops walked back to their flashing vehicle. The younger one still watching Bongi. Their siren blared as they drove off.

From behind me swirls of Deep Purple drifted over the blistered lawn. Electric organ and guitar. Terence had unplugged his headphones. *Sweet child in time* . . .

I waved the fine in the air, furious. 'They gave us a fine! Apparently Bongi needs a license – a cat license, because he climbs trees.'

Terence hung his head and his shoulders began to shake. He wiped his eyes and started to laugh again, 'Shit, this town. I don't know whether I'm laughing or crying.'

Thabazimbi lay subdued on the red rocks, opening a lazy, hostile eye to any newcomer. Everyone knew everyone and everyone's story was an epic tale. The promotions on the local mines were predictable and the houses and the salaries awarded according to one's grading. My arrival to join Terence travelled the gossip heat waves.

'Oh, Sterlitzia Street!' The woman behind the post office counter raised a stencilled eyebrow in approval.

'Strelitzia Street,' I told her. 'Oyster-coloured, three bedrooms and a carport. It's like all the other houses.'

'The houses are the same. But what matters is who your neighbours are,' she informed me, sliding my box key under the counter.

The librarian fixed her rings of eyeliner on me as I sunk between the rows of books. Her voice penetrated my burrow: 'She's living with the *Engelsman*. She just arrived, from nowhere. They are not even married . . . in Sterlitzia Street.'

'We are a God-fearing people,' someone agreed.

S, St, Ste . . . Steinbeck. I pulled out the book I was looking for: *Arlington Road*. It contained Doc, my favourite Steinbeck character. Doc was kind, he waved at all the dogs in his small town. He knew them all by name. Perhaps if he lived in a small town like this, he would also ignore the people and wave at the dogs.

Terence, too, wilted in the heat. Every day he travelled out of town to the Red Earth iron ore mine to map the hot red pit. He trod the surrounding hills mapping the outcrop, which had been mapped a hundred times before. His days were organised tedium; mine at least were open to possibility. The Swaziland waterfalls, the lush green fields and tranquil forests lay now in his distant past. The routine, the hopelessness of it all stripped away at him, like the miners stripped the ore from the pit. All that had given him the stride in his step was gone: the close whisper of nature, the friendship of his field crew, his lonely caravan. On the Swaziland border he had been king of all the land he could see. On the mine he was just another worker.

To us. In Thabazimbi, us was not enough.

On his worst days, Terence just lay on the borrowed couch and listened to his music through his headphones; playing his life on fast forward. One evening like so many others, I watched him on the couch with his back curled to the world, his eyes closed, his headphones insulating him. The music was loud enough for me to recognise it: Led Zeppelin.

For five months I struggled to stay afloat. For five months I watched Terence do the same. I was tired. I was sinking, drowning. I could no longer keep my head above water. Deeper and deeper.

Down the hall and onto the bed; I curled my legs up to my chest. I felt too paralysed to move.

Later, I felt the bed sink.

'Is something wrong?'

Terence had unplugged his headphones.

When the levee breaks, I have got no place to go . . .

Was something wrong? Just that *my* levee finally broke. No more stacking of banks, no more retaining the dark waters. I let the river flood its course.

'I'm tired.'

'Tired. Of me?'

Tired of it all. Tired of this town, tired of doing nothing. Tired of his dark waters smashing into mine. Tired of swimming against the hostile flow of this town.

'Yes, tired of you too.'

Terence rested his face in his hands.

I closed my eyes and let sleep take me. When I awoke, the grey morning light was filtering into the room. I rolled over to see that Terence had wrapped himself in a carpet. His feet stuck out the bottom: a human hot dog. His face looked angelic in sleep. His hair was short and his chin recently shaven, the result of working in a conservative mine environment. I reached over and touched his cheek. His eyes opened, he rolled out of the carpet with a *thwump* and climbed up onto the bed.

'You were rolled in a carpet.'

'I got cold,' he curled up behind me. I felt his face against my arm

'*Blue are the life-giving waters taking for granted, they quietly understand. But I'm, I'm bold as love,*' whispered Terence.

'Hendrix. Your music collection is stuck in a time warp.'

'Of course, that's when the best music was recorded. I am though . . . bold as love. Robyn, lets get married.'

I rolled over to look at him. He was serious.

I slipped my fingers into his. 'We are going to have to leave this place.'

'As soon as we can.'

The chance to leave presented itself shortly. Six months after our arrival, the transfer Terence had repeatedly asked for was granted. Red

Earth Company needed a geologist on the desolate west coast, not to explore for iron ore but for limestone, an essential ingredient in the steel-making process. Terence was being sent back into exploration.

Terence was granted another rattletrap of an Isuzu bakkie, and with our possessions loaded high, and Bongi sitting between us, we left. In the back, stacked in one of my boxes, were my black notebooks, stained with tunnel dust and sweat. Since my days in the tunnel, they had remained closed.

On our journey down to Lutzville, we were married in a small stone church in the Karoo by an easy-going minister. The ceremony was attended by close family and a few friends. Terence wore a waistcoat printed with blue roses. I carried a bunch of wild blue flowers and wore a dress the colour of copper. We were twenty-six and twenty-seven years old, and never before had something felt so right.

Before we reached Lutzville, the blue flowers had dried to drooping bruises and Bongi had slept on my dress for the whole journey, so it was stained with paw prints and smelt like spaniel. We drove west, from the thick green bushveld of Thabazimbi to a land of vast sand. A semi-desert. Lutzville lay close to the wild west coast. We found a house to rent on a farm, ten kilometres out of Lutzville, fifteen kilometres from the coast.

The farmhouse differed from the house in Thabazimbi. It smelt of freedom. The dry air blew through the open doors, through the square rooms and farm-size kitchen. The house itself was ordinary, boasting no imaginative architecture. Only the setting was extraordinary. It overlooked the Olifants River, which twisted its way like a green snake through the brown valley below. Eucalyptus trees towered behind the farmhouse, and beyond that, vast expanses of sand sunk and rose in sunset colours.

The desert sands welcomed us with wide-open arms in Lutzville. All memory of hanging time and red iron-ore pits was erased. Each morning we woke up to watch the sun light up the valley and smelt the west coast sea. Peace, quiet hope; it saturated our whole world.

Terence spent his time driving and walking the vast areas. I had begun to study part-time. *The Depreciation of the Copper Price in the Mineral Market* was an abstract concept, however, and the reality lay in the sands and sunsets, the wild west coast and its wine and seafood. In our inner sunshine.

As the farmhouse was set in a dip, we could not receive TV or radio. We shared a farm line, but our phone seldom rang. Lutzville remained our first point of contact with the outside world. The town had a post office, a small hotel and a school. We bought our food from the small but sufficient supermarket. There was even a coffee shop, which sold second-hand books. The town itself was centred around a large, authoritative church.

The Sunday after we arrived in Lutzville, we had driven into town in the hope of buying an English newspaper. We parked outside the coffee shop, which served as a small general dealer as well. There was a sign of a coffee pot hanging from a post, and the name: *Die Koffiepot*. A bell jangled as we stepped inside. A woman stood behind the counter. She wore an ocean of purple, each layer of cotton a slightly different shade to the next. Hair had escaped from her tangled grey bun. She eyed us over her half-moon spectacles and tucked a strand of hair behind her ear.

'Benjie, more coffee,' someone called.

She shot a look to the corner table, to a group of three men. Two of them looked dishevelled, their hair and beards long and tangled, and one wore a black eye-patch. The third, in contrast, was younger, handsome, tall and clean-cut.

'Benjie,' the young one called again, grinning.

'You boys just wait. I'm busy here. An English newspaper, well, we are sold out of those already. Only get a limited amount. But,' she ducked under the counter, 'you can have my copy, I've already read it.'

Benjie slipped the coin Terence placed on the counter into the layers of her skirt.

'Ray, what you up to?' she barked.

The man with the eye-patch had drifted to the bookshelf to inspect the second-hand magazines. 'Nothing Ma'am. Just, you know, looking.'

'Ray,' she looked over her spectacles, 'what have you been smoking? Look at your eye.'

Ray patted his patch.

'The other eye, you fool. Ray, sit down. I'll bring you boys your coffee and breakfast in a minute.'

We retreated from Die Koffiepot with Benjie's copy of the *Sunday Times*.

We drove past the church. Its large wooden doors were open and the congregation was spilling out onto the lawn: men in dark suits and women in bright dresses with coordinated hats and shoes. In the centre of the lawn, a woman twirled in a wide red skirt, her broad-rimmed hat trailing a red ribbon. Her white gloves fluttered like butterflies and came to rest on the dominee. She tugged his limp hands towards her bosom. The church and its congregation slipped away as we circled the block and returned to the isolation of our farmhouse.

We had been living in isolated peace for almost a month when the phone rang unexpectedly. Terence and I looked at each other.

'Hello?'

'Robyn?' her voice sounded as if it came from a hole in the top of her head.

'Yes.'

'My name is Mittie. I heard you moved into the old farmhouse. I think – no, *we* think that you should meet some of the women in town. You must come for coffee tomorrow. Be there at ten, at the coffee shop, there is only one, Die Koffiepot.'

I replaced the receiver slowly. I had enjoyed my anonymous presence.

Terence laughed. 'Coffee? They just want to suss you out.'

The next morning I selected a green dress and flat sandals, clothes that would not attract comment. I waved Terence goodbye with a long face. He continued to work at his desk, scratching the growth on his chin to hide his smile. In front of him, lined up along the window ledge, were all the bowls I had made in the Thabazimbi pottery studio, each one more colourful and lopsided than the next.

Thabazimbi. I had also been invited for coffee by the Red Earth Company wives, while their husbands attended a company braai. Each husband's position on the mine was the centrifugal force to the orbiting wife. Company benefits, street addresses, mine divisions were discussed. I was easily categorised: C3, Geology, Sterlitzia Street – one garage three bedrooms. Not married.

'Not married,' whispered a voice, 'still got a house in Sterlitzia Street.'

'Oh, Sterlitzia Street,' said another voice brightly. 'My husband is a C2, you know.'

I had suggested going to the bar for a cold beer instead of drinking coffee in the hot, overstuffed lounge of the Thabazimbi Hotel. Silence.

A woman crossed her ankles and told me with a sleek smile, 'My husband would never allow me to sit in a bar.'

By the time Terence had returned home I was sitting on the borrowed couch, sipping a glass of lukewarm red wine. Terence had apologised; only geologists had been invited to the braai, not wives or girlfriends. He had leapt back as I threw my glass against the wall. The red wine trickled down the oyster-coloured paint. I *was* a bloody geologist. Or had been.

But Lutzville was not a mining town, there were no gradings and no mine. Lutzville would be different. I took a deep breath and pushed the door to the Die Koffiepot open. Benjie peered at me over her spectacles, her grey hair in a tangle. A pencil was tucked behind her ear. With her head she motioned to a coffee table behind the bookshelf.

A woman sat with her hands placed neatly beside a large hat. I recognised the hat – its red ribbon was no longer fluttering after the dominee. Fingers that no longer wore little white gloves jiggled at me.

'Robyn, Robyn, over here! Benjie, another coffee.' Her bright red lips pulled apart to flash me a smile. She raised a soft hand, knuckles up: 'Mittie.'

I took it, wondering if she expected me to kiss it, and shook it firmly. 'Robyn.' I sat down.

'Robyn, the other ladies will be here later. But we can start talking. Benjie,' she sang, 'where are those coffees?'

'Coming Mittie, coming,' Benjie plonked two cups in front of us and departed.

The coffee had spilled onto my saucer. I decanted it back into the cup.

'Eeeee!' Mittie shrieked, looking out the window.

One-eyed Ray was staring at us over the window's modest frill. He left a wet nose-print as his good-looking crew-cut friend pulled him away. They both laughed and he patted Ray on the shoulder and the two of them parted ways. A matted brown-and-white sheepdog trotted beside Ray, wagging his tail.

'Those diamond divers,' said Mittie and leant closer to me, 'I don't know *why* she lets them in here.'

Benjie was busy sorting old books from a box. I thought I saw her smile as she dusted off another cover and placed it on a shelf.

'Robyn,' Mittie clutched my wrist, 'tell me. Tell me about yourself. Where do your parents live?'

'Johannesburg.'

'They are divorced?'

'No . . .' I looked at Mittie in surprise.

'But you said they come from Johannesburg?'

'Yes,' I frowned, not following her logic.

Where did my father work? And *did* my mother work? What *is* it my husband does? Mittie interrogated efficiently, with the ruthless precision of a detective. While she worked me over, a variety of ladies drifted into the coffee shop. They sat down at our table, listened over a cup of coffee and left. The inquisition was only interrupted to fill each newcomer in, as if they had missed the start of a rather boring soap opera. Some of the ladies were introduced to me, others not.

The last one flicked her long blonde hair over her shoulder as she stood and said, 'It's not just you people from the city who are busy. We are very, very busy. I must leave now, to fetch the kids from school.'

'I'm not busy,' I told her, but she had already left.

An hour later Benjie served me my third cup of coffee. This one was not slopped into the saucer. Mittie was looking pleased – her interrogation must be going well. Mentally I was trying to count the number of women who had drifted in and out. Seven, eight?

'What cars do you drive?' Mittie was annoyed; she did not like having to repeat herself.

A hand rested on my shoulder. It slipped beneath my elbow, encouraging me to rise to my feet. My eyes rose from the worn leather moccasins and over the ample layers of purple and blue cotton, to Benjie's mauve eyes. Her wrinkles creased naturally, the first honest smile I'd seen all morning.

'Come with me, Robyn. I have a book for you. I know you will enjoy it. *I* enjoyed it.'

'Benjie, we have *not* finished,' said Mittie.

Benjie crooked a finger. 'Follow me.'

Smiling apologetically at Mittie, I followed Benjie. Mittie snatched up her hat and handbag and left. The young crew-cut diver entered and held the door open for her. Mittie flapped her hat at him as if chasing a fly and sauntered out.

'Levi, you're early. Not working today?'

'Not today, Benjie. Sea's not right. We've been watching her for days. But she's just not right. She'll be too choppy and we won't see a god-damn thing.'

Levi sat at the counter. Benjie placed a cup of coffee in front of him and pushed the sugar bowl in his direction.

'Now, where was that book? Somewhere here I think, in one of these boxes,' Benjie slapped a cloud of dust off one of the boxes and opened it, 'Yes, here it is.'

She lifted a book whose cover portrayed a woman in a Victorian dress clinging to a heavily moustached soldier in a red jacket. *Passions Aroused*, read the title. She slipped on her glasses, 'No, not this one. Although . . .' she licked her lips, 'it does look like a good read.'

Levi laughed, displaying an even set of white teeth. 'Benjie, what do you want those books for, when you got me?'

'You,' she looked at him over her spectacles, 'need some of the swagger knocked out of you. Would you like me to do that for you?' She lifted the thick book over her shoulder.

Levi sipped his coffee, still laughing. He glanced at me. His eyes were startling, as crisp as the cold Atlantic Ocean.

Benjie dropped *Passions Aroused* back into the box and dug deeper. She pulled out another paperback and wiped the dust from its cover.

I peered over Benjie's shoulder. She smelt strongly of talcum powder.

'There, *Sophie's Choice*. I read it, loved it. You will like it too.' She thrust the book into my hand.

'Tea,' Benjie suddenly announced and ducked into the kitchen.

'What are you doing here? You and your . . . husband?' asked Levi.

'My husband is working on an exploration project. He's a geologist, well actually, we both are, but he's the one working here.'

Levi fixed his aquamarine eyes on me and a smile spread across his healthy, tanned face. 'Well shit. Know anything about diamonds?'

'Some,' I shrugged.

'Anything about the saltwater babies? The ocean diamonds.'

'Some,' I repeated, smiling.

'Wait here. Benjie will be a while with the tea anyway. She does the spooky thing with the tea, *whoo whoo*.'

Ignoring my puzzled look, Levi twisted off the stool with an easy movement and bounded outside. In a couple of minutes he returned with his eye-patch friend, who was wearing a raincoat over his shorts and T-shirt and cheap plastic flip-flops.

Levi pushed him towards me. 'Show her, Ray. She's a geologist.'

Filthy yellow dreadlocks fell over Ray's scarred face. He fixed his green eye on me and rasped, '*Lift up your skirts and bare your legs, your nakedness will be exposed and your shame uncovered.*'

Levi smacked him on the side of his head, 'Stop that, you sorry bastard. Show her the map.'

Ray passed a grubby coil of paper to me. He sniffed, looked around and sniffed again. His nose led him back into the kitchen where presumably Benjie was still making the tea.

Levi unrolled the map. It was a detailed contour map marked at ten-metre intervals. There was very little else on the map, other than a coordinate system, a scale and a north arrow. Red crosses had been drawn in places.

'Bottom of the ocean,' said Levi, 'Valuable map. Got it from one of Big Brother's diamond mining ships, results of their seismic surveys. They don't mine in our shallow waters anyway. Got it through a friend.'

I looked at the map. The contours rose and sunk in channels and potholes, not unlike something you'd see on land.

'The diamonds are heavy, they sink into the gullies and potholes, that's where we suck them out with our hoses.'

I nodded. 'That's the way I understand it.'

'This map doesn't cover a very large area. Thing is, we've mined out most of these channels. Crossed them off on the map. Found some fucking lovelies too. But we've sucked through the gravel in pretty much all the gullies on this map. So what I'm asking you . . .'

We both looked up as Ray returned, eating a sandwich. He went to the magazine rack, helped himself and sat down at one of the tables.

'. . . can you recommend any other areas we should mine?'

I stared at the map. All the major channels and potholes had been crossed out.

'What about the smaller gullies, something narrow like these?'

'They're bloody small.'

'So are diamonds.'

Levi laughed. 'Right you are. The little beauties.'

Benjie arrived with a teapot and a cup. She placed them on the counter.

'I wouldn't really know. Most of it has to do with luck – as you'd know better than me.'

'Exactly. So pick an area. Any. Make a lucky guess.'

Benjie tapped a teaspoon against the teapot making her point.

'Go on.' Levi pushed the map towards me, flashing his even white teeth.

'Oh . . .' I circled the air with my finger and dropped it on the map. 'There – no, shift it to a gully. There.'

Levi marked the spot, rolled up the map and tucked it under his arm, 'Not the tea, Benjie. Spooky.'

Benjie shot him a stern look, 'Time for you boys to be on your way, Levi. And take Ray. Make him put his plate in the kitchen.'

Benjie stirred the pot and then poured the tea into a cup. She drained it back into the teapot and peered into the bottom of the cup, slipping her spectacles further up her nose. 'Ooh, uh . . . mmm, not good.'

I waited, speechless.

'He got a moustache?'

'Who?'

'Your husband?'

'Oh, no, why?'

'Good, good, not a husband.' Benjie turned the teacup around, 'or a boat . . . you have a boat?'

I shook my head.

Benjie signalled the divers to leave: 'Beat it.' Levi gave a friendly wave and Ray shuffled behind him, sinking his hands into his coat.

'See you later, boys.' She turned her attention back to the cup. 'No, a moustache. I can feel it is a moustache. The future.' She showed me the contents of the cup. The damp tea leaves were curved into an arc.

'Could be a moustache. What does it mean?'

'I have found . . .' Benjie said slowly, her mauve eyes watching me, 'that the visions that come to me in the tea tend to be warnings.'

'Well, I don't even know anyone with a moustache.'

'You will,' she put the cup down. 'Two rand.'

'Sorry?'

'For the book.'

'Oh, the book.' I fumbled in my pocket and gave her the coin.

She placed it in the folds of her skirt. 'Close the door on the way out, don't let it slam. The wind blows away my magazines.'

While this semi-desert hosted a fringe community of farmers, the coastline kept others: the fishermen and diamond divers. Evidence of the diamond search was to be seen in the piles of reworked gravel along the coastline. Many of the divers worked from the beach, frogmen wading out into the cold Atlantic Ocean with generator-driven hoses to suck up the gravel. Others worked from boats in deeper seas.

The divers could be seen here and there. Their search for the elusive *blink klippies* – bright little stones – was a hard, rough, wild existence. Their eyes took on a certain look: as hard and shiny as the prey they sought; washed with the wide, moody distance of the ocean. Scanning, scanning, always in search of the Big Find. The promise of riches, the promise of the easy life. That easy life seldom came; only a living was made, in large, irregular sums. Gamblers of the ocean.

We saw the divers along the coast, we saw them in town. They could not dive every day. The sea was too choppy or too murky, perhaps. Even the promise of bad weather kept them on shore, and the lure of the cold Atlantic was postponed for another day. Time moved slowly between dives, so come weekend they could all be found at the only bar in town, the Lutzville Hotel.

Terence continued to explore the vast tracts of semi-desert. Sometimes I went with him. In the distance I would see him bend down to pick up a stone or sift the sand through his fingers. His hair grew long, he seldom shaved, and his face, arms and legs turned brown. He was once again surrounded by as much land he could hold on to. He lost too much weight, but was once again fit and lean. He refused to eat in the day; he said it was too hot. He drank water instead. At the end of each day he smelt of suncream and sweat.

The land was too dry to support much livestock and the farmhouses were therefore widely dispersed. The odd encounter with a farmer was always friendly, but we continued to enjoy our solitude on the farm. After Mittie's initial meeting, I never heard from her again; I was relieved. It was only after we had lived near Lutzville for two months that Terence and I began to feel the need for other company. So when Friday night came around, we headed for the Lutzville Hotel bar.

By seven 'o clock the place was already busy. Men jostled at the bar – diamond divers. The bar itself was heavy-duty, built for survival, with a heavy wooden counter and stools nailed to the concrete floor. The walls and the ceiling were painted a navy blue, and in places someone had attempted to paint a few silver stars. A motionless glitter ball hung in the centre. Terence and I headed for an empty spot near the end of bar, and sat down next to the diver I recognised from Benjie's shop, Levi.

As we sat down, Levi shot up and shouted across the bar, '*Jy het jouself amper gekak!* – You almost shat yourself!' He lifted his long denim leg and smacked his knee. '*Amper gekak, man.* When those sharks cruised over us today. Your eye man, it grew big. I thought you were turning into a Cyclops. I thought your eyebrows were going to swim away. Like two little fish!' He wiggled his forefingers over his eyebrows.

A few divers behind him laughed. Across the bar sat one-eyed Ray. Ray's yellow dreadlocks fell over his face as he studied his beer.

'Ray, Ray, Ray,' Levi waved a dismissive hand, 'they won't eat you, they're just inquisitive. They just like to come and see what we're doing. Hey,' he said, noticing us, 'welcome, geos.' Levi signalled to the waitress, a young girl with a blonde ponytail who stared at him through her eyelashes, to bring more beer.

'We haven't officially been introduced. Levi.' He held out his hand. His fingernails were neatly clipped, his fingers long and elegant.

Terence. Robyn. We shook his hand.

'What is it you're doing here?' Levi asked Terence.

'Exploration.'

'Diamonds?'

Terence shook his head. 'No, limestone.'

Levi tilted back his head and laughed, 'Fuck limestone. What's that worth? Now diamonds, those beauties are worth a whole lot more.'

Terence kept his smile. He didn't bother to reply.

'Levi? Strange name,' I said.

'Short for Leviathan,' Levi replied.

'Seriously? Your name is Leviathan?'

'It is now. Ray gave me that name.' He cocked his dark crew cut. 'You're obviously not familiar with the Old Testament. No? No?' Levi looked at Terence and then at me. 'Well, nor am I. But Ray is, reads it all the time. He gave me the name. Leviathan the sea-monster.'

Levi slid us down two beers, held up three fingers to the waitress. She placed another three bottles on the bar, turned and wrapped her apron slowly around her waist. Levi ignored her. He glanced across the bar at his one-eyed friend. 'Ray – he's been my diving buddy for years. Crazy as fuck. He's my best buddy, my lifeline. But shit, is he crazy.' He laughed and shook his head.

Terence and I glanced at Levi's object of affection. Ray still sat staring into his beer. He was not wearing his eye-patch and his left eyelid was closed. He pushed back his mat of yellow hair and took another sip of beer.

'Doesn't say much, Ray,' commented Levi.

Ray patted his knee and clicked his fingers. From the back door the matted brown-and-white sheepdog slunk in. One of its eyes was sewn shut, the other stared up adoringly at its master. Ray ruffled its filthy head.

Levi hammered the counter. 'Tonight the drinks are on *me*.'

A fresh round of beers was delivered onto the bar. I slid one down to Terence, but he had drifted off and was talking to an old man sitting at one of the sleeper-wood tables, who, with his neatly clipped grey beard and worn clothing, looked like a fisherman. The two appeared to know each other, and Terence laughed and sat down opposite the man.

'Drinks are on you then?' I turned back to Levi.

'That is correct. And I have something to show you.' From under his T-shirt, he pulled out a string necklace, with a small cylinder attached to it. Levi screwed it open and carefully tipped the contents into the palm of his hand. He signalled for me to come closer. I leant forward.

'Take a look at this fucking beauty. Go on, pick it up, hold it to the light. Here, take a look at it through this lens. But don't wave it around. Seven sweet carats.'

Levi handed me the diamond and, from his pocket, a lens. Turning my back to the bar crowd, I studied the diamond. It was a classic offshore beauty: a perfect octahedral crystal (the shape of two pyramids secured to each other's base) and the colour of champagne. I held it up against the light. The diamond was clear, without too many fractures and inclusions. I clutched it tightly before handing it back.

'It's beautiful.'

Levi tipped it back into the cylinder, which he screwed shut and slipped under his shirt.

'Worth a fortune. This baby is going to change my life. You know where I found her?'

I shook my head.

Levi nodded. 'Yup. In the gully you randomly chose on my map. That's where we were today. Just me, Ray and another couple of divers. We sucked up most of the gravel – it was only a small pothole. Then those fucking sharks cruised over us. Shit. I thought we were done for. We got out of there fast. Later, when we sifted through the gravel on the boat, that's when we found her.'

Levi pulled out a neat cigarette case, opened it and offered it to me. It was filled with hand-rolled cigarettes. I shook my head.

'Go on, the finest. Tonight we celebrate.' Levi lit up and took a deep drag. The sweet smell of grass filled the smoky bar. He held the joint out for me, smoke drifting from his hand. It smelt herbal and calm.

'What geologist doesn't want a spliff?'

He placed the neat, white cylinder between my fingers. Strains of Paul Simon drifted through the bar. I took a deep drag, held the smoke in my mouth and let it filter out slowly from my lips. Not bad. I turned to look at Terence. He was watching me. He raised an eyebrow over a quizzical smile. The fisherman tapped his arm.

'You can spot your diamond divers a mile off,' I told Levi. 'You get a certain look.'

'We get it from watching the sea too long. The sea has to be just right. Not too choppy, not too murky. That's when the sharks come out. Like today, we shouldn't have been down there. The water was murky. We didn't see those sharks until they were almost over us. It was shit scary.' Suddenly Levi laughed, stuck a flat fin hand on his head, and moved his shoulders through the water. 'Jaws – *doom doom . . . doom doom.*'

'What do you do with yourselves when you're not diving?'

Levi tapped the ash into an already overstuffed ashtray and handed the joint back to me. 'We smoke a bit of this, we watch the sea.'

'Has it been worth it?' I was beginning to feel calm, relaxed, a little hazy.

'I – we – make a lot of money. At times. But while we wait, we spend it, mostly here. But with this fucking beauty my life is going to change. I'll get a bigger boat, I'll get a bigger crew. From now on, life will be a fucking cruise.'

Another beer appeared in front of me. I took the joint back from Levi. 'Uh, thanks, keeps you sober, I think.'

I looked around to look for Terence but a crowd of divers had gathered around the table and I could no longer see him.

Levi sat for a moment in silence, and then shouted across the bar, 'Ray, why are you so quiet? What the fuck's got into you? Still *lekker geskrik, heh?* No sharks here, bro.'

Ray looked up. One green eye shifted across to us, the other remained closed. His skin was weathered and sunburnt. He drained his beer, revealing dark holes where some of his teeth should've been.

'Old one-eyed Ray. You see his dog's only got one eye too? What a laugh, the two of them. Man, he's crazy. But don't ever make Ray mad. No, not ever. I've seen Ray mad. Someone kicked his dog.'

The shaggy dog put his front paws up onto his master's lap. Ray rubbed his chest, keeping his one eye fixed on the wet bar surface.

Levi clicked his fingers at the barmaid. 'Sambuca, babe, make it the gold.'

The girl lifted a bottle of clear fluid from the shelf and placed it on the bar with two glasses. Levi shook the bottle and gold flakes twinkled through the liquid. He decanted it into the two small glasses and slid one over the wet bar surface.

'Go on, any geologist should love this. Pure, loving gold. Not as beautiful as diamonds, those little fucking beauties.'

I sipped the drink. It tasted like liquorice. I stuck out my tongue to see if I could see any of the gold flakes. My eyes squinted, I couldn't see any. I turned to Levi to show him my tongue. Perhaps he could see the gold flakes.

'Ith the everyday things in life that are preciouth,' I told him, my mouth thick with tongue. 'Ith the gold that eathes the jointh. Carter, my old both, thold me that.'

He refilled my glass. I drank it. I ran my fingers along the edge of the bar. Perhaps I had collected one blind eye from Ray and the other from his dog. I blinked slowly and turned to Levi, my focus tilting with his sea-wave eyes.

'You okay? Here, have some more.' He handed me his joint.

I shifted back onto the bar stool, one cheek at a time, and took a drag on his joint. A row of sticky glasses marched in front of me. Levi was refilling one of them.

'I think I, maybe, have had enough.'

I hiccuped with fright as I turned around.

'Wo-oh Ray, don't creep up on the lady like that.' Levi pushed Ray's yellow dreadlocks away.

A green eye fixed on me.

'*In my wrath I shall unleash a violent wind . . .*' Ray said in a hoarse, deep voice.

'Not here brother, not here,' Levi cackled.

'*. . . and in my anger hailstones and torrents of rain will fall with destructive fury . . .*' Ray leant closer, his hand reached out as if to touch me; it hovered in mid-air. '*Woe to women who sew magic charms . . . in order to ensnare people.*'

Ray pulled back, sniffed and scratched his sandpaper chin. He grinned, revealing his oddly spaced teeth. His dog slunk between my legs.

'Ray.' Levi stood up to embrace him.

Someone turned up the music; Paul Simon infiltrated the smoke. As if washed by the current, one by one the divers gathered around Levi. They formed a wave of swaying figures behind me. Together they roared with Paul Simon: '*He's a poor boy, empty as a pocket with nothing to lose. Sing ta na na, ta na na na . . .*'

Levi broke loose and beat the rhythm on the bar, *doef doef.*

Ray let out a guttural cry: '*Yeah, we've got diamonds on the soles of our flippers . . . diamonds on the soles of our flippers . . .*'

Terence was at my side, holding my elbow. I smiled warmly at him and sang, '*Sing ta na na, ta na na na.*'

'Time to go, angel, things are about to get messy.'

I stumbled down from the bar stool and giggled.

Levi broke loose from the wild, weaving divers. 'Hey Robyn. He's working and you're not?'

I nodded and caught hold of the bar.

'But hey, you brought me some luck with that map. Look, I know of someone up north who's looking for two geologists. Let me give you his number. A big exploration company. You can give him a call, his name's Bill but I call him Chief, most people call him Chief.'

Terence pulled at my arm and I stumbled after him, looking back at Levi. He had already locked arms with his sea-world friends. They swayed to the roar of their voices, rising and crashing against each other, waves washing up onshore: '*Diamonds on the soles of our flippers . . .*'

Terence led me out of the bar and into the pale green lobby. It was suddenly quiet. Two sad palm trees drooped over a blue, plastic fish pond. Inside, the algal water was as thick as pea soup.

'Oh my, welcome to Miami,' I gyrated my hips around the pool, an imaginary pineapple on my head.

Terence pulled me out of the giddy circle. 'God, you're a lump. Can't you walk?' He slipped one of my arms around his shoulders and put his arm around my waist, steering me out the front door.

Outside on the street I could smell the west-coast sea. The car door opened and I sunk onto the seat. The door closed behind me.

I shut my eyes, only to feel the world roll and sway in nauseating motion. There was a knock on the window and I rolled one eye in its direction. Aquamarine eyes; Levi. Terence leant across me and unwound the window.

'Hey, you guys, you forgot Chief's number.'

A piece of paper passed hands above me. I heard Terence slip it into his pocket.

'Look, we had a rough day out there. A big day. We're just letting off a little steam. Getting rid of some energy. Don't pay us much notice. But give Chief a call, he's a good guy. And I know he's looking for people up north.'

'Thanks. We'll give it some thought,' said Terence, 'when the missus sobers up.'

I heard him start up the engine, the bakkie rattled and with a lurch we were off, rising and sinking on the waves of the west coast.

CHAPTER SIX

Hot, Heavy Rain

We sat around a table made of heavy sleeper wood. Chief and his second-in-command, Riaan, sat at the head. Riaan's two geologists, Morné and JJ, sat on one side, Terence and I on the other. We were in the thatch lapa; around us prefabricated offices circled us like wagons in a Voortrekker laager.

This exploration camp, Spioenkop, was hidden in the thick green bushveld, a stone's throw from the town of Naboomspruit. It was an hour's drive north from Pretoria and less than an hour's drive west from our projects in Marble Hall. The afternoon was humid and hot; I could smell the rain brewing.

'As this is our first Month End together,' said Chief, 'let me welcome our new arrivals, Terence and Robyn. They will be taking on the two platinum projects near Marble Hall. An old friend of mine gave them my number – Levi. A wild bugger. However you know him, we won't hold against you,' Chief laughed and scratched his unruly brown beard. His good-humoured green eyes flickered onto us.

Chief was slim and wiry, not much older than forty. His brown hair stood on end, obviously not combed that day.

'I met Levi on the west coast, working on that heavy mineral sands mine. I used to go out on his boat with him, take my fishing rod while they dived. Coolbox full of cold beers, feet up. Waiting for the big fish to bite. Aah, that was the life.' Chief leant back with the good memory, hands behind his head. 'Damn fish never bit. But I watched the guys work. Pretty interesting actually, watching them sort those gravels. They toss most of it back overboard and sort through the smaller stuff to get those diamonds.'

Riaan cleared his throat. He sat so close to the Chief that their elbows met. His diary, like Chief's, lay open to the date: 30 April 1994.

'All right, Tiger, where was I? Terence and Robyn . . . the two of you, like Morné and JJ, will be reporting to Riaan. You'll be needing field supplies – everything from vehicles to spades, picks, tape measures, that sort of thing. But just remember to check everything with Riaan *first*.'

Riaan nodded. His black hair was military short, his eyes as dark as wet seeds. A thick moustache was pinned to his upper lip. I thought of the tea leaves at the bottom of Benjie's cup. Curved like a boat. Riaan's khaki shirt sleeves were rolled to the elbows, revealing sinewy brown arms.

Sitting next to Riaan was JJ, a long, pale young man with a freckled face. His hair was a nondescript colour and his front teeth slightly protruding, and he stooped forward as if he was always trying to make himself shorter. JJ said very little but nodded often. Beside him sat Morné, who was slightly older and bald, apart from the semicircle of brown fuzz that grew around the back of his head. His round paunch squeezed up against the table. He chewed on strongly scented mint gum.

Riaan looked at Terence and then at me. He held my glance. I was reminded of the TBM laser, which marked its grinding path through the mountain.

Chief slurped his coffee and laughed. 'Those were the days. Deepsea fishing. Couldn't find the damn bait those west-coast fish would bite though. Old Levi ran a tight ship – well, tight boat – there were always cold beers for me on board. Not that the divers drank on the job. No sir, but they certainly made up for it afterwards.'

Riaan continued to study me.

'Right, folks,' Chief pulled himself back to the present, 'We'll discuss all the technicalities of your projects at next Month End. When we have some results to look at. Have a good month and we'll see you here same time, same place, last day of the month. Morné, don't arrive the wrong day like you did last month.' Chief slapped the table and chairs slid back as everyone rose.

JJ laughed. He looked at Riaan and stopped.

Riaan stepped forward as I walked past. 'Just make sure you check *everything* with me first,' he said softly.

Back in Lutzville, Terence had found the piece of paper from Levi. We had studied it together, standing out in the front garden over-looking the Olifants River Valley below. The paper was frayed at the edges and the numbers were almost illegible. I sipped my coffee while my head hammered its good morning to me.

'It would be an opportunity for us to work together. You could work again,' said Terence.

I nodded. That hurt my head. 'What the hell did I drink last night?'

'Beverages,' replied Terence.

I sighed, carefully. 'I do need to work again. Soon.'

'It's been peaceful here, but . . . we should speak to them.'

'I know. Living here has been wonderful, but I guess it can't last forever.'

Terence put an arm around my shoulder. 'I'll call. . .' he studied the paper. 'Chief.'

Chief was cheerful over the phone. We gave him our details. He asked if he could call us back later in the day, after he had spoken to his second-in-command. He phoned that afternoon. Could we arrive immediately? The company, MinSearch, were exploring for platinum, they needed another two projects in Marble Hall started without de-lay. In fact, they had a caravan ready and waiting at a campsite close to the projects. We should go straight there. It was Chief's good hu-mour and cajoling over the phone that finally swayed us to leave the semi-desert of Lutzville.

We drove north on the day of South Africa's first democratic elec-tion: 27 April 1994. We had voted in Lutzville and then driven through one small town after the other, winding our way through South Africa. Past the shongololo lines of people, growing with the length of day. Everyone casting their vote; the vote of democracy, the vote of freedom. Within days the election results were announced. The African National Congress had won and Mandela was president. No, Mandela was King. Voices rose ululating from the country-side. But beneath the euphoria was a shudder of fear: how would the right wing react? How would they fight to topple the government?

Finally, we drove through the town of Marble Hall and into the caravan park Chief had described, situated ten kilometres out of town. The park was set in a small valley, beside the rather insignificant Moses River. A few caravans were scattered in the long green grass. When I saw our caravan, my heart sank. It was tilted to one side and looked rusted and lonely. In the windows, the orange blinds hung at odd angles, giving it a bleary-eyed expression. Torn canvas, in red and white carnival stripes, sunk from the caravan like a joke fallen flat.

The caravan park was scattered with thorny acacias. The other caravans looked less decrepit, their lonely inhabitants sitting outside in the late afternoon, drinking. Terence looked at our new home while Bongi snorted excitedly through the long grass. Neither of us wanted to be the first to say anything.

Inside, the caravan smelt of rot. Mould had grown into every corner and begun to eat away at the surfaces. I touched the closest blind and it fell off its hinge. My spirit sunk a notch lower. So little space to live in, and so dirty . . . On cue, the clouds opened up and the afternoon showers began. Hot, heavy rain.

I sat on the mattress and unpacked one of the boxes. I unearthed my black notebooks and stacked them on the shelf behind the mattress. The only new entries since the tunnel were a couple of attempts at sketching the semi-desert landscape around Lutzville. They had not worked well; I had found it impossible to capture the sense of space and dryness. I stacked my novels beside the notebooks, in the order I planned to read them: the two Milan Kunderas first. On Terence's side I stacked his books – all Paul Auster. He was reading no other author at the time. I left his CD box unopened; he would want to unpack them himself. He had collected over three hundred. Besides his music from the seventies, he had started collecting the blues, the older, the better. The moaning, groaning kind of blues, all the way back to Robert Johnson. His classical collection was growing too, showing a preference for violin concertos. I aligned all the book-spines neatly and sighed. The mattress felt soft and damp beneath me.

I looked up as Terence climbed into the caravan.

'I think you should take a look at the office.'

From his expression, I didn't particularly want to. I followed him anyway, through the long grass to the small hut in the centre of the park. It was built from loosely cemented river boulders, held together by a black tin roof.

A stranger was also heading for the hut. His stomach protruded ahead, riding on his thin, bandy legs like a camel's hump. Foam spewed from his mouth; he was brushing his teeth. Behind him sat a sleek-looking caravan, with a blue lightning bolt frozen against its gleaming white surface. I looked back at our dismal home with a frown.

Inside the hut, the stranger studied us while still brushing his teeth. It was as humid as a sauna; the black roof soaked in the heat. The rain drummed softly above us.

The man spat out and introduced himself: 'Morné. You'll be taking over my project, I'm being moved to another. And you,' he waved his toothbrush at Terence, 'will be starting a new project.' Then he raised his chin and shouted out the door, 'Move it, Ben! I haven't got all bloody day.'

Outside, a man of a similar build to Terence, the neat, balanced kind, was attaching the caravan to a bakkie. He looked middle-aged, and was wearing a red cap and blue jeans. He dropped the tow hitch and walked to the office.

Morné hoisted up his tight khaki shorts, shook their contents and sat down. He rocked back on the chair. 'Give them a finger and they take the whole hand. Just remember that,' he sniffed. 'This boy can get lazy, you have to watch him. He's been working for me, but I'm leaving him here.'

Standing at the door, Ben kept his eyes lowered.

'Well,' Morné rocked forward, 'I have to get going.' He opened the desk drawer, removed a pistol and leather holster and attached it to his shorts.

Terence stood with his arms crossed and his feet apart, his chin rigid.

'Don't you have some work to hand over to Robyn, seeing as she's taking over your project?'

I said nothing. The sooner he left, the better. Were all their geologists like this?

Morné gave Terence a blank stare and stood up. 'What's there to show?'

'The geology maps, for a start,' Terence replied. We all looked at the colourful maps hanging from a couple of nails hammered into the wall.

'Nah. Haven't had time to look at those. Don't forget we have a Month End meeting at Spioenkop. That's next week. It's an hour's drive from here, near Naboomspruit, but I can do it in forty minutes. Ben knows the way.'

Terence, Ben and I watched him leave.

'Pleased to see him go?' I asked Ben.

Ben chuckled, '*Ou knopkierie*.'

'*Knopkierie*?' asked Terence, thinking of the traditional walking stick with a rounded ball of a handle.

Ben made an oval shape with his hands over his flat stomach, depicting Morné's paunch on skinny legs.

The oppressive, humid heat suddenly felt lighter as we laughed.

I looked across at our caravan and fell silent. 'Where do *you* live, Ben?'

'*Daar agter*, back there where the black people live.' He pointed behind a row of trees.

'In a caravan?'

'No, they have rooms.'

Over the next week, Terence and I studied all the maps, familiarising ourselves with the geology and the network of roads which led through our field areas. We threw out the broken furniture and bought some second-hand chairs from Marble Hall. It was clear that no work had been done by Morné.

I called Chief.

'You will, in effect, be starting from the beginning. You'll need to construct a geology map to see if there are any Bushveld rocks there,' said Chief, referring to the rocks of the Bushveld Igneous Complex, known world-wide for their platinum content. 'The area of Terence's project has already been mapped. He'll need to conduct a couple of soil-sampling programmes over the area. Ben will be needed on Terence's project to do that. We'll talk about this in more detail when we meet you at the Month End. Then you'll be able to meet the rest of the crew. You've met Morné, so then it's just me, Riaan and JJ.'

A week later, Ben directed us from the campsite to Naboomspruit. We drove out of the town and onto a muddy track. Immediately we were enclosed by thick, green bush. Deeper and deeper we drove into the thorny tangle. At the end of the track, the bush cleared and the lapa and offices became visible.

'We are here,' instructed Ben. 'Spioenkop.' He did not sound happy.

'Aah, welcome,' a wiry man with an unkempt brown beard popped out of the lapa. 'Your first Month End. I'm Bill, but call me Chief. Everyone calls me that – one of the benefits of the job.'

The second week in Marble Hall, a few days after the Month End, I drove out to my field area for the first time. The farms were small, little more than a couple of fields each. Most of them were planted with maize, tobacco or sunflowers. Each farmhouse was within view of its neighbours. The project area was set in a valley, enclosed by ridges of orange granophyre, a fine-grained granite. A river twisted through it. I noticed with dismay that the area was covered in thick, black soil with very little outcrop. This project was not going to be easy to map.

I was already nervous about mapping. Apart from in the tunnel, my mapping experience was limited to what Terence had shown me on the hot, red slopes outside Thabazimbi near the Red Earth mine, his collar up and his hat pulled low to protect himself from the sun. The midday heat had been unbearable while we walked perpendicular to the strike of rocks, mapping our path on an aerial photograph.

I drove with one hand, the other hand holding a topographical map as my finger traced the lines of farm boundaries and secondary tracks. I would start mapping in the south. I turned off onto a muddy track, still wet from the previous afternoon's thundershower.

The mud was dark and fine, and the tyres of the battered Toyota skidded. I stopped and shifted into 4x4. Slowly I continued to grind along the track. But the mud was too fine, too slippery to grip and the tyres gently slid off the track and into the ditch running alongside it. Shit. The tyres spun in reverse. The bakkie would not budge. I turned off the engine. The maize plantation smelt foul, decomposing. Too much rain, too much water, too much heat. I climbed out, slipped and slammed my knee against the door. *Shit*; my eyes smarted from the pain. I sat down in the mud and pulled my knee up to my chest.

A rustle from the rotting maize startled me. A large reptile's head appeared, looked right, then left, and trundled out onto the track. From head to tail he was about two foot long, black, with a large yellow mark on his back, almost as if a tin of paint had toppled onto him. Beautiful. He stopped when he saw me. I kept very still. He tilted his head and continued to walk, swinging his fat tail from side to side as he did so. I watched the last of him disappear into the foliage. Calmer, I rubbed my knee.

The monitor lizard had dragged a few rotted maize leaves behind him. I picked one up. It might work, I decided, and pulled myself up.

I jammed armfuls of maize leaves under the tyres and climbed back into the bakkie. I started the engine and slipped the vehicle into second gear. The tyres gripped and the vehicle edged back onto the track. *Bump.* Now what? I climbed out and peered under the bakkie. Two flat depressions marked where I had driven over a metal irrigation pipe. Oh, *no* . . . I closed my eyes. I would need to tell the farmer. I hadn't even started working in the area, and already I might have made an enemy.

I drove to the closest house and parked outside a six-foot fence crowned by a coil of barbed wire. The gate lay open, the heavy chain unlocked. Two steps into the property, I froze.

A Rottweiler stood in my path. His lips flickered over heavy, yellow teeth. I stepped back. His growl rumbled a notch louder. Drool dangled from his chops. *No sudden movements, no reaching out and especially don't move towards the house. Never show a dog your fear.* But it was too late.

'Hello,' I called. 'Hello?

I heard footsteps crunch behind me. I did not dare turn around.

The footsteps came closer

'Samson!'

The Rottweiler's growl grew louder.

'Samson!'

The dog sunk to the ground and licked its paws like a puppy. I eyed it suspiciously and slowly turned around. A stocky man with a rifle slung over his shoulder stood behind me. He lifted the rifle off his shoulder. '*Wat wil jy hê?*' – What do you want?

I explained who I was and about the damage to the pipe.

His brown eyes did not stray from my face. After a long silence he nodded.

'I will refund you,' I offered lamely.

'Which field?' he asked.

I explained again. The farmer spat on the ground. The dog sat up and growled.

'Samson!' The dog lay down. 'That's not my field. That's Freddie's, the next farm. Head along that track through the bush, past my kaffirs. Freddie's place is deep in the bush, you won't see it from the track.'

He snorted a laugh. 'Those kaffirs think they have democracy, that they have freedom. Well, they work for me. If they want freedom, they can go and work for Nelson Mandela.'

Behind him the front door creaked open and a face and part of a skirt appeared. A girl or a young woman, I could not say for sure. Her skirt was torn. Following my glance, the farmer turned around and swore at her. She ducked behind the door, but a few seconds later, when his back was turned, her eyes reappeared.

The farmer swung his rifle back over his shoulder, 'Next time, geologist, don't walk through my gates. My dog could've killed you.'

I edged back out of the gates to my bakkie. I drove along the instructed track past a row of decomposing farmworkers' houses. Without doors or windows they resembled scorched faces, the eyes put out, the mouths screaming. A woman leant over a fire, stirring a pot, with a baby strapped to her back. Young children stopped playing to watch me drive past. I gave a sad wave. One child lifted a hand in surprise, and the woman stopped stirring to inspect me. I was not to stop, she did not want trouble. Her eyes said it all.

The bush grew denser, the trees thornier. A mangy horse crossed the track in front of me, its skin shivering and rippling under the constant irritation of flies. At the end of the track an old tractor, rusted and without wheels, lay outside a derelict house. The smell of diesel was overwhelming.

A man's face appeared at the tractor window, round and suntanned. His hair and beard were wild, tangled. He squinted at me, raising a hand above bushy eyebrows. A second face appeared, smaller, pinker. The door of the tractor shell opened and a stranger climbed out and walked over to me. He was barefoot and wore a shirt with missing buttons. His shorts had a broken zip, and a string of leather replaced a belt. Most surprisingly, a small baboon rode on his shoulders, clinging nervously to his ears. I stood waiting beside my bakkie for him.

'Freddie?'

He gave a nod. His eyes were devoid of expression; they appeared to be focusing separately, one trained on me and one circling the bush behind me. He scratched a callused foot on the back of the other leg and pulled the baboon down from his neck. He cradled it in his arm. An arm, I noticed, which was short and underdeveloped. The hand was small, like a child's, and two of the fingers were missing. It clutched the baboon's fur.

'Freddie Tontelbos. This is my farm Doringhoek. This is Niki, she's my baby.'

I launched into an explanation about the water pipe. Freddie's eyes wandered around my face.

When I had finished, he picked his teeth with his good hand. 'That pipe is old and the maize is rotten. Too much rain. The pipe was broken anyway.' His eyes shifted into focus for a second, 'I'll bring tea. Wait in the lapa.'

I stood inside the lapa looking up at the mangy thatch and the skeleton of wooden cross-beams. Freddie appeared with two mugs, which he placed on a broken braai grid with a packet of sugar. Then he removed Niki from his neck and sat in one of the broken garden chairs, inviting me to do the same. He stroked Niki's stomach and the small baboon closed her eyes with contentment.

'She seems so tame,'

'She has her own bed, own bottle. Her own blanket.' Much like Freddie's gaze, his words sunk and dipped, drifting around each other as if attempting to sort themselves into order, into sense.

'Where did you find her?'

'I shot the mother.'

The tea soured in my mouth.

'I shot her. *Kolskoot*. Bullseye. A troop of baboons came onto my farm, so I took out my gun and I tried to shoot them. But they ran away too quickly. Last came a mother with a small baby. She was slow. I shot her as she tried to climb through a fence. *Kolskoot*. I took the baby from her. It was hanging onto the mother's dead body. Niki is my baby now.'

'Baboons are protected animals. It's illegal to shoot them or keep them as pets.'

Freddie was not affected by my indignant tone. 'This is my second baboon, I got my first the same way too. She grew too big, so I let her go back to her *klomp* in the hills. They say that once a baboon has been with people, the troop won't take it back. But it's not true. When I released her in the hills, they waited for her. Took her back, no problem.'

'I should go,' I placed the mug back on the braai-grid. 'You're sure I can't refund you for the pipe?'

'You with that mining company, MinSearch? The one with Riaan Groenewald?' Freddie asked.

'Yes, I, er . . . work for Riaan.'

'I know him. We were in the Border War together.'

'The Namibia-Angola border?' I remained seated.

Freddie nodded. 'I was at the base camp when they brought him in. His patrol had been attacked by the Angolan troops. They shot his friend right through the brain – ' With two fingers, Freddie aimed a gun at his own head, '*Pow*. Riaan went a bit crazy in the head after that. They sent him back home, said he was a danger to the rest of us. But then, we were all a bit crazy out there. Then, ten years ago, they wanted us to shoot the kaffirs. Now since democracy this year, they want us to live with them. Wait in the bank queue with them.'

Thunder rumbled through the dense bush, the promise of after-noon rain.

I tried to catch Freddie's eye, but his focus was as unsettled as mist. I stood up. I was feeling unsettled too.

'Thank you for the tea.'

Ignoring my departure, Freddie rocked Niki, humming a couple of notes. Just as I opened my bakkie door, he muttered, 'He was crazy, crazy in the head.'

Our second Month End came to a close late in the afternoon. Chief asked us to stay and sleep in the spare caravans, rather than drive back at night. We could braai and have a few beers, he announced with satisfaction. Those that lived in Naboomspruit, close to the Spioenkop, namely he and Riaan, could go home afterwards.

JJ turned the boerewors over on the grill.

Riaan stood next to him. 'It's a fucking mine JJ, a fucking mine. And you are going to find it for us.' He wrapped his arm around JJ. '*You* are going to find us the mine.'

Beside them, Morné stood watching the flames. He popped his gum, took a sip of beer and rested the can on the top of his paunch.

Terence sat to one side, leaning against the lapa wall. Chief had strolled over to him and was discussing recent cricket results. I saw Terence say something that made Chief laugh.

Riaan snapped a glance at Chief, the jealousy naked on his face. 'It's a fucking mine, JJ,' he said, raising his voice.

I sat close to the fire, stroking Bongi's long ears while he stared, transfixed by the sausages. Each time JJ turned the grid over, his snout lifted and sank. Riaan grabbed JJ's shoulder and shook it again, laugh-ing. He had a high-pitched laugh, a weird sort of barking. A hyena laugh.

I stood up; I wanted to sort out my work for the following day. In that way, we could leave as early as possible the next morning. Bongi glanced back and forth between me and the sausages, and finally selecting me, charged ahead along the narrow concrete path. Distracted by the rich bush scent, he snorted off the path and disappeared. I strained my eyes to see the dim lights of the prefabricated offices ahead of me. The sound of crickets was deafening. I heard something slither in the long grass beside me and flinched. The entire area seemed alive with snakes; I saw and heard them daily in my project area.

A rough hand grabbed my arm.

'I'll see you in my office. Now.' Riaan.

I swallowed. What?

Riaan stood behind his desk, his hands resting flat on its surface. Surrounding him, his office was filled with memorabilia – defining who he was in his own eyes. Those eyes that were now fixed on me. A photograph of soldiers hung near the door: the South African Defence Force; the Parachute Battalion. Riaan stood in the centre of the group, his arms crossed, his eyes hidden by sunglasses. Other photographs: Riaan skydiving, his face distorted by the rush of falling air. Riaan white-water rafting. Riaan abseiling. Behind him hung his lieutenant stripes, framed. A small South African flag sat on the corner of his desk. The old flag: orange, white and blue. Above his crammed bookshelves, dominating the wall, hung his degree: *Masters in Exploration Geology,* awarded to *Riaan Jacobus Groenewald.* Black volcanic rocks were displayed in a cabinet, labelled *Bushveld Igneous Complex, N. Transvaal.*

'Fuck you,' Riaan said softly. He slammed his desk and shouted. 'Fuck you!' He straightened up, stepped out from behind his desk and walked over to me. He stopped an inch from me, and peered into my face. 'Fuck you,' he repeated, his tone sarcastic, almost conversational.

I glanced at the rock specimens. What could I use to defend myself? The rain started to drum against the prefabricated office roof. Riaan cocked his head, his eyes still hooked into mine.

'Did I not tell you to check *everything* with me. Did I not?'

We stared at each other. I was slipping into his eyes and drifting between the dark matter of his soul.

'The pipe? You don't offer compensation to a fucking idiot like Freddie Tontelbos. Chief told me you asked him. And you don't call Chief, you call me.' Riaan spun around to the door. 'Fuck off.'

Morné stood at the open door. He took a sip of his beer, grinning. A spectator to a blood sport. With two long strides, Riaan bounded over and slammed the door shut. 'That fucking moron. Halfwit.'

I looked at the shut door, then at Riaan, then back at the door. Riaan stepped back elaborately, allowing me to pass. I moved towards the door, my mind screaming at me not to turn my back. I took slow, deliberate steps to the door and opened it. Morné stood in the rain. The beer can he was holding shook as he laughed. I walked past him and hurried back along the path towards the fire.

Terence was scanning the dark. I saw his eyes relax as I stepped into the radius of the fire. What? I could read his face.

I jabbed the side of my head and mouthed, *he's mad*.

Terence gave a cautious nod, his eyes flicked behind me.

'Hey, Tiger, where you been?' Chief shouted at Riaan. He handed him a beer. 'Boy, you're a real spitfire today. Come on, relax, have fun.'

Riaan smiled, exposing sharp white teeth. He raised his can: 'To finding the fucking mine. To finding the big fucking one.'

The drink flowed; the bar in the lapa was well stocked. The group around Chief grew tight, the laughter louder. Riaan's hyena bark became shrill and crazy, bloodthirsty.

Chief started to sing: '*Oh show me the way to the next whiskey bar, oh don't ask why, no don't ask why, for if I don't find the next whiskey bar . . .*' His voice was surprisingly good. He threw himself into an Irish jig.

'Fucking *Engelsman*,' laughed Riaan.

'Bloody Dutchman, listening to your sakkie music. Dancing like windmills.'

Chief pumped Riaan's right arm stiffly, the two men jolted around the fire in a macabre dance. For a moment it looked as if they were wrestling, and then the dance continued. Bongi gave a low growl. I gave him the last of my hot dog to keep him quiet. Terence slipped his hand under his collar.

Riaan suddenly ripped himself out of the dance and looked at his watch, 'Fuck. It's late. Time to go, Chief. Back to the wives.' He dug in his pocket and delivered a roll of peppermints. He popped a handful into his mouth and crunched. Chief laughed at him.

'It's not funny, Chief, she'll fucking kill me if she knows I've been drinking.'

Chief and Riaan walked clutching each other. '*Oh if I don't find the next little girl, oh don't ask why, oh don't ask why . . .* ' Chief's voice grew softer in the night.

That night the rain continued. It hammered a steady rhythm on our makeshift caravan. *Rat-a-tat, rat-a-tat.* When I slept, I dreamt I was floating down a river. The rain was warm on my face. I floated easily on my back while the current spun me around and around.

Terence shook me. 'You awake?' he whispered.

'Mmm, am now. What time is it?'

'Five. I can't sleep, let's head back now and we can be back at Marble Hall before sunrise.'

As we drove, the rain washed down in sheets against the faulty windscreen wipers. *Flak flak.* Seconds in time were frozen by the brilliant flashes of lightning. Terence drove while Bongi slept with his head on my lap. *Flak flak.* As morning came, the sky softened to a dull grey. It continued to rain. Our tyres washed through pools of water.

'I'm sorry.'

'For what?' asked Terence

'That I was the reason you gave up your job in Lutzville. To work with . . . these people.'

Terence put his hand on my knee, 'It's not your fault.'

'Oh yes it is.'

'No, it's not. I wanted to take this job, I wanted the experience in platinum exploration.' Terence sighed. 'We've only been here five weeks. It's all new. It will get better.'

As we neared the Marble Hall campsite, the traffic became busier. Cars were parked along the side of the road. Flashing lights, cars, caravans and a small crowd stood in the rain near the Moses River bridge.

We recognised Ben's red cap from a distance and parked beside him. He was fighting to secure a plastic sheet over the back of one of the Toyota bakkies. Beneath the plastic I could see the office chairs, boxes. Ben turned around when he saw us, wiping the rain from his face.

'The river . . .' he began. We followed his glance to the campsite below. It was covered with muddy brown water, at least a foot high. All the caravans had been towed out and lined the road. All but three; the centre one was ours.

'I got back too late,' said Ben. 'It was too wet for me to tow the caravan out. The bakkie was getting stuck in the mud. I had to hurry, I took the things from the office, the papers and the furniture. And I took some things from your caravan, your books, your music system and some clothes. Whatever I could find.'

'My CDs?' asked Terence.

Ben shook his head.

A figure pushed his way through the growing crowd towards us. Freddie. He was grasping a wet Niki around his waist. 'Your caravan?'

I nodded, speechless.

'*Die dam het gebreek*. The dam broke,' he shifted Niki to the other arm so he could point with his good one, 'about twenty kilometres upstream. It washed away everything, cattle, homes. The water is still getting here. It will get here soon.'

Flashing lights arrived with the traffic cops. They blocked off the bridge: no more vehicles were to pass. Having parked safely up the hill, with Bongi closed in the car, we waited on the bridge. Ben, Terence and I stood watching our caravan. Freddie found us once again. A visible current was forming in the water.

'It's rising,' said Ben.

We nodded. It was flowing faster and faster. Suddenly the walls of the office hut crumbled and the roof washed away. It wrapped around the tree trunk and was caught. The last of the hut sunk beneath the water.

Freddie let out a whoop and jigged Niki up and down.

Waves rippled on the water surface. The campsite was now a broad river. Our caravan began to rock and then sway. Suddenly it pirouetted in its new-found freedom and began to bob down the river, dragging its faded red and white tent behind it. Twisting, dancing, it floated in circles. Curling, twirling, as light as a dancer. Graceful.

'Woo-hoo,' shouted Freddie, '*daar gaan hy!*' He pushed Niki up onto his shoulders, braced his feet apart and, in the driving rain, began to madly rotate his arms. '*Roei, Robyn, roei!*' Row, Robyn, row.

One by one, the two remaining caravans lifted up on their toes and, like bridesmaids, followed behind the red-and-white veil.

Terence began to laugh.

CHAPTER SEVEN

Fermented Oranges

Three months after moving to Marble Hall, Terence and I walked into the town's local bar. The only other two inhabitants of the bar sat at the counter, their backs to us. They looked identical, except one was much smaller than the other. From the front, they had the same flat heads and small pink ears, their hair resembling the worn bristles on a scrubbing brush. Their snub noses, loose jowls and protruding lower lips were also similar, I noted with satisfaction as they turned around to look at us. The bulldog and his master returned to their game of checkers.

'Want to play a game of pool?' asked Terence.

I shook my head, 'I'm not much good.'

'I thought you were the original barfly,' teased Terence. 'You should play better pool.'

'Not anymore.' I sat down beside the bulldog.

The dog's eyes rose and fell with the checkers. His master scratched his backside; his shorts had slipped down sufficiently to expose the cleavage of his buttocks.

'Help yourself.'

'Excuse me?' I asked.

'Help yourself. Bartender's not here. Cold beers behind the counter, leave your money at the till. Three rand a beer.'

Terence found two beers, left the money at the till and sat down beside me.

'I think we'll call this the Bulldog Bar,' I whispered to him.

Click, click click, the man continued his game. A long string of spit attached the dog to the board.

'You're looking for minerals.' A statement.

'Yes,' Terence replied.

'You're with that mining company, MinSearch. What you looking for?'

'Platinum, or any other precious metal we can find,' said Terence.

'Nothing here. They've all been here, mining companies, geologists, the lot. Haven't found a damn thing. Not a damn thing.'

'Perhaps,' Terence agreed. 'The results haven't looked that promising so far.'

'Where you staying?' *Click, click, click.*

'On a farm, ten kilometres out of town,' I replied.

'You'd better be careful.'

'It's close to town.'

The bulldog beside me shifted its stiff legs, impatient for the game to continue. I patted its flat head. It snorted and gazed at me with watering eyes.

His master looked up. 'A farm's a farm. No farm's safe around here. Farm killings. You'll be attacked. You better have good security.'

The person most surprised by the flood had been Riaan. The flood got to us before he could, but he was quick to follow. MinSearch, he assured us, would not compensate employees for private possessions. Not our clothes, nor Terence's music collection. They were not insured for that.

Chief had smiled and shrugged, 'Riaan would know.'

'We have our own insurance,' Terence had informed them with a cold stare.

'Well, that's all right then,' laughed Chief. 'Then you just need to find another place to stay.'

We found accommodation in an old farmhouse, not far from the old caravan park. From a distance the house looked grand: an ornate balcony surveyed a sweeping green lawn. Oak, lemon and apricot trees clustered in conversational groups on the grass, while birds, lizards and monitors gathered around the fish pond to drink. Orange trees and cotton fields surrounded the property. White cotton burst from the pods, and the scent of oranges permeated the air.

Inside, the farmhouse had fallen into decay. Only a few of the rooms were habitable, while the rest lay unused. The carpets had begun to rot and the plaster was crumbling. The most pleasant room was long and narrow and ran the length of the sunny side of the house. This was the new office. Ben slept in the cottage behind the house; he said it was much better than his room at the campground.

We now lived on a farm; we could be farmers.

Chief waved away our concern. 'You'll be safe. The farm killings, they're only after guns and money. You have neither.'

'Who are *they*?' I asked.

He shrugged, 'No one knows. Immigrants, farmworkers, trouble-makers from out of town. No one knows. But you'll be fine. Don't worry.'

But the newspaper headlines continued. Farm killings: not daily events, but at least weekly. All the farmhouses in the area were barricaded with humming six-foot fences, and dogs gnashed their teeth at padlocked gates. Houses with guns and money. In contrast, the derelict shelters of their farmworkers lay wounded and open, doors and windows missing. Desperately poor. When I took food to the farmworkers living closest to us, they accepted it with surprise and suspicion, their eyes distrustful. I did not know what to think. These suffering people were not guilty of the farm killings, but who was? And were we safe? Was I merely building on the fear of the farmers, already so solid in its foundations? Was I adding to the six-foot fences, adding to the gun collections, adding to the brutal dogs? Not a farm in our area lived without fear. Not a farm lay unprotected. Except ours. We had no fence, no barbed wire and no gun.

Were we safe?

Farm killings, the headlines and hatred washed into a river of fear, overflowing. Until the river flooded, flooded me, flooded the whole area. I drifted on it.

My geological map had progressed after three months. Outcrop remained difficult to find. The best places to see outcrop were along the riverbanks, now that the water level had subsided. The network of canals that fed off this river also proved to be useful, as the canals cut through the thick soils to the bedrock.

The rock exposed by the canal and river, however, was so altered and rotten it was barely recognisable. The platinum-bearing rocks of the Bushveld Complex resembled the surrounding hills of granophyre: orange, soft and crumbling. How was I to tell them apart? With time I was to discover the answers to my map lay elsewhere. In the centre of the fields, hidden by tall crops, were tiny islands of rock, little bigger than anthills. These hills were home to the indigenous plants, and here the rock was not weathered. With each new discovery, I found a missing piece to my puzzle.

A few weeks later, on a warm wintry morning, I drove through the maize plantations into an unexpected burst of colour. Fields of yellow optimism surrounded me, the faces of the sunflowers rising slowly with the morning sun. A rocky koppie rose from the centre of the sunflowers. I looked at my map. Lovedale Farm. Ahead of me the track led to a clump of large trees and the farmhouse. I would be able get permission to visit the field there.

I parked in the shade of the pine trees. A muffled, lazy bark greeted me: *raowff raowff*. An old black dog shuffled over. His muzzle and the circles of fur around his eyes had turned grey, so he gave the appearance of an aged ghost. *Raowff raowff*.

'That the best you can do, Spook, old boy?'

He wagged his tail.

'Timmy, Timmy! Stop that. Don't be rude,' a woman bustled out from around the side of the house. She stopped when she saw me. Large red gardening gloves hung from her hands. She wore a man's blue shirt, covered in soil, over a denim skirt and a white blouse.

'Oh my goodness, Timmy!'

Timmy looked up at his mistress, wagged his tail again, and then shuffled to the back door and collapsed on the lowest step.

'Robyn Hartley,' I held out my hand as I walked to her.

'Yes, yes, the geologist. Freddie Tontelbos told me about you. You know, the crazy one with the baboon.' She wrestled her gardening gloves off and shook my hand. Hers was small and soft.

'That Freddie has lived here, well, forever. We've just learnt to live with him – the way he drives up and down the roads. Sometimes drives into one of the fields and sits there for the whole morning. We've just accepted him, we had to.' She gave me a bright smile. 'We, it was then. Now, just me.'

She took off the shirt; beneath, her blouse was crisp and white, the collar fringed with white lace.

'Come inside, come inside,' she ushered me towards the kitchen door. 'Move, Timmy. Move!'

Timmy had fallen asleep; his snores rose loudly and gently.

'Aai *liewe hemel*, it was always Hennie's dog.'

I stamped the mud off my boots and stepped over the dog.

In the kitchen I collided with her soft bosom. She had turned around.

'I'm sorry. I forgot to introduce myself. Lizzie. Lizzie Pienaar. Are you going to have coffee or tea?'

I stepped back to focus.

'Coffee, thank you.'

I looked around as Lizzie filled the kettle. The kitchen was spotless; the stainless-steel sink shone her reflection. A pot simmered on the stove. My stomach gave a quiet growl: it smelt delicious. A stack of small Tupperware containers rose in a tower beside the stove.

'Much easier than cooking every night. One pot of stew and it lasts the whole week. I just pack them in the freezer. I have such a big freezer.'

Perhaps concerned I may doubt her, Lizzie opened the freezer door and I peered in dutifully. It was empty other than a row of single-portion, frosted Tupperware containers.

'I don't like to make a fuss cooking. When I have guests, yes. I love to cook. Roasts and puddings. And I bake. Cakes, *beskuit* and biscuits. But now, for who?'

I cleared my throat. 'I just dropped in to ask permission to walk on your farm. There's a koppie . . .'

But Lizzie was crouched down on the floor and clanging her way through her metal tray filing system. She pulled out one she liked: stainless-steel with elaborate brass handles. She placed it beside the kettle. Rustled in a drawer and rolled out a white linen cloth embroidered with roses. Her hands slowed down as she straightened the cloth. Her fingers trailed over the roses.

'I have come to ask permission ,' I began again.

She held up a hand to silence me. 'Of course. Let us not waste time speaking about things like that. Biscuits or *beskuit*?'

'Ah . . .'

She pulled the lid off a large biscuit tin and placed a few biscuits on a plate. Beside them she arranged a couple of rusks.

'Both, just in case,' she dusted her hands on the broad backside of her denim skirt. Soft brown curls with grey roots rested on her collar. Narrow, girlish wrists tapered from plump arms.

Lizzie suddenly looked up at me, aghast. 'What am I thinking? A guest and you are standing in my kitchen! Go and sit down in the lounge. Go, go.'

She ushered me through the kitchen doorway. Timmy shuffled up the stairs and followed me into the living room.

The carpet in the lounge resembled the fur of a neglected Maltese poodle. The light, which filtered through frilly net curtains, was respectfully subdued. Plump, green velvet sofas surrounded a wooden coffee table. Photographs lined the mantle of an unused fireplace. I sat down tentatively on the edge of a sofa. A room reserved for guests.

'Timmy, move. Shoo.'

Timmy remained in the doorway. He moved his grey rings of focus from me to Lizzie and thumped his tail. Lizzie edged around him, carrying the tray.

'Good farm coffee, the way we Afrikaners make it best.' She poured thick, dark liquid into a fragile teacup and handed it to me. Only after I had taken my first sip did she sit down opposite me and pour herself a cup.

'Are these sunflower fields yours?'

'No, not any more. They were Hennie's. He farmed them for twenty-six years. He was the only one in this valley who could grow sunflowers successfully. Others tried. Then he taught them, you know. *All* about sunflowers. Now we have beautiful sunflowers on many of the farms. I rent our land to a neighbour now, and he farms the sunflowers. Hennie knew this neighbour. Freddie Tontelbos wanted the land for his *skraal* cattle. But I said, not over my dead body. Or Hennie's,' she added softly. 'I said to myself, Lizzie, you only give that land to someone who can keep the sunflowers growing.'

I inadvertently glanced up at the pictures above the fireplace.

'My children and grandchildren. I have two sons. They both live in the city now. One is an accountant and the other draws pictures of bridges, what do you call that?'

'A civil engineer?' I offered.

'Something like that. Anyway. Neither of them wanted the farm after Hennie . . . was gone. So what could I do? I had to rent out the land.'

Lizzie looked out the window and struggled out of her seat, *'Liewe hemel,* look what time it is. It's Samuel.'

I stood up to leave.

'No, no, don't leave. We have not had time to talk. Stay. Stay, I won't be one, small minute.'

Lizzie hurried into the kitchen. From my seat I could see an elderly man climb the stairs to the back door. He removed his hat and walked into the sitting room. His clean shirt was frayed at the collar.

'Samuel *maar jy's vroeg.* You're early,' Lizzie complained.

'Missus Lizzie.' A deep voice.

Apparently delighted Samuel had arrived, Timmy got up and did a little shuffle around him, a stiff-legged sort of dance. Samuel bent down slowly and patted him. Timmy collapsed onto his feet and fell asleep. Snores rose almost immediately.

'I have a guest, Samuel. A guest. I won't be long. I have made coffee, I'll give you some coffee and you can start by pruning the roses. The yellow ones first. And then, after my guest leaves, you can take me into town.'

Lizzie hurried back into the lounge with a mug, filled it from the coffee pot, selected two rusks and two biscuits and placed them on a saucer. Samuel took the mug and saucer from her. He steadied the saucer with both hands.

'Wait, I'll be with you now-now,' she told me.

'Missus Lizzie, *die skêr?'*

'Oh, on the counter, Samuel. What am I thinking? The pruning shears are on the counter.'

Samuel pushed the dog with his foot. Timmy looked up, his grey circles blinked at us. *What, what, me asleep? Never.* He rose stiffly and ambled after Samuel into the garden. Through the net curtain, we saw them walk across the lawn.

'*Ou* Samuel,' Lizzie sat down, 'he used to work as a driver for Hennie. He worked for us right from the start. But now he just helps out in the garden and drives me into town twice a week. I never learnt how to drive, Hennie always drove. But now Samuel does. Have some more coffee.'

'No thanks, really,' I replied as she refilled my cup.

'Now where were we? So many distractions.'

'You were telling me about Samuel.'

'Aaai Samuel. He is so good with the roses. When *he* prunes the bushes I get so many roses. The rose bushes seem to like him. All the colours, pink, red, that sunset orange and my favourite yellow. They are beaut-*ti*-ful.'

I glanced discreetly at my watch, 'I think I should be getting back to work now. Thanks for the coffee.'

The smile melted off Lizzie's face. I remained seated. Lizzie bent her head and slipped her fingers together on her lap.

'He's dead,' she said eventually. 'I was there when Hennie died. I was there.' Lizzie looked up at me. Tears had pooled in the corners of her eyes. They slid down her cheeks. I stood up and walked over to her.

'You okay?' My hand looked dirty and brown on her crisp white blouse.

Lizzie's shoulder began to shake and a large tear dropped onto her hands and ran down her knuckles, one by one. I crouched down and put an arm around her shoulders.

'We were driving into town. We were taking the sunflower seeds to the depot. Hennie was driving the truck and Samuel followed behind us in the bakkie. An oncoming minibus taxi overtook on a solid white line. It came from nowhere. Hennie did not see it, he swerved and the truck rolled. We landed in a ditch. Hennie just lay over the steering wheel. They told me his neck was broken immediately. Aaai Hennie,' she pulled the cloth off the tray and dabbed her wet cheeks. 'It was Samuel who helped me out of the truck. It was Samuel who came with me in the ambulance. They tell me this, but I don't remember any of it. It was Samuel.'

'You are going to be okay.'

Lizzie nodded slowly. 'Two years last month, on the fourteenth. You *must* see the garden,' she snapped a wet hand around my wrist, 'I have not shown you my garden. Just give me one, small minute. I need to wash my face.'

I studied the photographs above the mantelpiece while I waited for Lizzie. The smiling grandchildren. The posed family portrait. At the edge of the row was an old black-and-white portrait of a young man. Handsome, other than his ears which protruded slightly. The glint in his grey eyes and indented dimple betrayed a good humour. Ink trailed in a confident scribble across the bottom right hand corner.

Lizzie. Lizbeth. My dear Beth. Love Hennie.

I placed the photograph back on the mantelpiece as Lizzie walked back into the room. I followed her out into the garden, and we strolled across the thick, even lawn to Samuel. He knelt in front of a bed of roses. His leathery hands, black as coal on the outside and pale as peaches on the inside, clipped a yellow rose and placed it on a damp newspaper. Timmy lay beside him; he inched forward to sniff the rose, and fell asleep with his head on the newspaper.

Lizzie inspected a new bud. 'They are beaut-*ti*-ful Samuel.'

'Good at this time of the year, Missus Lizzie. Especially the yellow ones. *Die geel ene.*'

Lizzie picked up the yellow rose from the newspaper, and sang in a soft, high voice, '*I just received sweetheart your yellow roses. They tell me that we're all through. I'll place them near your photograph and as the petals fall, they'll hide from you my lonely tears that should not fall at all* . . . Do you know that song?'

I shook my head.

'Hennie used to always sing that song to me. I love yellow roses. This bush has been giving us yellow roses, well, ever since I can remember. *Hulle is mooi,* Samuel. They're lovely.'

Lizzie walked me back to my bakkie, carrying the yellow rose.

She took a deep breath, 'I love the sunflowers at this time of year. I never want to leave. This is my house, my farm.'

'Do you not worry about the safety? About the attacks?'

'Aaai Robyn. The farm killings. But I cannot live in fear; besides, Samuel is here to protect me. And Timmy. Samuel lives very close to the house. And this land is his too, he worked it beside Hennie. They built this farm together. If I leave, where will Samuel go?' Lizzie smelt the rose. 'My sons want me to move to Pretoria. What must I do there? People say the farm killings are the workers. That I don't believe. They say it could be illegal immigrants or just *skelms* from out of town. I don't know, Robyn, none of us do.'

I climbed into the bakkie and started the engine. The sunflower faces had risen with the afternoon sun.

Lizzie handed me the rose through the window. 'Put it in cold water. It will last longer.'

I touched her hand as I took the rose. Timmy had awoken and stood on swaying legs beside Samuel. *Raaowf raaowf.*

Terence, Chief and Riaan already sat around the table in the lapa at Spioenkop. Our fourth Month End was about to begin. Terence looked grim.

'Terence, don't worry. You guys are as safe as, well, houses,' Chief laughed at his own joke and slurped his coffee. 'You've got nothing anyone would want in that house. No guns and no money. You don't have to worry. You don't have a gun, do you?'

'No, we don't have a gun,' said Terence.

'Good,' Chief dipped his fingers into his coffee and wet down the wayward pieces of his beard, 'Right, let's get on with the Month End . . .'

'There are farm killings in the Marble Hall area every week, *more* often than every week,' I protested.

'Robyn, you're safe. Right, now that we are all here, let's start. JJ, why don't you begin?'

JJ had begun nodding before Chief had finished his sentence. He rolled out his map and began to mumble in an even tone, his pale face expressionless.

'It's a fucking mine, Chief,' Riaan interrupted him.

'Hold off, Tiger, let him finish.'

JJ continued, falling silent whenever Riaan slammed the desk, grabbed his shoulder and shook him, slapped him on the back. Eventually JJ produced a couple of rock samples, which Riaan grabbed, marching out in the daylight to inspect them under a hand lens.

'There're fucking sulphides in this, Chief. I *told* you it's a fucking mine.'

'Hold your horses, Tiger. Let's see if those sulphides contain any precious metal.'

JJ bobbed his head, glancing at Chief and Riaan.

'Just wait and see. I told you JJ will find us the mine.'

'Sit, sit. Okay Morné, go ahead.'

Morné hoisted up his tight shorts, popped his gum and explained that he did not have anything to show that month, leaving Terence and I to unroll our maps and deliver our results. We presented our monthly work without too much comment, other than Riaan thumping JJ intermittently on the shoulder. Finally we all stood up to leave.

Riaan leant forward as I walked past. 'I told the Chief that farmhouse is safe. And if I say it's safe, it's fucking safe,' he said in a low voice, within JJ's hearing but not Chief's. 'Don't go doing anything behind my back.'

Terence prodded my arm, signalling me to keep moving. He did not look at Riaan.

In the next couple of weeks, Terence and I increased our efforts to get a transfer. No, the MinSearch Human Resource Officer informed us, they only transfer staff after they have completed an initial twelve-month orientation in one fixed area. The official transfer form (a K23) needs to be signed by the geologist's senior and then approved a further two levels up. Only then would he consider a transfer. His aim is to streamline the process of staff transfers. Focus the human resources.

We cannot get that paperwork signed, we cannot remain here until the end of the year, I insisted. There was a hesitation. The gold mines always need geologists, the young man informed me, two kilometres under. No, I replied emphatically, we wanted to stay in exploration. By the way, he said, just before I hung up, where is Spioenkop?

Meanwhile, around us, the newspaper headlines continued. Farm killings. The fear, the barbed wire, knives and guns, rape and murder. We had to leave.

At night the sound of silence became more one of listening, and the scent of oranges became the smell of fear. In the dark the shadows in the orange grove grew arms, shifting back branches to watch us, watch our silhouettes through the thin curtains. We locked the security gates we had installed onto the doors and bolted the windows. And listened to the shadows as they creaked and moved, as they loaded their guns and sharpened their knives. As they departed with the first sign of light, the first chirps from the birds.

The sun brought the hoopoes, who marched stiffly across our lawn, sinking their beaks into the rich soil. Bongi chased the lizards up the trees, and having lost them, lay in a branch surveying all the creatures below. Every morning Terence and I pulled on our boots, usually still damp from the previous afternoon's rains, climbed into our respective 4x4s and went to work.

Terence and Ben were working hard. The two of them got along well; there was a comfortable silence between them, a trust. Ben took to smiling more and telling more of his elaborate jokes. He usually forgot the punch line and began laughing before the joke was completed, which somehow was always more funny than the joke itself. Ben especially liked Bongi. A dog that could climb trees, in his opinion, was a very clever dog, and he made us promise that should Bongi have any puppies, he would get one.

Although numerous samples had been collected and tested on Terence's project, there was little evidence that the platinum-bearing rocks were present. Terence brought in an entire team to dig trenches to take samples closer to the bedrock. There were still no encouraging signs. The project looked like it would be brought to an end soon.

On my own project, I had discovered that Lizzie's fields hid many tiny knolls of unweathered outcrop – every new track I took led to another outcrop. Perhaps the sunflowers took a delight in keeping them hidden from the human eye. My map would be completed shortly. In this area, the Bushveld Complex was indeed present. Whether there was platinum within these rocks still had to be determined, but there seemed to be sufficient evidence that the project should be taken further. Riaan was delighted. His initial excitement over JJ's project had subsided. JJ's rock samples had been sent for analysis and the results had proved that they had no platinum content; the sulphide seen was merely pyrite. I was the new flavour of the month.

In one phone call, Riaan's hostility switched to camaraderie. I was now on his team, within his army. His favourite geologist, he joked. The closer he edged, the more wary I felt. As he had suggested, I was watching my back.

⌐

I drove slowly along the canal on the outskirts of Lizzie's farm. The first signs of spring added a gentle buzz to the air: birdcalls, a distant tractor. The morning sun felt pleasant on my arm and cheek. I had been mapping the area for just over four months, and the map was almost complete. The Bushveld Complex rocks appeared to sweep through the valley in an S-shape.

I had seen Lizzie a few times over the last month; she had waved to me from her garden. I had been meaning to stop and visit again, I would soon, but I was also anxious to complete my map. Finish it and leave Marble Hall.

A monitor lizard slipped off the canal wall and landed with a *plop* in the water. He swam down the canal using his thick tail as a rudder. I smiled, eased the 4x4 back into gear and continued along the track. A few metres ahead of me, a black water pipe lay across the track. Plastic, I noted; I could drive over this one.

My chest jammed into my throat as my foot slammed on the brake. I kept very still. Not even moving my eyes. Especially not that – don't give it any movement to attack. Its neck flattened as it pulled its head back and opened its mouth. Black, black mamba. A metre of snake raised off the ground, two metres left coiled on the ground, its black eyes swaying level with mine. Ready to strike.

The mamba shot off the ground like an elastic band. I watched it spiral past me in slow motion, right over the bonnet and the windscreen. Plop. It landed in the canal. Its head raised high, it rippled along the black water out of sight.

Breathe, I told myself, *breathe*. I pulled my arm into the vehicle; it had gone cold. I flinched as a piece of grass caught in the door tickled my head. Get out of here, just get the hell out of here. I slammed the gear lever into reverse and backed wildly along the track. I almost collided with a small blue bakkie.

Freddie climbed out. He walked towards me, Niki riding on his shoulder. He stood at my window. I stared at him. He lifted a callused foot and extracted a long, white thorn without wincing.

'Hey, geologist,' his eyes drifted around me.

I emptied my lungs. *Black mamba!*

'Hey geologist. She's moving. Her van is there. Her *boy* was attacked.'

'Who? What are you talking about?' I slowly focused on Freddie.

'Lizzie Pienaar. She is moving to Pretoria. I've spoken to her, told her to stay. But she's going, the van is already at the farm.' Freddie cradled Niki, rocking her. His three-fingered hand looked like a chicken claw. 'She's been here forever, just like the sunflowers. I told her to stay.'

I left Freddie standing in the track and drove immediately to Lovedale. A removal van was parked beneath the pine trees. There was no sign of Timmy. I stood back as a couple of men carried a plump green sofa past me.

'Lizzie?' I knocked on the back door.

As there was no reply, I walked in. I found Lizzie in the sitting room, empty other than the mangy white carpet and a box she was packing.

'Aai, *liewe hemel*, Robyn.'

'You're moving. Can I help?'

She shook her head, 'It's almost all gone now. Everything's gone except for me. But then I'll be the last thing to go.'

She eased up onto her haunches and wiped the neat brown curls from her face. Her face contorted. '*Arme ou* Samuel.'

'What happened, Lizzie?' I sat down.

Lizzie wiped the dust from a photograph and placed it carefully in the box.

'Samuel was driving back from town, with my shopping. He was hijacked. They held a gun to his head and told him to get out. Two men climbed into the bakkie and drove it off and they made Samuel . . .' Lizzie's voice broke. 'They made Samuel climb into a kombi and they drove him to a koppie in the sunflower field. They blindfolded him and tied his hands and feet. They pushed him onto the ground and held the gun at his head. Then, I don't know . . . they heard someone or saw someone. And they ran away. One of the workers from the other farm found Samuel and brought him back here. They were going to kill him, Robyn. Kill him. He told me that he tasted the ground in his mouth and he felt the red ants bite his face. And he knew they were going to kill him.'

Lizzie stared into the box as she spoke. Her fingertips trailed its edges.

'Where is Samuel now?'

'Gone, Robyn, gone. He's too old for this. He has taken the bus up north to live with his daughter. He tells me it is far enough, where the red ants won't bite. Aaai Robyn,' she wiped a cheek, 'who will look after the roses now?'

'And Timmy?' I asked softly.

'He was an old dog, Robyn. An old dog. After Samuel left he would not get up, he just lay there. And then two days later, he went to sleep and never woke up. Timmy was always Hennie's dog, and I suppose then he was always Samuel's.'

Lizzie stood up as a removal man entered the room and took the box from her. She blew her nose and followed him out, anxiously reminding him to be careful. I slipped out of the back door and drove off. I don't think she noticed.

Feeling in no mood to map, I drove back to our farmhouse. Terence was already home. He walked outside to greet me. Bongi scuttled down a tree and attacked my boot. I picked him up and flung him over my shoulder, his wagging tail smacking my face. I put him down and leant against Terence. Home.

'Bad day?'

'Of sorts. One of the farmers on my project was attacked, well, one of her workers. She lives alone.'

We opted to sit on the farmhouse stoep, drinking beer and eating olives. The setting sun cast a soft glow over the ample lawn and surrounding orange groves. Birds chirped loudly, a chorus led by the loud *kweeh* of a lourie. A faint breeze rustled the apricot trees closest to us. It began to get darker. The first star appeared, and then the Milky Way lit up. The birds had long since quietened; only the crickets called. The breeze still rustled the trees in the garden, but the rustle seemed louder, more human. Twigs broke in the orange grove and made us think of the weight of a foot. Behind us the security gate lay open: an easy escape. Even if neither of us would say it.

'It's full moon,' I commented.

'No, not quite. There's a bit missing from the lower left-hand corner. Not quite full.'

Thin strands of cloud drifted over the moon. It grew darker. There was a noise in the garden. Bongi sunk onto all fours and leopard-crawled forward, growling.

'Get inside,' Terence grabbed Bongi's collar and pulled him after us. He bolted the gate, closed the door and locked it.

'Bongi could have heard a lizard,' I tried to reassure him, 'or Ben.'

Terence shook his head. 'No. Ben's at the old campground, visiting friends.'

We both stood very still, listening. Nothing.

Terence marched from empty room to empty room, switching the lights off and on. Finally he went to the office, dug through the selection of field equipment and selected a lethal panga.

'If you're worried, we should call the police.' I followed him into the bedroom.

'And tell them what?' He placed the panga beneath his side of the bed. He pulled off his boots, stripped to his shorts, and lay down. I lay down beside him. Bongi, now relaxed, slept curled at the bottom of the bed.

In the dark I could hear Terence shift uneasily, straining to identify any unfamiliar sounds.

'We have nothing here to take. No guns or money,' I told him. 'No guns or money,' I repeated to reassure myself. I closed my eyes, my attention drifted and I fell asleep.

I dreamt I was walking down the dirt track past the farmhouse.

It is late afternoon and I am alone. I wonder where Bongi is. The smell of oranges is strong. Horrible, as if they are fermenting. The trees are laden and the ground between the trees covered in rotten fruit. On the track ahead, I see three men walking towards me. I am afraid. There is no time to run away. There are three of them and only one of me. There is no sign of Terence, no sign of Ben. The three men part as I walk through them. They smell of smoke and sweat. I can hear they have stopped walking to watch me. My neck hairs pierce me.

Awake, I lay very still, my breathing rapid. From his even breathing I knew Terence was asleep. Footsteps – I could hear footsteps, slow and careful. Footsteps behind our bedroom wall, footsteps on the stoep. Quietly, I reached over and touched Terence's arm. He woke up immediately, rolled over and picked up his panga. The metal blade caught the dim moonlight. Heel toe, heel toe . . . the footsteps were coming closer. Louder. They were at the front door.

The door handle creaked. All the way down. Silence. I could feel his weight against the door, his breath against the wood. Slowly the handle creaked back up. Terence and I lay on our backs, quiet. Footsteps again. This time, less careful. This time, walking away. They faded; as incomprehensible as shadows evaporating. Terence continued to grip the wooden handle of the panga.

'Who *was* that?' I whispered.

'Someone. I'm calling the police,' Terence slipped out of bed.

We sat waiting for the police in the sparse lounge. Terence paced up and down. His figure must have been visible through the thin curtains. The police did not arrive until two hours later, at the first light of day, the first sounds of birds. One of them was drunk. They stumbled around the house, peering into dark corners with a flashlight. There was nothing to report. As they left, they sounded their siren and flashed their lights. Terence and I watched them leave from the stoep.

'God, I can't live like this anymore. Perhaps we *should* get a gun.'

'No. Live by fire, die by fire. Anyway, guns are what they are after.'

'Then we must leave. We can't carry on like this, Terence. The fear is driving me crazy.'

Later that morning I phoned the head office of MinSearch. '

'We are leaving,' I told the Human Resource Officer.

He hesitated, then told me, 'I'll call you back.'

The phone rang ten minutes later. 'MinSearch need two exploration geologists in Namaqualand. Based in the town of Springbok.'

'Your forms, all the levels of approval?' I asked.

'No, in extreme situations we can bypass them with the standard Q form.'

'Why did you not do that in the first place?'

'We'd run out of standard Q forms and needed copies.'

'Copies . . . right. Anyway, what the hell is a standard Q form?'

'Oh, they're mostly outdated. We seldom use them. We have replaced them with forms Q 1 through to 23, in order to streamline the process of managing our human resources.'

Over the next couple of weeks, I completed my map and wrote the accompanying report. I drove all the familiar routes again. I drove past the humming electric fences and sprinkled lawns of the farmers. I drove past the wounded shelters of the farmworkers. For five months I had been a solitary figure driving between the farmers' six-foot fences of fear and the farmworkers' broken walls of poverty. The farmers eyed me with distrust as I drove past. It had not taken them long to label me: *kafferboetie*, kaffir lover. The farmworkers did not want me to stop my bakkie either. I was to keep my white hands on the steering wheel of my white bakkie and drive past. They did not want trouble.

Riaan found out about the transfer within days. He called the farmhouse.

'Fuck you.'

'Riaan.'

'You've been speaking to head office, that HR prick. You and Terence have got a fucking transfer.'

'I understand so.'

Riaan's voice became less hostile, negotiating: 'It's safe there. I've told you, and Chief's told you, its safe.'

'We've actually heard someone trying to break in here.'

'Bullshit, they're only after guns and money,' I could almost hear Riaan's mind ticking over.

'We're taking the transfer.'

'You've gone behind my fucking back. Behind my fucking back!' His tone was coarse again, a rusty blade.

'Oh, this is ridiculous.' I put the phone down. It rang immediately afterwards. I left it. The third time it rang, I picked it up.

'Don't *ever* put the fucking phone down on me. I . . . am *not* ridiculous.'

Riaan was the one to hang up.

Terence and I visited the Bulldog Bar for the last time. The man and his bulldog were once again playing checkers. The bulldog snorted with excitement as his master jumped a win, and then looked up to give me a watery look. I patted his flat bristles and he returned his attention to the game.

'Back again,' said the bulldog's master, without looking up.

'For the last time. We're leaving soon,' I said as Terence handed me a pool cue and we began to play on the small, uneven table.

He sunk four balls on his opening shot. I looked at him, annoyed, chalked my cue, took aim and missed the pocket.

'Nothing here, could have told you. They've all been through here, mining companies, the lot.'

The naked light bulb hanging above the pool table cracked and fizzled. Blown. Not disappointed that we had to stop the game I was losing, I sat down next to the bulldog.

'Better you get off that farm.'

'We heard someone trying to break in. It was the final straw. If they had really wanted to get inside, they could have easily.'

'When?'

'Thursday, last week,' replied Terence, sliding a beer over to me.

'That was the night they got a farm three kilometres south of here. No survivors. Even the farmer's workers. Shot.'

Three days later, five months after our arrival in Marble Hall, Terence and I attended our last Month End. Riaan was waiting for our vehicle as we approached Spioenkop.

'Want me to stick around?' Terence asked as he climbed out of the bakkie.

I shook my head, 'It's okay.'

Riaan watched Terence collect all his goods from the front seat and leave. Terence walked around the corner of the building and leant on a wall, within my sight but out of Riaan's.

Riaan caught my arm, 'Don't *ever* call me ridiculous. I am not ridiculous. This company is ridiculous, the managers are ridiculous, but *not* me.' He doubled over, his hand over his face.

'Anything wrong?'

'Fucking migraines.'

I stared at his back, 'Can I get you anything?'

He waved me away, 'Just get your fucking map and report together for the Month End. For what it's worth.'

Terence and I strolled to the lapa. I sat between Chief and Morné. Morné, as usual, smelt as if he'd been rolling in mint. He popped gum in his mouth.

Chief's unkempt hair stood up at right angles. If I looked around the table at the unshaven chins, torn shirts and JJ's obvious hangover, it did not seem out of place.

'Well, you chaps will be off. Sorry to lose you, but . . . hey, we all move around. Heard from Levi by the way, bought himself a bigger boat, got himself a bigger crew. But they weren't finding those little beauties. No, the taxman took it all away. He's back with his smaller boat and original crew.' Chief glanced around. 'Where's Riaan? Ah, there you are. Awfully Christian of you to join us, sir. What's the matter, Tiger? You've gone all pale. The fight knocked out of you?'

Riaan popped two tablets into his mouth and took a sip from Chief's coffee. He flicked Mornay's shoulder. Mornay stood up and sat next to Terence. Riaan sat down in his place, next to Chief.

Chief drifted on to more technical matters, discussing boreholes they were planning to drill. Around us the birds in the bush sounded louder and the air smelt sweet with optimism. Bongi lay on the lapa wall, cleaning the burrs from his paws. He saw me watching him, jumped off the wall and ran to me, wiggling his tail with an obscene grin on his face. As he settled beneath my chair, I patted him and closed my eyes. Mentally, I had already left. Left behind the farm-house, the rotting fields of maize and the brown waters that flooded the valleys in fear.

CHAPTER EIGHT

Slumber of Boulders

I walked onto the vast plain of sand. Sand to the horizon, as far as I could see. Behind me the granite domes formed a shield at my back. When I had last looked back, Terence was a distant figure standing on them.

The sky around me began to wash to a navy ink. The first star, as bright as a diamond, appeared above me. A star to wish upon.

I wished everything would stay exactly as it was at that moment. Exactly.

I could see forever, to the curvature of the earth. A deep breath. I drew all the space inside of me. Bongi's paws thundered across the sands and circled me. He slowed down to a trot and walked back with me to Terence.

By the time I reached the granite domes, Terence had made a fire and was lying on his back on a large boulder, his feet in the warm sand. He poured a glass of wine and handed it to me.

'Cheers, to us.'

'To us,' I clinked his glass and climbed up onto the rock.

Above us, the Milky Way trumpeted, a blaze of brazen victory. Calling through the empty plains of sand, reverberating off the stark granite. Deafeningly loud in its beauty.

'My God, it's so bright. I can see the whole of Namaqualand. There's Orion,' Terence pointed.

I lay on my back with my head on his chest. 'And there's Scorpio. See the tail? With the sting? I'll give you that constellation.'

'Scorpio? I didn't know it was yours to give.'

'Oh, the stars are everybody's to designate. They just don't know it.'

'Mmm, I don't know if I'll find it again,' Terence rolled over and put an arm around me. He leant his bristly chin on my arm, 'Perhaps it'll find me.'

We lay under the stars, pointing out the shooting stars in whispers – as if we did not want to alert the universe to our presence; startle its solitude and stop its performance. Until our eyes felt heavy with sleep and we gathered up our possessions and drove home, using the pointers of the Southern Cross as a marker. Within ten minutes we bumped onto a tar road and from there, it was just a twist and a turn before we rolled into the small heart of Springbok. The main road was quiet and dark. Second turn to the right, and the bakkie crunched up the gravel driveway to the little green house wedged between the butcher and the optometrist. I climbed out, my head still dizzy. Spinning with stars and space.

On our arrival in Namaqualand, two weeks ago, we had immediately been directed to the edge of town, to the MinSearch offices. The offices consisted of a building painted a school grey and various sheds storing field supplies, vehicles and trays of core. This office did not have a name; it was merely called Namaqualand. Muis was in charge. He was, more or less, the equal of Chief at Spioenkop.

Muis sat in his office across a large, empty wooden desk. He was a small round man with bright, predatory eyes framed by large black-framed glasses. He knitted his fingers together, leant forward and gave us a quick jab of a smile.

'Welcome to Namaqualand.'

It was difficult to decide what Muis's most striking feature was. He had a strong nose which swept up into elongated nostrils. His thick, brown hair poured over his head, an equal length all round, cut into a bowl-shape and obviously trimmed by a wife. His mouth was small, V-shaped and flashed smiles on and off, much like a light switch. His blue eyes, I decided, were the most remarkable. They were quick and bright and reminded me of a bird of prey's.

'So,' Muis flashed a smile, 'Who cooks in your house?'

Terence frowned, 'What?'

'Who cooks in your house?'

'Both of us,' I replied warily.

'But who cleans in your house?'

'Both of us,' Terence's reply was brusque.

'But . . . *who* wears the pants in your house?' Muis's face went red. We remained quiet.

'Terence,' said Muis, after he'd finished digesting his joke, 'I want you to explore various base metal anomalies in the Namaqualand area. It will require you to take a caravan and spend nights out in the desert. I can't give that job to a woman.'

I bristled.

'Robyn, you must look after the eight drill rigs for our copper programme. They are all in the vicinity of Springbok.'

I sank back in my seat, placated. Wow, eight drill rigs.

'You'll get to work with Laurie. Laurie, like me, is a true Namaqualander. We've known each other since we were boys. Laurie knows more about these granites than anyone else ever will. He may not have a degree in geology, but you'll learn a lot from him.' Muis's smile was suddenly charming. 'You'll find Laurie down at the core shed. You can go and meet him now while I show Terence some of the maps.'

I walked down the stairs from the office to a core shed. Beside the shed was an open-air shelter, protected by a tin roof. Various core boxes were laid out on trestles. Two men, one young and one old, both wearing blue overalls, edged past me carrying a core box. They laid it down on a set of empty trestles and walked back into the shed. Another man with a shock of white hair peered into the box. He was wearing a grubby lab coat from which grew two long, sinewy, nut-brown legs with knobbly knees. He patted his coat pocket and re-moved a flattened packet of cigarettes. He carefully extracted one, cupped a gnarled hand and lit it. He dropped the match and ground it into the concrete with his veldskoen.

'Laurie?'

He glanced up at me, his eyes registering both caution and surprise. He lowered his gaze and popped the cigarette from his mouth, nodding. 'Laurie, yes.'

I introduced myself and shook his hand. Laurie's eyes met mine. They were big and brown and looked as if they could easily be hurt. I thought I'd be able to get along well with those eyes.

'Muis told me I'd find you here.'

'Then you've met him. The little shit. '

I smiled.

'Concordia granite.' Laurie picked up a bucket and wiped a wet rag across one of the cylinders of rock in the nearest core box. 'Concordia granite, my old friend. The best-looking granite of them all.'

Each core box was a metre and a half in length and contained four rows of rock core. The granite Laurie had wet looked bejewelled. He touched the rapidly drying surface where a black rock interrupted the granite. 'This is the mafic rock which intrudes into the granites. It's this mafic rock that carries the copper.'

The younger of the men in blue overalls, a man with a cocky swagger and teasing eyes, sauntered up and flicked Laurie's coat. '*Gee vir my 'n* smoke. *Moenie so schnoep wees nie, man* – give me a smoke.'

Laurie looked irritated. He gingerly pulled out the pack again, removed a cigarette and handed it over, then turned his back on the young man.

'Don't you introduce me, Laurie?' He looked at me, lighting the cigarette. 'I'm Hannes and that there is Ou Johannes.' He pointed to the older man who was sitting on a pile of core boxes, sipping tea. Ou Johannes lifted a hand and his dark face wrinkled into a smile. Hannes tapped Laurie on the shoulder again, and Laurie repeated the procedure of extracting a cigarette, with even more reluctance. Hannes took the cigarette to Ou Johannes, lighting it on the way.

'They work for me but they smoke all my cigarettes,' Laurie sighed, leaning both arms against the core box. Smoke drifted from his fingers. 'This core is from Pinkie's drill.'

'Who?'

'Pinkie, the other seven drills belong to a big drill company but the eighth drill is Pinkie's. The other drills finish a borehole in four, five days. But Pinkie takes, maybe, four weeks.'

'Then why does Muis keep him on?'

'Pinkie's a Namaqualander. Like me. Like Muis. We all went to the same school here in Springbok, and stayed over during the week because our parents lived far away on farms. Yes, I went to the same school back then as Muis and Pinkie, even though I'm a *bruin* Afrikaner.' Laurie took a deep suck on his cigarette and slowly exhaled. 'It was easy for my father to bend the law. Not many knew. I have green eyes and in this Namaqualand sun, all white people go brown. Brown like me.' Laurie's white hair fell forward and he smoothed it back. 'Pinkie's father worked for Muis before he got sick and now Pinkie does. It has always been that way. When Pinkie's father died it was just natural that Pinkie took over the drill. But Pinkie is also . . . sick.'

Laurie picked up his clipboard and wrote, in impeccable handwriting, *Concordia Granite*. He underlined it using his matchbox. *Quartz, feldspar, plagioclase*; he listed all the minerals in the rock without looking at the core box in front of him.

It was easy to settle in Namaqualand, there was enough space. Or Namaqualand settled into Terence and me; the sand, the granite and the dry heat. Within a month we felt at home, within three we felt like true Namaqualanders.

Terence spent some nights away, never more than a week. His work took him further north, away from the Namaqualand granites, into areas more harsh, more barren. He found a shady dry river-bed to set up his caravan. From there he walked long distances, checking out various anomalies that had been detected earlier in a regional soil-sampling program. Signs of copper, lead and zinc. There was often a simple explanation for the metal presence: a decomposing farm tractor, a metal dump, drainage from an existing mine. Terence walked from area to area marking off the anomalies on his map. His hair and beard grew long and scraggly.

He had two young assistants, recent graduates, who helped him occasionally. One was a long, thin young man who took himself very seriously and had a continuous phlegm-hacking cough, which he spluttered out between taking drags on his cigarette. The other had hair as blond as Terence, a bouncing gait to his walk, was easy-going and talkative. The latter occasionally mapped with Terence in the field. In the evenings, camping in the dry river bed, they drank warm beer and Terence taught him chess.

Bongi stayed with me, keeping by my side. He lay under the core tables as I logged, or wedged himself under my desk as I plotted the positions of the new boreholes. He drove with me to visit the drill rigs. If I did leave him for a few hours, he stayed with Laurie. Over the last three months, an understanding had grown between them. Laurie spoke to Bongi about confidential things, like the possibility of diamonds on the farm he owned, or how to tell the Namaqualand granites apart. On days when he felt irritated by the heat, or perhaps by memories, he spoke to Bongi about Muis. If Laurie did not hate Muis personally, then he hated Muis for tipping the scales – for shifting the balance they had had as boys. Laurie worked for Muis, as he had done for almost twenty years. And every day he was reminded of this, everyday it agitated him like sand against an eyeball. *Muis*, even the word agitated Laurie. Every time he said it, he snapped his tongue. Muis (*click*).

'Bongi, that little shit Muis (*click*) thinks because I'm a brown Afrikaner he can tell me what to do.'

Bongi would flick his tail, not bothering to look up. He'd heard it all before.

On a Thursday afternoon, Laurie and I stood logging the core side by side. More accurately, I was logging the core and Laurie was smoking and contemplating the rock. He had been contemplating the same core box the whole morning, even though Hannes and Johannes were stacking the incoming core boxes from the drill rigs at an alarming rate. With eight drills continually running, the core mounted easily. Keeping up was constant work. I usually spent only the mornings logging with Laurie, but lately I was spending most of my day with him. Trying to hurry Laurie was of no use. He refused to work faster, and gave each tray of core the time and attention it deserved.

Laurie sighed, 'Rietburg granite, my old friend. See here, Robyn.'

I reluctantly put down my clipboard. We needed to be working.

'Look at the beautiful blue quartz crystals.'

I inspected the rock. 'It is beautiful.'

'This tray is from Pinkie's drill. It's the only box we've received from him in two weeks.'

'He's sick again, isn't he?'

Laurie nodded. 'Each time he goes to the big hospital in Cape Town and they cut away the cancer but it always comes back. The doctors tell him to stay out of the sun. He wears long sleeves, he bought the biggest hat he could find. But the cancer always comes back.' Laurie looked up. 'Shit, it's Muis (*click*).'

Muis marched down the stairs from his office and trotted over to the core shed. His chubby thighs rubbed together.

'Morning.'

'Morning,' I replied.

'How's the core today, anything interesting?' Muis asked cheerfully. He tried to peer down his nose at me, through his black frames. He still had to look up.

'No, not really,' I replied.

Laurie remained quiet.

Muis inspected the mounting piles of core boxes behind us. 'Backlog. You must work faster, especially you, Laurie.'

Laurie's face flushed.

'Which drill is this box from, Laurie?'

'Pinkie's drill, Muis.'

Muis frowned. 'We've had no news from him for a while. Laurie, you and Robyn should take a drive out there today and see what's happening with him. He always chooses the remote sites to drill, but it means he's far from town if he needs anything.'

Laurie nodded, keeping his eyes on the rock.

Muis folded his arms and studied both of us, smiling. I felt Bongi slink against my legs and sit down.

'Robyn.'

I sighed inwardly. I knew that tone.

'Robyn, what sort of woman dresses like that?'

I began to work. I was wearing an old, oil-stained T-shirt, torn on the lower seam from lifting a box of core. My khaki shorts were dusty. I wore my leather hiking boots. I dressed like everyone else.

Muis laughed, 'So tell me Robyn, what sort of woman dresses like that?'

Bongi's chest began to rumble; it grew louder as Muis walked over to me. I nudged him with my boot.

'What sort of man would marry a woman like you?'

Muis was grinning. Was this a game?

I smiled flatly. 'Well, I wouldn't marry you either, Muis.'

Muis stood in front of me, with his short arms sunk deep into his trouser pockets.

'*What* woman dresses like that?'

Bongi lunged. He sunk his teeth in Muis's trousers, ripping the fabric, and tugged back on his haunches, growling. Muis backed away, dragging Bongi with him. Not making one sound. Step, drag. Step, drag. Only when Muis was away from the core shed, did Bongi release his grip. He ran back to me, wagging his whole body in delight. Muis marched up the stairs and back into his office. Guilty as charged. The door swung closed.

Laurie's shoulders were shaking beneath his laboratory coat. He looked up and wiped an eye and started to laugh again. 'Bongi is now my best friend. I think, Robyn, when they gave the democratic rights to everyone, the blacks, the Indians and us brown Afrikaners, they forgot to give it to dogs too.'

I laughed with my hand over my mouth, 'Bongi, that was *very* bad. You'll get me fired, you little monster.'

Laurie took off his laboratory coat, folded it neatly and placed it on the edge of the core tray. 'Let's drive out to Pinkie's drill. Give Bongi a break from Muis.'

Laurie drove the red 4x4 bakkie, Bongi sat between us. As the office was situated on the outskirts of town, it was only a few minutes before we were driving through the desolate beauty of the granite domes. Starry branches of kokerbome dotted the domes, guarding their lonely positions in the harsh landscape. Occasional fields were still scattered with spring daisies, orange, white and yellow. Laurie drove an obscure route around the domes and into the infinite rocky distance. An hour and a half later he stopped. 'Look, there she is.'

Ahead of us was an enormous mountain of granite. On the very crest was a tiny black frame. Pinkie's drill rig.

'My God, how will we get up there?'

'There is a route.' Laurie shifted the gear lever from high to low four and, slowly, we started to inch our way up the dome. 'Pinkie always finds a way. How do you think he gets the drill rig up here?'

I clutched my seat as the powerful engine tackled the steep climb. We swung this way and that, following red spray-painted arrows on the rock. Bongi was tossed from Laurie to me, trilling and yelping, beside himself with excitement. Eventually the vehicle levelled and an old caravan and drill rig came into view. There was no one to be seen. Laurie parked beside the drill.

I stood on the crest of the granite dome. I could see forever. I could even see the west coast, over a hundred kilometres away. I stretched out my arms; the space was enough to make me dizzy with delight. Bongi darted around the drill rig.

Laurie looked around, 'Pinkie?'

Silence.

'Pinkie?'

The expanse of granite domes gazed back at us.

'Pinkie?' Laurie called for the third time.

I spun around as the caravan door swung open on rusty hinges. A small figure wearing a large white Stetson stepped out. The hat cast a deep shadow over his face. Despite the heat, he wore overalls covering his arms and legs. A colourful scarf was wrapped around his neck and another around the hat. He shuffled towards us in clumsy, steel-tipped construction boots.

I held out my hand. 'Pinkie?'

A hand emerged from his blue overall sleeve like a tortoise emerging from its shell. I shook it. The skin on his hand was as fine as tissue paper. It was dented between the thumb and forefinger, where flesh had been removed and the skin had healed over a vacuum. Pinkie nodded, touching the broad rim of his Stetson. White gauze was attached to his nose. The skin on his face looked scarred and red. His left ear lobe was missing. I quickly lowered my gaze; I did not want to be caught staring.

'Pinkie,' Laurie greeted him. He patted his breast pocket, removed his cigarettes and offered them to Pinkie. Pinkie took the cigarette and placed it gently between his lips. Laurie lit it and then one for himself. Smoking, they contemplated the quiet drill.

'She's down.'

It was the first thing Pinkie had said. His voice was dry, a hoarse whisper. 'She needs a new drill bit, the crew are in town buying one.'

'How long have they been gone?' asked Laurie.

'Three days.'

Laurie nodded. Three days.

'They must wait for it to come from Cape Town,' Pinkie explained further.

'You can see forever from here,' I commented.

Pinkie eyed the infinite escarpment with resignation. Yes, forever.

Laurie pointed at the green shade-netting tent erected near the drill. 'You using that, Pinkie?'

'It doesn't help. Every time I go back to the doctor they find more. It seems I can't hide. The sun will find me through the tent, through the caravan, through this hat.'

Laurie nodded sympathetically, his thick, white hair flopping over his forehead. He smoothed it back. The two men smoked in silence. Laurie finished first and ground the butt into the granite. Pinkie followed suit.

'Muis wanted us to find you.'

Pinkie gave a dry cackle, 'Muis. When we were little, I remember I used to pick him to be on my side of the rugby games. Because no one else wanted him. Now, he picks me. Because no one else wants me to drill for them.'

Laurie nodded. 'Big, important Muis. When he came back from the university in Pretoria he was the big, important geologist who gave me this job. Twenty years later, it's all the same. Except now he's the top boss.'

'He's not so big, Laurie. He's just Muis. Remember when the three of us chased that rabbit on your farm. We had my father's gun. Muis tried to shoot it. He missed it by a mile, he always was a terrible shot.' Pinkie gave a dry, open-mouth laugh. 'That rabbit got away from Muis. The rest of us didn't.'

'Back then he was just Muis. He used to go on and on at us,' Laurie made a little beak with his hand, pecking at the air, 'push us as far as we would go. Then we'd fight back and he'd run home, crying like a girl. We'd shout, *Klein Muis, hardloop tuis.*' Laurie was quiet. 'We are all older now,' he said.

'But maybe not so different, Laurie. Let me tell you a thing or two, sweetheart,' Pinkie pocked a scaly finger at me. 'Number one: granite is, in the most cases, better company than people. Like Laurie, I know every granite in Namaqualand. I know what type of drill bit to drill it with, I know when to drill it fast, when to drill it slow. Every granite, I know. This granite never lies.'

'People lie?' I probed.

'You could say that. That doctor, and my father, they told me I had a sensitive skin. A skin for sissies. That I needed to be in the sun to make it tougher. Only many years later, when I got really sick, did I learn the truth. This sun can also kill you. Who would've thought that?'

Laurie offered him another cigarette and he took it, placing it in his chafed lips for Laurie to light. He spoke through pinched lips, 'Look at Laurie, his skin is too brown to burn. I wish I had Laurie's skin.'

Laurie and Pinkie finished their second cigarettes in silence. Then Laurie nodded and walked back to the bakkie and climbed in. I followed, calling Bongi, puzzled. Pinkie shuffled behind in his steel-tipped boots.

He held the door open for me and tipped his hat. 'Next time sweetheart, next time bring a battery for my radio, a big one. It's all I have to listen to out here.'

'When will the drill be up and running?' I asked Laurie as we headed down the granite dome, wondering if we had somehow gleaned this information on our visit.

Laurie shook his head as he grasped the shaking steering wheel, 'It's not the drill bit he's waiting for. Pinkie's sick again, he'll start up when he's feeling better.'

'How do you know?'

'Pinkie only smokes when he's very sick. Otherwise he won't touch a cigarette.'

'But why is he out there? There's no one to look after him,' I asked, outraged.

Laurie sighed as he shifted into the next gear. 'It's the way Pinkie wants it. He would rather be out there, in the middle of Namaqualand, than in town. It's the only place he'll get better.'

'He should never have become a driller, Laurie. How can he be expected to stay out of the sun?' I asked as the vehicle lurched off the dome and onto the relatively smooth track.

'Drilling is all he knows, Robyn. It's all his father knew. His father died of the same cancer thing and then Pinkie took over the drill. All Pinkie ever wanted to do was drill. And all he ever wanted to drill was Namaqualand granite.'

Back at the office, I jogged up the stairs to the grey office building, Bongi at my side. I pushed the door open. Muis was busy talking to Ou Johannes. He looked at me; his eyes slid down to my chest and a small smile spread onto his face like butter. He said something to Ou Johannes and cupped his hands in front of his chest. He chuckled. Ou Johannes looked shocked, confused.

I let the door swing closed behind me, shutting out an indignant Bongi.

'What was that you said?' I asked Muis.

'Not for your ears,' he laughed again. He walked to his office and started to close the door. I followed him in.

I had no idea what I would say. I sat down. Muis frowned at me then sat opposite me.

'Muis.'

'Yes,' he switched the friendly, hospitable Namaqualand smile on. Knitted his fingers together and leant forward.

'I see you treat the other geologists, the other staff, with respect.'

'I do,' his smile grew.

'But not me.'

'Why do you say that?'

'Well, what about the comment you've just made to Ou Johannes about my breasts?'

'You heard wrong,' he jumped up, slamming his hands on the desk.

The anger started to drain from me. I was feeling calmer by the second.

'What about the comments about the clothes I wear? And asking me who wears the pants in my house?'

Muis's blue eyes looked cautious. He was quiet. I thought he was about to sit down again, when he suddenly marched around the desk and sat in the chair next to me. His arm touched mine.

'It's time we did a performance review of the work you're doing. I have been wanting to tell you what a good job you've been doing.'

I looked at Muis, surprised.

He pulled a file out from the shelf behind him. He thumbed through the pages.

I stood up, pushed myself past his small knees and opened his office door and looked back.

Muis was sitting on the wrong side of his desk, the file on his lap, his mouth open. His bowl-haircut looked monkish. I closed the door behind me.

Bongi pounced on me as I left the building. He charged ahead of me down to the core shed, back to Laurie. I felt light, breezy. I picked up my clipboard and began to work.

'You spoke to Muis?' Laurie popped the cigarette out of his mouth.

'You could say that.'

Laurie brown eyes studied me while he tasted the nicotine in his mouth. 'About Pinkie's drill?'

I smiled up at him. 'More or less.'

Eight months after our arrival in Namaqualand, the eight drill rigs assigned to me continued to grind core. Seven, actually. Pinkie's drill produced core at intervals. When he was well, we received a box of core every five days, but otherwise, we would not hear from him for weeks on end. His health came and went. Trips to the hospital in Cape Town, five hundred kilometres south, were common. Each time Pinkie returned with new gauze patches. Copper was discovered in moderate amounts in the core, providing enough promise to continue drilling, but nothing large enough to be of any real interest.

While I plotted and planned the positions of the future boreholes, Laurie was content to contemplate logging the core. He continued to make no compromise on the time he spent with each box of core. As I needed the information from the boreholes drilled to plan the next, I frantically helped Laurie log the core. Bongi and Laurie were happy to watch me work.

After my conversation with Muis, the change in him was as instant as a light switch. He spoke to me in cordial tones. He greeted me with a smile. There was no more reference to the clothes I wore, who cooked in my home. I could not understand the sudden change; I just had to accept it.

Terence had walked to most of the anomalies that showed the presence of metal and now was spending more time in the Namaqualand office, writing up his results. The two young graduates had since moved; the one with the bouncing step had been transferred to Spioenkop and was now working for Riaan. The hacking cougher had returned to university to study computer science, having discovered that the future was in IT, not dirty rocks. Hannes now accompanied Terence when he did go into the field. Hannes worked hard but he also amused Terence. He hummed tunes and radio advertisement ditties throughout their work, so that the two men walking the long, hot distances now had a marketing rhythm to their footsteps. While Hannes was refreshing their hard treks with soap bubble troubles and cowboy slogans for cigarettes, Ou Johannes had no one to carry the other side of the core boxes. Laurie and I were needed to help shift the core boxes back and forth. Laurie was indignant about this; this was not part of his job description.

On a warm sunny morning (like most mornings in Namaqualand), Laurie and I leant over a core box, inspecting its contents.

'Concordia granite, my old friend,' announced Laurie.

By now properly tutored and familiar with the subject, Bongi wagged his tail. He jumped up with delight as Terence entered the core shed.

Terence bent down to pat him. 'There are some men here to visit Muis. Apparently they arrived on a private jet at the airfield outside town this morning.'

'Big, important men.' Laurie patted his chest pocket, this being enough reason for a cigarette break. 'See here, Terence, Concordia granite. Typical; look at the pink feldspars.'

Terence peered into the box, ever inquisitive as to the core drilled that day. He pulled out his hand-lens and picked up a piece of broken core to inspect more closely.

'Shit, Muis (click),' said Laurie.

We all looked up. Muis was trotting down the stairs to the core shed. His face looked flushed and angry. Behind him strode two men. One was dressed in tailor-made beige trousers and a blue shirt, the sleeves rolled up to the elbow. His hair was neatly clipped, a slightly wavy strawberry-blond, his skin was pale and his walk calm and confident. A man accustomed to being in charge. Behind him was an older man in a dark suit, carrying a briefcase. His hair looked as if it had greyed prematurely. Strawberry Blond walked over to the core laid out in the trestles and peered into the boxes.

Laurie slunk away. The two visitors paid us no attention. S. Blond pulled out a hand-lens. Geologist: Terence and I both immediately identified him.

'You say this is the copper-bearing rock?' he asked Muis. His accent was clipped, British. 'How many drills have you got going on this?'

'Eight.' Muis looked like he would burst.

'*Eight* drill rigs,' S. Blond commented to the dark suit, shaking his head. He replaced the core carefully. He walked from tray to tray, inspecting a sample from each. Finally he dusted his shiny brown shoes with his hanky. 'Well, Muis,' he pronounced it Miss, 'I think I've seen enough. Let's go back to the drawing board, so to speak.' He led the way back into the office. Muis and the dark suit followed.

'Big important men with important business.' Laurie appeared from the shadow. He spat the last of his cigarette out and wiped his mouth, 'I have logged this core for twenty years. I know these granites like the back of my hand. But *he* comes in here for twenty seconds and knows everything.'

'Don't think I've ever seen Muis so mad.' Terence folded his arms, watching them enter the office. 'I wonder who they are.'

'Name's Blond. Strawberry Blond,' I said.

'Muis's mad because they're more important than him,' said Laurie.

'Here he comes again,' noted Terence.

Muis marched down the stairs, arms swinging, and over to us. His eyes were watering with fury. 'Robyn.'

'Yes.'

'What is happening with Pinkie's drill?'

I flicked through the sheets on my clipboard. 'The last core we received from him was . . . over two weeks ago. He may be sick. Has no one sent a message?'

'We need to know. *They* need to know. Take a drive out to his rig and find out what's going on.'

'I'll go with you,' said Terence.

I drove through the remote dusty tracks. Terence and Bongi sat beside me. After eight months I knew my way around the quiet network of roads almost as well as Laurie. As usual, Pinkie had chosen the site furthest from town. It was an hour later that we drew close to the site. Pinkie's drill rig was nestled in a depression, hidden between two granite domes. It lay silently beneath the hot blue sky. I parked next to the old caravan.

'Pinkie,' I called.

No reply. I peered into the green shade-net beside the drill. It was empty apart from Pinkie's grubby white Stetson. I picked it up.

'Pinkie?' I raised my voice.

A lanky young man appeared from behind a rock. He limbered up to us.

'Where's Pinkie?' I asked.

The man-boy shook his head. White gauze was pasted onto his neck, under his angular jawbone.

'Who are you?'

'Pinkie's boy.'

'Where's Pinkie?'

Pinkie's son touched the gauze on his neck, 'Pinkie died three days ago. On Friday.'

I looked at the black, oily drill rig and at Pinkie's hat in my hand. 'I'm sorry. I did not know.'

Pinkie's son nodded. His Adam's apple bobbed as he swallowed. He rubbed a greasy palm into his eye sockets.

'I'm really sorry,' I offered him Pinkie's Stetson. He shook his head.

'Take that,' he told Terence.

'What?'

He pointed to a core box, three-quarters full. 'The men in the Land Cruiser did not want to take it.'

'Which men?' I asked.

He shrugged, 'They said they were with you.'

Pinkie's son and Terence loaded the core box onto the back of the bakkie. Bongi jumped up behind them and licked the boy's hand.

He left his hand dangling for Bongi to lick. 'It's the grease. Grease for the drill rods,' He wiped his hands on his torn jeans and held it out for Terence to shake and then me, 'The next box will be mine.'

I glanced quickly at him. 'What do you mean?'

'The next box of core will be mine.'

'Oh . . . you're taking over the drill?'

He shrugged once again. 'It's what I know.'

We watched him slink off between the boulders of granite as if seeking their solace.

Back at the MinSearch Office, Terence and I unloaded Pinkie's box of core and laid it on a set of trestles. Laurie, finished for the day, walked over to us.

He looked at his watch. 'It is ten to five. Ten minutes before I can go home. If I walk very, very slowly back to my car, I can be out of the gates by five 'o clock.'

'Laurie, Pinkie died. Three days ago,' I told him.

Laurie stopped moving as if he had been hit by an electric shock. He fumbled for his pack of cigarettes. Shielding his back to us, he lit up.

'Laurie?' I walked up to him.

He nodded quickly, his thick white hair fell over his forehead. He walked over to Pinkie's box of core. 'Concordia granite, my old friend. Pinkie, my old friend.'

We stood in silence around the cheap pine box. Pinkie's hat in my hand.

Laurie looked at the red and white packet in his hand; it was three-quarters full. He placed it on the edge of the box and walked very, very slowly back to his car. I picked up the cigarettes.

'I'll smoke them for Pinkie,' Hannes held out his hand. His eyes were sad. He hummed the line of a cowboy tune and mumbled something about real flavour for a real man. I handed him the pack. He walked back to Ou Johannes who was sitting on a pile of core boxes. Between them, they lit up and smoked quietly.

'What's this?' asked Terence.

On the core box, where it had been hidden by the packet, was a name stamped in green ink: TURNSTONE.

'Don't know, never heard the name before.'

'I'll ask Muis. You should tell him about Pinkie. He won't know yet.'

I nodded.

Muis was sitting alone at the drafting table as Terence and I walked in. Scattered around him was an assortment of maps and files.

He looked up as we entered. 'They're taking over. MinSearch has been bought by a British company called TurnStone. Did you know anything about this?'

We shook our heads. Muis studied us to see if we could be lying.

'Bought?' I repeated.

'Bought. Acquired. Take-over. Those bastards want my office. They can have it, they can have all of this,' Muis gestured around the room. 'I don't need this. I have my own farm. But . . .' he wagged a finger at us, 'what I want to know is *why* there was no warning. They just came here out of nowhere. There was no warning. *Who* do they think they are?'

'Muis,' I interrupted.

'What?'

'Pinkie died, three days ago. We just found out.'

Muis sunk his head into his hands and sat there for a long time. Eventually he looked up and pulled off his TV-shaped spectacles. He wiped away a tear from his red eyes. '*Arme ou Pinkie.* We were all Namaqualanders.'

I offered him Pinkie's hat. He took it, fingering the rim. He almost smiled, but his face contorted and another tear rolled down his cheek. He wiped it away, 'Pinkie's silly cowboy hat. We were boys together; Laurie, Pinkie and me. I have known Pinkie and his father since . . . since forever. We shot rabbits together. Pinkie could hit them every time. I would miss by a mile. That always made Pinkie laugh. So hard he could no longer shoot. *Arme ou Pinkie.*'

'Terence,' Muis did not look up, 'I have unlocked your office. Turn-Stone locked everything and took the keys. But I have spares. You can pack away your files, take what you need. The rest is their property now.' He threw up his hands. 'They are closing the exploration offices and will be starting their own projects. There are only two positions open for geologists; you and Robyn can apply for them, but most of the geologists with MinSearch will be applying for them.'

'Why only two positions?' asked Terence.

'They have a different approach, or so they told me. Top-of-the-range technology and minimal staff. Well, good luck to them,' said Muis, meaning quite the opposite. 'I won't be applying. Nor will Laurie. We'll go back to our farms, we'll go back to sheep farming.' He turned the hat in his hands. 'Laurie and I are true Namaqualanders. We would never survive anywhere else. Just like Pinkie.'

He stood up and walked into his office, closing the door softly behind him.

Terence and I were called to Cape Town a week later. TurnStone would like to interview us. We drove the five hundred kilometres south, into the bustle of highways and byways. The mountains, the trees all a lush green in comparison to brown Namaqualand. Suddenly we were among millions of people. Terence selected the right off-ramp and we drove through the city centre to the foreshore. It was a modern building, glass and terracotta coloured plaster, with strange steel appendages that gave it a rocket-like appearance. It was tall, but not too tall. Ten stories, small enough to be exclusive. The tenth floor was rented by TurnStone. We were nodded past the security boom into the underground parking and from there took the lift up to the top floor.

TURNSTONE, read the engraved glass doors. A buzz and the doors automatically opened. Strawberry Blond stood waiting for us in the lobby.

'Lawrence Sutherland,' he introduced himself, extending a manicured hand. 'Welcome to my humble empire. Only joking, I'm one of TurnStone's Directors. Responsible for, amongst other things, managing Africa. I am still busy accumulating a top team for our mineral exploration. Through acquiring MinSearch, TurnStone obtained many strategic alliances and crucial joint ventures. Their exploration strategy? Well, I think you'll see we do things a little differently here at TurnStone. We use the best technology available and focus on specific ventures. Only ones that will boost bottom-line share price. We also farm out whatever work we can, so you may consider our exploration staff a little minimal. We like to think we make up for it with our approach. Most importantly we are *only* looking for world-class mineral deposits. Shall we get on with it then? Robyn, why don't you come through to the boardroom, and Terence, make yourself comfortable here.'

Lawrence and I sat around a large, oval oak table. Behind him lay a panoramic view of the Cape Town harbour. More than once, the view distracted me from his questions, so that at some point he turned to look with me, 'It is a beautiful city. We really could not have obtained better premises.'

He filtered through my replies with polite precision and then rose to usher me out. 'We have a good number of candidates to interview for these positions. We'll keep you posted. Would you send Terence through?'

⟨

Terence and I returned to Namaqualand not very hopeful. Someone else would get the position. Someone who would raise shareholder value with one fell swoop, or whatever it was that Lawrence had said. Someone who would sit in those pristine offices and comfortably survey the city harbour below.

The Namaqualand office was a hive of activity. A removal company was packing up the contents of the offices, and a truck was parked outside the core shed. Laurie watched Hannes and Johannes stack the boxes onto the truck. Hannes was whistling a tune, one familiar to me but not one I could immediately place – although it brought to mind clear liquor, palm trees and islands.

'A maize-meal company is taking over the buildings. This shed will be filled with bags of mielie meal. Johannes and Hannes will be staying here, working for them. Lifting the bags of mielie meal instead of core boxes.'

'And you?'

'I am going back to my farm. My farm is next to Muis's farm. But my farm has better water than his. His windmills are always breaking. He is going to need my water.' Laurie looked satisfied. He smiled. 'The big, important man will need my help now. Shit, Muis (*click*).'

Muis walked up to us. 'Laurie,' he said, 'you knew these granites better than anyone ever will. I was always grateful that you were here to help me.'

With that, he turned and marched back to the office.

Laurie fumbled for his pack of cigarettes. 'Well, I'll be damned.' He concentrated on lighting up, but I could see he was smiling. 'Once a Namaqualander, always a Namaqualander.'

That night Terence and I drove out into the lunar landscape. We sat on our favourite boulder and made a fire. Above us the sky lit up and sang its chorus of stars. Terence poured wine into our glasses.

He looked up. 'Look, there's Scorpio. There's the tail.'

PART THREE

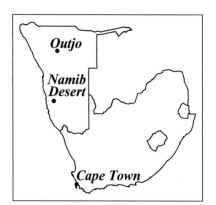

CHAPTER NINE

Flying Solo

Nausea lurched around my empty body. I prayed for the day to
end. After which I would *never* fly in a single-engine Cessna
again. For three days I had been buffeted by thermals – three infi-
nitely long, sickening days. We were currently flying over TurnStone's
license area in Namibia and the pilot had dropped from five hundred
feet above ground level to two hundred.

'Any lower and the thermals will knock us clean into orbit,' the
pilot shouted above the drone of the engine.

I curled away into a tight ball and rested my head against the vibrating door. I no longer wanted to look at the ground. I no longer
cared.

A month earlier, Terence and I had received a call from Lawrence
Sutherland.

'Congratulations, you and Terence have been selected for the two
positions within TurnStone. Of course, this is an opportunity you
could not possibly afford to miss. I interviewed many geologists from
MinSearch, including the lot from Spioenkop, and I must say, I couldn't
imagine any of them working for us.'

Terence and I drove to Cape Town, leaving behind the isolated
splendour of Namaqualand. We were trading the granite beasts for
plush offices overlooking the city and the harbour.

'It's an opportunity for us to work for an international company.'

We can gain international experience,' reasoned Terence as we drove. Then, with more than a drop of irony, he broke into the Peter Gabriel song: '*Big time, I'm on my way I'm making it. Big time. I' m heading for the big, big city. Big time . . .*'

In the TurnStone office, a couple of days later, Terence and I stood around a vast map table with Lawrence. Terence's hair was almost military short and his chin was shaved. I thought the short hair suited him. He wore khaki chinos and a shirt he had ironed that morning, but he drew the line at a tie. I too had cut my hair short, and wore a raw silk shirt and tailored trousers.

Behind the map table was an enormous window, which displayed a view of the entire Cape Town harbour. The rest of the offices, including mine and Terence's, faced Table Mountain. The table was littered with maps and reports, centred around one large map of Southern Africa.

Lawrence drummed his fingernails on the table. 'These two blocks are our recently acquired license areas. We have already flown a geophysical survey over them in order to identify the most encouraging areas, possible copper deposits. Copper is the one commodity that we can still hope to find an enormous, world-class deposit of. Something big like Chuquicamata in Chile.'

I looked at the two red blocks. Each held an enormous chunk of ground, one a large portion of northern Namibia and the other a fair bite of Botswana.

'We get generous long-term funding for developing projects like these. Spent over a million pounds flying these surveys. But now it's time to get the show on the road. Deliver some results, find those world-class copper deposits. So that we can boost the bottom-line profits and send TurnStone share prices through the roof. And since I'm a major shareholder, we *want* share prices to rocket,' Lawrence winked.

He was a handsome man, of sorts. Particular about his clothes; he was dressed in a studied, casual get-up that day. His soft, black cotton shirt was rolled to the elbows, revealing pale, freckled skin, unaccustomed to the African sun. All his movements were smooth and casual; he smiled frequently and yet his hazel eyes never seemed to change. They were always watchful, as if programmed to absorb all data at high resolution. His cell phone rang.

'Excuse me,' he said and stepped away from the table. He stood with his back to us, his one hand in his pocket, facing the view. 'Kirkby, yes . . . no, that's not what I said, what I . . .'

'Shit,' I whispered to Terence, 'what the *hell* have we let ourselves into?'

'Just don't forget to find the world-class copper deposit,' muttered Terence. His smile was a little feeble though. He looked seriously worried. As was I.

'The areas are huge, a whole portion of the country,' I said.

'That's because we don't want to miss the deposit,' said Lawrence, stepping back into the conversation. 'The larger our license areas, the more chance we have of hitting the jackpot. Robyn, you'll be looking after the project in Namibia, while Terence takes care of the project in Botswana.'

'One geologist per project?' asked Terence.

'That's correct, we don't have much staff to go around. But with modern-day technology that's not really needed. The geophysical survey we flew will already have selected the most promising areas anyway. Thing is, no one has actually seen the ground we've obtained a license for. That doesn't look good to investors, so I want one of you to fly over the license areas and record anything you see. Access roads, including dirt tracks; dams; rural settlements. Anything we wouldn't see on our topographical maps. Robyn, why don't you go? We'll charter a plane for you.'

I swallowed. They would *hire* a plane for me.

Lawrence's cell phone rang again. 'Hello? Kirkby. Yes, could you hold for a second?'

He smiled at us. 'Welcome on board. I'm sure I made the right decision hiring the two of you. I know you won't disappoint me. Well, we all have work to do.'

Lawrence strolled down the corridor with his cell phone to his ear. 'Kirkby?' He walked into his office and closed the door.

Terence and I stared at the map in silence. Terence's arms were crossed and his chin tucked into his neck. He sighed.

'I'll be working in Namibia and you'll be in Botswana,' I repeated. He nodded.

'For a *lot* of the time,' I added unnecessarily. 'How much time are we going to be spending apart?'

'We'll make a plan to see each other whenever we can. Don't worry about that now. I think we have enough to worry about. Modern technology or not, these areas are very big for one geologist to cope with.'

But I did worry. 'He seems very sure of himself, of the company. Of the way they're approaching things.'

'They've got the finances. They can afford to do everything on a big scale.'

'I guess so.'

A scheduled flight took me from Cape Town to the capital of Namibia, Windhoek. From there, the smaller, internal airport was just a taxi trip away. I walked out onto the runway with my bag slung over my arm, a roll of maps in my hand. An early morning breeze cooled the promise of a hot day. It was impossible to continue to feel apprehensive on a day like this. I could smell adventure in the air; it rose like the sun's warmth off the asphalt runway.

In the corner of the airfield stood the only plane: a small, blue, bow-legged bird. A single-engine Cessna. I walked towards it. A tall, wiry man was checking her wings. From the back I could see he was wearing dusty leather boots, khaki shorts and a checked, short-sleeved shirt too small for even his skinny shoulders. A shapeless felt hat completed the outfit. He turned to look at me, pulled his hat off to study me more clearly. He had an unruly brown beard and unkempt hair. A pipe was clamped between his teeth and his ears – well, his ears were large and red and stood out from the side of his head like two red danger cones. His eyes were a clear blue, as washed-out as the cloudless sky behind him. His face as eroded as a contour map of dry land.

'Louwtjie,' he announced between clamped teeth

'Robyn Hartley. May you . . . er, smoke here?' I asked.

He pulled out the pipe and stared at me. 'Get in the plane.'

I obeyed, heaving my tog-bag ahead of me.

Louwtjie closed the door behind me and tugged the handle twice. He then walked around the plane, going through a routine check, before climbing in beside me. He popped the pipe out of his mouth and tucked it into his pocket. He smiled.

'It's not lit, don't worry. Welcome to Louwtjie's airline. Just sit back and relax, refreshments will soon be served.' He signalled to the cool box on the back seat.

Permission for take-off granted, crackled over the radio.

The engine started to whine and the propeller spun, slowly at first and then faster and faster. Rocking from side to side, we taxied along the runway. Suddenly, we were airborne. Louwtjie scratched his beard and tenderly adjusted the dials. I studied the disappearing city of Windhoek with excitement.

The buildings dissolved to khaki bush, the roads to rocky hills. Suddenly the plane lurched heavenward, leaving my stomach hanging somewhere below. The engine spluttered and we dropped like a stone to our former height. I looked at Louwtjie, terrified.

'Thermals!' shouted Louwtjie. 'Terrible at this time of the year. Wait until we fly at a lower level over your project areas, we'll be knocked around like a ping-pong ball.'

We flew east first, planning to cross the border into Botswana. The first day we would fly over TurnStone's license in southern Botswana. The second day we would fly north west, back into Namibia, and spend the night in the town of Grootfontein where we would be able to refuel. The third day we would fly over TurnStone's project in northern Namibia and return to Windhoek.

Hour after hour the plane droned hiccuping over the thermals. The days blurred, one day's nausea building on the last. Khaki colours, the smell of fuel and dust. Each day began with the plane rising with the exuberance and clumsiness of an airborne beetle, and ended by thankfully dropping onto the runway of a small town. For three days, I plotted our path, using a handheld GPS (Global Positioning System). On my map I recorded everything I saw: *road access, rural settlement, game fencing, dams, small town, cattle farm.*

On the afternoon of the third day, Louwtjie pointed below us at the heaving ground. 'We're flying over TurnStone's project in Namibia now.'

I stared at the ground. We were flying over a small town.

'Outjo,' shouted Louwtjie, 'I know this town, far too well.'

I closed my eyes and leant against the door.

Louwtjie shook me roughly by the knee. 'We're not flying this way again, you'd better take notes.'

I curled further away from him and swallowed the sour liquid that had squeezed up into my mouth.

'Suit yourself. Just remember one thing, one name actually: Abel Kalomo. He's a farmer here who can help you. Abel by name and, *fokken hel*, able by nature. '

I rolled my head to look at Louwtjie through hot, watering eyes. He looked so comfortable, so cushioned in the third dimension. Every time the plane lurched he just steadied her, reassuring his blue bird, aiming her for the horizon.

My stomach started to spasm, heaving uncontrollably. Oh God, I was going to be sick. Hot tears ran down my cheeks

'Robyn.'

I shook Louwtjie's persistent hand off my shoulder.

'We'll be landing in Windhoek in just over an hour. Then it'll be over.'

I imagined being on sturdy, steady, solid ground. Ground that held you, ground that never dipped, sunk, lurched, heaved or fell. Solid, reliable earth. The plane caught a thermal and we rocketed into orbit. I fell forward and gagged.

Louwtjie grabbed one of my hands and placed it on the second control stick in front of me. I glanced feebly at him.

'Take the controls!'

I shook my head. What was he thinking? I couldn't fly.

He sat back and rested his head in his hands, leaving his stick unmanned.

I jolted upright, my eyes wide, my knuckles clenched around the stick. 'Take it. Take the plane. I can't fly.' I sounded deranged.

Louwtjie leant forward and wrapped his hands around mine. Gradually he eased the stick out towards my stomach, and the nose of the plane lifted. Gently he eased it back in and the plane levelled. He tilted the stick to the left and right, the plane dipped. He levelled her. 'There. Now fly.'

Louwtjie leant back and placed a boot on the control panel. The frayed end of his green shoelace taunted the corner of my eye. What was he doing? Was he crazy? I would kill us both.

Our world swayed with every motion of my knuckles.

'Aim for the horizon. Keep her steady.'

'Take her.'

No reply. Every muscle in my body aimed for the shifting horizon ahead of me. Swimming in fear, drowning in air-sickness, I flew us towards that line dividing sky and land. It staggered, swinging right, then left. Always levelling back.

For half an hour I clung to our lifeline, that stick, not trusting the propeller to keep us in the air; expecting the wings to spiral earthward, tearing the sky open with a whine. The terror, the sickness. My stomach heaved against the control stick.

The hills of Windhoek appeared in the distance.

'Bring her lower. Steady . . . that's right . . . level.'

I ripped my eyes from Louwtjie back to the advancing horizon. Take her, *please.*

The plane was heading into the Windhoek mountains, their stark beds folded in monstrous creamy swirls. They sparkled in the setting sun.

Then, as if a ray of light breached a cloud, elation burst through my terror. I was flying, I was really flying. Flying through these stark, beautiful hills.

'Bring her lower.'

My elation drained away. The city was now in sight. The tall buildings in Windhoek and the cars grew rapidly larger.

We are going to die. Take her.

And yet, I wanted to hold on to this feeling of flight. Go down with this bird, riding on her stiff, blue wings.

'A little lower . . . steady. Steady her wings, take her lower, Robyn, a little to the right . . . yes . . . lower.'

Lower. The landing strip at Eros was in sight, straight and narrow, marking our destination. Marking our death. Lower, I could see the runway opening up.

'Right,' Louwtjie's boot slipped out of sight, 'I'll take her from there.' He turned on the radio and called, 'Permission to land.'

Permission to land, crackled back.

The runway rose up, the tyres screeched and the plane eased clumsily onto the runway. Louwtjie taxied to the small airport building. The engine died down.

He grinned at me. 'Best thing I could have done, to make you fly. Kept your mind off your stomach, didn't it? Want me to help you with your bag?' he opened the door and unfolded his long, wiry frame.

I looked down at my hands; they were still clenched around the control stick. I cracked each knuckle loose and climbed out of the door, and sank onto the flat, steady land.

Louwtjie slung my bag and his over his shoulder. 'Best thing I could've done. Besides, I didn't want you to get sick, it takes weeks to get rid of the smell.'

He strode in a lopsided gait towards the airport building. Tripping and skipping behind him, feeling as if my knees would buckle at any moment, I followed him. I had flown over those stark, twisted beds of rock. I had flown. A smile cracked from ear to ear. The sheer miracle of flight had lit a star inside of me. Pinned it to my soul. I would fly so much better in my dreams now.

From the air, Outjo was just another small town safely tucked between dolomite hills. On land Outjo was hot and dry, quiet and dusty. At midday on Saturday, the town had already shut down for the weekend; the only places that would remain open until Monday morning were one of the two fuel stations and a small corner cafe that provided emergency cigarettes and fizzy cooldrinks. The silence hummed behind the consistent click of the fuel pump, the numbers whizzing by. I stood leaning against the Land Cruiser.

The first time I filled up, the attendant was surprised. He checked beneath the vehicle to see if there was a leak – no vehicle took *that* much petrol. Second tank, I explained, and he pushed back his green cap (the only part of the uniform he wore), shook his head and laughed.

Second tank and so much more, this top-of-the-range, navy-blue Toyota Land Cruiser. This Blue Baron. Fitted with a bull bar, roof rack, off-road tyres, winch and an already used high-lift jack. Inside the luxury interior, a roll cage had been fitted – an added TurnStone safety feature. A satellite tracking device had been fitted to mark my position and a cross-country radio kept me in contact with any other Turn-Stone vehicles in the field – currently only Terence's in Botswana – and with the office in Cape Town.

Lawrence had signed a blank cheque and handed it to me. 'Get two field vehicles. The best you can get. Get them fitted with the whole outdoor canoodle. Oh, and . . . buy two. One for you and one for Terence.'

Terence had glanced at me and raised his eyebrows. So there would be some benefits to this job. We had studied our options and selected the Toyotas. Terence chose white, I had wanted navy blue. Of course I loved the vehicle. It sailed through the soft sand like a ship and on tar it was equally steady. I felt self-conscious about its cost though – I knew it alienated me from the local farmers. It was too big, too brutish: a large, snorting rhinoceros which rocked from side to side when I put my foot on its accelerator.

Within weeks of our arrival, Lawrence had requested that we head out into our field areas: Terence into Botswana and I into Namibia.

'Time is of the essence,' Lawrence insisted. 'We need to commit ourselves to the realisation of TurnStone's exploration potential. Focus on our strategy and make our inroad into Africa.'

Lawrence spoke like that. An entirely different language: Corporatese.

'When will Terence and I be able to see each other again?' I asked.

'Well, to begin with, you and Terence need to be out there to get your projects started. Get the show on the road. So it *might* be a while to begin with. . . but in future,' he smiled and adjusted his collar, 'you'll be able to organise your time.'

I had been in Outjo for two weeks. It was just over a month since we had joined TurnStone. Bongi had travelled to Botswana with Terence. We had decided it would be easier. Terence would be staying in an old farmhouse, far from any town, while I would be accommodated in a small lodge on the outskirts of Outjo. They had a room for me, but no dogs were allowed.

Every other day Terence called me over the radio. The conversation was stilted. One of us had to finish speaking before the other could start. Over. Our words travelled the airwaves, audible to whoever cared to tune in.

'Bongi's settled in. The heat is too much for him though, and he stays in the shade of the old veranda. Over,' said Terence.

'Does he climb the trees. Over?'

'No, not really. He's tried. But they're too thorny. Mostly he just runs between them, chasing the birds. Over.'

We described our situations as best we could. But we limited our conversation to news and advising each other on work, saving a few endearments for the end.

Lawrence called twice a week. His conversations were long monologues: there was no danger of cutting him short or repeating the word 'over' too often.

'I've hired a young geophysicist,' he told me. 'Name's Spyder. He's a bit of a lunatic but he's the brightest. I've had him review the geophysical surveys flown over the project areas and select the most promising targets. You'll meet Spyder soon enough, but he'll get back to you with his results before then. Over and out.'

The second tank finally full, the attendant tipped the peak of his cap and I drove off, towards the outskirts of town. Since arriving in Outjo, I had driven the network of dirt tracks, armed with a copy of the Namibia one-in-a-million scale geology map, trying to orientate myself. I still had not driven all the roads and tracks. Over a hundred kilometres long and over sixty kilometres wide, the area was vast; too big for one geologist.

The radio beeped and I pulled over to answer it, pressing the PTT (press to talk) button. 'Vehicle 3033, Robyn here, over.'

'Robyn. Name's Spyder. So you're out there in the middle of no-where. Is it another fucking beautiful day in Africa? Oh yes, we're not meant to swear over the radio. *Hee haw hee haw.* Over,' his laugh sawed through the Cruiser.

'Yes, it's another beautiful day in Africa, Spyder. Over,' I smiled.

'I have ze vays and means to mek you talk, voman. I have all ze an-swers dat you vant. Over.'

'Mmm, Lawrence told me you analysed the air surveys. Over.'

'Yup,' Spyder's voice immediately dropped an octave and sounded serious, 'I've analysed various frequency decays and done a layered earth inversion of the resistivities . . .'

'Er, Spyder, I don't mean to interrupt, but just the results would make more sense to me. Over.'

'Oh . . . all right. I have a list of the four most promising targets here. I'll list them in priority . . .'

I opened my notebook and, while Spyder dictated, took down the coordinates. Spyder used TurnStone's local grid coordinate system, so no one else listening to the radio would be able to make sense of the localities. Then I studied my map and wrote down the following:

1. *Wag 'n Bietjie – landowner, L. Barendse*
2. *Soetwater – A. Kalomo*
3. *Moedhou – E. Nangula*
4. *Soutpan – J. Pretorius*

Over and out, Spyder signed off the airwaves. I studied the list. The first farm, Wag 'n Bietjie (wait a minute) was named after a thorny bush that flourished in overgrazed land. Its tiny thorns hooked into your flesh in such a way that it was only possible to extract your-self by backing out of the *wag-'n-bietjie* bush. The second name, A. Kalomo, had been mentioned to me by Louwtjie. I reached for the Namibian phone directory, which I kept under the passenger seat, and flicked through its yellow pages. Outjo, Barendse. I punched the number into the radio.

Over the radio, the conversation was laboured. Mrs Liddie Barend-se was indeed the owner of Wag 'n Bietjie. She sounded suitably thorny. Only after a long hesitation did she agree to see me and yes, now would be an acceptable time. Her voice had become dry and decisive.

The warm breeze ruffled my short hair as I drove; it felt much better short, so much cooler in the heat. The road, although dirt, was smooth and graded. Twenty minutes later, as Mrs Barendse had instructed, I took the left turn where the road forked and stopped at the first farm gate. The name was marked on a board wired to the gate: *Wag 'n Bietjie.*

I untangled the heavy, unlocked chain and drove through. My neck began to tingle as I secured the last of the chain back around the gatepost. I turned around very carefully, scanning the bush. There – our eyes locked. His were big and brown, framed by long lashes. His horns twisted into a massive crown. Kudu – kudu bull. He stood his ground, unafraid, ears flinching. The left ear was torn, battle-scarred. A twig cracked behind him and the flank of a female kudu passed through a clearing. The bull turned away and followed her. I watched him melt into the bush.

From the gate, the track led in a straight line to a koppie, from where the farmhouse surveyed the land from an advantaged height. I parked at the base of the koppie, outside the six-foot fence. I walked through the open gates, up the steep driveway to the house.

Two figures stood watching me from the stoep. I lifted my hand and waved. The figures remained motionless. I shifted my maps to the other hand and trotted up the stairs. A woman of about sixty stood outside the front door. Beside her was a younger man, presumably her son.

'Mrs Barendse?' I held out my hand.

She fixed me with her grey eyes. She was a good-looking woman, with thick, wavy grey hair combed back from her face. She had defined cheek-bones and her chin was prominent, almost stubborn.

Her eyes softened as she shook my hand. 'This is my youngest son, Ludie.'

Ludie stood a good head and shoulders above his mother. He was lean and wiry, olive-skinned. His brown eyes were opaque, registering no obvious emotion. He stared at my extended hand for a drawn-out moment and then finally shook it. His grasp was loose and dry.

I followed Mrs Barendse through the front door and into the sitting room. I felt as if I had been dragged underwater. Light filtered from the net curtains onto the dusty grey walls. The carpet was a grubby green, the sofas a worn blue. The room was cool; a wooden fan spun from the ceiling. *Flaka flaka flaka.* I was offered the armchair beside a wooden display cabinet, which had the stoic expression of the senior member of the family. Its glass doors revealed stacked teacups, chipped and mismatched. All predictably in shades of blue. A green urn and an ornate wooden box sat on the lowest shelf.

With the announcement of tea, Mrs Barendse retreated into the kitchen. I heard the rattle of an aluminium kettle and the flare of a gas stove being lit. Ludie sat in the centre of the three-seater couch opposite me. He leant back with his arms over the shoulders of the couch and spread his legs wide. He was wearing shorts and canvas army-style boots. The sleeves of his stained T-shirt had been torn off and the sinewy contours of the muscles in his forearms could be seen.

Ludie sucked his teeth as he studied me, producing a sound rather like a mosquito.

'What do you farm here?'

Ludie sucked his teeth again, as if extracting the thought. '*Beeste.*' Cattle.

Mrs Barense entered carrying the tea tray. I stood to give her a hand. She gave a vehement shake of her head and I sat down. Without putting it down, she offered the tray to me and then to Ludie. Her arms began to tremble beneath the weight. Ludie slowly helped himself to four teaspoons of sugar, stirring slowly while he kept his sullen eyes on me.

I unrolled the map onto the coffee table. I pointed out the vast prospecting license belonging to TurnStone. I showed them the boundaries of Wag 'n Bietjie in the centre of the map. The tiny block constituted only about a hundredth of TurnStone's total license area. I explained how their farm had been selected from the aerial survey; that the areas of interest detected on their farm had the slim chance of being copper deposits. Finally, I requested permission to drill a borehole on their land.

'What if you find something?' asked Mrs Barendse.

'You must remember that only one in every hundred prospecting projects ever finds anything good enough to mine,' I replied carefully

'But what if you *do* find something good enough?' she repeated.

'Well, I suppose TurnStone would offer to buy your farm. You'd get legal advice and you could ask a good price . . .' I drifted off, worried I had alarmed them.

'You can buy the farm,' said Mrs Barendse.

'*Oor my dooie liggaam.*' Over my dead body. Ludie fell back into the couch.

I shifted a land access contract closer to them. 'This contract explains that you own the surface rights of the farm and the state owns the mineral rights, but that you give permission to TurnStone to access your property in order to prospect.'

The contract lay between us, looking too white, too bright. Too contractual, too city, just like the Cruiser I had parked outside.

Silence.

'Who will you be visiting next?'

I looked at my list, 'A. Kalomo on Soetwater.'

'Ah, Abel,' Mrs Barendse nodded.

Ludie sucked his teeth, *squeak.* I glanced at the contract. *Flaka flaka flaka*, the fan waved overhead. No contract was about to be signed then. They would need time to think it over. I rose to leave.

Mrs Barendse rose quickly to her feet. 'No, don't go. Stay and talk to Ludie. He does not get the chance to speak to many young people and . . . not girls.' Cooling from a blush, she shot a glance at her son. 'Ludie, tell Robyn about your holiday.'

She retreated back into the kitchen. I sat down dutifully. Ludie picked his teeth with the nail of his little finger.

'Where did you go?'

'Orange River,' he replied, staring at the carpet.

I frowned. If I was boring him, I should leave. He stood up suddenly and walked over to the cabinet beside me. He withdrew the wooden box from the lower shelf and placed it on the coffee table between us. He opened it.

Ludie held a fistful of yellowed newspaper clippings, which he arranged carefully on the table. He sat forward, leaning his sinewy arms on his knees.

'*Blacks have less cognitive reasoning,*' he read, and then explained: 'They have smaller brains.'

I snorted in disbelief.

Ludie selected another clipping, sucking his teeth. '*Education standards drop with introduction of black pupils.*' He looked up at me. 'Kaffirs can't think for themselves. And Africa is filthy: *Aids Epidemic in Africa.*' He held the last clipping in his hand as his mother entered carrying a tray with two glasses of water. She slid them onto the coffee table and retreated into the kitchen.

'Where *did* you get those?'

'Newspapers. I have been collecting them for years. I keep them in this box.'

'I should go.' I stood up.

'I've been thinking . . .'

I looked at Ludie. From the kitchen behind us I could hear something thick bubbling on the stove, *gloob gloob*. The sweet smell of peaches filled the room.

'About this Aids. So many black people are going to die and there is no room in Namibia to bury them all. So I've been thinking. *Squeak,*' Ludie leant back in the couch. 'We must bury them all standing upright.'

Gloob gloob, the smell of peaches was overpowering. *Flaka flaka.*

'There'll be more room to bury all of them if we bury them standing upright,' clarified Ludie, concerned that I had missed the point, 'you know, like a six-pack.'

'Uh-huh,' I picked up my map roll. I left the access agreement on the table.

Mrs Barendse intercepted me at the door and pushed a jar into my hands. 'Peach jam. Take it. I make it myself.' She wiped her hands on her apron.

'Thank you.' The jar was still warm.

'Ludie,' she called, 'did you say goodbye to Robyn?'

'*Ja*, Ma,' he sounded irritated.

She smiled and shrugged as if to say *what can you do?*

'I'm going to see Abel Kalomo tomorrow. He's the second landown-er I need to talk to. I've also heard he's a good person to meet because he knows the area so well.'

Mrs Barendse nodded. 'Abel, his farm is not far. Half an hour's drive in the other direction from Outjo.'

'Do you know him?'

'We all know him. Abel by name and able by nature, is what they say.'

'So I've heard. I'll call you, and . . .' I lifted the jar, 'thanks for the jam.'

Time was of the essence, as Lawrence kept emphasising, and now that I had my list of priority targets, I was to waste none of this essence. Early the next morning I headed out to visit my second landowner, Abel Kalomo. His farm, Soetwater, was forty kilometres west of Out-jo, where the thorny bush suddenly merged into rows of citrus trees. The trees were heavy with oranges; the sticky-sweet smell saturated the air. The name of the farm hung on a wooden signpost beside a road stall which looked as if it was going to collapse beneath the weight of oranges. I slowed down and turned onto the farm track, which twisted through the orange plantation. I hadn't got far when I saw a white bakkie at the end of a row. I parked and walked towards it.

Standing at the back of the bakkie in a mounting tide of oranges was an enormous man. His workers continued to unload baskets of oranges at his feet. Oranges thundered out of their baskets. He dabbed his forehead with a hanky, looked up and saw me.

'Robyn, you phoned,' he bellowed, and using an arm to balance himself, sprung out of the bakkie and landed smoothly on his feet. Nimble for such a heavy man. He pulled in his large stomach and tucked in the tails of his shirt as he strode up to me. His flesh was dark and smooth, carved from teak.

He pumped my hand. 'Abel Kalomo.'

My hand looked small and pale engulfed in his, a fragile new shoot growing from bark.

'My hands are filthy,' I said, slipping my hand out of his grip.

'Nonsense.' He grabbed back my hand and pumped it as if it was a windmill he was trying to start. 'People like you and me, we get dirty.' His face split into a grin. He was as bald and dark as the southern hemisphere at night. Two sharp eyes, two stars.

'First, welcome to Namibia.'

I smiled, taken aback. I never thought of myself as a foreigner to Namibia – not like, say, Lawrence. I loved this country. But I was a stranger on Abel Kalomo's land, he was reminding me; and yet, he was making me welcome.

Abel shouted back at his farmworkers. One tossed him a large orange. He caught it in one hand, and dug his pink nails into the fruit. He peeled it in three swift motions, revealing its soft white down, and handed me half. I bit into the segments; juice ran down my chin. I wiped it with the back of my hand, which now smelt of cow-shit and orange.

'Good.'

Abel laughed, a deep laugh which rumbled from the base of his formidable stomach. Like distant thunder with the promise of rain.

'Good, yes. Bigger and sweeter than last year. Who's that?'

I looked behind me and saw a rusted red bakkie parking behind my Cruiser. Mrs Barendse stepped out.

'Liddie,' Abel yelled and motioned her towards us, saying more quietly to me, 'Now I wonder what brings Mrs Liddie Barendse to visit old Abel.' He winked, flashing one of his stars.

Mrs Barendse was holding the contract I had given her the day before. She nodded at both of us. 'I'd like to hear what Abel has to say about this land access agreement. He has experience in such matters.'

Abel ignored her envelope. 'Liddie, how's your boy?'

Liddie gave a deep sigh and shook her head, 'Sick some days and on other days he's fine and working on the farm. We don't know what's wrong, the doctors have taken so many blood tests.'

'But, what can you do? Keep trying. What else can you do?' Abel reached out and squeezed her shoulder.

Mrs Barendse coughed. 'We should get on with this, shouldn't we? I have a lot of work waiting for me back at the farm.'

'There's always too much work on a farm. Let us go to the house then,' Abel gestured the direction with his hand.

Mrs Barendse and I followed Abel through the rows of orange trees. I noticed a coolness had settled in the air and looked up to see that a few clouds had drifted over the sun. Their borders were wrapped in orange rind.

'What is TurnStone looking for?' Abel asked me as we walked.

'Copper.'

'Copper,' he repeated, entering a clearing.

Abel's farmhouse was enclosed by orange trees on one side and lemon trees on the other. Their citrus scents blended. We trotted up the stairs onto his stoep and sat down on a collection of odd chairs surrounding a shaky wooden table

'Now let's see this Land Access Agreement you spoke about over the radio, Robyn.'

I handed him his copy. Abel slipped a pair of spectacles out of his breast pocket and put the fragile apparatus on. The glass was missing from the left eye. I pointed it out to him.

He leant back, his belly shaking with laughter, 'No, no, Robyn. That's my good eye. That eye doesn't need help, only this one.'

Abel read the document. His expression was now earnest, even frightening. When he'd finished, he rose and went into the house. He returned with a file, which he paged through.

Suddenly he jabbed a large forefinger onto a page. '*This* is a copy of the agreement used by a previous company who worked on my land. Yours is similar, I'd say it's fair. At any rate, Liddie, you and me, we can't do much to keep them off our land. The state owns the mineral rights and we only own the surface rights.'

Mrs Barendse nodded and looked at me. 'Where do I sign?'

I pointed to the line, pleased. My first access granted. She ripped a small, neat signature across the line and handed the contract back to me. *L. Barendse.*

Liddie stood up and gave Abel a nod. 'Thank you, Mr Kalomo, I must go now. There's work waiting for me on the farm. And today Ludie is in bed.'

Abel rose, almost knocking the fragile table over in the process. 'Then you must go, Liddie.'

We watched her neat, slim figure disappear between the orange trees.

Abel smiled, 'That woman; hot, cold, hot, cold,' he sighed. 'But that boy of hers, he needs help.'

'Ludie?'

Abel nodded, 'Strange brew of beer that boy. Killing himself from the inside out, if you ask me. But then you didn't,' he smacked his hands on the table, 'and it's time for me to go back to my men. Let me sign this copy for you.'

Abel's signature was large and round-looped. I tucked my second signed agreement under my arm.

'You call me, Robyn, if you want any advice about the area or the people.'

I nodded, thanking him. 'Yes, a pilot, Louwtjie Boshard, mentioned that you would be the person to speak to.'

Abel frowned and, as if a cloud had blocked out the sun. His face looked fearsome. 'You know Louwtjie?'

I explained he had been the pilot to fly over the project areas.

Abel shook his head as I spoke. 'Louwtjie, now we go back a *long* time,' he patted me on the shoulder. 'I must get back to my men now. You can find your way back?'

After Abel had left I ambled through the orange trees and back to my Cruiser. I drove back with my windows open. I was almost back in Outjo before the last of the sweet smell of oranges had blown away.

Just as the town's water tower came into sight, the radio crackled.

'This is 3033, Robyn speaking. Over.'

'Robyn, Lawrence here. I'm calling to clarify your progress, over.'

'I've just received permission to work on two of the farms. Over,' I replied, pleased.

'And what about the others?'

I hesitated. 'I'm still working on them. I haven't had time to get hold of the other farmers yet.'

'Robyn, time is of the essence. The manager of TurnStone's Australian division, Kirkby Jones, will be arriving in Africa next month and I expect to show him the core from your first borehole by then. In the meantime, I'm sending a senior geologist out there to assist you. An excellent geologist, he has extensive international experience and will be a benefit to us all. He'll stay for a month in Outjo and then travel over to Terence's project. Over.'

'Another geologist? Over'

'Yes, Antonio Conté, he'll be arriving next week. I need someone out there I know and trust. Well then, keep at it. Over and out.'

'Over and out,' I replied into empty airwaves. Lawrence had already ended the call. I frowned, what *did* he mean 'someone he could trust'? And when would I be seeing Terence again?

CHAPTER TEN

Inertia of a Windmill

Antonio looked up at the young Damara waitress. 'Aah, thank you, a *continental* breakfast. So much better than the English, which is so heavy on the stomach.' He patted the ever-so-slight bulge above his belt.

The waitress, a beautiful girl not yet twenty, tilted her head and laughed. She exited the room glancing over her shoulder.

'You seem to have won *her* over quickly.'

'Don't worry, you know that the dogs that bark, they don't bite.'

Antonio had a strong Italian accent, his words lilted up at their tail. *Don't-a worry.*

He winked, 'My wife, she knows that too . . . and so do my three daughters.'

Perhaps worried he had become too familiar too soon, he blushed. His face turned a rosy pink, the colour of the scar that ran up his left cheek to his ear. He self-consciously pulled a small knife from his pocket and peeled his apple.

Antonio had a pleasant face, despite the scar, which only seemed to add a foreign glamour to him. His dark hair was greying above his temples and combed neatly back from his face. It was his voice, I decided, that made him handsome. It rolled off his tongue like honey. The type of voice women like, the type that makes you feel like its sole confidante: a trusting tone, a disarming sincerity.

Antonio lifted the knife up to show me its blue stone handle and said, one geologist to another, 'Lapis lazuli. Much admired stone from

Chile. My father comes from Chile, he gave me this knife when I was a boy. My mother is Italian. The first six years of my life we lived in Chile and then we moved to my mother's country.' He peeled his apple in one long twist. 'It has been a long time since I worked in the field. I've been assisting in diplomatic relations for mining companies all over Africa for the last couple of years, using my language skills. I am,' he tucked away the knife, 'very happy to be back in the field.'

It was two months since Terence and I joined TurnStone. Of those two months, I had spent six weeks in Outjo. Antonio had turned up late the previous night, and had waited until breakfast to introduced himself. I had been sitting in the corner of the lodge restaurant, away from the other couple of guests, sipping my second cup of coffee. Through the window in front of me I could see spectacular plains of shrubby bush – not a sign of a house, a windmill or a human being. Smelling the unfamiliar scent of woody aftershave, I had looked up to see a stranger standing beside me. Middle-aged, wearing neatly pressed trousers and a checked blue-and-white shirt, and holding a large cotton hat, the type cricket players wear.

Antonio finished his breakfast in a leisurely manner and then excused himself to wash his hands and collect his maps. I waited in the Land Cruiser for him. Ten minutes later, just as I was starting to glance impatiently up at the rooms, he appeared looking fresh and organised. A map was folded up under his arm.

He smiled at me through the window. 'If there is one thing Italians love,' – he pronounced it *lorve* – 'it is to drive.'

'Would you like to drive?' I offered the steering wheel.

'If you don't mind. Do you mind?'

'Not at all,' I replied, unsure whether I did. It was *my* Blue Baron after all. I slid over to make room for Antonio.

He started the engine. 'Oh man, listen to this baby.'

'I know.'

I opened my window as we drove off. The day's warmth was beginning to replace the morning freshness. Antonio closed it from the driver's panel and turned on the air conditioner. Unpleasant, icy air blasted me.

'Do you mind? I don't like the dust,' he smiled at me.

'Dust?'

'At my age, I like a little comfort. These grey hairs, I earned them.' He turned up the air conditioner. 'I like it nice and cool . . . aaah. Unless, of course, you want the window open. Do you want the window open?'

'No, I'm fine,' I said, and turned the air vent away from me. I loved the dry, warm air. The dust smelt like freedom; the heat baked a calm serenity onto the vast landscape.

Antonio drove through the small town and stopped when he came to the crossroads. 'Where are we going?'

'A farm called Wag 'n Bietjie. Only one borehole on this project has been drilled so far and that's on Wag 'n Bietjie. The drill's moved to the second farm, belonging to Abel Kalomo, called Soetwater. They've just started the borehole there, and – '

'And what have you found?' Antonio quickly interrupted.

'Not much, I'm afraid. Nothing, in fact; not a sign of copper. The borehole on Wag 'n Bietjie hit dolomite for the first fifteen metres, but from then on the entire borehole, all hundred and thirty metres of it, intersected graphite. I must speak to the farmer, Mrs Barendse. Explain the results and pay her the compensation for the borehole.'

'The graphite is just as conductive as copper. Copper, graphite, groundwater, they would all cause an identical signal in the airborne survey. I don't trust this geophysics, this new-fangled technology.' Antonio sounded heated.

'Spyder pretty much agrees. The graphite could cause the anomalies.'

We drove in silence for a while.

'This er . . . Mrs Barendse – is she nice?'

'She is. I've met her youngest son. He, well . . . you'll meet him. I haven't met the older son.'

Once on the open dirt road, Antonio pressed his foot on the accelerator, and the speedometer rapidly rose to over a hundred kilometres an hour. I shifted uncomfortably in my seat. The road was good, flat and graded, but one still had to be careful. All the locals knew that. A sudden twist in the road was all it took to roll a vehicle. The only rolled vehicles towed through town, and regularly at that, were rented by tourists.

'I think you should slow down.'

Antonio looked at me with surprise and a little annoyance. The needle dropped a fraction.

'The farm gate is up ahead,' I warned him, 'you can start to slow down. Yes, that was it. You've driven *past* it now.'

Antonio came to a stop, turned the Cruiser around and drove back to the gate. I opened it, closed it behind him and climbed back in the vehicle. We drove the straight, undulating track to the farmhouse, and then Antonio began to turn up the steep driveway.

'No, park *here*,' I insisted. 'Park outside their fence, *here* under this tree.'

Antonio stopped the Cruiser and looked at me. His eyes caught the light. He was clearly enjoying himself.

A young man stood at the top of the driveway leaning against a battered red bakkie. A rifle was slung over his shoulder. He looked identical to Ludie – long, thin and olive-skinned – except for two things: he had a narrow strip of black moustache above his upper lip and his stance was cocky, whereas Ludie's was hangdog. He thrust out one hip. His smile looked as if it could slip off his face.

'Morning,' I said as we reached him, 'I've come to see your mother. I phoned this morning.'

Ludie's brother's eyes slid down my body and his smile broadened. He chucked his head in the direction of the house.

'Let's go,' I said to Antonio.

Antonio, however, stood transfixed, staring at the back of the bakkie. I followed his gaze and swallowed. A tiny black hand clutched at the sky. Frozen. It was hairy. Baboon.

'Let's go,' I said more softly, touching Antonio's arm.

Mrs Barendse stood waiting for us at the front door. At the sight of her, Antonio brightened. She was wearing a yellow cotton dress and a touch of lipstick. Antonio bowed slightly as he took her hand. She whisked a glance at me. I shrugged.

She gestured to her lanky son who had followed us up the stairs. 'Have you met my eldest son, Tobie?'

'Not introduced.'

Tobie squeezed my hand gently and his eyes hung on my lips. I wiped my mouth as I followed his mother into their sitting room.

Ludie was sitting on the three-seater couch. His face was the colour of sour cream and his lips had a bluish tinge. He rolled his head to us.

'Ludie, have you said hello to Robyn?' his mother's voice held a hint of reproach.

'Shuddup Ma,' Ludie mumbled.

Tobie sat down next to his brother. Ludie, the paler version of Tobie. Antonio and I sat facing them across the coffee table. Mrs Barendse excused herself and retreated into the kitchen. Tobie and Ludie stared at Antonio, Ludie's mouth hanging slightly ajar. Who was this stranger? This *uitlander*, foreigner, with the accent? Who was this neat, too-clean, too-groomed man?

'You've been hunting,' I said to Tobie, trying to break the awkward silence.

Tobie's smile slid back on his face. 'Just baboons.'

'Why?' I asked, allowing distaste to slip into my voice.

'They are *nuuskierig*. Inquisitive. They mess with the water pipes, so we shoot them.' Tobie's thin moustache flattened above his grin.

Ludie's eyes shifted onto me. 'They are easy to shoot this time of the year, when there is little rain. We fill the water tank with just a little water, just enough to cover the bottom. The troop of baboons climb down into the tank to drink it. But they can't climb out. That's when we stand on the wall and shoot them. *Bam bam, bam bam.*' He lifted a weak arm to fire an imaginary round of bullets.

'And the dead one in your pick-up?' Antonio asked with alarm.

'We're going to stuff it with poison and lay it out for the leopards to find,' replied Tobie. 'We've killed seven leopards on this farm already. My father and me, seven. They're clever, they're not easy to kill. You have to lay out poison for them. Lay it out with the lambs so when they come down the mountains to rip the milky stomachs out of the lambs, they eat the baboon. Then they die.'

The brothers were smiling. I glanced at the stoic cabinet beside me, as if this senior member of the family should step in and take some control of the conversation. The cabinet and its green urn remained silent. Antonio and I looked up with relief as Mrs Barendse entered the room carrying a tray. She served me and then Antonio.

'What are these?' he asked.

'*Beskuit* – rusks, home-made.'

Antonio took a bite. 'This is good, very good.'

Trying not to, Mrs Barendse looked pleased.

'I've brought the compensation for the borehole TurnStone drilled,' I said, sliding an envelope onto the table.

'Did they find anything interesting?' asked Mrs Barendse.

I shook my head. 'Not yet. TurnStone may decide to continue with prospecting on Wag 'n Bietjie, but so far the results don't look that good.'

'I went to the see the drill and looked at the rock they drilled. It was all black. I wiped my hand over it.' Ludie lifted a hand as if the evidence of the black graphite was still there.

'Graphite, just like the lead of a pencil,' explained Antonio, accepting another rusk from Mrs Barendse.

'Well, if you need to continue prospecting you have my permission.'

Both sons glared at their mother.

'*As Pa jou nou kon sien,*' said Tobie. If Dad could see you now.

She waved him away. 'This is still *my* farm and they need *my* permission. Not yours. *Jou Pa is lankal weg.* Your father is long gone.'

'To you maybe.' Tobie's tone was bitter.

'Tobie, you are never here, always in the city with your girls. And Ludie is sick most of the time. How can I cope with the farm on my own?'

'If you sell, you'll regret it.'

'Will I?' She lifted a sardonic eye at Tobie.

'We'd better get going.' I rose, keen to remove myself and Antonio from any domestic argument. I faced the brothers. 'We've only been prospecting on your land, we don't want to buy the farm.'

'That's what you say.' Tobie placed his hands on his worn shorts, as if resting them on holsters. He had the same sharp chin as his mother.

'Stay and talk to Ludie,' Mrs Barendse asked me.

'I'm sorry. Today we are really busy. Perhaps another time.'

Her face fell. 'I'll walk you down.'

Mrs Barendse walked between Antonio and myself. I kept my eyes averted from the dead baboon as we walked past the red bakkie.

'Ludie is sick,' I said to Mrs Barendse.

'Yes,' she wrapped her arms around her body, 'He is going for more blood tests today. I'm driving him through to the Windhoek hospital.'

'What is wrong?' asked Antonio.

'We don't know. Every time doctors say his blood is thin and they give him a blood transfusion. He gets better for a while and then he gets sick. We still don't know.'

We stood at the navy Cruiser. I shook Mrs Barendse's hand. 'I hope Ludie gets better soon. Thank you once again for your permission to work on Wag 'n Bietjie.'

'His father,' she cleared her throat, '*Their* father died of leukaemia three years ago. We discovered it when it was too late and there was not much we could do.' She kneaded her hands together as if to get the circulation going. 'He was a hard man, my husband. Tobie was his boy but he never had much time for Ludie. I've been running this farm ever since he died.'

For the first time, her face showed signs of strain.

'What is this from?' She pointed to Antonio's cheek.

He touched his face self-consciously. 'Oh, it was a long time ago. I was a boy, in Chile. Difficult times; my father and I were just in the wrong place at the wrong time.'

She nodded. 'These things happen.'

'They do.' Antonio gently shook her hand. 'Thank you for the *beskuit*, Mrs Barendse,' he said, pronouncing the word carefully.

'Liddie,' she corrected, and smiled suddenly.

'Liddie,' Antonio repeated as I drove off Wag 'n Bietjie. 'A pretty name. She has nice eyes, don't you think?'

I rolled my eyes and laughed.

'What?' he looked at me innocently.

'You are *such* a flirt.'

He laughed. 'As I said, the dogs that bark . . . such a lovely lady with such . . . sons. I don't think she would mind *you* as a daughter-in-law.' He shot me a teasing glance.

'Lucky me.'

'That baboon. Terrible. What are they thinking?'

I shuddered. 'I don't know, I can't believe those brothers.' I braked suddenly. 'Look!'

Antonio lurched forward and looked at me, thoroughly annoyed. He threw up his hands. 'What?'

'Look, there, in the bush. In front of us.'

'Aah.' Antonio fumbled in his neatly ironed breast pocket. He removed a pair of delicate spectacles and slipped them over his strong, continental nose. They hung on a silver chain. 'Aah, beautiful. Kudu.'

The Kudu bull watched us beneath its immense crown of horns. His ears twitched, the left one nicked. Gingerly he stepped out and froze in the centre of the track. His hide rippled and his long white beard shivered like mist. Behind us, tyres ripped up the track and skidded to a halt. With a muscular jolt, the kudu disappeared into the bush, leaving only stirrings of dust.

Tobie's red bakkie drew level below the Cruiser. A rifle lay across his lap. The dead baboon bounced in the back, its one hand reaching for eternity.

'You seen any kudu? I saw one heading this way,' Tobie shouted from his window.

'No,' Antonio and I replied. Our voices overlapped emphatically.

Tobie sliced his vehicle back through the dust and swung around. He tore off in the opposite direction.

Antonio slipped the spectacles off his nose. 'These are my wife's. I lost mine and have not got around to replacing them. But it's strange. As they are not mine, I don't see so well through them. What was that we saw?' He chuckled softly.

Antonio and I drove to Soetwater. The drill crew had completed the borehole and recently cleared the site. All that remained were the last six boxes of core, which Antonio and I were to load up and take back to our shed. Antonio had been in Outjo for two weeks, in which time we had easily fallen into a routine together. There were a few changes to how it had been when I worked alone: we left later in the morning, we drove with the air conditioner on and our maps were always neatly stacked on the back seat, rather than in the disorganised jumble I was accustomed to.

We drove the familiar winding track through the bush on Abel's farm. As we neared the old drill site, we saw a Land Cruiser parked in the area where the drill had been. Battleship grey, but otherwise identical to ours.

'Who's this?' I asked slowly as Antonio parked beside the vehicle.

Two men were bent over the core trays, inspecting their contents. One straightened up. Lawrence. He dusted off his pants and leant against the grey Cruiser, smiling. Waiting for us to walk to him.

'Antonio, Robyn, good to finally be in the field with you. See some of the drill core. We thought we'd find our own way here – practise some of those rusty map-reading skills.' He pushed himself off the bonnet and shook Antonio's hand, and then, as an afterthought, mine.

Lawrence was wearing neat cotton trousers and a blue office shirt, minus the tie. His sleeves were rolled to the elbows, his top button undone. The shoes he wore, casual brogues, were hardly suitable for the rough field conditions of Namibia.

'We?' I asked Lawrence.

Lawrence opened his hand graciously as the other figure stood up. 'Kirkby and I. This is Kirkby Jones, who manages TurnStone in Australia. Based in Perth.'

Kirkby kept a few paces back, staring at us through two thick, square pieces of glass. His face was round, sunburnt, with a neat brown beard. The corners of his mouth were turned down, his coarse nose a little elevated. He wore a wide-brimmed khaki bush hat and a hunting waistcoat, which had dozens of tiny pockets. His legs were hairy and burnt brown.

He grabbed the sides of his waistcoat and pulled his chin in. 'Antonio.'

'Kirkby.' Antonio did not step forward.

'Robyn Hartley,' I introduced myself and held out my hand. Kirkby looked at it for a second and then shook it.

'You have, ah, come to see the core?' asked Antonio.

'That's right, Antonio. We'd like to be the first to see if there is anything promising on the ground. Our shareholders have a right to be notified immediately in such cases,' replied Lawrence.

Antonio glanced at me and back at Lawrence. 'Both boreholes have only intersected graphite, as we explained over the radio. We have explained the geophysical anomalies. There was no evidence of copper in either of them.'

'Well, we'd like to make sure of that, mate,' Kirkby told Antonio, and then looked at me. 'We'd like to inspect the core ourselves.' He had a strong Australian accent.

'Yes, well,' Lawrence intervened with his plummy vowels, 'actually we've just got here. Let's take a look at the core together, shall we?'

The four of us walked over to the core boxes. Lawrence bent down and broke a piece of core off and studied it under his hand-lens.

'You see?' Antonio was getting frustrated. 'Just graphite. There is not a sign of copper.'

I backed him up: 'There are some sulphides concentrated along some of the fractures, but that is all pyrite.'

Lawrence stood up. 'The entire borehole like this?' He wiped his hand over his mouth, worried.

'All two hundred metres of it, just like the borehole drilled at Wag 'n Bietjie.'

Lawrence turned to Kirkby. The two men stared at each other.

'Robyn,' Lawrence spun around, 'have this core sent to Committed Labs for analysis. Take samples at three-metre intervals. Both this borehole and the previous one. Antonio, show Robyn the standard TurnStone sampling procedure. I would appreciate it if you get it done as soon as possible.'

Antonio looked flustered. 'But, but we would see the copper. There is nothing . . .'

'It's probably just too finely disseminated to see with the naked eye, Antonio. Either that or it could be a black copper-bearing sulphide like chalcocite. You would not be able to tell that apart from the graphite,' said Lawrence.

'That's right, Antonio mate, there could be chalcocite.' Kirkby did not blink.

Lawrence twisted his platinum watch on his elegant wrist. 'Well, look at the time. Kirkby, we should get going if we want to cross the Botswana border before dark. Antonio, as I said, please ensure those samples get sent soon. It's vital we know their copper content before we have the annual TurnStone board meeting next month.' Kirkby and Lawrence climbed into the Cruiser.

'Are you going to Terence's project now?' I asked Lawrence through his open window.

'That's right. We'd like to see the core he's drilled on his project.'

'I've been out here a while, Lawrence. I need a break to go home. At least to see Terence.'

Lawrence scratched the side of his nose. 'Robyn, I did warn you starting up the projects was going to be a busy time. Things should slow down once we know the direction in which we are heading. In future you and Terence must learn to organise your time. Learn to coordinate your projects more effectively.' He started up the engine and the grey Cruiser pulled off.

Antonio and I watched them depart. I was angry. I tried not to dwell on Terence, but the mention of his name had made my chest painfully constrict.

'Pah,' Antonio threw up his hands, 'it cannot be too finely disseminated to see with the naked eye! For this to be a copper deposit, the core needs to contain two or three percent copper. At *least* one percent. Let me tell you this, Robyn, we would see that. Perhaps there is chalcocite present? I don't know about that either. There is very little chalcocite in this area. It only occurs in specific environments. It is possible, there is a fraction of a chance, but I think it is highly unlikely. I would expect Lawrence to know better. That man, Kirkby, he is an idiot. What would he know? But Lawrence should know better. He has seen core from the best copper mines all over the world. Chile, Australia.'

'What the hell did he mean, organise my time?' I asked Antonio, as we loaded the boxes of core into the back of the Cruiser.

'Chalcocite in this area? Is it possible?' Antonio strapped down the boxes.

'How the hell can I *organise* my time?' I climbed in and slammed the door.

Antonio shrugged as I started the engine, swung the Cruiser back onto the track and drove to Abel Kalomo's house.

Abel was not home. Antonio and I agreed to try the farmhouse again the next morning. We drove back to our small lodge to shower and eat dinner. After dinner, I excused myself and went to sit in the Land Cruiser. Antonio was in the lodge kitchen instructing the Damara staff on the finer points of Italian cooking. 'More olive oil. You must always add olive oil. And garlic,' was the last thing I heard him telling them. Someone laughed. The scene sounded jovial but I wanted to speak to Terence. The evening was the best time to call, when voices were somehow clearer and the radios dialled through more easily.

The radio beeped at the agreed time. Eight-thirty.

'Radio 3033. Robyn here. Over.'

'Hi.' Terence. 'How are things going? Over.'

'Okay. Missing you. Lawrence and a manager from Perth were out here today. They were heading for your project. Have they arrived there? Over.'

'Not yet. Thanks for the warning. You sound down. Over.'

'Not really,' I lied. 'It's just good to hear your voice. Over.'

'Mmm, let me tell you about some of the farmers I've been meeting then. There are fewer here, the farms are vast, most of them use planes to get to the closest town. I met one farmer today; he was sitting under a tree with his shirt open and the scars of a recent triple-bypass operation showing. He had an oxygen tank next to him and wore these hospital stockings with flip-flops. He seemed very proud to tell me he'd just come out of jail for shooting a farm worker.'

'Wow. He sounds . . . unbelievable. Over.'

'They're not all like that. The farmer who's renting me this house is a nice guy. A tough nut really. He was extremely difficult to begin with, but now that we've got to know each other, it's easier. He's invited me to join him and his wife for lunch. She's a doctor with a pilot's license. Actually, each member of the family has a pilot's license. They use the family plane to get from farm to farm, and to do their monthly shopping in Maun. Last week they gave me a lift to Maun. Bongi went too. Over.'

'Bongi? In the plane? Over. '

'Of course, their dog goes too. They told me to bring Bongi. They said the dogs enjoy the view. And he did. Over.'

200

I laughed. 'The most well-travelled dog.'

The radio fuzzed, crackled. Our connection was broken. I tried to call back but there was no reply. We would try again in a couple of days' time, at the agreed time. Eight-thirty.

Antonio had retreated to his room. I did the same, climbing into bed with a technical paper titled, '*Isotopic dating of low-grade metamorphic events in northern Namiba: Implications for the orogenic evolution of the Pan-African Damara Belt.*'

I quickly fell asleep.

The following morning, after Antonio had had his continental breakfast ('something light on the stomach. Not this Anglo-Saxon bacon and eggs. So heavy!') and I had finished my second cup of coffee (I never ate breakfast), we drove back to Soetwater.

Abel was waiting for us on his stoep. 'Antonio, Robyn!' he bellowed, then trotted down his stairs and popped his big, bald head into my window. 'Antonio,' he grinned.

'Mister Abel.' Antonio gave a gracious mock-bow of his head.

Abel's head sunk, shaking from laughing. 'This man from Italy, Robyn.' He grabbed my shoulder. 'I'll lead the way, okay? I'll take you to Mrs Nangula's farm, you will not find Moedhou otherwise. There are no real roads or road signs. Do you know what Moedhou means Antonio? It means hang in there, never give up.'

Abel's white bakkie drove back onto the Khorixas-Outjo tar road and then suddenly veered off onto the hard, white calcrete, following no obvious path. I swerved after him, trying to keep up. We drove for a while through an erosional donga. When it narrowed, Abel veered up the side, weaving between trees and shrubs. About an hour later he stopped beside a broken gate. I pulled up beside him. There was only a gate, no fence attached to it, and the only tracks leading through it were wild and skinny. Donkey carts. A lid from a twenty-litre paint drum was wired to the gate. *Moedhou*, it read in pink letters.

Moedhou, hang in there. I could see why. The land differed from Mrs Barendse and Abel's farms. The trees were taller, but the bush was thinner. There was no grass and the ground was hard and white, capped in calcrete. The farmhouse was situated close to the gate, just a drive over a bump and a dip, on a piece of barren ground. A couple of trees sprinkled sparse shade over it, and a windmill stood about a hundred metres away. The house, which was small and uneven, was painted bright pink.

A tiny old woman stood outside the house. She was carrying a large round rock, which she placed at her feet when she saw us. She waited for us, immobile. She wore a traditional Herero dress made of blue silk, which shimmered in the blinding light. Influenced by Victorian fashion, the dress was floor-length, with a pinched bodice, puffed sleeves and an enormous matching bow-shaped hat.

We parked under the scarce shade of a tree and walked to her. I slipped my sunglasses off, resisting the urge to protect my eyes from the harsh light – I did not want to appear anonymous. The silence hummed. Deafening, quiet silence, heavy and hot. Not even the windmill creaked. But then, there was no wind to move it. Abel lifted the sagging garden gate – another gate with no fence attached to it – and held it open as Antonio and I walked through. We stepped through a random pattern of stones to get to the old woman. The boulders were smooth and round – river boulders. How many thousands of years ago did enough water flow through Moedhou to round these boulders?

The old woman squinted at Abel. 'Abel, I thought I heard a car, but then I thought it must be the wind. Often I think I hear a car, but it is always the wind.'

'This is *Mevrou* Nangula,' Abel told us.

I shook her hand. It was as frail and dry as a leaf skeleton. Her face was lined by deep gullies, her skin as dark as Abel's. Her eyes narrowed as she stared at me – *what is it you want?* She turned to Antonio, who took off his sunglasses – the type that made him look like a Mafioso – and bowed slightly.

'Antonio Conté.'

Mrs Nangula slit her eyes. '*Uitlander.*' Foreigner. 'Abel,' she turned to him, her thick layers of skirt swishing in the white dust.

'Mama Nangula.'

'Abel, the windmill is broken again. We have no water. Lucky is trying to fix it.'

Abel shook his head and marched off in the direction of the windmill.

Mrs Nangula lifted her skirt as we climbed the three steps into her house, revealing her tough bare soles. Inside, the house was dark. My eyes adjusted slowly as I stood in the doorway, and I made out a small window divided into four panes. I could smell stew cooking. A faint sound of a crackling radio babbled from another room, in a language I could not understand, probably Damara or Herero.

'Sit down,' commanded Mrs Nangula; the crack of leather on the worn shoulder of a donkey. Antonio and I moved in the direction she pointed. I could now see three floral sofas circling a small coffee table; small chairs for a small woman. Antonio and I sat down. The coffee table stood on a worn animal skin. Cheetah. I traced a finger down the black tear-streaks draining from the empty sockets. No other animal is faster . . . but not fast enough to escape man.

Mrs Nangula disappeared through another doorway. I looked at Antonio while we waited for her. He looked perfectly at home in Mrs Nangula's floral chair. A smile hinted at the corner of his mouth, beside his scar. His hat rested on his knee, his toe tapping to a tune playing in his head. He stood up to help Mrs Nangula as she reappeared with a tray carrying three large tins.

7-Up, thirty-three percent free, flashed the cans. Mrs Nangula placed the tray on the table, bypassing Antonio's hands, and sat in the sofa between Antonio and myself. I cracked open my tin and drained half the fluid – finding Moedhou had been thirsty work. Her blue dress glistened in the light from the window.

I reached out and touched the fabric. 'This is so beautiful.'

'I make the dresses myself. People think only Herero woman wear these dresses but I am a Damara and I wear these dresses.' She took a sip from her Seven Up tin. Her wrist was slim, a girl's; but her hand was old, the knuckles large. She slid her feet under her skirt, 'My mother was Herero, my father Damara. My grandmother was Damara and my grandfather was German. I can still remember him. He had a brown beard and was as white as . . .' she looked around the room and her eyes settled back on me, 'as you.'

I went through my routine explanation: how we had chosen farms with the most chance of having a copper deposit, and that we wished to drill a borehole on Moedhou.

'Copper,' Mrs Nangula sucked her lips, 'We don't need copper, we need water. Why don't you drill another hole for water?'

Antonio shrugged apologetically. 'This company only drills for minerals, not water.'

Mrs Nangula stared into her 7-Up tin as if it was a third whisky at a bar. She sighed heavily. *''n Goeie vrou is so skaars soos hoendertande.'*

I laughed; the expression sounded so strange in Afrikaans. I translated it for Antonio: 'A good woman is as rare as hen's teeth.'

'I would never say so myself,' he remarked.

Mrs Nangula slid a look at Antonio and chuckled; dry seed-pods falling onto hard ground, scattering onto the white earth. Thirsty. The laughter dried up, she shook her head. 'The reason I say that is my son Lucky. His wife has left him. Where will he find another wife, a good one? That is why I say a good woman is as scarce as hen's teeth.

'I have three sons, no daughters,' she continued, sounding pleased about the latter, 'although, Lucky is not my real son. When I was younger and my husband was still here, an old man and a young boy brought us vegetables from a nearby farm. They came on their donkey cart every week. One day, the young boy came alone. I heard the clippety-clop of the donkey cart and stood on the track waiting for them. That was when I saw the boy was alone. The old man had died. So Lucky became my son.'

'That *is* lucky,' I commented.

She looked at me sharply. '*He* is Lucky.' She shrugged her tiny shoulders in their large blue sleeves. 'What could I do?'

Suddenly Mrs Nangula jumped forward in her seat. 'This,' she said, pointing at the cheetah skin, 'we killed this. It ran behind the buildings and we caught it. We threw stones at it, all of us, until it died.' Her thin arms pummelled the air.

Antonio's eyes softened.

'But there are no more cheetah left here anymore, are there?' I touched the charcoal tear marks again.

She shook her head. 'No.'

Having explained our business and finished our drinks, Antonio and I stood up to leave.

'Wait,' commanded Mrs Nangula, 'I have something for you.'

Her skirt rustled as she left and reappeared with a tight roll of paper, stained from handling. I unrolled it; a twenty-Namibian-dollar bill and a list fell out. *Flour 200 g, sugar 250 g, coffee 200 g, windmill oil.*

I nodded. 'I'll be passing by here next week, Mrs Nangula. I'll drop your groceries off then.'

Antonio and I followed Mrs Nangula out into the blinding sunlight. Dozens of brown cattle had gathered at the windmill. Abel and another figure, presumably Lucky, walked over to us.

'It's no good, Mama Nangula. No good. The windmill is bust for sure this time,' Abel told her.

'Lucky,' jabbed Mrs Nangula, 'that true? We just need more windmill oil.'

'Not this time, Mama. Our pump is not strong enough, or the water is just too weak. But the cattle are thirsty, they have not drunk in two days.'

Lucky was a good-looking man in his mid-twenties. His white T-shirt was stained with oil, his jeans cut off at the knee. He wore open sandals.

'I know, I know,' she waved away an imaginary fly, 'These people must drill us water.'

'We are drilling for copper, not water,' I reminded her.

Mrs Nangula sat down on a large boulder. From the ground she gathered a couple of pebbles, rearranged them around her feet, sorting and resorting them.

'They must drill us water,' she told Lucky. She looked at me sharply. 'Where else are you drilling?' she demanded.

'We've just finished drilling on Abel's farm and before that we drilled a hole on Wag 'n Bietjie.'

'It's the farm owned by Liddie Barendse,' clarified Abel to Mrs Nangula, 'the one with the sick boy.'

'Hmm, sick, you say? Her boys are *bad*.'

Abel nodded. 'His mother says it's his blood.' He looked at the windmill stricken with inertia and sighed. His voice lowered to a threatening rumble: 'Mama Nangula, your cattle will die if they don't have water in the next day. They will not eat if they are thirsty and their tongues will swell. We cannot fix the windmill in that time.' Abel looked at Antonio and I. 'We need your help. Do you have tools in that vehicle? Wire cutters.'

I nodded. We had everything in that vehicle.

'We must cut the fence where Moedhou meets my farm Soetwater. We must drive the cattle through there. They can drink on my farm'

Antonio's face brightened. 'Operation Sabotage. Man, oh man!'

Antonio and I followed Abel's bakkie through the sparse bushes. Lucky stood on the back of Abel's bakkie shouting directions at him. Abel came to a stop at the corner of Moedhou, and Antonio and I parked beside them. I rummaged through the back, found the tool box and removed a pair of wire cutters. Antonio grabbed them and marched up to the fence. Lucky pointed at the wires. Antonio braced himself; *twang*, the first wire sprung loose, *twang*, *twang*. Operation Sabotage completed.

'Wait here, Antonio,' Lucky instructed him, 'Abel and I are going back to get the cattle.'

Abel's white bakkie sped back to the windmill, to the thirsty cattle waiting at the empty trough.

Antonio and I stood waiting at the Cruiser, the heat shimmering off the white calcrete. A rumble of hooves vibrated the earth; a distant cry – *waa waa*. A cloud of dust rose and dozens of cattle thundered through it. They came to an abrupt halt when they saw the fence. Eyes rolled back in fear. Antonio took off his cotton hat and slapped his thigh, *waa waa*, he shouted, trotting behind them. The first beast shifted and trotted through the broken fence.

Waa waa, Lucky shouted from the back of Abel's bakkie.

Waa waa, Antonio galloped after them. Hooves and dust, with Antonio in pursuit.

And me with my head in my hands, laughing at Antonio.

CHAPTER ELEVEN

Stones and Bones

'There are Namibian Germans and German Germans,' said Herr Winkler, proud owner of the Outjo Coffee Shop, 'und I am a Namibian German. We are citizens of Namibia. We live in Afrika and we speak Afrikaans and some of us, ja, we speak Herero or Damara. We love the bush and the wide open space. German Germans, hah, they are Europeans.'

He held his pencil expectantly above his pad. Abel, Antonio and I sat at one of his tables, studying the menu. It had only been four months since Terence and I had joined TurnStone, but already it felt as if my world pivoted around Outjo.

'Just coffee, thanks,' I said to Herr Winkler. They served good coffee there, German coffee.

'Me too,' Abel patted his moon of a stomach, 'I had a big breakfast this morning.'

We all looked at Antonio. He was busy writing on his hard hat with a black marker pen. Finished, he laughed and held it up. *EnGLaND Go HoMe!!!* He smothered his laugh with an adult cough. 'Last night England lost to Italy on penalties. Man, oh man, I am so happy when those bloody Anglo-Saxons get beaten!'

Herr Winkler coughed.

Antonio looked up at him. 'Just coffee, just coffee. Italians don't eat heavy things in the morning. Just fruits.'

Herr Winkler had the skinniest legs I'd ever seen. He snapped them together and retreated into the kitchen.

'Germans,' whispered Antonio. 'So particular, but at least they can cook. Not like the English. They do not know how to cook. Never heard of garlic and olive oil.'

'How is your work coming along. Robyn?,' asked Abel. He leant his weight back on the small cottage chair. It creaked.

'Have you ever seen that T-shirt –' Antonio continued, ignoring the conversation, 'on the front it says, *A perfect world: German technology, Italian lovers, English police, French cooks.* And then on the back it says, *An imperfect World: English cooks, Italian police* . . . and, wait for this, *German lovers!*' Antonio pinched his nose, and his eyes watered in his attempt to restrain his laughter.

Herr Winkler coughed and placed the tray on the table, and then departed in a huff.

Abel laughed into his coffee, shaking his head. 'This man from Italy, Robyn.'

'I've been back in Cape Town for a few weeks and Antonio visited his family in Italy, so the work's been held up,' I told Abel, 'but we're planning to continue drilling the targets soon. To be honest, there's been nothing too encouraging in our results so far. No sign of any copper yet.'

It was the first time Terence and I had returned to Cape Town since we began working for TurnStone four months before. We had looked forward to spending time together in the city, but that had been ruined by the long hours of work at the office. Arriving late every morning, Lawrence worked until all hours of the evening. Discussions dragged on until the sun had set over Cape Town and the lights in the harbour below began to twinkle. We worked feverishly trying to coordinate contractors and landowners, compile reports and give presentations to the stream of strange faces that trickled through TurnStone's engraved doors. We prepared maps and approved costs. Before we knew it, it was time to head back into the field.

On our last day in the office, Terence and I stood around the map table, heads bent, papers and maps shuffling. Before us lay the spectacular view of the harbour on a clear winter morning; we hardly glanced up at it. Through the glass doors, we could see Lawrence working. He was talking on the phone, pacing up and down the length of the telephone chord. He ran his hand through his short hair, then slammed down the phone. He walked to his door, opened it, then had second thoughts and walked back to the phone. His clipped voice filtered through the open door.

'Kirkby. Yes, yes, I know. In six months we've practically spent our budget for the year . . . I know we'll have to explain that, Kirkby, damn it, I *know* . . . Of course it's cost us millions of dollars, of course. The air survey alone cost two-thirds of our budget. Listen Kirkby, it's the right geological setting, there are existing copper deposits in the area to prove it. Things should have progressed further than this. Those results are crucial. Today's discovery is tomorrow's market. Even a *potential* of a discovery will justify our expenditure.'

There was silence while Lawrence listened. Once or twice he opened his mouth to interrupt but closed it again.

'We need to know our worth, we need to know how much our projects are worth. It's a priority that we ascertain our assets. They are the bottom line of any company's value . . . You're right. Assets, even *potential* assets,' said Lawrence finally. He glanced up and caught my eye. He excused himself, closed the door and returned to the phone. A minute later he put it down. I saw him sink his hands into his deep tailored pockets and stare out at the harbour. He rocked back and forth on the balls of his feet. I pulled my attention back to Spyder's geophysical map.

'Morning,' said Lawrence, strolling over to the map table. He leant his elbow against it in a studied sort of way. 'Great potential, this area. We look forward to seeing the results on these projects. Any word from the laboratory yet, Terence?'

Terence rubbed his set jaw. 'The samples are still being processed by Committed Labs.'

'Good, good. The laboratory results for the your Namibian project, Robyn, should be coming through any day now.' He pushed himself up and slipped his hands into his pockets. 'We have the highest hopes for these two areas. They have been carefully selected for their potential; we use state-of-the-art technology, we have good drill targets. Now all we need are the copper results. We also have the best team. Small but organised. With Antonio and Spyder's input we should be able to find our deposit.' He turned to leave, and then paused. 'Just remember; it's essential that we increase our asset potential. Exploration works at a loss and we need to justify these losses with some encouraging signs of a mineral deposit.'

We watched Lawrence wander into the kitchen, pour a cup of filter coffee and help himself to a pastry. He was met by an accountant he had recently hired, a small woman with three chins and eyes I did not particularly like. They walked back to her office and closed the door behind them.

Terence's eyebrows lifted and contracted into two peaks – two blond horns he grew when he felt extremely pressured. I would have felt some sympathy, if I hadn't felt so sick with pressure myself. The areas were just too large for such a small team.

'It's a long-term thing,' said Terence. 'Exploration takes years. They're expecting results within months, it's ridiculous. You have to take a methodical approach.' He sighed and pulled a couple of large maps across to the light table.

The next day, Terence and I stood in the airport. He wrapped his arms around me and pulled me close. 'It won't be long, you'll see. We'll have more free time the next time we come back. We'll go away for a weekend or something.'

I nodded. My flight was about to leave. I buried my face into his neck and then wrenched myself free. I hadn't looked at Bongi, who sat droopily in his dog box, under the influence of a sedative, waiting to fly with Terence to Botswana.

'Robyn,' Abel called, 'your mind has floated elsewhere. It's not here with Antonio and me.'

'Sorry, just thinking back to Cape Town.'

'And your husband,' Abel chided.

'Of course.'

I thanked Herr Winkler as he placed a fresh pot of coffee on the table. He was cheerful again; he had forgiven Antonio. He almost collided with Mrs Barendse as she walked into the shop.

'Liddie,' called Abel, 'come and have a cup of coffee with us.'

Mrs Barendse was wearing a floral blouse and trousers. She walked over to our table. Her face looked pale and pinched. Antonio stood up to offer her a chair, and she thanked him and sat down.

'Abel, Robyn, Mr Conté,' she greeted us.

'Antonio,' objected Antonio, rather loudly.

'Antonio,' Mrs Barendse nodded. She hugged her elbows.

Abel looked concerned. He leant forward and touched her hand. 'Liddie?'

'It *is* leukaemia. They've finally made a diagnosis. What is the worst thing that could happen? Leukaemia. As if I have not already lost my husband to it.'

Antonio looked distressed, and caught my eye.

I reached over and touched her other hand. 'He must be going for treatment.'

Mrs Barendse nodded. 'The doctors say he must go for chemotherapy. They have . . . hope. He starts with their treatment next week. I have to drop him off at the hospital in Windhoek and leave him there for a while.'

'Liddie,' Abel's hand engulfed hers, 'Liddie, listen to me. You need to come with me to visit old Mrs Nangula. She can throw the stones and bones for him.'

Mrs Barendse shook her head.

'She has helped me many times. Think about it, Liddie.'

Mrs Barendse pulled back her hands and stood abruptly. 'The farm . . .' she looked at me, but then shook her head and walked out of the Outjo Coffee Shop.

Abel sighed as he extracted his wallet from his shorts. 'She must see Mama Nangula.'

A month later, Antonio and I stood in the small shed we had rented in Outjo. It was wedged between the fuel station and the tourist shop, which sold gemstones and curios. The shed had few windows; they were all narrow and high. Thin strips of light filtered through the suspended grey dust. Rows of neatly stacked core trays lined the shed like coffins. Trays of black graphite. Quiet. In six months, we had not had a whisper of copper, not an innuendo of a mine.

Antonio and I had only recently returned to Outjo. Antonio had been back to Italy to see his family, and Terence and I had met in Windhoek for a few days, coordinating work we both had to do at the Windhoek Geological Survey. Terence had looked well: fit, healthy and tanned. I know I looked the same. This work kept us outdoors and active. The drilling phase would hopefully come to an end on our projects soon, we promised each other. Then we would spend more time in Cape Town. We would spend more time together.

Antonio slapped his clipboard down on a core tray, dislodging a cloud of fine dust. He waved his hands in the air. 'At first I logged everything in great detail, Robyn. But now, what's the use? Every bore-hole looks the same. Graphite, graphite, graphite. This is the cause of the geophysical anomalies. Let me tell you that. This new-fangled technology cannot tell a copper deposit from graphite. *Four* bore-holes. Graphite,' Antonio emphasised.

I shrugged. 'But as Spyder says, we have to drill them to find out what they are. There is no other way of finding out. Our next bore-hole is on Mrs Nangula's farm.'

Antonio cheered up at the thought of this.

Footsteps echoed in the shed. We turned to look in their direction. No one ever visited us in the core shed. A long, thin figure, hazy in the filtered dust, treading between the coffins of graphite like the Grim Reaper. He stopped a little distance from us and pulled his floppy hat off. Louwtjie, the pilot.

'Well, I'll be damned,' I said.

He grinned. He looked more bedraggled somehow, as if he had been living in the bush. His hair had grown longer, almost covering his large red ears. His beard looked mangy. As usual, his checked shirt was too small for his skinny frame. It had torn under the arm.

'Came to see how your flying lessons were coming along.'

'What are you doing here?'

'Ah, I get around,' he peered into the closest core box. 'Not much copper here, I see. Just graphite. You're drilling big *fokken* pencils.'

Antonio stared at Louwtjie quizzically. I introduced them and they shook hands.

'Listen,' Louwtjie turned back to me, 'brought you something. I was at the post office and they asked me if I'd come this way and drop this off for you.' He handed me a sealed, brown envelope addressed to me.

I took it and slit it open with my pen. I pulled out the sheets of paper and read them.

'What is it?' Antonio leant over my shoulder.

'Lawrence has sent me the results from Committed Labs,' I said slowly, scanning the page, 'but . . . this can't be. The results are very high. Look at this, the core drilled at Wag 'n Bietjie: two percent copper in one sample, one percent in another . . . and look at this – two point seven percent copper!'

'What?' Antonio snatched the page from me. 'It is impossible! There is no copper here. This cannot be true. Perhaps the Laboratories have made a mistake. I must call Lawrence.'

I shook my head. 'It doesn't make sense. Unless the copper is present in a sulphide as black as the graphite, too black to see. Unless chalcocite *is* present.'

'No,' Antonio opened his hands, 'no, not here. Other copper-bearing sulphides would be present too, not just chalcocite. Pah, I must call Lawrence.'

'Why don't we get the lab to run the samples through again? Check them. Perhaps they were confused with others. Ask Lawrence.'

Antonio marched outside.

Louwtjie stalked between the trays: a praying mantis. 'I'd say he's right. There's no copper in this core. *Fok*-all copper here. Just graphite.'

'You seem to know a lot about rocks for a pilot.'

'That so?' his blue eyes twinkled.

'Many talents? Not just a pretty face?'

He laughed, '*Fok* no, I used to work in this area. I know it like the back of my hand.'

'Work here doing what?' I leant back against the core tray, knowing the black graphite would mark my already filthy shorts.

Antonio came bursting in, agitated. 'You missed this, it was still in the envelope, a letter from Lawrence.' He handed me the page. 'How *can* this be true? No, no.' He stormed out again.

I scanned the letter, which was addressed to me.

Congratulations on the promising results . . . encourage further interest and funding in Africa . . . for immediate results we must move quickly and shift our attention from drilling to taking soil samples. It is a priority to take soil samples on the farm adjacent to Wag 'n Bietjie, to find out if the possible copper deposit extends over a large area . . . have the soil samples taken by Simon Says Samplers (I recommend them highly) and get them sent to the same laboratory, Committed Labs, for analysis. Regards, Lawrence.

Antonio walked back in, looking appeased but still red. 'He wants those soil samples taken in case the laboratory has *not* made a mistake. In case chalcocite *is* present. He said he cannot fund the samples to be reanalysed by the lab.' Antonio tossed up his hands. 'What more could I say?'

I studied the map. 'The farm adjacent to Wag 'n Bietjie is . . . Soutpan.'

'That's Jakkals Pretorius's farm. He owns a butchery in town here, *Die Vleis Paleis*. It's just up the street.'

I looked at Louwtjie, 'You really do know everyone around here.'

'Of course, not that they all remember me.' He slapped his floppy hat against his thigh. 'I'll be seeing you, Look after yourself, old crow.'

'Wait,' I called, but he had already gone.

'Old crow,' I mumbled to myself, indignant, as I studied the lab results again.

Lawrence was right: the area was geologically attractive. It was the right depositional environment for a copper deposit. TurnStone had used state-of-the-art technology to fly the geophysical survey. They had good targets. They had drilled them. And now, finally, they had promising copper laboratory results. It all looked good, except for one thing: the naked eye. The core showed no sign of the two most common copper-bearing sulphides – chalcopyrite, the colour of gold; bornite, blue as peacock feathers. They would have shone out of the core like street lights on a moonless night.

I found a copy of a land access agreement and the regional map amongst my notes, tucked them under my arm and walked up the street to the butchery. The light outside was practically blinding compared to in the shed, and I stepped into the dark butchery with relief. My eyes adjusted to the change. A small woman with blonde ringlets and red lipstick stood behind a counter. Behind her hung a freshly slaughtered carcass. I could smell the blood.

'May I see Jakkals Pretorius?'

She tilted her head flirtatiously. 'He's on the phone. He'll be with you now.'

I looked past her and the carcass to a dirty window. Through it, I could see a grey spiral phone cord and an enormous stomach.

There was a grunt and a click. A man entered, dabbing his watering eyes with a hanky.

'*Dis weer mevrou Barendse*,' he told his assistant. 'She has slaughtered more of her cattle. She wants to know if we can use more meat. That's the second lot in two weeks. She can't have that many more left. I suppose we can always use more meat. Make biltong.' He looked at me. He had a large, red, bulbous nose and eyes the colour of tap water.

'Johan Pretorius, call me Jakkals.' His handshake was loose and heavy. He moved from behind the counter to stand in front of me. I stepped back, preventing his huge belly from pressing against me. He was barefoot, the skin peeling off his feet in onion rings. His toenails were long, jagged and yellow.

'I work for a prospecting company, TurnStone. I've come to ask permission to take some samples on your farm Soutpan.'

Jakkals licked his lips. 'I'll come with you.'

'Thank you, that's not necessary.'

'When you work, I'll come with you, girlie. We can have lunch, I'll bring some boerewors from *Die Vleis Paleis*.'

'This is the contract giving us permission to work on your farm. If you're happy that we take the samples, you can sign on the last page.'

Jakkals thumbed to the last page and signed while looking at me. 'Girlie, I'll be going with you.'

I nodded, despite the *girlie*. It was his farm after all. He slid the clipboard back to me; a shrivelled stick of meat lay on it.

'*Droë wors,* eat it girlie. I made it myself.'

I took a bite of the dried sausage and chewed. A thick layer of fat lined my mouth. 'Good,' I lied, slipping the rest of it into my pocket. 'I'll call you as soon as the crew from Simon Says Samplers arrive.'

The blonde woman's red nails chirped a silent goodbye. Jakkals wore the faintest of smiles.

As I drove, Mrs Nangula's groceries rustled in the breeze on the back seat. All the windows were open and my hair fluttered in my face. During the seven months I had worked for TurnStone, it had grown longer. Seven months, and yet the fieldwork had shown no sign of subsiding. Lawrence continued to promise it would. But really, he always added, you must learn to organise your time. If he used that phrase again, I swore to myself, I'd throttle him. Antonio had travelled across the border to Botswana two weeks ago and was currently working with Terence in Botswana. Terence told me over the radio that Antonio was enjoying Botswana, but that he and Bongi kept their distance. Antonio was more of a cat person and Bongi was suspicious of his Italian exuberance.

I leant back against the seat and let the country wash past me. I thought of Terence. I sighed and slipped a cassette into the open mouth of the player. Terence had made a tape of some of his favourite songs and mailed it to me. *Dangerbird, he flies alone,* Neil Young's voice rose, raw and brittle.

I turned up the volume. That's how I felt. Alone. As much as I loved Namibia, as much as I loved meeting the farmers, Terence's absence was gnawing a hole inside me. Nothing but our broken conversations over the radio.

And he rides the wind back to his home, although his wings have turned to stone.

In town, in Outjo, every time I saw a glimpse of sandy blond hair in the corner of my eye, my heart lurched. Terence. But it never was. No miracle had carried him across the border to Namibia. Broken radio signals, broken words and broken hearts. Terence's shadow had crept into my heart, and curled into a tight, hurt fist. That raw guitar . . . I felt my teeth clench.

The radio beeped. I turned off the tape.

'3033, Robyn. Over.' Silence while my voice travelled the airwaves.

A crackle. 'Robyn, angel. It's Terence here. Over.'

'I was just thinking of you. Over.'

'Listen Robyn. I'll call later tonight but I wanted to ask you if you had seen this month's edition of *African Discovery*? Over.'

'No, I wouldn't be able to get it out here. Over.'

'There's an article submitted by TurnStone discussing their exploration approach in Africa. It includes a discussion of your Namibian Project and lists all the elevated copper results from the drill core. Over.'

I was silent for a while. 'But . . . both Antonio and I are not sure about those results. They should *not* be published. Over.'

'I know. I know, Robyn.' Terence hesitated. 'The share price of TurnStone is on the rise. The article puts it down to the current mineral market. Pretty broad term, doesn't mean anything actually. Over.'

What was he saying? That the two were connected?

'TurnStone has other joint ventures in Africa and Australia. An exploration project in such an early stage would not affect the share price . . .' I drifted off, suddenly recalling Lawrence's words . . . *Tomorrow's potential discovery is today's market.*

'It can't be connected,' I said emphatically, more to myself.

'Robyn, we'll talk about this when we see each other. Okay?' Terence interrupted.

He was right. Radio waves are public airwaves, and although it was unlikely, anyone could be listening in. A sign loomed ahead on the road. *Soutpan, Jakkals Pretorius.* I slowed down and stopped outside the gate.

'Okay. We'll talk about it when we see each other. When will that be? Over.'

'Soon. Soon I hope. The drill crew here needs a break. And we should be able to meet in Cape Town for a couple of weeks. Over.'

'I look forward to it. Over and out.' Understatement of the year.

'Over and out, angel.'

I looked at Jakkals's gate. It was unlocked. This was a good opportunity for me to look at the farm before the crew from Simon Says Sampling arrived. I opened the gates, drove through and closed them behind me.

Soutpan – salt pan – was flat and more grassy than Mrs Nangula's farm and the trees were taller. It was surrounded by a horseshoe ridge of quartzite which glinted the sun's hot reflection. I parked in the scant shade of a tree, tucked my geological hammer into my belt and slipped my black notebook into my pocket. My hand-lens, compass and pen were attached to a string hanging around my neck. I climbed the steep ridge, the familiar weight of my hammer digging into the arch of my back, keeping my eyes on the ground for any sign of green copper staining. I reached the crest of the ridge, wiped the sweat from my brow and looked up.

The world unfolded before me. Beyond Soutpan lay desolate plains that rose into flat, sedimentary mountains. A turmoil of warmth; a living sunset of sands. Not a sign of human life. Not a fence, not another farm. This dry expanse. 'The land God made in anger', the early German settlers called Namibia. Anger? Never. I slipped the notebook out of my pocket and wrote:

Let God's country ease the worry from my mind
and bleed the anger from my veins.
As the dust and the sun settle
over these dry dusty plains
let me feel peace again.

These were the words that had blown to me when I first walked across the runway to Louwtjie's blue bird of a plane. They were etched into my memory by now, synonymous with Namibia. Word for word, I said the words each time I returned to Namibia, leaving Terence for more indefinite weeks or even months. Now for the first time I wrote the words down, so I would never forget them.

I walked back down the ridge to the dusty Land Cruiser. I drove off Soutpan feeling calm. The land had soaked into me, the space had drenched me. The Cruiser bumped back onto the tar road. I drove a further twenty kilometres east towards Khorixas and then swerved off along the donkey-cart tracks to Moedhou. Using these tracks, the dongas and trees, I found the broken gate leading to Mrs Nangula's pink house.

Mrs Nangula stood waiting in her stone garden for me. She wore another traditional Herero dress, this one made of black silk with enormous red fire-cracker flowers exploding over it. She watched me shift her grocery packets into one hand and struggle to open the garden gate.

'Mrs Nangula.'

'I thought it was the wind,' she said, 'but then it was you.'

I placed her packets at her feet, on the blinding glare of calcrete.

She leant forward and wrapped a soft hand with a steel grip around my wrist. Her brown eyes squinted at me. 'How come when I ask you to buy two hundred grams of sugar you buy five hundred? When I ask you to buy five hundred grams of mielie meal, you buy a kilogram. You never ask for more money. Why do you buy me windmill oil for free?'

'You already gave me money.'

'But not enough.'

'Don't worry about it.'

'Is the windmill oil a gift then?' Her tough, scrawny neck stretched and sunk, reminding me of a lizard raising its neck to the sun.

'Yes, a gift then.'

'The windmill is broken again. Lucky is trying to fix it.' She lifted the packets, shrugging off my offer of help. 'A good woman is as scarce as hen's teeth,' she muttered as she went indoors.

'Robyn.'

I turned to see Lucky walking from the windmill towards me, wiping his hands on a rag. He smiled broadly.

'Problem with the windmill?'

'It's the water pressure, it's too dry on Moedhou.' His grin broadened. 'I see you brought Mama more shopping.'

'She keeps me busy.'

'Mama, our mama,' Lucky looked at me from the corners of his eyes, in a teasing sort of way. 'Mama tells me you have been buying her gifts. That you buy the big sugar and you don't ask for more money. That you buy her windmill oil. She says to me, *Lucky, I am telling you,*

Robyn likes you. She wants you for a husband. Why else would she buy me these things? Mama, she's crazy.'

I could feel my face warm to a blush. I was not sure if I was more embarrassed at being called Lucky's suitor, or being caught in the awkward light of giving charity – 'TurnStone will drill on your farm. They can pay for some of your groceries until then.'

'My goodness Robyn. Taking from the rich, giving to the poor,' smiled Lucky. 'You are playing Robyn Hood.'

The front door of the pink house creaked open and out stepped Mrs Nangula. Her full skirt swept the dust as she walked across her stone garden. She stopped in the centre and waited.

'Mama's heard something,' Lucky told me.

Sure enough, a rumble grew closer and a large white bakkie drove up to the farmhouse. Abel Kalomo waved from the window. Beside him sat someone else, a white woman. She opened the door. It was Liddie Barendse. They walked up to Mrs Nangula, and Lucky and I joined them.

'Mama Nangula, Robyn, Lucky,' Abel greeted us.

Mrs Nangula ignored Abel. She studied Mrs Barendse instead.

'What's *she* doing here?'

'Mama Nangula,' cajoled Abel, 'we need to speak to you. She needs help. Your help. Her boy is sick.'

'Her boys are *bad*.' Mrs Nangula's voice swept like an unexpected gust of wind through parched, parched land.

'Mama,' Abel's voice was sterner, 'her boy, her youngest, has sick blood. He could die.'

Mrs Barendse's face was pale, bloodless. She shifted her gaze to the windmill behind the house. 'You are having trouble with your water?'

Lucky nodded, glancing at his mother.

'I could help with a pump. I have a spare pump on my farm.' There was a slight edge, a pleading, to her voice.

'A pump may help. But it is the water pressure. We need a new hole,' replied Lucky.

'Mama Nangula,' Abel turned to the old lady again, 'Lucky is your youngest. If he were sick, you would want someone to help him. You would not want to lose your youngest boy.'

Mrs Nangula wiped her tough soles on the ground. She cracked the knuckles on her hand and said something in Damara to Lucky. He nodded and left, returning immediately with an empty old paint tin, stained with pink paint, and a small skin bag. He placed the tin on the ground and his mother sat on it. The bag he left at her feet.

Mrs Nangula's hands worked quickly, collecting small pebbles at her feet and rearranging them constantly. She touched them all with a finger and then, content, hissed something to Lucky again. Lucky walked into the house and returned carrying an old rusted tin of 7-Up filled with water. Mrs Nangula poured a little water on one small, round, grey stone.

'Hot, hot, his blood is hot, must cool his blood. Hot like the sun, hot enough to burn. Wet the stones, wet the stones, pour water on the bad blood, pour water on the bad boy.' She poured more water on the stone and touched them all again. 'Cooler, cooler, make his blood chill. Cold.'

Mrs Barendse stood beside Abel, immobile and as expressionless as when she arrived.

Mrs Nangula's head hung forward, as if her neck was not strong enough to hold the enormous, bow-shaped Herero hat. Her hands rested on her knees. 'Go,' she said.

No one moved.

'She can go,' Mrs Nangula told Abel, 'his blood is cooled. It was hot like the sun. Not you,' she shot at me as I turned to leave with Abel and Mrs Barendse. She spoke to Lucky in Damara.

'Mama wants you to stay. She will throw the bones and stones for you, in payment for the windmill oil. Kneel here.' He pointed at the ground.

I looked at the departing figures, and then did as I was told.

Mrs Nangula lifted up the bag and untied the leather thong. She picked up a couple of pebbles from the ground, leaving the wet one to dry in the sun.

She handed me the bag, 'Shake.'

I shook it, a little timidly.

'Empty it,' she waved at the ground in front of her bare feet.

I scattered the contents. Seed-pods, stones and bones. I stared at their abstract pattern and looked up at Mrs Nangula. She leant forward, resting her elbows on her knees. Her eyes glistened like a young girl's.

'A good man, a good marriage. He loves and respects you. You love him. See here?' she pointed at two seed-pods lying beside a round pebble. 'Marriage as solid as a rock.'

I nodded. She looked up at Lucky's retreating figure and allowed herself a silent chuckle.

'No money trouble.' She pointed to a blackened coin I had not noticed amongst the thrown contents. 'No trouble with your car . . .' her gnarled finger touched one long, thin bone and then another, 'and no trouble with the police.' She scratched her nose and leant closer. She sniffed. Her pink tongue flickered over her lower lip. She sniffed again. 'Trouble.'

I edged forward on my knees over the white calcrete to look at what she was pointing at. A tiny, yellow vertebrate bone lay on the outskirts, far from the other objects.

'A man in your world, but not too close. Trouble.'

'Who?'

'A man with a smile but a knife in his hand. See the way the bone lies? With the round side to the sky and the sharp side under?'

I shrugged. 'I don't know him.'

'No, you know him, but you think that you don't know him. A man far away, but with money and able to see far from where he stands.'

She gathered the stones and bones and put them back into the bag. I got to my feet and dusted my knees.

'Wait.' She dug into her skirt and pulled out a coil of paper, wrapped in an equally worn Namibian twenty-dollar bill, and handed it to me. Another shopping list.

CHAPTER TWELVE

As the Dust and the Sun Settle

The last of the coals warmed my legs. The sky was tangerine, evidence of the day's arrival. For over seven months I had worked for TurnStone. By now, reality smelt like the dry Namibian bush, looked like the expanse of land that surrounded me and sounded like the long-awaited calls from Terence. I stood around the fire with half a dozen bush-wise men. Long, tangled hair harnessed in headbands or pinned back with fly-style sunglasses. A few of them were smearing suncream on their burnt noses. Around us a collection of sagging khaki tents reminded me of sleeping jackals.

Bull, the crew's leader for Simon Says Sampling, stood next to me. Like his name, Bull was solid and square. He had been named by his crew for his ability to blunder through the bush. His hair was shorter than the other men's, black and curly and secured with a grubby red headband. His T-shirt was torn and filthy, his leather boots scuffed and broken. I knew Bull's cautious respect for me was laden with irony – this woman in her luxury 4x4, sleeping and eating at the local lodge. But I liked Bull. I liked the way he worked.

'Where's Eddie, Bull?'

'He's still getting up.'

I looked at my watch, annoyed.

With the tip of his boot, Bull knocked the lid off the three-legged potjie which stood to one side of the fire. 'Springbok in there. We picked it up off the road yesterday. Hit by a truck, I guess. When we found it, it was still warm. I said shit, tonight we eat game. Can't waste good meat. Shit no.'

We looked up to see Eddie approaching. He was still wearing his tracksuit and the laces of his boots flapped as he walked.

'Not that Eddie would eat it, said he had his own grub. And I said *shit*, all the more for us,' said Bull.

I tucked a loose strand of hair behind my ear. It had grown long enough to tie back into a ponytail. I was aware it made me look younger than my twenty-nine years – too young to supervise this wild collection of men.

Eddie stood staring into the fire, sipping a mug of coffee with both hands. His face was long and horse-like, his skin a translucent white. In his early twenties and a recent geochemistry graduate, Eddie had the dubious job of quality checking all the soil samples taken by Bull and his boys. Bull needed no quality checking, and both he and Eddie knew it.

I handed Bull and Eddie each a map of Soutpan. Bull scanned the map. Eddie's copy hung from his hand.

'Soutpan is the farm, Jakkals Pretorius is the owner. I've arranged permission for you to work there. You can begin taking the samples as soon as you're ready. The sample positions are marked on the map, they're to be taken at fifty-metre intervals.'

Eddie slurped his coffee, loudly.

'Before you leave, we need to have a brief meeting about safety in the field.'

Eddie rolled his eyes.

'Sorry, Eddie. It's TurnStone rules, and Simon Says Sampling are working for TurnStone.'

'Move it, boys,' Bull shouted at his crew.

Tall and short, the men shuffled closer to the fire. Tough, hairy bastards. I liked them all, with the exception of Eddie.

Bull's men double-checked the contents of their first-aid kits and the procedure for managing an accident was discussed – the lines of communication, the nearest clinic. All cut and dried.

'A reminder about safety, mostly to do with driving,' I finished off. 'You'll be working a hundred kays from here. It's a long drive there and back. Don't rush it, give yourselves time. TurnStone are paying for it anyway. And no driving in the dark, so leave well before sunset. Remember your seatbelts. That's all, thanks for your time.'

Boots shuffled and the men dispersed. Bull and his team departed for Soutpan and I for Mrs Nangula's Moedhou.

As I drove I fingered the necklace Terence had given me.

Just a week before, Terence, Antonio and I had stood around the map table in TurnStone's Cape Town office. Terence was unpacking rock samples from his field bag.

'Ah,' he exclaimed, pulling out a small, wooden box, 'I forgot to give this to you. I bought it in Maun.'

He handed me the box. Antonio looked up from his map and stopped working.

The box was hand-carved and it smelt of foreign wood. A distant land. Inside, coiled like a glowing worm, lay the black and copper necklace. It carried a small charm, an elephant carved from bone.

'I thought of you when I saw it. I know how much you love elephants. I was told all the telephone wire was nicked in Maun and there's a flood of copper-wire jewellery on the market.'

I rubbed my fingers over the elephant. It had a sharp trunk. 'I love it.'

Antonio shook his head. 'Myself, Terence, I never bring my wife presents. I travel too much. No, it would spoil it for her. My present for her is me.'

Terence laughed. He brushed away the hair at the back of my neck and fastened the necklace.

'No,' insisted Antonio, 'next thing your wife will be expecting gifts. Then she'll want to see your baggage before she sees you. I'm telling you, Terence. Keep yourself as the gift.'

'Don't discourage him, Antonio. I expect gifts.'

'You see, ah?' Antonio threw up his hands. His eyes glinted.

'Dammit, Kirkby!'

We turned around to look through Lawrence's glass doors. Kirkby stood facing Lawrence across his desk. Lawrence appeared agitated; he had raised his voice. The report he had slapped down was as thick as a telephone directory.

'Dammit Kirkby, I know. Expenses are mounting. But we *have* something to show for it! We have promising copper results. The results of our persistent, hard-hitting approach. These results are our *poten-*

tial assets. Of course we consider them assets. And we have a letter of intent. It's a serious approach.'

Lawrence dropped his voice, so we could no longer hear him. Kirkby thrust his hands into his pants and nodded with a thick-lipped expression, staring at Lawrence through his glasses. Even though he was in the office, he still wore his field get-up: khaki pants and field boots; his waistcoat with its many pockets.

Lawrence opened his door and walked over to us. Kirkby hovered behind, clearly wanting to return to the sanctity of the office.

Lawrence placed an open envelope in front of Terence. 'Well done, Terence. We've just received the results from your project in Botswana. Committed Labs have sent them through. Now we have copper signatures on both the Namibian and Botswana projects. Well done, chaps. I knew I could count on you.' He turned to go.

'Lawrence . . .' I hesitated as Lawrence turned around, then took a deep breath, folded my arms and continued: 'As we mentioned before, those results from Outjo look too high. Both Antonio and I have seen the core and we don't think the copper content can be that good. The lab must have made a mistake . . .' I trailed off.

Lawrence's eyes looked bright, hard. 'I think I've told you that Committed Labs are reliable, Robyn. In fact, I don't think I could have made it any clearer.' A smile smoothed over his bland, handsome features. 'Really, Robyn, Committed Labs are an excellent laboratory. They have been a partner to TurnStone's exploration from the start. Have they not, Kirkby?'

Kirkby fixed me with his glassy stare, 'They know their work, mate.'

'I wouldn't worry, Robyn. It's natural to question positive results. And it's good you do. It's good science. However, we need to remember that our top-class team armed with state-of-the-art technology has delivered the results. And we should accept that.'

Lawrence and Kirkby retreated into the accountant's office. She looked up and gave a brief smile as they closed the door.

Terence flicked through the contents of the envelope. He was frowning.

'What's wrong?' I asked

'These results are also too high. I saw some evidence of copper-bearing sulphides along the bedding, but it can't be *this* high. I've got three samples here, taken at metre intervals, each with over a percent of copper.'

Antonio threw up his hands. 'This laboratory must be making mistakes.'

Terence tucked the pages back into the envelope. 'I don't think Lawrence wants to question the results.'

Antonio nodded. 'We all want to believe good news.'

'We need to send some samples to another laboratory,' said Terence.

'But Lawrence won't fund it,' I pointed out.

'We'll have to do so ourselves. We'll just send a few. Three or four.'

'Yes!' Antonio said loudly, and then lowered his voice, 'just a few and we'll analyse for copper only, not the other elements. That will make it cheaper. Robyn, you can send some duplicate samples from your next drill core from Outjo.'

I nodded. 'We could send them to those old laboratories MinSearch used in Namaqualand. They take a while to analyse, but their results are reliable.'

'Then Lawrence will see he has made a mistake,' said Antonio.

'Or will he?' Terence muttered under his breath.

While Bull and his men were getting started on Soutpan, I would have time to check on the drill on Moedhou. This was the last of the Outjo field work for the year. Then, according to Lawrence, we would be 'reassessing our data' in order to 're-evaluate our future approach', our 'way forward' – as always, he spoke as if in some secret corporate code; as if only the right phrase would open the right door. I was now pulling the elephant charm back and forth with irritation. I released it and swung onto the obscure track leading to Moedhou.

For once, Mrs Nangula was not standing in her stone garden. I parked beneath a tree and walked around her pink house, her grocery bags digging into my hands.

'Mrs Nangula,' I called.

Lucky appeared from a dark doorway, smiled and put a finger to his lips. With his head he motioned me around to the shady side of the house. I handed him the groceries and followed him – and then stopped in surprise.

Mrs Liddie Barendse sat on a rock beside Mrs Nangula. Mrs Nangula sat on her paint tin, arranging stones on the ground. She looked up, squinting into the light until she recognized me, and then went back to her work. I hung back. *Clunk clunk clunk*, she moved the stones around, her blue dress the colour of oceans lapping in shadow. A note changed hands and Mrs Barendse rose. She saw me and walked over.

'Mrs Barendse, how are you?'

She gave a nod, dismissing social niceties.

'How is Ludie?' I asked, more to the point.

'Responding to the treatment, the doctor says. Getting better. The treatment makes him sick some days, but other days he's okay. He's working on the farm. He's even been out hunting this week. Shot a kudu.'

'A bull?'

She nodded. 'A bull.'

No, please no.

'Ludie didn't kill it though, only wounded it. He tried to follow it, but he lost it in the bush. Robyn.'

I looked up at her.

'I got an offer for the farm, for Wag 'n Bietjie. It was a good offer, very good. I have accepted, I'm selling the farm. Ludie and Tobie are not happy but I've had enough. I cannot do this on my own any more.'

'But . . . from who?'

She shrugged. 'An agent approached me from Windhoek. I don't know who the buyer is. Ludie studied to be a mechanic, when he's better he can do that for a living; and Tobie – well, he's only interested in the city and girls.'

As Mrs Barendse left, I heard a rustle behind me. Mrs Nangula's soft sea of silk lapped across the calcrete. She stood beside me, shoulder height, watching Mrs Barendse's red bakkie drive away. 'You forgot windmill oil.'

'You didn't put it on the list.'

'The windmill is broken again. *She's* bringing me a new pump though.'

'Mrs Barendse?'

Mrs Nangula nodded. 'Not that it will help the water pressure though. We need a new hole. But where will we find water? Water is as scarce as hen's teeth.'

'I must go and check on the drill.'

'Wait,' she bent down and rearranged the stones in the closest stone bed. They clacked against each other as she mumbled. Words I could not understand, although the word Moedhou came up a few times. She straightened and stared at the stones. Sniffed and shook her head. 'Go,' she said, 'you can go and look at your drill machine. Next time, don't forget the windmill oil.'

She walked from the shadow into the sunlight. Her blue dress sparkled.

I drove through the bush, following the driller's trail, pieces of colourful rag tied to thorny branches, a trail which led to the grinding rhythm of the drill. I parked a slight distance from the drill rig, away from the activity of men and machine. Next to the drill lay the core trays, waiting for the geologist. I put on Antonio's hard hat, the one with *England Go Home* written across it, and replaced my hiking boots with steel-tipped construction boots. Safety regulations.

The driller, a pixie-faced man named Klippies – either for the rock he drilled or the Klipdrift brandy he drank – walked over to me. His smile revealed the gum outline of cheap false teeth. 'Drilling soft rock. Drilling through it at one hell of a pace. We'll soon be finished. Black rock, soft, sort of slippery.'

I nodded: graphite. The core trays confirmed this. I sighed. Once again, our geophysical conductor had been explained. I took three empty sample bags, broke off a piece of core and placed a bit into each bag. I labelled the bags carefully with a black marker, recording their depths and the borehole number. These three samples would be sent to the laboratory in Namaqualand. Personally funded. They would be compared to the standard set I would send to Committed Labs.

'We'll be finished by nightfall. Very easy to drill this,' Klippies shouted at me above the sound of the drill. His front teeth were missing – he held them in his hand. His grin broadened, more endearing for the gap between his teeth. His face had deep lines which radiated out from around his eyes and creased around his smile. 'Easy drilling, easy money.'

'Klippies, what's that?'

He shrugged, 'Don't know. Was here when we got here this morning.'

I pulled it out from the thorny branches. A few twigs were tied together to form a pyramid shape, possibly resembling the frame of a drill rig. They were tied with a blue, silky fabric, the same as Mrs Nangula's dress. Presumably scraps from her sewing.

'This is Mrs Nangula's,' I said, fingering the cloth.

'The old lady? She was around here yesterday, just standing in the bushes watching us.'

'I'll visit her on the way back,' I told him.

Klippies looked at the false teeth in his hand, 'New. Can hurt. Don't know why I bother. My wife told me to get them. More useful without.' He stuck his tongue against the gap and gave a shrill whistle.

The chief driller looked up. Klippies sliced a finger across his throat. Cut the drill. Shut her down. The driller nodded.

I took the pyramid of twigs back with me.

I drove back to the pink house with a weight in my stomach. I had to tell Mrs Nangula that we had not drilled the water she wanted, the water she so desperately needed. I drove past Lucky. He was busy trying to start the windmill pump and did not look up. I parked outside the house and walked the pattern of stones to the back door. Mrs Nangula stood waiting for me. She ushered me into her kitchen.

'Mrs Nangula. We have finished the borehole. We'll clean up the site.'

She clutched my wrist holding the twigs. 'Finished?' she squinted up at me, 'Where is the water?'

'They did not drill water.'

'We *need* water. The cattle are thirsty. The cattle could die.'

'Mrs Nangula,' I hung my head, 'I wish we had drilled you water. But we did not. It was just soft, black rock.'

She released her grip. Her lizard neck stretched out and her eyes bored into mine. Her full skirt swished the floor as she left the kitchen. At the door she turned. 'My cattle will die. And you say you are sorry.'

I looked at the twigs in my hand, sighed and placed them on the counter, beside a basin of soaking beans. I saw myself out. Lucky was wiping his brow as I climbed into the Cruiser. He gave a friendly wave.

I drove back to Outjo, giving the odd heavy sigh and then shaking my head. Moedhou, with its dry thirsty calcrete plains. Moedhou, hang in there. Moedhou, with no relief.

I stopped at the Outjo Coffee Shop and ordered a large pot of German coffee. Not even seeing Herr Winkler's skinny knees snap to attention cheered me up.

'You're sad.' The chair opposite me creaked.

I looked up. Abel. I nodded.

'Why?'

'We finished drilling at Moedhou. Mrs Nangula expected us to drill water. I was hoping to, but we didn't.'

'No, you didn't,' Abel leant back in his chair, 'and you are disappointed.'

'Mrs Nangula counted on me.'

'She did, did she?'

I looked Abel in the eye. 'Yes, she did.'

'Mama Nangula hoped you would find water, Robyn. She wanted you to find water. But she did not expect you to find water.'

I looked at Abel.

'The stones and bones, Robyn. They never lie. They told her long before you did. No matter what she did, the stones and bones told her the same. Over and over.'

'She knew?'

'Of course. But it does not change much. When you want something badly enough, you don't want to listen.'

'If I had struck water, then she would have had to question her skill reading the stones and bones.' I attempted a smile.

Able laughed, rocking back. 'Now you are beginning to understand. There are always greater things at work. Greater things than

---

231

you and me. And Robyn, with your work, you are here today and gone tomorrow. Who will be left to help old Mama Nangula?' he slapped the table, 'Me, Robyn, that's right. Me. And Mrs Barendse. Yes, even old hot-cold Liddie. She has given Mama a pump. It will help in the wetter season. In the dry season, well, she will still have a problem.'

'I don't want them to suffer.'

'It's a thirsty country, Robyn. You know what they say about Namibia: 'The land God made in anger.' It's been a thirsty country for thousands of years. That's what makes it Namibia. People and animals, we get thirsty out here. One Robyn with one drill is not going to change that. An army of people with an army of drills is not going to change that.'

I sighed. 'I know you're right.'

'Of course I'm right. And I must go. No coffee for me, Herr Winkler.'

'Hah,' Herr Winkler looked at Abel in disbelief and then shrugged. 'Another time maybe. In Africa there is always another time, ja?'

I woke up at the lodge the next day. I looked at my watch: six 'o clock. I needed to hurry. It was the second day that Bull and his men were working on Soutpan, and I had to ensure it was all going smoothly. I had also promised to visit Jakkals Pretorius on his farm.

Soutpan was forty minutes' drive east from Outjo. I turned off at the signpost and onto the flat plain of grass and trees, enclosed by the horseshoe ridge of white quartzite. Dust hung in the air. Travelling slowly ahead of me I could see Eddie's twincab bakkie.

I drew level with him. 'Hi.'

'Just finding Bull.'

'You're heading in the wrong direction – they're working on the other side of the farm.'

Eddie shrugged. His shoulder was bony and resistant.

'Don't you have a GPS?'

He shrugged again. 'Batteries are flat.'

'Please stop.'

He reluctantly stopped the twincab. I dug into my cubbyhole, found a spare pack of batteries and carried them over to him. He took them without looking at me.

'You may as well follow me, I'm going there anyway.'

I drove to the centre of the plain, to where Bull's old-style Land Cruiser bakkie was parked. He was unloading equipment from the back. His face was pale and clammy.

'Got the shits man, all of us. From the springbok.'

Eddie laughed.

'I've got some Imodium in my vehicle.'

'Yeah, give it to me. We've finished our supply.'

I found the Imodium in my first-aid kit and gave it to Bull. He took it without comment, slipping it into his pocket. There was no use in asking him if they would continue to work. They would. Generous field incentives would keep them working.

'I'll be up at the farmhouse if you need me. I'll drop by later.'

Eddie lit up a cigarette as I left, leaning back on the bonnet of his twincab, watching Bull work.

The farmhouse on Soutpan was not difficult to find; the main track led directly to it. The house was small, with a larger shed next to it. A couple of tall trees cast shade over both of the buildings. Beside the house, a windmill turned slowly. Jakkals stood barefoot outside his house, waiting for me. He wore an island-style shirt, on which palm trees lay silhouetted against a bright yellow and orange sunset. The shirt buttons strained against the azimuth of his belly.

He held my door open. 'Come inside, girlie.' He patted his watering blue eyes with a hanky.

Jakkals led me through the back door into a confined kitchen. He closed the door behind us and bolted it. My eyes dropped onto the lock.

'Sit down, girlie.' He pulled out a kitchen chair from a cramped table.

I eased myself between the table and wall, facing Jakkals and an old-fashioned iron kitchen stove. He opened the stove, stoked the small fire and placed the kettle onto the plate. The kettle boiled almost immediately. He filled two cups and placed one in front of me.

I sipped the grey liquid and grimaced. The coffee was weak and sweet, not strong and sour the I way I like it.

'Stay for breakfast, girlie. I've got boerewors from the butchery here.' Jakkals pulled a length of pink sausage out of a plastic bag. It hung from his fist like a fat python. With the other hand, he rolled it into a coil and threw it into a pan. The sausage sizzled.

Ill-fitting cupboards lined the kitchen wall. They eyed me from their hollow air-vents, stupid and single-eyed. Perhaps the walls were skew and the cupboards were upright, I couldn't say for sure. A frilly net curtain hung over the window beside me; tiny red and blue pots and pans whizzed over it with gay poltergeist abandon. The edges of the frill were worn and grubby. The curtain was a woman's choice, yet the rest of the kitchen looked sparse and masculine.

'Where is your wife?' I asked Jakkals.

The palm trees on his back shifted as he flipped the sausage. He muttered something.

'What?'

'Dead.'

'Oh, I'm sorry.'

It was getting oppressively hot in the tiny kitchen. I pulled the net curtain aside to open a window, but the glass was sealed into the wall. There was a crunch of footsteps along the gravel path. Only when the figure was almost at the backdoor did I recognise him: long, skinny and familiar. Louwtjie. I frowned at him quizzically from under the curtain. He winked a sharp, blue eye at me and patted a finger over his lips: *Ssh*! He knocked at the door. Jakkals wheezed, shifted the pan off the stove and unbolted the door.

'*Morê Oom. Tannie*,' greeted Louwtjie. '*Oom*, I am Cornelius Jacobus du Plessis and I work for the Agricultural Division of the Municipality of Northern Namibia.' He waited a full second for his title to sink in. 'I have come to look at *Oom's* cattle to inspect for diseases. But I cannot stay long *Oom*. I have paperwork to do.' Louwtjie's pink ears shifted, animated. Paperwork.

'My cattle don't have diseases.'

'Yes *Oom*, it's just a routine inspection. Boerewors,' he noted and took a seat at the table. I caught his eye and sipped my putrid coffee to prevent myself smiling.

Jakkals sliced the boerewors and divided it into three portions. When I protested, he cut two-thirds off mine and loaded it onto his plate. He placed a plate and a cup of coffee in front of Louwtjie who accepted it without comment, as if they were playing out an accepted routine of country hospitality. Jakkals squeezed in beside Louwtjie and began to eat.

Louwtjie hit the ground running: rainfall statistics, drought, cattle and diseases. He steamed on, shovelling the boerewors into his mouth. Jakkals's eyes glazed over.

Within minutes, Louwtjie ejected from his seat, his plate empty. '*Oom, Tannie*, I must go. I have official paperwork to do.'

Jakkals sighed, pushed himself out of the chair and opened the door for Louwtjie. Then he bolted the door closed behind him. I shifted the curtain to see Louwtjie climb into a rusted, beige Land Rover. The engine rattled as he started it and the vehicle trundled out of sight.

'I must go too. Some of the crew are not well. I must check on them,' I told Jakkals.

Jakkals picked up the boiling kettle and held it over my cup.

I placed my hand quickly over it.

'You shouldn't do that girlie, I could have burnt that pretty little hand.'

I quickly dropped both hands under the table. 'I must go. Thanks for breakfast.'

Jakkals gave a long, soulful sigh. He placed the kettle on the table and sat down. He dabbed his eyes. 'We must go and shoot kudu now, girlie.'

'No, I don't think so. I need to get back to work.'

'You promised me you would shoot kudu with me. A kudu bull was wounded on Wag 'n Bietjie. I've seen his blood trail on my farm now. We must find him.'

With an added effort, I managed to push myself up from behind the table. 'I don't like hunting. I did *not* promise I would shoot kudu with you.'

Jakkals stood up, suddenly quick for his size. 'I will show you the roads, the tracks on the farm, which are not on your map.'

I hesitated. Knowing the private tracks on a farm was always useful. It would help Bull load up all the samples. 'Well, thank you. I'll follow behind you in the Land Cruiser.'

Jakkals unbolted the door.

Outside, I took a deep breath of clean, sun-soaked air. Although hot, it was certainly cooler than the kitchen. I walked towards the Cruiser.

'No, we'll take my bakkie, girlie. I know the tracks.'

'Er, no. It's easier for me to follow, I can just leave . . .'

'We'll take my bakkie, girlie. I'll bring you back here.'

I looked at his small, pumpkin-coloured Nissan bakkie, tilted over to the driver's side. 'I can't take too long.'

I climbed into the bakkie and closed the door. From the driver's side, Jakkals reached across me, his thumb sliding over my knee as he picked up a rifle. He placed it on the seat between us.

All farmers had guns. All farmers carried guns. I remained quiet as Jakkals swung onto an overgrown track which led away from the grassy plain and into the surrounding thick bush. The flat, hard calcrete allowed Jakkals to drive at speed.

As the bakkie lurched over a bump, the rifle fell against my shoulder.

'This thing isn't loaded, is it?'

'Why?' Jakkals steered the bakkie around a sharp corner.

'Because I don't want it to go off and get shot, that's why. Why do you have the rifle? I *said* I didn't want to go hunting.'

The bakkie jerked to a halt. Jakkals picked up the rifle and aimed it slowly out the window. 'Look, there he is.'

Sure enough, there in a clearing was the kudu bull. It turned to look at us. The nicked left ear twitched. There was a bloody wound on its shoulder. Jakkals took aim.

'No!' I shouted out the window.

With a rolling leap, the kudu bull jolted into the dense bush.

Jakkals slowly lowered the rifle. 'If he can run like that, he's not seriously wounded. Ludie's bullet must have just grazed his shoulder.'

'Take me back, now.'

'You promised we would shoot kudu, girlie.'

I was quiet. With each move, I just seemed to get more tangled into this sticky web. The more I struggled, the more tangled I became.

'Take me back,' I tried not to reveal my rising panic.

'*They* said you want to shoot kudu with me today.'

'Who?'

'The boy with the twincab.'

'Eddie?'

He nodded.

'Well, I don't. Take me back. Now.'

Jakkals suddenly swung his sunset belly towards me. '*Gee my 'n soentjie* – give me a little kiss.'

'*What?*' My hand slipped to my ankle to find my geological hammer. I had forgotten it. Shit.

'Robyn, my little bird, my little sparrow,' his pale eyes streamed, 'I get dizzy looking at you, girlie. I just want to touch your soft skin. They said you wanted to shoot kudu with me.' He lifted a finger to my face.

I leant back. 'Start the bakkie. We are leaving. Now.'

Jakkals put his hand on the ignition keys. He dabbed his eyes with his hanky, 'I just wanted to touch you, girlie.'

The heat of the afternoon buzzed through the window in the form of a lazy fly while we waited. It landed on my cheek. I did not move. Then the sunset on Jakkals's stomach swelled as he sighed.

'I just wanted to touch you,' he repeated. He started the ignition and drove us back to his farmhouse.

I climbed out beside my Cruiser and, in an attempt to sprinkle some normality onto the situation, bent down to window level to thank Jakkals for breakfast. He stared ahead. Then his tyres squealed as he tore off. Jakkals's bakkie, the colour of pumpkins and sunsets, disappeared through the white dust.

From behind me, Louwtjie's Land Rover appeared. As it passed me, he winked and leant out the window. 'No diseases on this farm. But you can never be too careful. Listen old crow, you and me need to talk some time.'

'Yes. Wait!' I shouted after his trundling Land Rover. I sighed as it disappeared along the track.

I climbed back into my Cruiser. I needed to find Eddie. Fast. I found the crew not far from where I'd seen them that morning. Bull and his men were dispersed in a line, sieving samples of soil and spading them into half-kilogram bags. Eddie leant against his vehicle, smoke trailing from his fingers. He took another puff. He smoked like a school boy.

I slammed the door shut behind me. 'What was that about?'

'What?' asked Eddie

'Approaching the landowner and telling him I wanted to go hunting with him?'

He shrugged.

I crossed my arms and waited.

'I don't know. Clients, kind of, get in the way while we're working. You know what I mean.'

'Get in the way?'

'Yeah, you know, stick their noses in while we're getting the work done. Better to have you off busy doing something else.'

'That right?'

'Yeah.'

'Simon Says are working for TurnStone, okay? We hired you to do a job. And you'll comply to our sampling program and safety standards. Got that?'

Silence.

'You'd better have.' I turned back to my Cruiser. Shit. Shit, shit, *shit*. A flat tyre, now, of all times. And those off-road tyres were large and heavy.

From the toolbox in the Cruiser I took a pair of gloves and a spanner. From the bull bar, I unscrewed the high-lift jack. Without it, jacking up a heavy vehicle like this was impossible. I jacked up the Cruiser, removed the nuts of the flat tyre and placed them in my pocket. They jangled like loose change. Now for the hard part: lifting the tyre off the bolts. I sat down and slid my legs under the tyre. I strained my arms against it. It would not budge. *Shit.*

From the corner of my eye I could see Eddie. 'I will . . . not . . . ask for help,' I forced the words through my teeth as I strained against the weight. The tyre lifted and fell onto my lap. *Ooof*, I grunted. I rolled it off with a heave and towards the back of the vehicle. I bent my legs, hauled the tyre up onto my thighs and with a final heave lifted it into the back. I jumped back out of the way as I rolled out the spare. Behind me Eddie laughed.

Panting with the frustration of my powerless arms, I reversed the procedure. Lifting the tyre onto the bolts with a strength I did not have. That finally done, I secured the nuts, pumped down the high-lift jack and threw the tools into the back of the Cruiser. I drove off Soutpan without looking back.

As the kilometres between me and Soutpan grew, the tension in my body eased. My thoughts drifted to Terence. When would I see him again? Would it be weeks, a month, even two? My hand slipped to the charm around my neck. On impulse I dialled his vehicle over the radio. Late afternoon was a bad time to call; the radios seldom connected. But this time I dialled through.

'3034, Terence speaking. Over.'

'Terence, hi, just calling to say that. How are you? Over.'

There was silence at the other end, then a crackle. 'Okay. The drilling is continuing. They've had a few hold-ups. I don't know when they'll finish.'

My heart sank. He would not be able to leave his project while they were drilling. And I would not be able to see him.

'One of the farmers died yesterday. He had cancer of the liver. They flew him to the hospital in Gaborone a week ago. But he died yesterday. I saw his family today. Over.'

Terence was embroiled with other worlds. With other lives.

'I'm sorry to hear that. How are you? Over.'

There was silence again.

'I'm just tired,' he eventually said. 'They're having trouble drilling. There is just so much sand to drill through to get to the bedrock. The boreholes keep caving in, we must line them or something. Look, I have to go. I'll call you later, okay? Over.'

'Okay, later. Over and out.'

'Love you.'

'I know,' I replied, but the call had already been severed. Just like my heart.

As I drove, I watched the sun sink low on the horizon. The day had just slipped away. The sky warmed to the colours of the sand on Soutpan. Orange, yellow, pink and magenta. The words I had written down earlier that week came to mind. *Let God's country ease the worry from my mind, and bleed the anger from my veins, as the dust and the sun settle . . .*

I drove into Outjo and saw the one small supermarket was still open. I parked. Inside the shop I walked down the quiet isles. What did I need? What did I want? I had bought all the magazines already. They were stacked in my room on the spare bed next to my geological papers. A world of smiling, beautiful women, whose lipsticks matched their nail polish. I did not wear either, but that didn't stop me buying the magazines. I walked past the toiletries. The small shelf in my bathroom was already cluttered with jars and bottles I did not need. What did I think? What were they preserving me for? But buying things made sense: I could expense them to TurnStone. I could make Lawrence pay for some of the misery I was feeling. Pay for separating me from Terence for such long periods.

I drove back to the lodge armed with cheese, bread, a bar of chocolate and the only magazine I had not read, the *Farmer's Weekly*. At the lodge I closed my door behind me and climbed into bed. Boots, sweat, filth and all. I felt so tired. I ate the bread and cheese looking at pictures of hefty cattle. A lonely heart's column; *single man looking for single woman*. She was to be young, big to medium build, with an appetite for farm life and the outdoors. I checked the column again. Yes, lonely hearts, not lonely cattle. I fell asleep with the magazine over my face and the open chocolate bar squashed against my cheek.

My sleep was scattered. I dreamt all the stars went out, one by one. *And the world is desolate. Lost. Empty. Cows shuffle their hooves in the dark, mooing. Thirsty. There are no stars to watch us from above. There is just . . . nothing. I understand technically, of course, why the stars have gone out. There are formulae to explain it all. Formulae that balance, and hint at the greater knowledge that lies out there. But that is all. This scientific explanation gives no comfort. So what if I understand it? It makes no difference to the bleakness I feel. How can you continue to exist when you can no longer look up and see the stars looking down on you?*

I awoke with a jolt, feeling disorientated. It was late, almost eight in the morning. It would be quickest to grab a cup of coffee at Herr Winkler's shop and head straight to Soutpan. I picked up my field bag and walked out to the Cruiser. I stepped aside for some tourists wheeling their suitcases past me. They stopped to stare at me – at the black tyre marks on my legs, and then at my cheek. I wiped it and stared at my brown fingers. I licked them. Just chocolate.

A voice called out to me as I parked at Herr Winkler's shop. A familiar voice, a distant rumble of thunder. Abel. He wrapped his hand around my shoulder and squeezed, 'You look tired, tired like a donkey.'

I shook my head, which made me dizzy. 'Just bad dreams, Abel.'

He squeezed my shoulder so that it almost hurt. 'Bad dreams, hmmm.' His large dome of a head filled my vision, blocking the sunlight. 'Robyn, dreams are like Mrs Nangula's stones and bones. There are messages there, if you care to look.'

'I dreamt the stars went out.'

'The stars, Robyn. That is a bad dream. Just remember if you look very, very carefully, you will always see things coming.'

My mind popped and fizzled as I watched Abel leave. I was really not feeling too well. I put on my sunglasses. I would forget coffee. I needed to get out to Soutpan immediately.

'Robyn,' Abel was halfway down the street.

'Yes.'

'I have someone who wants to talk to you,' Abel called. 'I will speak to you about him later.'

I climbed back into the Cruiser and started the ignition. I sighed, rubbing my fingers deep into my eye-sockets. Colours spun. Then I sunk back into my seat and drove out of town, onto the open road. I slipped a cassette in, a tape I had bought in Outjo – a good find, given the limited selection. Juluka, Johnny Clegg and Sipho Mchunu. 'Tatazela'; the wild Zulu rhythm thumped about, beating off the Cruiser walls. Slamming into me. I jigged about, starting to wake up.

I turned up the volume. Opened the windows. My foot hit the brake. The vehicle veered. I grabbed the steering wheel. The Cruiser, as steady as a ship, eased to a stop at the side of the road. I ran back.

'Eddie!'

He stood in the middle of the road. Blood ran down from a gash in his forehead.

'Oh fuck,' he sobbed.

'Eddie,' I could hear the panic vibrate in my voice, 'What . . . where?'

I looked behind him. Through the bush, rolled well off the road, was the steel belly of the twincab. One of its tyres was still spinning. There was a movement in the bush.

'Eddie, wait here,' I pulled him off the road to the Cruiser.

Juluka continued to pound through the open doors. Eddie leant back against the Cruiser, swaying slightly. He held his head in his bloodied hands. I blundered through the bush towards his vehicle.

'Anyone here? Anyone else here?'

A groan, and Bull pushed past me. He held his wrist lamely, his face an odd shade of green. 'Just me.'

'You hurt?'

He shook his head. 'Just my arm. I told him he was driving too fast.'

I sunk onto my hands and knees and peered through a broken window. Torn seats with a bloody smear. There was no one else. A wallet was lying on the roof. I picked it up. Bags of soil samples lay scattered around the vehicle.

'Support your wrist with your other arm. No other injuries? No? Okay. I'll get you both to the hospital now.' My voice was smooth, syruping my panic.

Eddie had crawled into the back seat. I turned off the thump of music. Eddie's moaning rose.

Bull, with his good hand, helped me secure a seat belt around Eddie. 'Sit still, you arsehole. A seat belt has already saved your life once today.' The belt clicked into place.

Bull climbed into the passenger seat and winced as he pulled his seat belt over. 'Collarbone, I think. Shit, this should keep me out of the field for a few weeks. A month.'

'Just relax. I'll have you at the hospital as soon as possible.'

I checked my safety belt, twice. Quiet now, I drove into town. The syrup had dried up. I had to think, focus. The best clinic was past Outjo, seventy kilometres south, a private clinic in Otjiwarongo. I drove fast, but not too fast. Willing Otjiwarongo closer.

'Why?' I asked just once, 'Why the hurry?'

Bull shook his head.

Running, doctors, patients and eventually bandages and comforting sounds.

'Only superficial injuries, nothing serious,' explained the doctor. 'The worst injury is the cut on the young one's forehead. The older one has a broken collarbone. They're lucky, very lucky.'

Eddie was sedated. Bull sat up in bed with his arm secured to his body in a sling. I handed him the wallet.

'Thanks,' he said, and placed it on the table beside him. As the doctor left, he lit up a smoke. He looked strange leaning back on plump, white pillows – still dirty, unshaven, his torn field boots crossed at the ankle.

'Does it hurt?'

'Like hell, actually. Just waiting for the painkillers to kick in. Should be back on the job within a few days.'

'Don't be crazy.'

He started to shrug, then winced. 'The others can carry the samples. I'll supervise.' He took another drag on his cigarette. 'You asked what the hurry was. Your boss, Lawrence Sutherland, was the hurry. But still, old Eddie here didn't have to drive like an idiot. He did that all by himself.'

'What are you talking about?'

'TurnStone wanted the samples sent to Windhoek. They wanted us to offload them in a shed in Windhoek by nightfall. I understand someone from Committed Labs will pick them up in a few days' time.'

'I thought you sent them directly on to Committed Labs.'

A nurse popped her head around the curtain and sniffed. Bull held his breath and lowered the cigarette out of sight. She stared at him and then at me and finally left, barking at the male nurses not to smoke on the premises.

Bull exhaled with a smile. 'No, apparently not this time. We like to try to keep the client happy.' He glanced at me, as if that was the last concern on his mind.

'You mean you listen to whoever is paying you.'

'Exactly.'

'Those painkillers kicking in?'

'You bet.'

Leaving the men in the hygienic hands of the small-town clinic, I drove back to Outjo. I parked in a quiet street and punched Turn-Stone's number into the radio.

Lawrence's voice was crisp and tight. 'Why did you not follow Turn-Stone emergency procedure and call me first? Over.'

I closed my window, sealing myself in. 'I wanted to get the men to the hospital as soon as possible. Over.'

'Procedure states: step one, call the most senior member of staff *immediately*.'

'There was not much you could do from Cape Town,' I cut in.

'Step two, the senior member of staff will mobilize an emergency response. Over,' Lawrence threw his vowels roundly at me.

'Look, we were half an hour's drive from the closest hospital. The men were not seriously injured. I could get them to hospital faster than anyone else.' I rubbed my forehead as I spoke. 'They said they were in a hurry to drop samples off in Windhoek by the end of the day. Your request. I didn't know anything about it. Over.'

'We needed to get samples analysed before our annual audit. Our accountant's request. Financial matters for next year's exploration budget,' he replied tartly. 'But I thought I had made company procedure clear. I could not make it any bloody clearer. Step one: call the most senior member of staff immediately.'

I remained quiet.

'Where are those samples, over?' he suddenly asked.

'What, over?'

'The samples loaded on the vehicle that rolled. Where are they? Over.'

'I presume they're still there, over.'

'Have them secured and sent to Committed Labs immediately. And in future, follow procedure.' And then, as if extracting a cancerous piece of flesh, he added, 'We need better control out there. This is what comes from putting a junior, female geologist in control.'

I pushed the PTT button, 'The fact that I am female is of no consequence. And I have experience.'

But the line was dead, Lawrence had ended the call. Beneath my sure words, my voice staggered. My world was tilting. I sunk my head into my hands. A knuckle rapped on the closed window. I looked up to see Abel peering through the window, his eyes sheltered by his hand. I opened the window.

'Robyn. What can I do?'

I was silent for a second. I wanted to bury my face in his chest and cry like a child. I wanted to tell him that two men had nearly died on my project today. I wanted to lean against his friendship. I wanted his strength.

'Nothing, thanks,' I shook my head, 'the men have already gone to hospital. They are not seriously injured.' I gave a humourless laugh. 'Quite a day.'

'You're hurt.' Able popped his large head through the window. I leant back as he lifted a finger to my face. 'What's this?'

'Nothing. Just a scratch from a *wag-'n-bietjie* bush and that, oh, just chocolate.'

'Robyn, Robyn,' he shook his head as he extracted himself from the window. He leant against the Cruiser's rear view mirror. Large muscles, dark as coal, bulged from his shirt sleeves. 'I have someone who wants to talk to you.'

I was quiet. I did not feel like talking to anyone.

'You know him. He is staying on my farm Soetwater. Come and visit him there. But you must come at night. *Hy loop bedags deur die bos* – in the day he's walking through the bush.'

'I'm not meant to drive at night, company rule.'

'Come tonight.'

We looked at each other. He waited.

'I'll be there after seven.'

After Abel had left, I dialled the number of Terence's vehicle. There was a crackle.

'3034, Terence speaking. Over.'

Relief flooded through my veins. 'Terence, it's me. Just calling to hear your voice. Over.'

'Everything okay there, over?'

'No, there's been an accident. Simon Says rolled a vehicle,' my voice caught.

Silence. Terence was always one to think before he spoke.

'But no one is hurt? Over.'

'No one is seriously hurt. Some minor injuries but no one is hurt. They were lucky. Over.'

'This is good.' Three simple words that carried such weight. Damn right it was good. Otherwise what? Death. Funerals. Bodies to fly back. Soulless. Starless.

'Terence,' my voice cracked.

'Yes, angel.'

'It's really good to hear your voice. Just to know you're at the other end of the line.' I leant my head against the steering wheel, rubbing my fingers tightly into my eyes. 'Terence?' I called.

A crackle, a buzz. Our line was dead.

The sun was setting. The day had disappeared, just like the day before. Time was running on fast forward. I drove back to the lodge and closed myself into my room. There was blood on my shorts. Eddie's blood. On impulse I pulled off my clothes and threw them into the bin. Standing under the shower, I let the hot water massage my back and scalp. It stung the fine scratch on my cheek. I let the water calm my shaking hands. A field mouse with a brown stripe down his back crawled up from the drain and drank the shower water, as he did most nights. I poked him with my big toe and he darted back down the drain. After a long while, I switched off the tap and roughly towelled myself dry. Clean laundry was folded into a neat pile on the spare bed. I selected a pair of jeans and a tracksuit top. They smelt clean and felt soft and luxurious, even the socks. I pulled my sturdy leather boots over them.

I drove out to Abel's farm. The sensation of driving at night had become unfamiliar. Forbidden. Yellow lights on a river of tar. I slowed down as the headlights blinded a hare. Further down the road I drove past a warthog with three babies. Their little tails stood up like radio aerials as they ran into the bush. Abel's orange stall came into sight; there were no oranges in it. I turned onto his track.

The lights in Abel's house were on. I knocked on his front door. Abel answered wearing only a pair of baggy shorts, presumably his pyjamas. He scratched his stomach, the dark side of the moon. 'Just keep driving, Robyn. He's camping in the bush, about two kilometres from here. You'll see his fire.'

'Who?'

'Louwtjie,' Abel chuckled as he closed the door.

Abel's instructions were simple. A fire flickered two kilometres down the track. It was the only light in a black, starry night; the moon provided just a sly slit of a smile. Louwtjie's Land Rover bakkie was parked near the fire. It was parked at an angle, with its rear tyres reversed up a termite mound. I parked the Cruiser a little distance from his camp, in the shadow of the moon. From the passenger seat, I picked up the six-pack of beers I had brought from the lodge.

There was an echoed splash and the distinctive squeak of naked flesh from the back of the bakkie.

'I'll be there now, Robyn,' he called, 'Just taking my bath.'

Thud, he jumped onto the ground out of sight. I heard him bang his boots on the tailgate, 'Must always check for scorpions. Those little *boggers*, they'll crawl in anywhere where it is nice and warm. *Fokken hel.*'

Louwtjie emerged wearing nothing but a towel wrapped around his skinny waist, army-style boots with their laces undone and a soft canvas hat. The hat cast a long shadow over his face. As he stepped closer to the fire I could see how pale his hollow chest was compared to the deep tan on his legs and arms.

'Can you actually bath in the back of that?'

'She can hold just enough water. Wait, I must just let the water out or she'll rust.'

He started the motor, the bakkie lurched forward and the tailgate fell open with a clang. His bath water spilled out. He took long, gangly strides back to me, holding his towel in place. 'Right, let's make ourselves comfortable. Cold, too,' he said as he took the six pack. 'Now that's more like it.'

Louwtjie pulled out a coolbox for me to sit on and made himself comfortable on a rock, his long legs stretched out in front of him.

'So, Louwtjie. Why is a pilot here? On Abel's farm?'

'Questions, questions. Have a beer first,' he opened two bottles and handed one to me. He drained half his beer in the first gulp and looked at my Cruiser. '*Fokken hel*, geologists now have vehicles like that. Palaces on wheels.' He hesitated. 'Pilot. Well, I have a license, take the odd contract here and there to keep me going. Like the one for Turn-Stone. But for most of my life I've worked as a geologist.'

'A *geologist*? Why didn't you say?'

Louwtjie pushed back his floppy hat. His large, red ears looked luminous in the firelight. His eyes shards of brittle blue glass. 'Been laying low. Been watching. I know this area well, like the back of my hand. I worked here in the seventies and eighties.'

'In Outjo? I would've seen your reports, in among the open files at the Geological Survey in Windhoek.'

'You would think. Not that I wrote actual reports, *fokken hel*. More like a diary. But they were all handed over to the survey. When I saw the area you were working in I wondered if you'd seen my work, so I went to check the survey records – and guess what? They were nowhere to be seen. So I sent a copy to your TurnStone office in Cape Town. Never heard a *piep* from them. That's when I got more, um . . . *interested*.'

'What did the report say?'

'Let me tell you,' Louwtjie pointed at me with his beer, refusing to be hurried, 'I worked this area every day for seven years. Looking for base metals, including copper. That's how I know Abel, and let me tell you one thing, you won't find a better friend than Abel. There's a man I trust.'

He leant forward and tilted the lid of the potjie on the fire. The sweet aroma of game swirled around me. My stomach clenched. I had not eaten dinner, nor lunch nor breakfast, I remembered ruefully.

'Abel told me I'd have company tonight and that it would not be his. So I cooked extra. Warthog. I think you'll like it.' Louwtjie stood up and his towel slipped, revealing one bony white hip. He collected some utensils from a box: a plastic plate, a spoon and a fork. He ladled some stew onto the plate and handed it to me with the fork. He then turned the pot lid upside down, filled it and sat down beside me. His spoon scraped the lid as he shovelled the stew into his mouth.

'So in your seven years here, did you discover any new copper deposits?'

'Have you?' Louwtjie slid me a look.

I rubbed my cheek. 'To be honest, I'm not sure what's going on here. We've had elevated copper results from the laboratories. They actually look quite good. But the core . . . we can't see any copper-bearing sulphides. You saw the core in the shed.' I shrugged. 'Perhaps it's chalcocite and we just can't see it in the graphite.'

Louwtjie opened another beer and took a long sip. His prominent Adam's apple bobbed. He wiped his mouth. 'No chalcocite here, old crow. No copper here either for that matter. Believe me, our methods were not so different. We flew an air survey, different technology then, but the results would have been similar. We drilled the targets. They were all graphite. The results were laid out in the diary I sent through to TurnStone. We even drilled a hole on Abel's farm. So what I cannot understand is why you buggers are still at it.'

'They believe there may be a world-class copper deposit here,' the fire spat a flame at me. 'So, no copper here.'

'*Fok* no. If anyone knows the geology here, it's me. For seven years my team moved from farm to farm. Mapped, took samples, drilled. If there was something here, we would've found it. We did it differently then though, no palaces on wheels, we camped from farm to farm. Seven years, we worked through the Angola-Namibia Border War. And this was one of the routes the Swapo troops took to get from Windhoek to the border. Those troops travelled at night, raided farms along the way for whatever they could get, guns, food, whatever. Farmers were shot. You cannot believe the fear the farmers lived in.'

'But you continued to work here?' I placed my plate silently at my feet.

'I had a job to do and I did it. I knew the paths the guerrilla troops took. I had daily contact with the police sergeant. And we took precautions; we stayed away from major dirt tracks, we never drove through a farm gate. We would take down the fence and make our own track. We also stayed away from the power lines, water tanks. Anywhere they would lay landmines.'

'But still . . .' My throat felt dry.

'I had a job to do and I did it.' His eyes, which had so recently sparkled with humour, were icy. 'The nights were the worst. We had to keep quiet, keep our voices down. Keep our camp dark and hidden. No fires, no music. We didn't want to attract the troops. Night after night, month after month. Sometimes we couldn't stand the silence any longer. We could not stand the fear. We used to go crazy some nights. We would make a fire, play loud music and get drunk and scream at the shadows in the bush.' Louwtjie flung his arms open wide and yelled, *'Come and get us, you fokkers. Come and get us. We are waiting for you!'*

A twig broke behind us and we both flinched.

'Just warthog,' Louwtjie said softly, 'just warthog. He can smell his brother.'

'And then one night they came. After months of being specially careful, they came. We hadn't even made a fire that night. Our camp was hidden. We were all asleep. And they came. They moved through our camp so quietly, none of us woke up. They took everything, all our food, all our water. Even our gun. Not one of us heard them.'

The flames crackled and the fire flared. My face grew hot and I shielded my burning cheeks from the fire.

'We saw their tracks in the sand the next morning. There were eight of them and not *one* of us had heard them.'

The smoke from the fire drifted over Louwtjie and me. Casting a spell of silence. We watched the fire. My beer grew warm in my hands.

'My crew walked out on me the next day. All of them. Packed up and left while I was in the field. They went back to our office in Windhoek, back to safety. The boss sent out the police to arrest me, the same bloody police sergeant I spoke to every day.'

'Why?'

'For putting the field crew at risk, he said. For putting their lives in danger. They thought I had left this field area years ago.'

'But . . . what happened?'

'They released me, eventually, when they realised I knew what I was doing. When they found out I had spoken to the police daily. I had taken precautions. Abel backed me up, he was not a man to argue with. He had connections. Abel got me out.'

A log collapsed on the fire and the sparks flared and rose into the air like yellow beetles. They hovered around us and then faded.

'Well . . .' I sounded sceptical. I silenced myself with a sip of warm beer.

'We had a job to do,' Louwtjie looked at me, 'and we did it.'

I nodded.

'So, no copper,' I said after a while. 'Louwtjie, I've had a long day. I need to sleep. Thanks for this information.'

I reached out to shake hands. Our hands met across the fire; the grasp held a second longer than was comfortable over the flames.

'I'll be seeing you, sometime, somewhere.' Louwtjie's eyes sparkled once again and he wiggled his beard playfully.

'I hope so,' I smiled.

I walked back to the Cruiser, feeling the heat in my hand subside in the cool night air. The Cruiser stood silent in the dark shadow. I drove past Abel's house, but his lights were already out.

CHAPTER THIRTEEN

Desert Varnish

'Desert varnish.' Prof popped the unlit pipe from his mouth. 'The iron and manganese are leached from the rock to form this hard, black metallic coating – desert varnish. You'll only see it in the harshest conditions like this. You can't tell what lies beneath it until you break it open and get a nice, fresh surface.'

Prof's words were partly swallowed by the wind. His face was hidden by the turban he'd wrapped around his head to protect himself from the sun and sand. The rest of us – Kirkby, Spyder, Terence, Antonio and myself – stood huddled around him. *Clang, clang*, Spyder pounded away with his hammer.

'And it's hell to break.' Prof bit his pipe and called, 'What've you got there, Spyder?'

Spyder held up a tiny chip of rock. 'Not much. Holy *shit*.' He whipped off his hat.

We all turned around.

Prof's mouth fell slack. '*Hemel en aarde.*'

Beyond the black mountain on which we stood, beyond the sea of yellow sand, beyond the lapping waves of the red dunes of the Namib Desert, a dust storm rolled and tumbled. A dust storm of the worst possible scale, obliterating the desert and sky. Rolling, churning, a fog of yellow smoke. Rising, sinking and howling towards us.

We all ran, following Prof's long thin legs down the mountain to the two dinky cars parked at the base. We dropped level by level, our clumsy boots nimble over the loose, black boulders. The doors of the two Land Cruisers slammed. Seconds later the storm engulfed us. The desert disappeared. Terence's mouth moved; I heard nothing but the hail of sand. *Taka-taka-taka.* I turned to see Spyder on the back seat. His large frame filled up most of it. His blond hair, torn apart by the wind, stood up at right angles from his broad tanned face, and his eyes looked red and astounded. Terence started the Cruiser and followed the red lights in front of us. Bumper to bumper we drove through the storm. *Taka-taka-taka.*

∧

Lawrence had arranged this excursion into the Namib Desert. At a drop of a hat, we were to leave the drilling, leave the projects. We needed a break, explained Lawrence, and a once-in-a-lifetime opportunity had arisen: to travel through the restricted Awasib desert with one of the world experts on Namibian geology. That was Prof. A once-in-a-lifetime opportunity, Lawrence emphasised; we would *all* be going. But at the last minute he had backed out. Shareholder commitments, he'd explained.

He'd watched Terence, Antonio, Spyder, Kirkby and I depart for the excursion from the TurnStone Cape Town office.

'Kirkby, you're to take my place as management representative. I'll be sure on my part to represent TurnStone's best interests. I trust you'll be gone for . . . three weeks?'

Kirkby fixed Lawrence with the gaze of a dead fish and said, somewhat mysteriously, 'It'll be three weeks. I know my work, mate.'

Lawrence was smiling, but he seemed edgy, preoccupied. A ship leaving the harbour distracted him. He touched his tie, a tie of impeccable taste, made of bronze and black interwoven thread, set against a cream shirt. Then he pulled his attention back to us. 'Time for you to leave. Have a good trip, all of you. I'm devastated I cannot join you. Quite devastated – it's a once-in-a-lifetime opportunity.'

We heaved our luggage over our shoulders and edged past Lawrence as he held the door open. He shut the door, etched with the TurnStone logo, firmly behind us.

∧

That was just two weeks ago. We had been living in the desert for only fourteen days and yet I could not remember a time before it. Time had spread out like the horizons around us. No longer measured by sunrises and sunsets, but rather by the survival of sandstorms, dehydration, sunburnt skin and eyes stinging from grit.

I wiped the sand from my eyes with the corner of my T-shirt as Terence drove. Not in my wildest dreams could I imagine Lawrence in these conditions. The Cruiser rocked as we drove, hit by another wave of sand. Terence, Spyder and I were quiet, wrapped in nature's yellow cloak of devil mystery.

Spyder fell over on the seat. 'That was wild, that was crazy man.' *Hee haw, hee haw.*

We followed the other Cruiser through the yellow mist. *Rat-a-tat.* Suddenly the veil started to slip away, and the blue sky stood shyly in front of us. We had driven through the dust storm. It was quiet. We heard only the hum of the soft tyres. In the distance, the red dunes of the Namib lapped onto the hard yellow plains. No words could describe the expanse, the size of the landscape around us. There was no shade, no water and no means of survival other than what we carried with us in the Cruisers.

I opened my window and my hair snapped across my face, stinging me. 'Pass my cap, Spyder.'

He leant forward and jammed it on my head. 'There you go, *woestynblommetjie.*' Desert rose – a rose-shaped crystal found in the sand dunes. I laughed at him.

Terence changed up a gear and the tyres whizzed, sounding like a hovercraft over water. His hair, which he still wore short, was as wild as Spyder's. The two weeks' growth on his chin had practically formed a beard. His face looked a little burnt, sensitive to the touch. But he looked calm, content, with nature leaning her heavy weight on him. He glanced at me and smiled. '*Woestynblommetjie* – crystallised from sweat perhaps.'

Slowly we arced towards a black mountain. We drove to its foot and around its craggy toes to our secluded camp. Prof and Antonio were already stacking wood alongside the fireplace.

'Where's the white Cruiser?' I asked as Terence parked.

'Kirkby has it. He said he wanted to tinker with the radio when he got back to camp.'

Hee haw, haw hee, Spyder collapsed. 'Tinker with the radio! Is that what they call it now? Tinker with the radio. Not Spank-the-monkey, Peel-the-banana or Shake-hands-with-yourself?'

'Really, Spyder,' I rolled my eyes, 'it's not *that* funny.'

'It is, it is!' He rolled over onto his back, *hee haw, haw hee.*

'I'm going to be the first one to use the water,' I said, gathering up my toiletry bag from under the seat.

Spyder sat up. He opened the door and jogged past me towards the sagging canvas tent. I hurried after him. It was better to be first with the basin of water than second, or worse, third. Spyder found the two plastic basins and decanted water into them until they were each half-full. Two basins was all the water we had to spare for washing every day.

I carried my basin around to a private space behind a boulder and stripped to my shorts and bra. The water felt cool against my hot skin, soothing. I washed off the slippery suncream and dust from my nutmeg-brown arms, and patted my sensitive skin dry. There was the familiar whir of the radio dialling. I turned around. It came from the white Cruiser parked a distance away – out of sight of the camp, but just within sight of my private bathing area. Kirkby stood at the open door. With nothing in the desert to hinder it, his voice travelled clearly.

'It's been almost two weeks, mate. It's a bloody desert out here. It's fucking harsh.'

Silence. A crackle.

'No, no ways, mate. I've told you. We can't stay out here for bloody ever. You've got the letter of intent for Christsake, now get this due diligence wrapped up. I don't give a damn if they're trying to beat you down. You told me you could justify the price . . . Listen, Lawrence, I told you, it's harsh out here, a fucking desert. Sort out the disclosure of assets. Sort it out, Lawrence. Over and out.'

I pulled on my cleanest shirt, jeans and sandals and walked back to camp. I handed Antonio the bar of soap and he trundled off, his torn shirt tails flapping behind him.

In the camp, Terence was lighting the fire and Prof was peeling onions on the camp table. His hands worked quickly, obviously accustomed to cooking. He had a long, dour face and grey eyes that dripped with humour. His wavy grey hair was combed away from his face. He handed me a penknife and a bottle of red wine as the sun sunk reluctantly behind us. No one turned to watch her go, even though she spread a tail of cosmic gold on her departure. Rather we looked up to welcome the cool, still stars.

As Prof, Terence and I prepared dinner, Spyder sat down near the fire and blew softly on his harmonica. He sucked and blew with serious concentration, producing a reasonable rendition of 'Whiter Shade of Pale'.

Leaving the dinner to cook, Prof sat down beside him, dragging the coolbox. With his fingers he beat a soft accompanying rhythm on the box. Terence stood staring into the fire. I refilled my tin mug with red wine and went to join them.

'Prof,' Kirkby's voice was loud and brash. He had put on a red, waterproof jacket which flared at the base, designed to be loose enough to throw over a backpack.

Spyder stopped playing.

'Prof,' Kirkby repeated, 'TurnStone have some pretty good exploration ventures in Africa. We'll be able to sniff out the larger mines. We definitely have some promising results, definitely.'

Prof nodded but continued to drum, his eyes on the fire.

'Yeah, mate,' Kirkby raised his voice, 'you might want to mention that to some of the larger mining companies you consult with. Yeah, you might want to mention something about the promising signs of copper we've had.'

'Hey, Little Red Riding Hood, you sure are looking good.' *Hee haw haw*.

Kirkby's chest swelled and he stared at Spyder slit-eyed. 'Best you can get, mate. This jacket came from Australia and it's survived trips all over the world. You don't get better quality than this.'

'Little Red Riding Hood,' Spyder repeated and blew a loud flat note.

I saw Prof's shoulders lift as he swallowed a laugh.

I strolled over to Terence. 'Kirkby was on the radio to Lawrence.'

'What about?'

'Prices and such. Difficult to know. He mentioned a due diligence.'

'Due diligence?'

I shrugged. 'Perhaps a joint venture. TurnStone has lots of those.'

Terence turned to look at Kirkby. His eyes followed him as he dragged a camp chair closer to the fire. 'He's called the office a few times. Doesn't seem to want to lose touch. Something must be going on.'

'Not much we can do to find out. Not here. Perhaps when we get back.'

Terence sighed and put his arm around my shoulder, 'This can't continue indefinitely.'

I leant against him. 'What can't?'

'Working like this. Months and months away from each other.'

A star shot across the sky, burning out.

Terence and I helped Prof carry the three-legged potjies to the fire. Within fifteen minutes a simple meal of pasta and sauce was ready and distributed amongst hungry hands. Spoons scraped plastic plates and the last of the wine rations were handed out. Blistered red feet stretched out towards the fire. The first to finish dinner, Prof placed his plate on the ground and leant back with a sigh. He popped his pipe into his mouth and lit it, and the smell of fruity tobacco filtered around us. Above us the Milky Way blazed.

'Prof,' Kirkby tried again, 'TurnStone has been getting some interesting copper results. Yeah, we've been pretty successful in Africa. Especially in Namibia. '

But Prof had closed his eyes, his pipe still in his mouth, and was dozing.

'Well, I'm going to sleep,' Kirkby stood up, irritated, 'and I suggest you all do the same. We have another early start tomorrow.' Kirkby clumped out of sight.

'Watch out for the big, bad wolf,' said Spyder.

Antonio looked up at the stars and sighed. 'Ah,' he suddenly sat up, 'something my daughter gave me just before we left.' He walked over to the white Cruiser and we heard him rustle through the cubby-hole. Something dropped and he swore. He returned to the fire smiling, sat down and closed his eyes.

In that silence, with the universe swimming above us and the surrounding desert asleep, a voice rose spinning towards the stars. Dipping in heartache and burning with pain, Pavarotti gave his finest performance of 'Una Furtiva Lagrima'. In the dark, with only the crackling flames and the Milky Way above us, we sat quiet and attentive. The fire flared and caught our faces for a flicker of time: still faces with quiet smiles. Faces in a time and a space we would remember forever. We sat like that until the last of the sound drifted from us and was washed up into the night sky, carrying with it all our peace and happiness. Soaked it up and tumbled it together and formed – in the very corner of our galaxy – another star. So small and insignificant in the scale of the universe. But there it was: one perfect, tiny star.

The music faded. Prof sighed and then rose. One by one figures left, retreating to stretchers laid out beside the Land Cruisers or, like Terence and myself, to sleep on the Cruiser's roof racks. I climbed up onto the roof, dragging my mattress and sleeping bag behind me. I pulled off my shoes and wiggled into my bag. A few minutes later, Terence joined me. He pulled me closer and we stared up at the orchestra of stars above us.

'Words cannot describe the size and beauty of this place,' I murmured. 'It's a pity you couldn't bring Bongi with you.'

'It's way too harsh for Bongi out here. He'd never survive.'

Terence was right, of course. He'd left Bongi with the farmer's wife, the doctor. Bongi was keeping their family dog, a ridgeback named Ella, company. Ella and Bongi now accompanied the doctor on her errands as she flew her Cessna from farm to farm. Terence's fingers trailed through my hair and got stuck. He gave it another attempt and gave up, patting my tangled hair away from my face.

'This place is incredible. I guess we have TurnStone to thank for being here . . . if nothing else.' He sighed. 'If nothing else. Not much else makes sense. The copper results from my project don't correspond with the geology. But Lawrence seems to trust them. You've received the results from your soil samples. What did they indicate?'

'The soil samples taken from Soutpan? The elevated copper values indicate there could be a copper deposit, extending over the two farms, of almost five kilometres in length. Lawrence is pleased.'

'Of course he is.' A minute later, Terence asked, 'When are you getting the results back from those duplicate samples you sent to the Namaqualand laboratories?'

'They take a long time. But it should be any day now.'

'We could try and call them over the radio.'

'We could, if you don't think it can wait.' I lay down against his chest. 'You know, Louwtjie prospected for copper on Wag 'n Bietjie in the seventies. I know that the technology was not as advanced in those days, but he didn't find a thing.' I closed my eyes, exhausted from the day, and fell asleep, breathing in the smell of sweat and dust.

I awoke just before sunrise. Wind ripped through the valley. In the past two weeks, we had had windy days, wind that stung sunburnt cheeks, wind that bit legs. But nothing like this. This wind smacked waves of sand into my sleeping bag. It tore into my ear, filling it with sand. The dust; I could hardly breathe. I tied a T-shirt around my nose and mouth and shook Terence. Only his eyes could be seen; he had wrapped a turban around his head. He sat up, spluttered and swore. The others were getting up, grey figures moving around, grabbing possessions and complaining. Terence and I climbed down, pulling our bedding with us. We threw it into the back of the Cruiser.

Prof was making coffee, bringing a pot to boil over the previous night's coals. He had a towel wrapped around his head, Arab-style. In fact everyone's face was hidden by drapes of cloth, towels, anything. It looked like a scene from Lawrence of Arabia, except that Lawrence was not there.

'What the hell do you mean, there's no breakfast,' shouted Kirkby through his turban.

'Ah yes, we have run out of food. My fault, thoroughly. This was not meant to be an endurance trip.' Even in these conditions, I could see Prof's dry humour was at play.

'You're bloody right it wasn't!' shouted Kirkby.

I'm not sure if Prof's eye flickered from a wink or a gust of sand as he handed me a mug of coffee. It still tasted of last night's red wine. 'We'll have to pack up,' he said. 'It's about time we started moving south anyway. The camp will never survive in this.'

'And us?' I asked.

'Us? Oh *we'll* survive,' Prof reassured me.

A wave of sand stung my ear, drowning out the rest of his sentence. I stood around the smouldering coals with Antonio and Terence, sipping my gritty coffee with my eyes closed.

The camp was quickly cleared and stacked. Vehicles were packed and ready to go. Something was missing.

'Where's Spyder?' I shouted.

The others looked around.

'There,' pointed out Terence. Spyder's stretcher was laid out behind a boulder. He lay asleep on his stomach. The wind tugged at his flimsy T-shirt and sand had collected in tiny dunes on his back and in his sleeping bag.

'Spyder, wake up.'

He sat up with a jolt, spitting out a mouthful of sand. 'What?' he looked at the packed vehicles. 'Hey, *woestynblommetjie*, you guys weren't planning to leave me behind, were you? Shit, looks like another fucking beautiful day in Africa.'

The two Cruisers drove in convoy, leaving behind our desolate campsite. Prof, Antonio and Spyder in the white. From the start Prof and Antonio had hit it off, the Afrikaner and the Italian. They took turns to drive, arguing about it amicably. Behind them, Terence, Kirkby and I followed in the navy Cruiser. As it was Prof's excursion, he had planned each stop carefully, and it wasn't long before his vehicle veered from the expanse of open desert towards a black mountain which rose like a volcanic island. My heart sank; we would have to leave the shelter of the vehicles again so soon.

We parked at the base of a mountain, secured our hats, packs and hammers and began to tread the black spines of desert varnish. As the sun rose that morning, its weight dropped onto us like an expected burden. Wind, sand and sun. A day of hell. There was no escape. No escape from the sun, no escape from the sand or the wind. Sand, sun and wind. In no particular order. Together and in combinations. Even through the thick, greasy layers of suncream, our skins became red and sensitive to the touch. The day's dry heat merely mounted on the accumulated heat of the days past; mounted it like a crazed, thirsty jackal.

A solitary hell for each of us, a desert of purgatory. Each of us following the other weary figures over the black vertebrae of the rocky mountains, while the glare of the red and yellow seas reflected below us. The black rock beneath our boots baked us, cooked us, slowly but thoroughly.

By midday I had had enough; more than I could take. I was, I told myself, officially dehydrated and worthy of medical attention, never mind more sun, sand and wind. No more bloody desert varnish. I trailed away from the group and sat in the very sparse shade of a kokerboom. Its starry branches pleaded beseechingly for some relief from the hot blue sky. Or at least I did. Behind me on the black spine of the mountain, the group, their heads and turbans bent into the wind, gathered around Prof. Geologists, I mumbled to myself, why don't they ever know when enough is enough? No rock could be that interesting, no rock could be worth this amount of physical torture. The black boulder I was sitting on scorched the bare skin on the back of my thighs. I leant back against the trunk of the kokerboom, which resembled sunburnt human flesh, and squinted into the sun.

No. I lifted my binoculars.

Yes. In this cruel, unforgiving paradise, in this world with neither river nor rainfall, there it was . . . treading one hoof in front of another. Gemsbok. Oryx. It stopped to look up at me, perhaps at the glint of light from the binoculars. A black-and-white face – the markings of a warrior. Sand Warrior. He returned to his rhythmic plod, carrying the weight of his horns, accepting his purgatory. He left neat dark tracks. His image shimmered and was soaked up by the sun.

I was dizzy, dehydrated. Around me, the boulders were too hot to touch. I picked up my hammer and struck the rock in front of me. Not for geological interest – my interest had long since evaporated, along with the water content in my body. I pounded against the desert varnish with sheer exasperation, for the heat that tore at me, for the sun that blistered me. I suddenly wanted to break through that black skullcap. Desert varnish. I wanted to see beneath the surface. *Pang, pang,* my hammer rung a metallic chime. The others looked around to identify the noise and carried on walking.

Pang, pang, I pounded the boulder. I wanted that rock to break, reveal itself. *Pang, pang.* Break it open. I hesitated and then, as if fooling the rock, gave it a swift, unexpected blow across its shoulder. A chip ricocheted off, revealing clear blue contents. I picked up the piece and rubbed my thumb over the fresh surface. Fine-grained, siliceous; a felsic volcanic. I looked up at the expanse of yellow sand interrupted only by the black islands of mountains. I looked up at the desert that could kill me with a hint of its breath.

The horizon had melted. I was feeling nauseous. I pulled my knees up to my chest, looking around for the others. They were nowhere to be seen. The best thing for me to do would be to climb down and wait at the vehicles. I stood up, slipped my hammer back into my belt and adjusted the water bottle strap around my neck. I started my slow descent, balancing boulder by boulder, my knees unsteady. The desert varnish was hot through the soles of my boots. The sun's rays ricocheted like bullets off its metallic sheen. The ground rose and fell with each step. Lower and lower; the dinky cars in the distance became bigger and bigger. The desert varnish shimmered and then folded its big black arms around me. The arms of Africa. I stopped to steady my knees, which were shaking uncontrollably now. I looked back to find the others. Still there was no sign of them. I continued my journey, boulder by boulder. I slipped and fell. My vision blurred. The Cruisers had risen up to greet me. But no, I was on their level. I pulled myself up with a final heave, walked over to the navy Cruiser and collapsed in its tiny strip of shade.

'My God, what is it they are doing?' Antonio appeared from behind the vehicle. 'What I need now is a nice cold rock shandy. The only good thing the Anglo-Saxons invented.'

'Don't,' I said to Antonio. I thought of cold, bitter liquid, the ice clinking against the glass. Antonio and I had enjoyed many rock shandies in Outjo.

Behind us we heard a rattle of keys. Spyder was opening the white

Cruiser. He carried a canister of water over to us. 'It's not cold, *woestynblommetjie*, but at least its not boiling.'

The water was warm, body temperature. Too warm to hydrate me. I handed it to Antonio. I watched the water run down his grey stubble and his dirty neck as he drank.

'And this?' Prof's skinny figure towered above us in his turban. Behind him trudged Kirkby and Terence.

He pulled out his field guide from his pack and flicked it open. 'Another three outcrops to visit before we head south.'

'I can't,' I said.

Prof looked at the others. No one said anything. Spyder scratched in the ground with a stick

'Sissies. I told you it would be a tough trip.' Prof smiled but he himself looked exhausted. 'Well then, we may as well head directly south. Take a break driving. We've a fair way to travel today anyway. We can stop at a few outcrops later in the day.'

Thank God. I crawled into the back of the navy Cruiser.

'Prof, I'd like to talk to you about the exploration potential of these rocks for copper-gold deposits . . .' Kirkby climbed into the white Cruiser with Prof.

Just about to follow Prof, Antonio looked at Kirkby and grimaced. He chose to travel with Terence and me in the navy Cruiser, leaving Spyder to travel with Kirkby and Prof. Terence started the engine, the air conditioner purred to life and we headed out of the yellow desert with its islands of black mountains, towards the red Namib dunes.

As the air conditioner blasted its chilly breath onto me, I scrounged under the seat and found some packets of nuts. I handed them out. We washed them down with water. I began to feel better. Sweat had dried in crystals along my hairline. I untied my laces and eased my sore feet from my boots.

'No more!' cried Antonio. 'It's too hot.' He looked over his shoulder and asked me, 'Where are we going, which route are we taking?'

I picked up the excursion guide and flicked to the date. 'According to this we drive about three hundred kilometres south, by which time we'll be out of the Namib desert. Prof has marked a couple of stops there, described here as younger granitic intrusions . . . What's this?' A page slipped out. My eyes skimmed it as I read slowly, '*The samples were sent to TurnStone's associate company Committed Labs and taken by their subsidiary Simon Says Samplers.*' I closed the booklet. *Kirkby Jones* was scribbled in the corner. 'This is Kirkby's copy. He left it in here. This is a letter to him from Lawrence. Committed Labs an *associate* of TurnStone? Sending our samples to an associate for analysis. How could you trust that? And Simon Says their subsidiary? Lawrence has *never* mentioned this.'

'They could tamper with the samples,' said Terence. 'Salt them with copper.'

'What? No,' Antonio waved his hands, 'no, no, no. Not salting.'

'We should call the Namaqualand laboratory. See if they have the results for Robyn's samples.'

I paged through my diary and handed Antonio the number. He switched on the radio and punched it in. The number dialled through.

Please do not hang up, this call is from a radio. I repeat, do not hang up . . . the recorded voice said. *Beeeep.*

'Charlie, delta, zulu,' shouted Antonio, 'Hello? Hello? Pah, they hung up.'

The voluptuous red dunes loomed closer, and before long we were driving on a track twisting through their naked curves. We sat in silence. Lawrence had wanted no other laboratory used, only Committed Labs; he had wanted no company to take the soil samples other than Simon Says Samplers.

Prof, having stopped to look at loose scree, was a good twenty minutes' drive behind us. Terence parked at the base of a large red dune. He switched the radio back on and tried the laboratory number again.

Please do not hang up, this call is from a radio. Do not . . .

'Hello. Namaqualand Laboratories? Yes. I am calling to inquire about the results for samples sent by a Ms R. Hartley. Over?'

A voice crackled back, refusing to give confidential results over the phone.

I took the hand piece from Terence. 'This is Robyn Hartley. Please may I speak directly to your lab technician? They do know me, I used your laboratory regularly when I worked in Namaqualand. Over.'

There was an extended hiss while we waited.

'Robyn? Yes. I'll read the results to you. Three samples, here they are. 0.09%, 0.02% and 0. 03% copper. That all? Keep in touch.'

Terence scribbled down the numbers.

Antonio switched off the radio. 'That is not copper. So little. But looking at the core, it would have been my guess.'

Terence shook his head. 'Have Committed Labs been salting the samples? Or TurnStone even. Have they been adding copper to the samples?'

'But *why*? We're just lying to *ourselves*. We should speak to Lawrence about this. Find out what this means.'

'Let's just . . . wait. Let's think about this first. We don't want to make any accusations yet. We can wait. Just keep an eye on Kirkby.'

We climbed out of the Cruiser and walked up the dune's arched S-curve. The red sand was fine; it filtered through my toes like sunshine. Cooler just below the surface. I fell onto my back and made an angel in the sand.

Antonio sat down beside me. 'You know, I have been all over the world. All over. But I have never seen a country as beautiful as Namibia.'

I sat up and dusted the sand from my hair. Terence was climbing at a pace up the dune, his hat jammed down low on his head. He always retreated to think.

'So much beauty. So harsh, Antonio. So desolate. And here we sit, while God knows what is happening with TurnStone.'

I looked at Antonio. His cricket hat was filthy; it drooped over his forehead. 'How long have you known Lawrence, Antonio?'

'Ah, a long time. Maybe twenty years. He has offered me work here and there. Only eight months ago, he offered me this permanent position with TurnStone.'

'But how well do you know him?'

'How well does one ever know one's colleagues, Robyn? One's boss?'

'Well, actually I think we all get to know each other pretty well out here.'

'Out here, of course. Where is there to hide? But then Lawrence isn't here. On the tenth floor of his neat offices, behind his silk ties. What would you ever see, Robyn?'

There was a soft crunch of footsteps behind us. Terence pulled my cap down lower. 'Your nose looks like it's burning.'

'I can't help it. Damn sun.'

Prof's Cruiser appeared down the track. He drove past us slowly and waved. We could see Kirkby in the back seat – head back, mouth open, fast asleep. Terence smiled.

'How do you sày? Let the sleeping jackal lie?' asked Antonio.

'Let sleeping dogs lie,' corrected Terence.

'Bloody language of the Anglo-Saxons, they keep changing the rules,' grumbled Antonio as we got to our feet and walked back to the Cruiser.

The route we drove twisted in and then out of the red dune desert. We drove onto hard, flat ground, and soon the odd shrub and sprout of grass appeared. Within an hour we had moved from the harshest of deserts into semi-desert. Within two, we were driving through land that looked like it could even support the odd goat. We drove always keeping Prof's vehicle in sight ahead of us. The occasional granite dome could be seen in the distance. Shrubs were clustered closer together. There was no more evidence of desert varnish. A shadow fell over us, and the semi-desert suddenly had a blue tinge.

'Look, clouds,' I exclaimed, straining my head out of the window.

As if in reply, the clouds churned and rumbled. Thunder. A fine needle stung me on my arm. Rain, in this land of no rainfall. The rain fell harder, faster. Terence turned on the windscreen wipers. The dust turned to mud on the windscreen and then washed clean as the clouds opened. Relief. Mist hovered over the cool plains of sand and shrub, the water evaporating instantly. Terence followed Prof along the track, around a granite rise and then through a depression. He came to an abrupt stop beside Prof's vehicle. There was a deafening roar. We climbed out to see a river raging across the track.

Prof walked over to us, his pipe clenched in his mouth, 'Flash floods, they're common when it rains. Nothing to collect the water in these dry parts. Water just runs off through the depressions in the land. There must have been a fair amount of rain further south and it's draining in our direction. But a river this size, it could take a day to subside.'

We stood watching the raging mass of brown water. Standing at its edge, Spyder tossed a stone into it. There was no way we could drive through that.

'Oh man,' shouted Antonio, delighted, 'we should try!'

Terence raised an eyebrow in his direction, aware he was half-joking.

'Don't panic!' someone cried and we all turned around in surprise.

Kirkby had woken up and stood in the middle of the track.

'What the . . .?' Prof chewed on his pipe like a giraffe.

'In emergency situations like these, the most senior member of staff must take control. And . . .' Kirkby hopped, pulling off one boot and then the other, 'the most senior member of staff here is *me.*'

He took off his socks and his waistcoat with its many little pockets. His shirt and shorts fell onto the growing pile of clothing.

Spyder walked up to us. He folded his arms and opened his mouth in exaggerated confusion, 'What is he . . . *doing?*'

Kirkby took off his large, square-framed spectacles and placed them on the pile.

Other than his underpants and his hat, he stood naked. He took his hat off.

His underpants were large Y-fronts. They were worn and yellow, with broken elastic around the waist.

'Now I'm panicking,' I said softly, and the others laughed.

'In situations like these we must not panic. We handle situations like these all the time in Australia. The most senior member of staff . . .' Kirkby hobbled towards us, bow-legged, over the rocky ground. He stood on something sharp and winced, '. . . must take control.'

Antonio threw up his hands at us. 'What is he doing? Ah, *what* is he doing?'

Prof pulled out his pipe, licked his lips, 'Lordie knows, Antonio.'

Kirkby hobbled past us, towards the stream. Standing on its bank, he turned to us and shouted again, 'Don't panic!'

He sunk one leg and then the other into the brown turmoil of water. Immediately he sunk thigh deep. His arms spun. He inched deeper into the water.

'We can't allow him to . . .' my voice was swept away with Kirkby. He was sucked into the water. His head disappeared.

The dark, desert waters had taken Kirkby.

Further down the river, Kirkby's cork head bobbed up. A silence suffocated our group. Then with a leap, Spyder jumped up onto the roof of the grey Cruiser. He doubled over and dropped onto his knees. He rocked. My head swivelled between the disappearing Kirkby and Spyder.

Pointing, Spyder shouted, '*Swem boet!* – swim!'

Kirkby's head popped up. He waved an arm and was sucked back under. Holding his ribs, Spyder climbed down from the roof of the vehicle and fell onto his knees in front of us. Tears streamed down his face, his mouth held in a silent scream of *funny*. I swivelled my head back to Kirkby. The noise of the raging brown water was deafening.

Kirkby washed into a curve of the river where its banks spread. He pulled himself to the edge on his hands and knees and slowly rose. He began his painful, barefoot, bow-legged hobble back to the group. Spyder had rediscovered his lungs and his laugh sawed its way over the frolicking waters. *Hee haw hee haw*. Kirkby got closer to the group. I gave Spyder a light clip on the ear. He abruptly turned off the laugh, stood up and cocked his head to a serious angle. Kirkby's pigeon chest swelled as he neared us. He placed his hands on his hips, 'No way, mate. No way we can cross that. The water is far too strong. We'll never drive across.'

'Really,' said Prof, 'I thought you were taking a bath.'

Kirkby's underwear had gone transparent. He limped back to his pile of clothing and found his glasses. He slipped them on and fixed us with the grey, glassy stare we had all begun to associate with him. 'Just don't panic. Remember company policy.'

Antonio winced. '*What* company policy?'

'The most senior member of the staff must take control. I am the most senior member of staff here.'

'Pah,' said Antonio.

Terence marched back to the navy Cruiser. I followed him and stuck my head through the window. He traced a finger over the map.

'Got a plan?' I asked.

Prof, so much taller then me, leant his head over mine. 'Ja, what's the plan? *Bogger*, that man hasn't even been to Namibia before this trip. Who does he think he is?'

'The most senior member of the staff,' I offered helpfully.

Prof laughed, pretending to tap the contents of his pipe out on my head.

'Twenty kilometres back along the track, there's a detour we can take,' said Terence, focusing on more serious matters. 'It will add over an hour to our journey, and we may have to drive through some private farm land,' he rubbed his coarse chin and shrugged, 'but there's no alternative.'

'Good man, Terence. Let's get going.' Prof hurried back to the white Cruiser, motioning Antonio inside. Spyder took a running jump and the three of them sped off, leaving Kirkby with us. Kirkby glared at the departing vehicle. He took off his underwear and walked over to us.

'God, Kirkby, must you?' I averted my gaze.

Kirkby found his shorts in his pile of clothing, pulled them up over his naked buttocks and drew the zip up, every so carefully. He fixed me with a stare. 'This is a *field* excursion and I travel light. This is my only pair of underwear. And they are . . . wet.'

'I suppose another pair of underwear would have weighed you down?' asked Terence, sitting in the passenger seat.

Within ten minutes we had caught up with the white Cruiser. They'd stopped next to a granite dome. Above us, the clouds had lifted and the rain had stopped, as abruptly as it had started. Prof leant against a boulder waiting for us. We all clambered around the boulders to find a shady place to sit and wait for Prof to collect his thoughts. I have always liked granite: it is somehow a clean rock, a rock that absorbs energy and filters it out in a distilled state. An old friend, granite. Familiar.

I thought of Laurie in Namaqualand suddenly. *Concordia granite, my old friend . . .*

'Rooiberg granite,' said Prof, lighting his pipe. 'One thousand one hundred million years old. Typically red in colour . . .'

Spyder hunched over his grubby notebook and wrote furiously.

I trailed my fingers over the large pink feldspar crystals. Terence and Antonio stood on either side of me. Both their legs were grey with accumulated grime.

Terence shielded his eyes. 'What's that? Dust?'

We all turned to look. A fine trail of dust. It was growing thicker. I handed Terence the binoculars.

'It's too small for a vehicle. A quad bike,' said Terence eventually.

The trail of dust arced towards us, the first sign of human life we had seen in over two weeks. As it drew closer, we could make out the quad bike. Something hairy sat behind the driver. They stopped in front of us.

A man in his thirties sat on the bike. Slim and long-limbed, he had long dark hair which trailed over his shoulders. Behind him sat a brown-and-white sheepdog. One of its eyes were sewn shut. The stranger gave us a sceptical smile and leant forward on the handle-bars, as if waiting for an explanation. There was something about the angle of his jaw, the movement of his long legs. Then he turned to look at me and I recognised him. Aquamarine eyes . . . the colour of that wild west coast. He squinted at me and then glanced up at Terence, as if something was tickling his mind.

'We're . . . er, geologists,' said Prof, 'on a field excursion. Just driving through, looking at the rocks.'

'Listen mate, we are on a very important geological excursion. We need to travel due south.' Kirkby stepped forward, interrupting Prof.

'This is a private track. This is a private farm.'

'Look, I told you we need to head due south.' Kirkby pointed east.

Prof shook his head with irritation and placed a hand on Kirkby's arm. Kirkby shook him off.

'This is private land. You have no right to be here.' He swivelled his eyes to me.

'Levi?' I asked. 'We met in Lutzville. The geologists you met at the bar. Robyn and Terence.'

A slow smile spread over Levi's brown face, and then those perfect white teeth were exposed. He bowed his head and chuckled.

'Well, I'll be damned. I thought I recognised you. And you,' he looked up at Terence and then scanned the rest of the group. 'Look, it's getting late. I don't know where you're planning to set up camp. But I've got a cottage here I've built for guests, tourists. You can stay there tonight. It has hot showers and I can cook you up some stew.'

'Man, oh man,' Antonio looked pleadingly at Prof.

But Prof needed no encouraging. He was already walking to the Land Cruiser. 'We'll follow you.'

Levi started his quad bike, turned around and sped into the trail of dust he had left behind. The sheep dog leant into the wind.

Antonio, Terence and I followed the Prof's Cruiser and Levi. The dust snaked through the landscape. Granite domes rose like stubborn beasts from the land.

'Where is the house? How big is this farm?' asked Antonio after a while.

'As big as the ocean,' I said.

'Huh?' Antonio strained to look at me on the back seat.

'Big,' I leant forward to watch Terence driving. 'I can't imagine Levi landlocked like this. We are hundreds and hundreds of kilometres from the west coast.'

Terence shook his head. 'Who would believe it? Out here, in the semi-desert. But it's been a long time since we saw him – over two years.'

The dust from Levi's quad bike and Prof's Cruiser continued to wind through the land. Still, there was no evidence of a cottage. The dust slowly slid towards a granite mountain, making for its rocky base. Closer and closer the mountain loomed, glowing an iridescent orange in the sunset.

We had come to a complete stop at the mountain base before we saw the cottage. It was built into the rock, blended into the mountain's shoreline with the sand. The walls were built from stone, perfectly camouflaged. Only the tin roof and the wooden doors revealed the cottage. Levi and his sheepdog waited for us at the front door. Prof, Spyder and Kirkby were already inside.

Levi ducked as he walked inside. 'Built from solid rock, built it my-self. I'm starting to bring tourists in here. The more adventurous kind. I've used the natural contours of the rock for shelves and stor-age places. You'll see. There's even a shower and basin in each room. Solar panels.' He led us from room to room. Each had a bed with clean linen and a small bathroom. Modern piping and shower noz-zles were fitted into the rock showers. Clean towels lay folded on granite shelves.

'Oh, clean sheets,' said Antonio with delight.

'Hot showers,' I added.

'Just like the Flintstones,' said Terence.

'Better,' Levi smiled at him, 'much better. Tourists are starting to hear about this place. But it takes time. Word has to spread.'

The sheep dog slunk between my legs and to his master's side.

'This was your buddy's dog – the one with the long dreadlocks. The one with one eye, like his dog. What was his name?' I asked.

The smile slid off Levi's face. 'Ray,' he said and turned abruptly away.

I caught Terence's eye.

Spyder emerged carrying a cold beer. At the sight of us he balanced his geological hammer on his head. 'Beam me down, Scotty. We seem to have discovered intelligent life forms. Cold beer. *Prrrrp.*'

He disappeared into the labyrinth of rock corridors.

'Fridge generated off gas in the kitchen,' Levi explained.

Each equipped with a cold beer, Terence and I followed Levi and his dog around the side of the invisible cottage and past the restau-rant (a protected enclave of rocks with railway sleepers wedged be-tween the boulders), and climbed an easy series of rocks up onto the cottage roof. The others were already there – Prof, Antonio and Spyder. The only one missing, not surprisingly, was Kirkby.

I reached out and patted the sheepdog. 'His coat looks fantastic. I remember how tangled and matted it was. But now he's silky. He looks good.'

Levi leant his arms on his sharp knees. 'I take good care of him. Most of the time it's just me and him. So I take good care of him.'

The sun sank behind the horizon like a heavy egg yolk.

'Now this is why I became a geologist.' Prof lifted his beer bottle, 'Cheers.'

We all lifted our bottles in a chorus of *cheers*.

'What's his name?' I asked Levi.

'Ray,' replied Levi. 'He didn't have a name before. Was just called Dog. Now he's Ray.'

Terence leant forward, 'Where is Ray?'

Levi rubbed his nose roughly with the back of his hand then sipped his beer, 'We lost him.'

'What?' I asked.

'We lost him. He drowned. He didn't come up with the other divers. We searched for four hours to find him. Found him drifting on the ocean floor, weighed down by his diving weights. His hair look liked the yellow seaweed, we didn't see him at first.'

The last of the light sprinkled cinnamon across the sky.

'Ray'd been smoking. We had a policy of no booze and no grass on the boat. Except for Chief's beers. But Chief found his stash under his mattress.'

'Chief?'

'Yeah, Chief, you know from Spioenkop. Works for himself now. He'd come along for the fishing. Yup, Ray was just too stoned to dive.'

'You left? You don't dive anymore?'

'No, sold the boat. I had made my money. Bought this farm from an uncle's friend. So I farm ostrich now. After that day we lost Ray, I don't know, I had had enough. Enough of the sea. I'll watch the sun set over it, but not much else. I'm done with the sea.'

We sat in silence, watching the sky warm to the colours of a spice market.

'You must love all this space and beauty,' I turned to Levi.

But he and Ray-the-dog had left. Slipped away as quietly as shifting sand.

Terence cocked his head in the direction they had gone. 'He's in the restaurant, making the fire.'

Below us in the distance was the familiar buzz of the radio. Kirkby's brash voice rose; he was obviously unaware how sound travelled through the desert.

'Right mate, Kirkby here. Practically got washed away in a flash flood today. Too right, mate. Thank God I was here, a senior member of staff. Had to make sure the others didn't panic.'

Silence.

'Practically there, Lawrence? Listen mate, I know you don't like to talk details over the radio but let me tell you, "practically there" isn't bloody good enough. You've justified the price. I don't think we should wait, Lawrence. No, mate . . .'

Silence.

'Right, the last lap mate, I know. I know. Final details . . . I don't give a damn about their lawyers, that's your game, not mine. You've got the shareholder vote. Sounds like the end of the line to me . . . well, don't hang about. I told you we were practically washed away in a flash flood. Thank God I was there.'

Silence.

'Don't get funny with me, mate. You don't need to send a speedboat to fetch us. Listen, we're coming back. No, I said we're coming back. It's the end of the line. Sort it, Lawrence, sort it . . . Yeah, all right, call us tomorrow. Early.'

Silence.

On the roof, no one said anything. Antonio sighed, rubbed the coarse stubble on his chin and stared out into the distance. Prof gave us a quizzical look. Spyder took a sip of his beer. His eyelids fluttered, evidence of matters in his sharp mind colliding. '*Prrrp*,' he said softly, 'Time to beam us up, Scotty.'

'Hey,' Levi shouted from below, 'I need some help with dinner down here.'

'Right,' Prof stood up, 'need me to catch the ostrich and wring its neck?'

'No need. I don't usually eat my birds. But this one I had to shoot a few days ago. She attacked the quad bike, almost killed Ray. The meat will be a little tough though.'

Prof, Spyder and Antonio clambered off the roof.

I pulled Terence's arm before he could stand up. He sat behind me and I leant back on his legs. 'What's going on, Terence?'

'With TurnStone? Your guess is as good as mine.'

'Those projects have no copper. We know that now. The results have been falsely elevated. What is Lawrence up to? Trying to make the shareholders happy? Is that it?'

'Nah,' Terence gave me a light shove and I sat forward. 'The shareholders will find out soon enough. My guess, within a couple of months. You can't keep something like that a secret. Not for long anyway. Other parties would become interested. The drilling would continue, the samples would get sent out to other laboratories.'

'What then?'

The sky had darkened and the first stars glittered like diamonds.

Terence stood up, shaking his head. 'Ask Kirkby.'

'Yeah right, he'll explain everything.' I followed him down from the roof. 'It's so beautiful here. I wish I could stay forever.'

Levi was cooking in a large, three-legged potjie. The smell of fried onions was appetizing. Ray-the-dog lay by his side, his one eye following every move. When Levi stood up and moved three paces to collect the next batch of ingredients from a flat boulder, Ray-the-dog lifted his head to watch him.

'Need help?'

'Cut those,' he pointed at the tomatoes.

I sliced through them. 'Do you miss the sea?'

'No.'

'Not at all?' Terence asked, dropping some more wood near the fire.

'Not at all.' He looked up at us. Those aquamarine eyes still reflected the moods of the ocean. Unpredictable.

He pushed his long hair back and fastened it behind his neck. 'This is my land now, this is my country. The west coast is almost three hundred kilometres away.' He pointed at the cottage. 'This here is now my ship, my boat. And she's right here at the bottom of the ocean.'

Dinner was served to eager hands. Wine, unbearably sweet but bearably cold, was served in tin mugs. We ate quietly, our voices muffled by the good stew, content from the wine. The dirty dishes were stacked in a bucket beside the fire. Spyder pulled out his harmonica and began to buzz on it. Ray-the-dog, who had been lying in the shadow of the firelight, sat up suddenly and began to groan, then howl. Spyder continued to play between laughs, sawing the notes back and forth to accompany the dog. I looked up at the stars. They were less bright; a slight breeze had picked up. And although where we sat in the boulder enclave was protected, the sky was clouding with suspended dust.

'Ray, enough,' Levi put a hand on the dog's head.

Enough. Enough for the day. We all trailed to our rooms, except for Levi and Ray-the-dog. They would sleep under the stars, between the boulders. All the rooms were taken. I showered in the rock shower beside our bedroom and with the unfamiliar feel of clean skin on clean sheets, fell asleep curled behind Terence.

I dreamt I was dancing in the desert.

Stars swirl above me; I can hear my muffled footsteps in the sand. The sand is still warm. My white vest reflects the bright moonlight. Robyn, someone calls softly, Robyn bring the knife. What knife? Then I see it, lying on the sleeper wood, glinting. I pick it up and carry it to the cottage. I walk between the boulders, the path getting very dark. I am scared I will trip and hurt myself. I clutch the knife, straining to see.

Hands grip me. Men's hands. They hold my wrists. I twist and strain. Above me I see a small figure silhouetted on a rock, the head a large shadow. A swish of heavy fabric. Then I know who it is.

'You say you are sorry, but my cattle will die,' says Mrs Nangula.

I twist to get away from the man.

'A man with a knife, a man with a smile. I told you.'

I look up. She is gone.

'Mama Nangula,' I cry.

'It's a thirsty country, Robyn. It always has been and always will be.' Abel. I look wildly around me but I can't see him.

The man's hands are hurting me. His hands catch the moonlight; I can see the strength in those knuckles. The knife may be pointing at him, but my hands will always belong to him. He will never release me. I start to sob with fear.

Terence was shaking me. 'Ssh, the walls are thin. It's just a dream.'

He pulled me closer and his hand fell heavy against my shoulder. He'd fallen asleep. I could hear the wind picking up outside. It started to whistle and rattle the windowpanes. Sand clawed at the door. I drifted off, and when I next awoke the grey light of morning shone around the curtain.

Terence was up, dressed, pulling on his boots. The wind cried when he opened the door and abruptly stopped when he shut it behind him. I rose slowly, brushing my teeth, dressing, packing my bag. When I opened the door, the land was obliterated. The sand sparked my flesh like electricity as I fought my way to the Cruisers. I was pleased we were leaving. I was no longer sure I liked this place.

Ray-the-dog sat at the back of the quad bike, flickering his one eye closed. His long brown-and-white hair whipped into a small hurricane. Levi was securing a water canister to his bike. The others, Spyder, Antonio, Terence and Kirkby were standing around the Cruisers. They seemed to be arguing, but the words were torn away and hurled into the desert. I reached the group.

'Call him yourself, mate.'

'What do you mean? Why now?' Antonio turned to Spyder and Terence for backup.

'I mean we have to leave. Now. Can't you understand English, you bloody I-talian?' said Kirkby.

I thought Antonio would explode. His chest swelled and his cheeks went red. 'What did you call me? What did you call me? You . . . you . . .'

'Enough.' Terence glared at Kirkby, shielding his face with his hand. 'I'll call Lawrence. Give me this new number you've been getting through on.'

Kirkby's grey eyes swum behind his thick glasses. He stood firm, his mouth sullen, seemingly unaffected by the sandstorm around him. The piece of paper cracked wildly in the wind as he handed it over to Terence. Terence climbed into the navy Cruiser and shut the door behind him. Antonio climbed in beside him, Spyder and I in the back seat. Just as I was about to shut the door, Prof appeared and squeezed in next to me. The howl shut outside, we sat in the eye of the storm, our hair still suspended by the wind. Our faces brown, burnt. Levi, Ray-the-dog and the cottage had disappeared, obliterated by sand. Kirkby stood looking at us, then he turned and was gone too.

A wave of sand hit the Cruiser. I was wedged between Prof and Spyder. Struggling for space, Prof found his pipe and popped it into his grey-stubbled mouth.

Terence dialled the number, and the radio beeped its code.

Please do not hang up, this call is from a radio, I repeat, do not hang up . . .

There was a reply.

'Lawrence, Terence here. What's going on? Over.'

'Terence,' Lawrence's voice was surprisingly clear, 'I presume Kirkby has spoken to you. I want you all to return to Cape Town immediately. Over.'

'Why? Over.'

'Nothing I want to discuss over the radio, Terence. I want you all to return immediately. Over.'

I tried to snatch the speaker from Terence's hand. I wanted to give Lawrence an earful.

Terence pulled it away in time. 'You want us to return today, over?'

'That's right. I want you all to take the shortest route back to Windhoek. I've hired a private plane, which is waiting for you at Eros airport. It will bring Spyder, Antonio, Robyn and you back to Cape Town. Kirkby is to catch the main Windhoek airline back to Johannesburg to pick up his link to Perth. He's needed there now. I'll arrange for someone to pick up the Land Cruiser at the airport and drive it down to Cape Town. The academic can drive the other vehicle back in his own time. Over.'

Prof jabbed me with his elbow, 'The *academic*.'

Terence hesitated and looked at Antonio, then back at us. He sighed. 'If we leave now, it will take six hours to drive to Windhoek. That's taking the shortest route. Over.'

'Well, splendid, the aircraft will be waiting for you. Over and out.'

Outside the wind gave a final shriek. The Cruiser gave another gentle rock. Inside, we all silently swayed from side to side.

Prof popped his pipe out of his mouth. 'Looks like the journey's over.'

CHAPTER FOURTEEN

Due Diligence

Antonio, Spyder, Terence and I sat around the large oak table in TurnStone's Cape Town boardroom. We were still filthy, torn and dishevelled from our trip into the desert. Lawrence sat across the table from us. For once he was wearing an ugly tie, a navy one with two orange arrows colliding.

Beside him sat two men: an older man with silver hair and bushy black eyebrows who had a tight, hard mouth, and a younger man, whose blond hair was trimmed for the fast track to success. The silver-haired man wore a dark suit of impeccable fit; his tie was discreet and tasteful. His spectacles sat low down on the bridge of his nose. The blond wore a yellow tie which he played with as he swivelled his chair back and forth, casting his blue eyes from one face to the next: Antonio, Spyder, Terence and me. Then in reverse.

Lawrence removed a black pen from his breast pocket and tapped the table. 'Good evening. Apologies that you had to return in such a sudden manner, but this is of the *utmost* importance.'

Earlier that morning, we had been driven from the remote wind-torn land of Levi's farm, leaving behind Levi, Ray-the-dog and Prof. Prof had wanted to stay on Levi's farm a few more days, and had agreed to drive the second Cruiser back to Cape Town in his own time.

We had all thanked Levi for his hospitality. When my turn came, I had patted Ray-the-dog. His one eye flickered in the sandstorm.

'Out here,' shouted Levi, 'out here you never forget how big nature is. Don't mess with her because she'll bite back. Not a day goes by here when I'm not reminded of that. It's the same as being out at sea; that little boat used to keep us alive. Here, this cottage is my only protection.'

Gritting his pipe between his teeth, Prof waved casually and hurried indoors, into the shelter of Levi's rock cottage.

Terence and I took turns in driving the navy Cruiser back to Windhoek. For the next six hours Spyder slept, Antonio wrote in his notebook and Kirkby sat staring out of the window in stony silence. By the time we rolled into Windhoek it was early afternoon. The Cruiser felt big, dusty and brutish in the streets of the small city. I drove the forty kilometres out of the city to the international airport to drop Kirkby off. Outside the airport doors, Kirkby took his bags from Terence without a word. The four of us watched him walk away. I then drove us back into the city, to the small airport for light aircraft, Eros.

At Eros we unloaded our luggage. A driver from a car rental company was waiting for us, and drove the cruiser away for safekeeping. Antonio, Terence, Spyder and I trundled through the airport doors into the small waiting room. It was empty except for a tall, thin figure slumped on a chair. He rose to greet us. Louwtjie.

'Why am I not surprised?' I asked.

'Maybe I'm the only private pilot they know. That's probably it.' He took my bag and a couple from Antonio's overloaded arms.

We walked onto the asphalt; a collection of weathered individuals. Louwtjie's familiar blue bird stood bow-legged at the edge of the runway. Antonio took the seat next to Louwtjie, the same seat from which I had flown. I sat between Spyder and Terence on the back seat. Spyder was a big guy, and it was a little cramped.

Permission granted, crackled the radio. The propeller began to spin, the plane taxied along the runway and we were airborne. Dusty green veld passed beneath us. The plane evened out, smooth. The engine churned, easy. There were no thermals. Spyder rested his chin in his hands. Terence leant back, staring out the window. The drone of the engine made conversation impossible. There was not much to say, not yet anyway. We could just wait, wait for our future to catch up with us.

Half an hour later, I strained my neck over Terence for a view. Below I saw the red dunes of the Namib desert, the late afternoon sun accentuating their voluptuous curves. We flew south over the Awasib desert, yellow, flatter. The black mountains of desert varnish. Further south, over the beauty of the vast Orange River, crossing back into South Africa. The broken west-coast shoreline.

'Look, Springbok. Namaqualand,' I said to Terence.

The slightest smile pulled at his mouth. He sighed. Beneath us, the granite domes rose and fell like a migration of giant tortoises.

'That's where we used to make a fire and watch the stars,' Terence pointed out a ridge of granite. He leant forward, his elbows resting on his legs, and took my hand in both of his. Deep in thought, his thumb rubbed repeatedly over my knuckles.

Louwtjie's aircraft droned on, following the contours of the coastline. Terence tugged my hand. Below was Lutzville, and a distance away, a tiny speck of a farmhouse. Our house. The Olifants River Valley snaked past it. The sands had lost their warmth, the sun was setting. The Cape mountains, Table Mountain. The first twinkle of lights and then the city of Cape Town. A length of red lights marked the light aircraft runway. The plane sank with an inappropriate gaiety and scuttled to a halt on the runway.

I was the last to climb out of the plane. I caught Louwtjie's eye.

He winked, '*Sterkte*, old crow. It appears things are coming to a head.'

'I guess we're about to find out what's going on.'

'Either way, don't worry. Remember you were in this for the land, the rocks. And the people. Not the Company.'

'I'll try.' I heaved my bag after me, weighed down with rock samples. I frowned at Louwtjie suddenly. 'You're not involved in all of this in any way, are you?'

'Me?' His blue eyes opened wide. He waved at me to close the door.

'Yeah, right.' I banged the door closed.

Terence, Spyder, Antonio and I filed into the airport. The men were unshaven. We were all dirty, our legs burnt red-brown. Our boots were dusty and scuffed, our hair wild. We made our way through customs and immigration. Travellers in neat suits wheeling small, compact suitcases glanced at us. A group of Asian businessmen crowded past me, separating me from the others.

'What . . . get your hands off me!' I heard Antonio's voice.

I pushed through the suits. A man in a black uniform stood beside Terence, Antonio and Spyder. Spyder was frowning, Terence was scanning the airport for me.

'Ms Hartley, if you'll join us . . .' Another uniformed young man was at my elbow. On his breast pocket was a red logo enclosing the words *Corporate Security*. 'A vehicle is waiting for all of you, Ma'am. Courtesy of Mr Sutherland. If you'll head this way.'

I followed the others out of the airport into the evening air. A warm wind was blowing, unusual for Cape Town. It swirled around our legs in moody gusts. Warm as blood. Around us, passengers grabbed their bags and coats. We followed the uniformed men to a large, grey car with dark windows, parked in a no-parking zone. The number plate was obscure: CPR SRT3. The boot was large; it accommodated all our luggage easily.

The two guards sat in front, Antonio, Spyder, Terence and myself in the two rows of seats behind. The driver manoeuvred through the traffic, the hooters and the city lights with ease, delivering us at the TurnStone building twenty minutes later. Glowing in the floodlights, the building's metal fins rose skywards, like a rocket ready for launch. The guard parked in front of the entrance and his colleague unloaded our bags. Then the grey car circled the parking lot twice, only leaving once we were in the building.

The lift took us to the top floor. TurnStone's floor. We dragged our baggage out of the lift to the engraved TurnStone door. Antonio held it open. I was the last in. I heaved my bags down with a sigh and turned around. Another black-uniformed security guard with the *Corporate Security* logo stood in front of us, in a soldier's 'at ease' position: feet spread, hands clasped behind him, his focus on the space behind us.

'You are not to move beyond this point. Mr Sutherland wishes to meet with you in the boardroom.' His eyes flicked to the right, in the direction of the boardroom.

'What is this? I want to go to my office,' Antonio demanded.

'Leave it, Antonio,' Terence touched his arm, keeping his eyes on the guard.

I walked up to the guard. His eyes remained distant, his position braced. I pushed myself up onto my toes and peered over his shoulder. Down the corridor, another guard stood in front of our offices. He wore a leather holster strapped across his chest. He was armed? I eased myself back on my heels and trailed after the others.

Terence, Antonio and Spyder sat alone in the boardroom. I sat next to Terence. The silence smelt volatile, a gas waiting to ignite. Terence rubbed the sunburnt skin on the back of his neck. Antonio folded his arms high against his chest and pulled his chin in. He sighed. Just when the silence threatened to explode, Spyder pulled out his harmonica and gave a soft blow. A few notes, sawed back and forth. It stopped abruptly when Lawrence strode into the room, followed by the two men, one older, one younger. The young one carried a briefcase, the older a leather-bound book.

Now Lawrence, having introduced the men – their names washed past me – promptly sat down, and the younger man with the yellow tie stood up. He opened his laptop computer, the lights dimmed and the screen rolled down.

Overhead on the screen, two orange arrows collided. Below, it read:

TurnStone Inc. – Leaving no stone unturned.
Global Mining Group (GMG) Inc. – World leaders
in mining technology.

Who were the Global Mining Group?

The next slide was a graph. Yellow Tie used his laser pointer to highlight the plummeting mineral price, cost and demand. His voice was loud, with a twang difficult to place. This current market, he prattled on, would explain GMG's strategy (except he could not pronounce strategy, he said *stragedy*, so that it rhymed with tragedy) of acquisition. Their Way Forward.

'*What*,' Antonio looked at the rest of us, 'is he talking about?'

Spyder grimaced in exaggerated confusion.

Lawrence stood up quickly. 'Yes . . . er thank you. I'll take it from there.'

Yellow Tie sat down. He looked annoyed.

Lawrence tapped his knuckles gently on the table. 'As you can see, TurnStone has been reassessing our strengths and weaknesses in our competitive line of business. We have long been looking for a partner who can combine their strengths with our weaknesses and vice versa. GMG have come to an agreement for a merger.'

Lawrence smiled at the silver-haired man, who seemed preoccupied with aligning his book at right angles to the table. 'For those of you who are not familiar with GMG,' Lawrence continued, 'they are a company with well-established assets in exploration and mining throughout the world. They have a collection of remarkable individuals with considerable expertise who have been able to formulate an ongoing strategy that continues to be competitive and cutting edge. GMG have had the foresight to see that the African continent will play a pivotal role in the future of exploration, and that is where we hope TurnStone's influence will be able to assist.' Lawrence smiled again at the silver-haired man, straightening the orange arrows on his tie.

'What does that mean for us?'

'Well, there we have it, Robyn. GMG have sufficient people to realise the merger potential and therefore will not be taking on Turn-Stone's exploration staff.'

'We're fired?'

'Released from work obligations, Robyn .'

'I knew something was going on. We were fools not to see this. Fools!' Antonio was red with anger. 'Those elevated copper results – pah. What copper? I told you there was no copper in that core. Tell him about the results from the other laboratory, Robyn.'

'That's right. We sent three samples to another laboratory for analysis. No copper. A *fractional* amount of copper.'

'I think that's enough, Robyn. You are all understandably tired and angry,' said Lawrence.

'Don't tell us we're tired. The hell you would know.' Terence stood up. 'You're right about angry. Committed Labs, your *subsidiary*, have been falsely elevating your results.'

'Fuck this,' Spyder stood up.

Lawrence's olive eyes looked like they could burst into flame; his face was pinched and pale, furious. 'Sit down,' he snapped, and then composed himself. 'TurnStone remain indebted to you for your contributions. I know you have all worked very hard towards making the company what it is today.'

The white-haired man rose, pulled his silver rimmed spectacles off his nose and looked at Lawrence. 'So . . . Mr Sutherland. I wonder if you would mind if I had a word now.' He had a deep voice, a laid-back Houston drawl.

'Please, Chuck, er Mr King, please add anything you think I may have glossed over.' Lawrence took a seat.

'Indeed I will, Mr Sutherland, indeed I will. Please,' he looked at the four of us, 'If you would kindly stay for just a few minutes longer. I think you may want to hear this.'

Terence and Spyder reluctantly sat down.

Mr King picked up the leather-bound book and then put it back down. 'Ah, where to start? I think Mr Sutherland has made it pretty clear that TurnStone no longer exists. A merger, Mr Sutherland called it. I would prefer to use the word "acquisition" myself. For Global Mining, of course. But never mind, call it what you want. But with any merger, or in this case acquisition, there is always a certain amount of blood shed and it gives me no pleasure to see you lose your jobs. That, I'm afraid, cannot be helped.' He held up a hand defensively in my direction. 'You may glare at me, Ms Hartley, but that I cannot change. What I want to bring to your attention is an extension of this point you have already raised. About the copper content of the samples taken from your projects.'

'Mr Sutherland,' Mr King glanced at Lawrence, 'while Global Mining conducted their due diligence of TurnStone, it was revealed that TurnStone has various promising copper targets in Southern Africa. Was it not?'

'We have had a focused approach and a great team, Chuck.'

'Indeed. Your disclosure document indicates possible copper deposits in Namibia and Botswana of . . . considerable potential. I would say you have listed *very* intriguing results. You are right, Mr Sutherland, that Global Mining does see the future of mineral exploration as being focused on Africa, and that our specific interest in TurnStone was the potential for a discovery of a copper mine at greenfields level. Still unexploited. Indeed, I'd say that TurnStone justified their price by indicating their exploration skill in Africa.'

'Skill and a little luck. One develops a nose for these things.'

'Quite, Mr Sutherland, quite. Today I received this document from Mr Louwtjie Boshard.' King held up the leather-bound book. 'A day after the acquisition was signed off, unfortunately, otherwise I would have brought it to your attention earlier. Mr Boshard spent seven years working in the same area in Namibia. Similar samples to yours were analysed by Mr Boshard, but his results differ immensely from yours. Which brings us back to the point already raised by your staff, your "great team", Mr Sutherland. Now, just to straighten the record and make sure we all remain on the best of terms, I have taken the liberty of sending a fresh set of samples through to our own laboratories. Just to, you understand,' he slipped his spectacles back on and peered over them at Lawrence, '*verify* your results.'

Lawrence had crossed one leg over the other. His foot was tapping. He did not look up.

'Should we find that the results do differ . . . well, I would have to agree that Global Mining's due diligence process was not thorough enough. That we were a little . . . trusting. We should have drilled our own boreholes, taken our own soil samples. But that's business for you today, Mr Sutherland, the young bulls want to charge at every opportunity.' He glanced at Yellow Tie. 'However, Mr Sutherland, should we find that your laboratory results were misleading in any way, I think you will discover American corporate law is far stricter than Britain's when it comes to revealing explicit warrantees. You will be held accountable. I'm just warning you, Mr Sutherland.'

'I assure you, Mr King, you are mistaken.' Lawrence stood up and straightened his arrow collision tie.

'Am I?'

A vein in Lawrence's neck was throbbing. He addressed the four of us. 'Given the current sensitivity of the merger, you'll appreciate that you will not be able to return to your offices. Any personal possessions will be posted to you. All reports, rock samples and the like are now the possession of the greater GMG.'

He left the boardroom, the doors swinging shut behind him.

Yellow Tie placed his briefcase on the table. *Click click*, he opened it and withdrew a handful of white envelopes. He placed them on the table in front of us. My name was printed in neat italics on the centre envelope. *Robyn Hartley.*

'Your notice in writing,' said Yellow Tie, licking his dry lips. 'Given that you cannot return to your offices, we would like you to be off the premises by seven o'clock.'

I looked at my watch. It was quarter to seven.

Terence slid the envelope back to Yellow Tie with force. 'Post that to me, along with my personal office possessions.'

'What . . . what? Who?' Antonio picked up the envelope and punched a finger into his name. He began to rip and tear. Piece by piece, he scattered the paper into the air.

'I'm afraid that will not change anything, Mr Conté. TurnStone no longer exist. You no longer have a position with TurnStone,' said Mr King.

'Pah. Dismissed. By who?'

'TurnStone, officially, Mr Conté.'

'I thought you said they no longer exist,' said Terence.

'It's a dog-eat-dog world,' said Yellow Tie. He sighed and looked at his watch.

'Is that right?' Spyder stood up, 'Then perhaps you'll be the next meal.'

'Jeffrey,' Mr King clenched a firm hand around Yellow Tie's shoulder, 'that is enough. Quite enough.' He looked at the rest of us. 'You understand the rest of us need to get on with the process of this acquisition. There is much work to be done. Shall we, Jeffrey? I'm sure the old TurnStone staff can see themselves out. I wish you all the best.'

The four of us were left alone, Spyder and Terence standing, Antonio and I seated. I released a deep breath. My envelope remained untouched on the table.

'There are things in my luggage I want. Notebooks,' I said.

'Well then, *woestynblommetjie*, we had better get them for you,' said Spyder.

We glanced at Spyder.

'Just move quickly. Take what you need from your bags,' he said.

Spyder sidled out of the boardroom and back into the entrance hall. He pulled out his harmonica and blew a note. Then he gave an exaggerated tragic sniff and mumbled something. The guard looked disconcerted; he concentrated at not looking at this large, sobbing, filthy man.

Then Spyder ducked. Under the guard's arm and down the corridor.

'Stop!' the guard shouted. The second guard jumped across the corridor, blocking Spyder's path, his hand on his holster.

'Okay, okay,' said Spyder, throwing up his hands in a mock gesture of defeat.

I bent down and quickly slipped my notebooks out of my bags. I wedged them into my waistband and pulled my shirt over them and stood up quickly. Terence held the door open and we all filed out, myself, Antonio and Spyder. We caught the lift down to the ground floor. Outside the warm wind was still blowing. Terence put his arm around me as we walked outside. The wind tugged at our clothes, swirled around our legs.

Promise Me Mountains

Panting, my hands on my hips, I continue to climb. Above me, the basalt cliffs crack skyward. The Shield of Lesotho. As treacherous as these cliffs are, as stark and forbidding, there are paths that twist through and behind them. My chest heaves, my eyes water and my legs ache. I am tired.

By late afternoon, I will have reached the escarpment. Terence, having driven from the campsite up the winding pass, will be there to fetch me with Bongi. He wanted to climb with me today, but I needed to be alone. Alone in these mountains.

Before I left, Terence had pulled me close. 'Be careful,' he said, his breath steaming in the cold morning air.

I lean against a boulder, catching my breath. A whole year has passed since that night at TurnStone. The night we walked out into the hot, moody wind and dispersed like autumn leaves on a lonely street. Ultimately our anger died, was carried away by the merger, the swarm of corporate bees.

Spyder no longer works as a geophysicist; he takes tour groups on adventurous excursions, the thrills-and-spills kind. Bungee-jumping, river rafting and the like. His tours often stop at Levi's farm in southern Namibia, where the guests may try their hand at riding ostriches – hanging on to the birds' long sinewy necks while their dinosaur claws thunder across the sands.

Antonio returned to Italy, to his wife and three daughters. He now works for the Italian Embassy, where his fluent language skills are much in demand.

Louwtjie? He no longer lives in the Namibian bush, at least not for the time being. Impressed by his honesty, Mr King of Global Mining hired him to pilot his private jet in Houston.

I understand Kirkby still heads the Australian division of the Global Mining Group, based in Perth. Lawrence, however, left soon after the merger. The circumstances around his departure are unknown. I understand he has interests in the large salt pans in Botswana, which he plans to mine. He has called his company Exposure.

Terence and I work together for smaller consultancies. Our office, always littered with maps and papers, overlooks the cold sparkle of the west coast. Sorting through this confusion of paper one afternoon, I came across my black notebooks. I spread them out on the floor. I paged through them, one by one. The daily tunnel maps, soil-sampling positions, a sketch of the kudu bull in Outjo. A rose petal, once yellow, was pasted beside the Marble Hall geology map. There was an attempt to sketch Mrs Nangula standing in her stone garden; across it I had written: *As the dust and sun settle, let me feel peace again* . . . I found a damaged photo of Terence and Bongi in Botswana; behind them, the bush is thick and green.

I tore. I pasted. I wrote. I discovered writing has a voice of its own. One that heals, one that reasons. The same voice that whispers over the crest of a sand dune. The same voice that resounds through these basalt cliffs.

Closing the last book, I asked myself, would I do it again? Would I ride to the *chug-boom* of the tunnel train, out into the dense, green bushveld and through the sweeping red dunes; past those who are part of the landscape, part of the contours, those who have been defined by the rain, the droughts, the cracked earth; and then on to TurnStone's deceit?

I would have no choice. The voice I answer to, resonates from deep within the earth's fractures. My fractures. This journey has been mine to take, and mine alone.

I climb the steep path, my feet slipping on the loose scree. I reach a ledge in the cliff face. Panting, I catch my breath. An ocean of cloud has gathered below me. I am distant, secluded.

A rasping cry startles me. A jackal buzzard drops off the escarpment down to my level. For a second it hovers, and then drops into the soft, white mass of cloud and is gone. I hold out my arms, I am high. The mountains hold me, keep me looking in awe at the world below.